SPUN YARNS UNWOUND: VOL. 5

HISTORICAL, MYSTERY, AND A DASH OF ROMANCE!

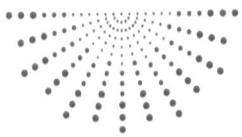

DEBBIE MUMFORD

WDM Publishing

HISTORICAL, MYSTERY, AND A DASH OF ROMANCE!

This volume of Spun Yarns Unwound contains a sampling of several genres of stories written by Debbie Mumford.

Debbie writes in a wide variety of genres, and this volume illustrates that beautifully. We start with a few historical tales, including a well-loved time travel romance novella, before moving on to contemporary times. Among the more recent settings, you'll discover everything from family drama to cozy mystery to romance.

So sit back, relax, and enjoy Debbie's eclectic tales!

COPYRIGHT

TWENTY STORIES BY DEBBIE MUMFORD

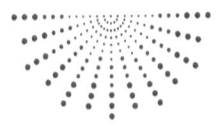

PART I
MISS BAINBRIDGE'S
SUMMER ADVENTURE

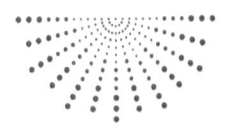

DEBBIE MUMFORD

BESTSELLING AUTHOR OF *SORCHA'S HEART*

Miss Bainbridge's
Summer
Adventure

SPUN YARNS
A Story of the Erie Canal

CHAPTER ONE

*M*iss Clarissa Bainbridge clutched her parasol and surveyed the packet boat that would carry her along the newly constructed Erie Canal from her home in Albany, New York to Buffalo, on the shores of Lake Erie. To think that she would view the glory of Niagara Falls in less than a week! The very thought caused her heart to race and her face to heat. To calm herself, she drew a deep breath and concentrated on the details of the boat before her.

The packet tied to the dock was long and narrow. The hull was painted bright red, and a long white cabin with a row of windows took up most of its deck. Red Venetian blinds covered the windows, adding to its gay appearance. The top of the boat was also a deck, very slightly rounded to allow rain to shed, and surrounded by a low iron railing. Already the packet's crew was stacking passengers' baggage in neat rows on that upper deck. At the bow and stern of the main deck were much smaller spaces, only a few feet above the muddy water of the Erie Canal. The captain and the helmsman would command the small deck at the stern as they manned the tiller. The forward deck, as well as the upper, would allow passengers a place to sit and breathe the fresh mountain air while enjoying the scenic delights.

Though the August day was warm and the packet's cabin would likely be close, Clarissa could hardly wait to board. She was tired of standing on the dock waiting for her adventure to begin. Not to mention anxious to be away from the odors of the near-by stables which housed the horses and mules that would plod along the towpath beside the canal, pulling the packet boats and liners to their destinations.

Adjusting her wide-brimmed straw hat and straightening the jacket of her olive green traveling dress, she noted that the crew had reached her bags and were loading them onto the upper deck. Surely the passengers would be allowed to board soon.

A moment later the steward called for the passengers to make their way to the gangplank.

"Have your tickets ready, please," the man called in a booming voice. "You'll need to show your ticket before you step on the gangplank."

Clarissa hurried to take her place in line, a little miffed that the gentlemen passengers did not immediately make way for her. Well, that was her own fault for insisting on traveling alone. Not having an escort to open the way for her was a bother, but the freedom to do as she saw fit more than made up for the momentary aggravation.

At first her mother had flatly refused to allow Clarissa to travel unaccompanied, but Clarissa had prevailed in the end. After all, only the wealthiest patrons could afford a place on the packet boats of the Erie Canal. The riff-raff had to be content with the slower, more crowded conveyance of the liners, squeezed in amongst the freight those vessels hauled. Clarissa would be surrounded by gentry, with her own sleeping berth—in a separate section for ladies only, of course—and meals prepared and served by the packet's crew. Her journey to the wilds of Niagara Falls would be a genteel and refined excursion to view the juxtaposition of nature's beauty and man's industry with her own eyes. For Clarissa Bainbridge couldn't imagine a higher form of technological achievement than the engineering marvel that was the 363 mile long Erie Canal.

When Clarissa reached the steward, she handed him her ticket without comment. He glanced at it, nodded, and handed it back.

"Very well then, miss. Would you like assistance boarding the packet?" he asked, glancing from Clarissa to the gangplank that was little more than a four foot wide board linking the dock with the packet's deck.

She almost accepted, but then remembered her desire to be free from male supervision for this journey and declined. "Thank you," she said, "but no. I can manage on my own." Holding tightly to her ticket with one hand and her parasol with the other, she stepped onto the gang-plank and boarded her packet boat to adventure.

CHAPTER TWO

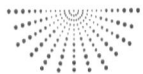

hree days later, Clarissa was ready for the voyage to end. She had seen lovely landscapes, to be sure, but she had also endured monotonous sections that lulled the senses and caused the hours to drag.

And she was heartily tired of the interior cabin. The novelty of watching the crew transform the sitting room into a dining room and later in the evening into sleeping quarters—separated into men's and ladies' sections by a thick curtain—had quite worn off. At least she was a lady and was not subjected to the extreme crowding that her male companions endured at night.

For while there were only six women to share the ladies' sleeping quarters, there were no fewer than sixty gentlemen. Since there were so few of them, the ladies each had lower berths, with no one sleeping above them. Not so the men. She'd seen their accommodations before the curtain was dropped. The gentlemen's berths were stacked three high with what had to be barely enough space between them to allow a man to crawl into his bed.

She shuddered to think of the close proximity… not to mention the smell since it was impossible to bathe on this boat.

Opening her fan, she waved it in front of her heated face. Two more days. They would dock in Buffalo in two more days. Then she would be free of this cramped, noisy, and too often dirty little packet boat.

"Very low bridge," the helmsman called, and Clarissa who was seated on the lower deck at the bow, glanced up to see a low stone bridge spanning the width of the canal. Above and behind her, she heard the men who were sitting on the upper deck scramble from their seats to lay flat on the deck. She'd experienced that scramble herself a time or two when she'd been unable to procure a seat on the lower deck, but had been unwilling to remain cooped up inside the cabin.

Smiling and fanning herself, she tilted her head back in time to see a young man climb onto the low stone wall of the bridge and prepare to jump.

Good lord! She hoped he wouldn't land on anyone. The passengers above would be unable to scramble out of the way, crouched as they were on the deck to avoid being scraped off into the canal's murky water. She passed into the shade under the bridge and immediately thereafter heard a thump and a yell as the newcomer landed on someone and both flattened themselves to avoid being hit by the stone solidity of the bridge.

Once the boat had cleared the obstacle, Clarissa jumped from her chair and climbed the stairs to see what was happening on the deck above.

A nice looking young man rose to his feet, dusted himself off, and offered his hand to a middle-aged man wearing a brown paisley waistcoat and a white shirt with the sleeves rolled to his elbows.

"Sorry about that," the young man said. "Hard to judge the landing when everyone is laid out to avoid the bridge."

The older fellow accepted the offered assistance and stood with some difficulty. "What were you doing jumping aboard in the first place?" If he sounded a bit testy, Clarissa couldn't blame him. She wouldn't have appreciated being jumped upon either.

The young man shrugged. "No docks nearby. This was as close as I could get to a packet boat."

"Well, you'll have to pay your fare, dock or no dock," said another deep voice. The captain had climbed the stairs at the other end of deck and now stood with his fists on his hips. "Come with me and I'll calculate your fee." The captain looked him up and down. "Our berths are full. You'll have to make do with a pallet on the floor."

"I expected as much," the new passenger said with a smile. He held out his hand. "Jeremy Pine."

The captain glanced at the man's hand, but didn't take it. Instead, he sniffed, jerked his chin toward the stairs, and said, "This way."

As the captain and the man retreated to the stern deck, Clarissa stepped down and resumed her seat.

"Well," she said quietly to herself. "That was unexpected."

CHAPTER THREE

*S*he couldn't have said why, but Clarissa found the newcomer unnerving. It wasn't his appearance; he was nice looking, to be sure, but she knew many young men with stronger chins, kinder eyes, and better grooming. It wasn't his manner; he was jovial and pleasant and went out of his way to be courteous to everyone, especially her. It wasn't even his speech, though his choice of words did strike her as a bit uncouth. But whatever it was, it jangled her nerves and kept her on guard whenever he was near.

She didn't trust him.

But other than his unorthodox method of boarding the packet, she had no reason to distrust him. Of course, the opposite was also true. But then, she had no reason to trust any of the other five ladies or sixty gentlemen who shared this cramped little boat with her. But none of them, nor any of the crew, concerned her. The newcomer did.

So she watched him.

She tried to be circumspect about her observations, but she watched him at meals, on the deck, she even tried to note where he placed his pallet every night, though that was not always possible, for once the curtain fell, it was not to be disturbed.

She carefully recorded all of her observations in her diary. Every. Single. One.

Her mother had given her the diary and made her promise that she'd keep a faithful record of her adventure and all that she observed on the way to and from Niagara Falls. But Clarissa doubted her mother had expected her to record the movements, expressions, and utterances of Jeremy Pine. A young man Clarissa would have never met had he not jumped from a bridge onto her packet boat.

At the very least, Mr. Pine relieved Clarissa's boredom with the plodding trip along the Erie Canal.

As they neared Buffalo, Clarissa's notes on Mr. Pine diminished. She didn't lose interest or cease to observe him, but he became quieter. Almost as though he desired to fade from other's notice. He drew into himself and his eyes narrowed. He watched everyone, and he noticed Clarissa watching him.

Clarissa stood at the rail of the forward deck, watching as the packet approached the dock in Buffalo. A shadow fell across her and she glanced around to find Jeremy Pine standing just behind her. Her heart pounded, but she remained still.

"You've been watching me," he said, moving to stand beside her. Too close beside her. "See something you like?"

She kept her gaze resolutely forward. "Not really."

He tapped a fist to his chest. "I'm wounded!"

"I doubt it," she answered, allowing herself a single sideways glance.

"Everyone else seems to find me amusing. Why not you?"

"Does it matter?"

He cocked his head and then turned to stare straight ahead. "I don't suppose it does. Still, our paths will part soon. I'd like to think you'll remember me fondly."

Clarissa turned to meet his gaze. "I doubt I'll remember you at all. Good day, Mr. Pine."

She turned and walked into the cabin, intending to gather her belongings, but stopped just inside the door, out of Jeremy Pine's sight. Listening intently, she heard him slip away down the narrow passage along the outside of the cabin toward the deck where the helmsman kept a steady hand on the tiller.

What could he be doing there? The passengers had been asked to steer clear of that small deck. Cautiously, she followed, but from inside the cabin. When she reached the back of the sitting room, she paused and eased open the door to the small galley where the captain's wife prepared their meals. Pressing her face close to the narrow opening she surveyed the room...

...and saw Jeremy Pine standing on tip-toe and reaching deep into an upper cabinet. When he pulled his arm out, he was grasping a small tin box which he quickly stuffed inside his shirt. Turning, he sauntered toward the door where Clarissa stood.

Without attempting to close the door, she turned and raced into the room, dropping into a chair and grabbing a book from a nearby shelf just as he pushed the door wide and stepped through.

Seeing her, he stopped short, then smiled and said, "Fancy meeting you here, Miss Bainbridge. I thought we'd said our farewells."

She glanced at him, hoping her cheeks weren't too pink. They certainly felt hot enough to give her away her exertions. "Indeed. I believe we've already said all that is necessary." She returned her gaze to the book... and noticed she was holding it upside down. Her breath caught, but she forced herself not to right it.

"Well," he said, "we'll be docking soon, so I'll leave you to your reading." He walked calmly down the length of the sitting room, onto the forward deck, and out of her sight.

Clarissa sat still for a moment, waiting for her heart to stop racing. Then she stood and walked through the galley and onto the stern deck. The helmsman stood at the tiller, carefully watching the horses as they plodded along the towpath, pulling the packet ever closer to its dock and the end of their journey.

How had Pine gotten past the helmsman unseen?

Or had he?

Clarissa bit her lip, suddenly unsure of what she should do. She'd expected to tell the helmsman of Pine's theft, but if he had allowed Pine to enter the galley without challenging him...

"Is there something you need, Miss? You shouldn't be back here."

She started, her heart racing again. "I know. I'm sorry to bother you, but I need to see the captain."

"And why would you need to see me this close to docking?" a gruff voice asked from behind her.

Clarissa whirled and found herself face-to-face with the packet's captain. She glanced over her shoulder at the helmsman before saying quietly, "If I could have a moment of your time, Captain, I'd like to speak with you... privately."

The captain raised his eyebrows, but gestured her into the galley and then through to the sitting room. "Now, how can I help you, Miss Bainbridge?"

She hesitated a moment, then blurted out. "Mr. Pine stole something from the galley. A small tin box." She gestured with her hands to indicate its size. "I saw him reaching into an upper cabinet and removing it."

The captain's eyes widened. "When?"

"Just a few moments ago."

The man turned and strode into the galley, going directly to the cabinet Pine had rifled. Reaching inside, he felt around, then withdrew an empty hand. His shoulders slumped.

"Well," he growled, "at least we haven't docked yet." Turning he spied Clarissa and smiled grimly. "Thank you, Miss Bainbridge. I'll take it from here."

Recognizing his dismissal, Clarissa hurried back through the sitting room and onto the forward deck. Relieved to find an unoccupied chair, she dropped into it, adjusted her straw hat to better shade her eyes, and watched the plodding horses while she listened to the commotion on the upper deck.

Voices shouted, but for once she didn't even try to understand what was being said. She had played her part. Now it was time for others to do the same.

CHAPTER FOUR

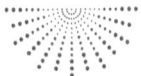

*C*larissa sat in a padded rocking chair on the wrap-around porch of the Endicott Hotel in Buffalo, New York sipping a cup of tea flavored with lemon and honey. Beside her, Mrs. Hargrove, a fellow passenger from the packet boat, practically bounced in her rocker.

"I can't believe you foiled a robbery," the woman said, her eyes round and her voice awed. "You must have been terrified! I know I would have been."

"Really, Mrs. Hargrove, it was nothing. I merely observed Mr. Pine doing something he oughtn't and reported it to the captain."

"But you were so calm," Mrs. Hargrove exclaimed. "My Henry was there on the upper deck when the captain apprehended the scoundrel, and he said that Mr. Pine said that he'd spoken to you only moments before and that he was sure he didn't know *what* you were on about." The woman paused to draw breath before continuing. "But the captain wouldn't hear anything against you and insisted on searching the man."

Clarissa took another sip of tea, resisting the temptation to speak in the opening Mrs. Hargrove had provided.

After taking a sip of her own tea, the woman continued. "And you know," she said, lowering her voice to a conspiratorial whisper, "when the search was done, Pine didn't have anything he oughtn't to. Well, my Henry thought it was all over, that you'd been mistaken and that Mr. Pine was innocent, but the Captain bellowed for the steward to take the tiller and the helmsman to come up."

"And?" asked Clarissa, curious now despite herself. She hadn't implicated the helmsman when she'd spoken to the captain.

"Well, my Henry says that's when everything went to… uhm… heck," Mrs. Hargrove said, her cheeks pinkening at the near slip of her tongue. "Evidently the helmsman jumped right into the canal, which is terribly muddy, and tried to make his way to shore. But the horseman left his team and waded in after him and the captain's son, who was helping the horseman, joined in and they caught him and dragged him back to the towpath."

Clarissa nodded. "Trying to get away simply confirmed his guilt."

"Yes," said Mrs. Hargrove. "He confessed and said it was all Mr. Pine's idea." She sat back, satisfied with the outcome. "My Henry says they're both locked up in the Buffalo jail right this minute." She paused before continuing dramatically. "And it's all thanks to you, Miss Bainbridge."

"Well," Clarissa said after another sip of tea. "I can't really take any credit. After all, I simply made an observation and reported it to the proper person."

"Perhaps," Mrs. Hargrove said, "but the captain says you can take passage on his packet boat anytime you like. That tin held all the money from all of our fares. The captain and his family would've been hard put to keep their boat if they'd lost it."

Clarissa sighed contentedly and took another sip of tea. She'd saved a good man and his family... and had quite the adventure. And she hadn't even seen Niagara Falls yet!

Mother was never going to believe the story Clarissa's diary would tell.

PART II
MISS BAINBRIDGE'S
CHRISTMAS PARTY

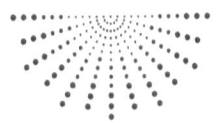

DEBBIE MUMFORD

BESTSELLING AUTHOR OF *SORCHA'S HEART*

Miss Bainbridge's
Christmas Party

CHAPTER ONE

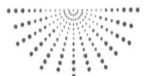

*M*iss Clarissa Bainbridge extended her white gloved hand to the footman and stepped into her father's well maintained black carriage. After tucking the woolen lap robe across her knees, she slid her gloved fingers into the depths of her white rabbit fur muff and sighed happily. Everything was in readiness for tonight's Christmas party. She had only to hand deliver one last invitation. Sir Gerald Lannington and his mother, Lady Helena, had only arrived in Albany yesterday evening, and this was Clarissa's first opportunity to issue their invitation. She did so hope they would be able to attend, despite the short notice.

After all, the party she had arranged would be the highlight of Albany's Christmas season. So many new trimmings in this Year of Our Lord 1830. Why gift-giving was now considered *de rigueur* and decorated fir trees were just coming into style, and Clarissa had ensured that her party was up to snuff in both areas! She and her mother and their maids had spent countless hours stringing popcorn and cranberries, making cut paper ornaments, and sewing small lace bags that would hold favors of hard candies and sugared nuts to be provided to each guest as a token gift as they gathered their great coats and pelisses to depart.

Everything was arranged to perfection, but the evening could only be enhanced by the presence of English nobility. It wasn't often that such refined personages deigned to spend Christmas in Albany, New York, and Clarissa was determined to add their glittering personalities to her party tonight.

She did so hope they would choose to attend!

Her carriage clattered to a halt on the cobblestone street, and Clarissa put aside the lap robe just as the footman opened the door. Allowing herself to be handed down, Clarissa gazed up at the stately townhome Sir Gerald and his mother had hired for their stay. The brownstone building rose two stories above a raised basement and boasted a small front lawn, now covered in a dusting of snow. A finely detailed cast iron fence and gate separated the yard from the street and a balustraded stoop rose to the main entrance.

Miss Clarissa Bainbridge lived in a townhome as well, but her family's dwelling was neither as broad nor as tall as this one, and her stoop was not nearly as grand as this fine example of Albany architecture. Of course, her family was not of noble blood, so allowances must be made.

Taking a deep breath, she nodded to the footman, who hurried to open the gate for her, and raising her skirts just enough to ensure good footing, mounted the stoop to the beautifully paneled and carved front door. Adjusting her pelisse and touching her fur trimmed bonnet to be sure it sat squarely upon her chestnut curls, Clarissa raised the iron door knocker and rapped twice. A few moments later, a liveried butler answered her knock.

"I am sorry, madam," he said, looking down his long nose at her, "but the family is not yet receiving callers. Would you care to leave your card?"

Clarissa inclined her head ever so slightly. "Thank you, Mister…" She paused waiting for him to supply his surname.

"Walters."

She smiled. "Thank you, Mr. Walters. Please see that her ladyship receives this invitation and my card." Pulling the items from the lining of her muff, she handed them to Walters.

He glanced at her card, nodded, and said, "Very good, Miss Bainbridge. You may be assured that her ladyship will receive both at her earliest convenience.

Clarissa nodded and was turning to go when her foot slipped on an icy patch and she landed in a most undignified fashion on a hard brownstone step. Before she could do more than pull her pelisse and skirts more decorously around her legs both Walters and her own footman, Jenkins, were at her side.

"I say, Miss Clarissa," Jenkins said, kneeling beside her, "are you well?"

Walters sniffed. "Of course she is not well, you dolt. She's taken a serious tumble." He offered Clarissa his hand. "Do you think you can stand, Miss?"

Clarissa accepted the proffered hand and made a brave attempt to rise. Pain shot from her ankle all the way to her heart the moment her foot touched stone. She cried out and collapsed again to the cold, hard surface of the stoop's top step.

Walters knelt beside her. "If I may presume, Miss, I'll carry you into the parlor and call one of the maids to assist you."

Jenkins planted his fists on his hips and glared at Walters. "Here now! If anyone is to take liberties with Miss Clarissa's person, it shall be me." He turned his gaze on the young lady. "Come now, Miss. I'm sure you'd rather I bundled you into the carriage and saw you home, wouldn't you?"

Clarissa grimaced. "Thank you, Jenkins, but I don't think I could endure the swaying and bumping of a carriage ride right now. Mr. Walters, you have my permission to attempt to lift me. If I am too much for you, I'm sure Jenkins will assist."

"Not to worry, Miss," Walters said. "A little slip of a thing like you won't be a problem." And placing one arm behind her back and the other beneath her knees, the butler lifted her carefully from the step and carried her through that lovely front door and into the parlor, Jenkins following close behind.

When she was settled on a sofa with her injured foot propped on a pillow, Walters rang for a maid. While he was explaining that the young lady had taken a fall and would need assistance removing her pelisse and fur hat, Clarissa turned her attention to Jenkins.

"If you would be so kind, Jenkins, please return home and inform Mother what has happened. Tell her that I've likely sprained my ankle, but that I should be home well in advance of the Christmas party."

Jenkins bowed. "Of course, Miss. Shall I come back to collect you?"

Walters, overhearing this remark, said, "That won't be necessary, young man. When Miss Bainbridge is ready to leave I shall order her ladyship's coach to convey her."

Clarissa nodded her thanks.

"Now, if you'll be good enough to make a detour and deliver a note to her ladyship's physician, I think we should retire and allow Ellen to help Miss Bainbridge out of her pelisse." So saying, Walters ushered Jenkins from the room and pulled the parlor's sliding doors closed.

CHAPTER TWO

*M*iss Clarissa Bainbridge rested at her ease on the thickly cushioned sofa in the front parlor of Lady Helena Lannington's Albany residence. Her ladyship's maid, Ellen, had taken Clarissa's pelisse and hat, smoothed her chestnut curls, and provided her with a cup of hot tea, sweetened with milk and sugar, and a plate of shortbread cookies, though Ellen had referred to them as *biscuits*.

Now Clarissa awaited the arrival of the physician, whom Walters assured her would come immediately on receipt of the note written on her ladyship's stationary. While she waited, Clarissa took note of her surroundings. While she understood that the Lanningtons had hired the brownstone furnished, she was nonetheless fascinated by the graciousness of the room. The walls were painted a pale, new-leaf green, with the woodwork a very slightly darker shade. The central area of the hardwood floor was covered in a Turkish carpet of tasteful design. Sheer lace glass curtains covered the two windows, their heavy, brocade drapes of deep forest green were tied back allowing light into the room. Matching brocade valances completed the window treatment.

The furnishings were classic and elegant. The sofa— upon which Clarissa now reclined, loveseat, and several arm chairs were upholstered in a vine and rose patterned damask, as were several ottomans. The circular tea-table, lamp tables, and sofa tables were of cherry wood and polished to a high sheen, as was the elaborately carved curio cabinet in the corner. The fireplace, with its merrily dancing flames, was as ornately decorated as the rest of the furnishings, and the intricately designed iron fire screen was a thing of beauty.

Clarissa had just finished cataloguing the room's decorations when she heard voices in the hall. Perhaps the physician had arrived? She hadn't heard a knock or the opening of the front door, but her mind had been rather occupied with memorizing the furnishings in order to share the details with her mother at a later time.

Footsteps sounded on the hardwood floors of the hall and then the parlor doors slid open. Walters stepped into the room, his back ramrod straight. He cleared his throat to assure her attention, and announced, "Sir Gerald Lannington."

The gentleman who entered the room wore a dark gray morning coat, matching waistcoat, white shirt, and dove-gray trousers. His dark hair was side-parted and he sported mutton chop whiskers. Clarissa knew Sir Gerald to be of marriageable age, but had not expected the man to cut quite such a dashing figure.

"Sir Gerald," Walters continued, "Miss Clarissa Bainbridge."

"Please forgive me for not rising, sir." Clarissa's cheeks heated at her inability to stand and offer Sir Gerald the required curtsy.

"Not at all, Miss Bainbridge." Sir Gerald's voice was a very pleasing baritone, and Clarissa watched through her lashes as he strode into the room to stand near the fireplace. "I'm only sorry that our stoop has caused you injury." He glanced at Walters, who remained near the parlor door. "Has the physician been summoned?"

"He has, sir."

Sire Gerald nodded. "Very well. You may go, Walters. Please have Ellen inform Mother of our guest."

"At once, sir." Walters departed, leaving the parlor door open, as was proper in mixed company.

Sir Gerald turned his attention to Clarissa. "If I may ask, Miss Bainbridge, what brought you to our door this morning?"

"Oh! In all the commotion, I quite forgot." Clarissa clasped her hands in her lap and glanced toward the open door, wishing Walters would return. "I brought an invitation for you and her ladyship to a Christmas party this evening. I'm afraid I gave it to Mr. Walters prior to my... uhm... my fall."

"I see. No doubt Walters has sent it up to Mother." He waved the matter away, but then glanced at Clarissa again. "I doubt we'll be able to attend. It *is* rather short notice."

"Of course," she said, "though you did only just arrive in town and I didn't want to offend by failing to issue the invitation."

His eyebrows winged up and he cocked his head. "I'm sure neither Mother nor myself would have taken offense, but it was very good of you to extend the courtesy."

He smiled as he uttered these words, and Clarissa wished for a fan. Not only did she need to cool her heated cheeks, but she would have appreciated the ability to hide her face... and perhaps peer at him from behind the safety of the fan's screen. Lord! She'd found the man dashing before, but when he smiled! Well, Sir Gerald Lannington was quite the most handsome man she'd ever seen.

CHAPTER THREE

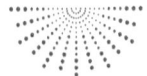

*S*ir Gerald Lannington observed the young lady currently resting on his sofa, considered the actions that had placed her there, and decided she was quite the most interesting person he'd encountered since arriving upon American soil. He and his mother had spent a month in New York City and had received numerous invitations to dinner parties, theatrical evenings, and even a ball or two, but none of the hostesses of those events would have dreamed of hand-delivering the invitation. That was what servants were for, after all.

And yet this pretty young female had made the effort to present herself at his door just to ensure that he and his lady mother would know that their arrival had been noted and that their attendance at tonight's party was desired. She'd undoubtedly assumed they would not attend. Not on such short notice.

And yet, the effort had been made… and an injury sustained.

Remarkable.

Uncertain of his next conversational gambit, Sir Gerald was about to withdraw to the window when he heard the unmistakable sound of his mother's footsteps. Two beats of her fashionable leather boots accompanied by the thump of her cane and the swish of heavy silk skirts. He crossed the room to the open door in time to usher his mother inside, waving Walters away as he did so. No need for a second formal announcement.

Taking his mother's free arm, he led her to an upholstered arm chair. When she was comfortably settled, he took his own seat and made the introductions.

"Mother, this is Miss Bainbridge." He nodded to Clarissa. "Miss Bainbridge, my mother, Lady Helena Lannington."

He noted with pleasure— odd, really. Why should the young lady's good manners please him?— that Miss Bainbridge refrained from speaking until Lady Helena opened the conversation.

"I'm told you took a fall on our front stoop, Miss Bainbridge. Are you quite comfortable?"

Clarissa inclined her head and lowered her eyes as she replied. "Yes, my lady. Walters and Ellen have taken pains to see to my comfort." She bit her lip lightly before continuing. "I must apologize. I had no thought to intrude upon your privacy and will be gone as soon as the physician has pronounced me fit to travel home."

While the two ladies spoke of trivialities, the weather and the dangers of icy steps, Sir Gerald studied the pair of them. His mother, a striking dowager with meticulously coiffed gray hair under a lace cap, and the lovely, petite Miss Bainbridge. The young lady's chestnut hair was modestly styled with ringlets falling to the shoulders of her pale blue morning gown. A stray lock had escaped, forming a small curl at her temple. He found that little curl absurdly charming.

"Don't you agree, Gerald?"

Sir Gerald startled. Yanking his thoughts from the contemplation of Miss Bainbridge's curls, and perhaps even the imagined softness of her lips, he said, "What? I'm sorry, Mother, I'm afraid I was wool-gathering."

"Honestly, boy," Lady Helena huffed. "Do try to pay attention when we are in company. I said, we are much too fatigued by travel to attend a Christmas party tonight. Do you not agree?"

Sir Gerald glanced at Miss Bainbridge, who had bitten her lower lip and fluttered her lashes in quite the most adorable fashion when his mother had rebuked him, and saw disappointment bloom in her lovely blue eyes. A sudden wish to please overcame him. He simply couldn't allow her to be disappointed. Not if it was within his power to prevent.

He turned to his mother. "If you are overtired, Mother, then of course you must remain in residence for the evening." He smiled at Miss Bainbridge. "But I would not miss this party for the world."

CHAPTER FOUR

iss Clarissa Bainbridge sat enthroned like a princess in a wing backed chair beside the Christmas tree. Her injured ankle rested on a cushioned footstool, and though she fidgeted, wishing she could see to the myriad last minute details before the guests began arriving at her door, she kept her seat. After all, Lady Helena's physician had been very firm. She would only be allowed to return home, where a grand party was scheduled for that evening, if she promised to stay off her feet. She was not to put weight on that ankle for at least the next several days.

She had given her word.

Of course she had given her word! Had not the very handsome Sir Gerald Lannington agreed to attend her Christmas party? How could she possibly miss what was now certain to be the event of the season? Even if missing said event would mean she was forced to remain in the Lannington household?

She would far rather attend the party, even if she did have to remain seated, than to spend the evening tucked up in an unfamiliar bedchamber.

Besides, Sir Gerald could hardly visit her in her bedroom, but she had hopes that he would condescend to converse with her for at least a few moments during the party.

So she sat as quietly as she could manage while her mother and their maids, Darcy and Emma, lit the candles on the tree. When her father joined them and laid a hand on her shoulder, she breathed out a happy sigh.

"It's a lovely sight," her mother said, pinching out her taper, and stepping to join her husband and daughter.

"I must admit, I had doubts about bringing a tree into the house," Clarissa's father admitted, "but it does make a pretty sight."

Clarissa clapped her hands, joy filling her heart. "It's absolutely magical."

Just then Jenkins, who was performing the role of under butler for the party, ushered in the first guests. As her mother and father moved to welcome the new arrivals, Clarissa studied the Christmas tree. Cranberries and popcorn. Cut paper and candles. A small, well-shaped fir tree. Who would have thought such simple ingredients could combine to create such a beautiful vision?

She was delighted that her family had been among the first to adopt what had seemed a somewhat outlandish idea, and now that she had seen it arrayed in all its finery, she was determined to make it a Christmas tradition.

"Your tree is quite the loveliest I have yet seen."

Startled, Clarissa turned her attention from the tree to find Sir Gerald standing beside her chair.

"Oh! Sir Gerald," she said, once again wishing for a fan to hide behind. She knew he was to attend, knew he had this effect on her. Why, oh why hadn't she thought to have Emma fetch her white lace fan?

Of course, she knew why the fan had been overlooked. Dressing in her best ruby red silk dress with white lace accent at bodice and cuffs had been difficult to manage while avoiding placing any weight on her injured ankle. Emma had had quite enough to deal with without intuiting that her mistress would be in need of a fan to hide behind during the party.

Clarissa lowered her eyes and hoped any pinkness in her cheeks would be attributed to the candlelit tree and the excitement of the party in general, rather than the nearness of the estimable Sir Gerald.

"I didn't realize you had arrived."

"I only just walked in," he said. Was that a twinkle in his eye, or simply a reflection from the candles on the tree? "You made such a pretty picture sitting here beside the tree that I had to give you my compliments."

Clarissa's heart leapt and she knew her cheeks must be flaming, but she couldn't deny his words pleased her beyond reason.

Glancing around the room, he gestured to a straight backed chair with a needlepoint cushion, and asked, "Might I be permitted to rearrange the furniture and join you?"

Clarissa's mouth went dry and her tongue felt glued in place, but she managed to whisper, "Of course."

A warm glow settled over her person as Clarissa watched the handsome young Englishman stride across the room. The very same young man who had seen her home after her morning's adventure. Who had insisted on carrying her inside— against her protests that it was unseemly, that Jenkins could unquestionably accomplish that task in his stead. The young man who had convinced his lady mother to attend the party this evening, and who was even now preparing to do her the singular honor of sitting beside her and keeping her company during the party, the gaiety of which now swirled around her.

As Sir Gerald hefted the chair and prepared to return, Lady Helena appeared at Clarissa's side.

"I do believe my son is smitten, young lady," the dowager said, thumping her cane to assure Clarissa's attention.

Clarissa quelled her nerves and turned a wide-eyed gaze upon the older woman. "Oh, Lady Helena! I'm sure you are mistaken."

"I most certainly am not." Lady Helena tilted her head and studied the young lady ensconced in the wing-backed chair. With an almost imperceptible nod, she continued, "I know my son, and his every mood." She patted Clarissa's arm and smiled. "Be careful of his heart, my dear, for it is the greatest Christmas gift you will ever receive." And stepping away, she made room for her son to place a chair beside the very pretty, and now visibly flustered, young lady.

And that is how a slip on an icy Albany stoop caused Miss Clarissa Bainbridge's Christmas party to become her final such seasonal event... for the next year she was no longer Miss Bainbridge, but Lady Clarissa Lannington.

PART III
THE TRAIL WHERE WE CRIED

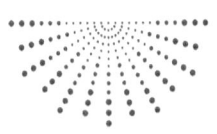

DEBBIE MUMFORD
BESTSELLING AUTHOR OF *SORCHA'S HEART*

THE TRAIL
WHERE WE CRIED

SPUN YARNS
A Short Story

CHAPTER ONE

he soldiers told us we would reach our destination within the week. I didn't believe them. My life had been reduced to an endless trail of misery. I would walk until I died, just as my mother and sister had. My father hadn't even begun the journey, dying of dysentery while still penned within that horrible removal fort.

The sun shone in a cloudless blue sky, but it shed no warmth. The snow had finally gone and this piece of road was packed and dry, but my blistered feet found no relief. The leather boots I'd worn on the day of removal had long since fallen to pieces. Now my only shoes were blood-stained rags.

I closed my eyes and plodded on, following my uncles and the mothers of my clan. I couldn't smell the sweetness of the day, only my own foul stink and the fetid odors of my people. I'd forgotten what it was to be clean and well-fed and content.

All of life's goodness had been stripped from us along with our homes and land. No joy remained in the world. Only tears and despair and this endless trail.

Once I was a daughter of the Tsalagi, Cherokee in the white man's tongue. A maiden on the verge of womanhood. Now I was nothing. A starving stick-figure without family or home or hope.

Sometimes at night, as I lay huddled on the ground with only one thin blanket and the warmth of my clan mothers' bodies to protect me from the cold, I dreamed of home; of what was no more. Of the father and mother and little sister who had loved me. Of our village, deep in the ancestral lands of the Tsalagi Nation. Of our fields of sweet corn, plentiful beans, and plump, healthy squash.

The Great Spirit gave those lands into our care and we loved them. The mountains and valleys carved by the wings of the Great Buzzard, the rocks marked by the frightful claws of Uktena, the horned serpent. The Creator set the first man and first woman of the Tsalagi in that land, and we had remained.

We were an ancient people, wise in the ways of the world. In times of ease and plenty, the white chief, our peace chief, led us with wisdom and compassion. When hard times caused other nearby nations to raid, the council of mothers called for war and our red chief, the war chief, led our men in battle to defend our homes and fields.

We were not a war-like people, but when the mothers decided the time had come, we were not afraid to fight.

This was the way of the Tsalagi. This was how it had always been.

Until the white Americans saw that our land was good and determined to take it for their own.

Now we had nothing. Only the clothes we had worn when the soldiers drove us from our homes. We hadn't been allowed to carry anything away. Everything now belonged to the state of Georgia. Our land. Our homes. Even the possessions within our homes.

Our Principal Chief, John Ross, had fought long and hard for our rights. Other nations had been removed from their lands, but John Ross and our tribal council fought, not with guns and knives, but using the American's own laws. Ross took our cause all the way to the American's Supreme Court ... and won.

We celebrated when news of that victory reached our village. The Chief Justice, a white man named John Marshall, had decreed that the Cherokee were a sovereign nation and that Georgia had no right to claim our lands.

But the soldiers came anyway and drove us into stockades like cattle.

The American President, Andrew Jackson, had defied the courts and sided with the state. The Supreme Court had ruled, but the justices had no power to enforce their decision. That power lay with the President.

Our nation was at an end. Our lands were forfeit. We were forced to march to a place no one wanted: the Indian Territory.

CHAPTER TWO

The Removal became a reality for me on a fine day in May, 1838. I had followed my charges, a group of rambunctious children, to a meadow beyond our fields. The morning sun shone warm on my back. The fields of corn bristled with straight rows of healthy seedlings. A cool breeze teased the ends of my long dark braids and birds sang in the trees at the edge of the meadow. The boys laughed and ran, already choosing sides for a game of stick ball. The little girls carried corn dollies and danced, practicing the steps of the Green Corn Dance.

I breathed in the sweet scents of home, the good dark earth beneath my feet, the green promise of corn and squash, and the fresh cool tang of running water. I settled in the shade of an ancient oak and smoothed my homespun skirts. Pulling my work bag from my shoulder, I rummaged within and found the pine-needle basket I'd started the day before. I would finish it now while I watched the children play.

I'd heard the rumblings of my elders, was aware that John Ross was concerned about something called The Removal, but I wasn't worried. Our village lay in the very heart of our lands, far from the grasping hands of the Americans. We held to the old traditions. Few of our people had intermarried with the whites, and those who made that choice had left our lands, settling on the fringes of the Cherokee Nation.

White missionaries came among us occasionally, but our elders chose to honor our own spirituality. We listened politely to their stories, shared our meals with them, and offered them shelter when they chose to stay, but we held to our own beliefs.

The one concession our mothers made to the outside world was that a few of our younger people learned English. When the missionaries came a few of us worked to learn their language. I learned quickly.

The sound of hoofbeats pulled me from my reverie. I called the children to me and stood between them and the approaching riders. My heart beat like thunder in my chest as the men came into view. I'd never seen so many horses and these were lathered from hard riding. The men wore blue uniforms, their faces grim and covered in hair like some of the white missionaries.

Bile rose in my throat, burning away my voice, but I stood firm as two riders broke away from the column and rode straight at us. Dust swirled in the air from the horses' hooves, clogging my nose and throat.

The soldiers dismounted. I'd never seen an American soldier before, but I'd heard stories. I knew that was what these men must be.

"You there," called the first, pointing at me. "Get those little 'uns over to the road."

I held my chin high and stood still, arms outstretched to protect my charges.

The second man stepped closer. "Did you hear what he said?" he asked. "Or are you too stupid to understand?"

"I understand," I said, swallowing my fear. I was determined to act like a woman of the people even if I wasn't one yet. "I will take these children back to the village. Back to their parents."

"No," said the first man, "you will not. These are no longer your lands. That village and these fields and everything inside those houses now belongs to Georgia."

"That's right," said the second. "We're here to remove you squatters from Georgia's land." He stepped forward, grabbed my shoulder and pushed me roughly. "Now get over to the road."

I stumbled and fell to my knees.

One of the bigger boys ran forward and hit the soldier who'd pushed me. The man swatted him to the ground like an annoying insect. The little girls wailed and the other boys surrounded their friend.

"Stop," I called in Tsalagi. I glanced toward the village and saw our men and women milling on the road, surrounded by white men with guns and swords. I wanted to puke, but swallowed the bile and stood, holding out my arms to the frightened children. "Come with me. We must join our parents."

The children surrounded me, clinging to my skirts and glaring at the blue-clad men. Holding my head high, I led the boys and girls to the road.

Only moments before they had been playing familiar games, safe on the breast of the land that had been ours for eternity. Now armed men pushed and prodded us down a road claiming that our land belonged to someone named Georgia.

My world had changed from whispering winds and birdsong to thundering hoofbeats and the clatter of steel.

What would become of us?

CHAPTER THREE

*W*e were herded into a nearby fort like so many animals. Soldiers armed with shining rifles watched over us every step of the way. I heard two of them talking, shaking their heads over the fact that the rough stockade — a *removal fort*, he called it — had been constructed just to hold us while the occupants of nearby villages were rounded up. Once all were accounted for, we would be marched to an internment camp somewhere in Tennessee.

Though the missionaries had told me my English was excellent, the soldiers' words held no meaning. I didn't understand what an internment camp was and I had no idea where Tennessee might be. All I knew was that my home was gone and I was penned inside high log walls with no shelter and little food or water.

The fort was a simple structure. Four tall log walls with a guard tower at each corner as well as one by the only gate into the stockade. Barracks for the soldiers had been built outside the walls. There were no buildings inside. No shelter for those of us confined within.

Our family claimed a few square feet near the western wall of the fort. The sun warmed us in the morning, ending the chill of nights spent in the open without blankets or extra clothing. By noon, the light and heat were no longer welcome, but punishments to be endured. When the wagons bearing food and water entered the fort, my little sister, Yellow Bird, and I would jostle for places in their shade while we waited for our family's meager allotment of rations.

As the sun moved past the edge of the log wall, our space would become blessedly shady and cool. Yellow Bird and I would revel in the relief from the blistering heat, until the coolness lost it's friendly succor and turned into our nightly enemy.

We huddled together in the darkness, Mother and Father holding Yellow Bird and me between them, sharing their warmth as best they could. Mother would sing us to sleep through chattering teeth, while Father reminded us how lucky we were that it was summer. Winter would've been unendurable.

And so the relentless days passed while other villages were decimated and other bewildered families were herded into the stockade. Father met often with the other men, while Mother joined the council of mothers, hoping for news of what lay ahead.

I tried to remain calm, to help Yellow Bird and the other children not to cry and whine. I told them stories of coyote and raven and sister fox, and made up quiet games to help occupy their minds. To occupy my own mind; to hold my fears at bay.

Until the day Father fell ill.

Mother shooed me away from our small area. "You father is not well," she said with a glance over her shoulder. "Take Yellow Bird to the center of the camp and ask Red Sorrel to care for her, then go to the mothers and ask if anyone has herbs for bloody flux."

A wave of fear washed over me. In our village, in the comfort of our home, bloody flux would be a fearsome enemy. Here, with little water and no medicinal herbs, it would be deadly. I gazed into my mother's eyes and saw the truth. Father would not live.

I wanted to scream, to run at the soldiers and beat them bloody for bringing us to this horrible place, but I held my breath and pushed my panic to a dark corner of my mind. If Mother could be calm, so could I.

Nodding my understanding, I took my sister's hand and obeyed.

No one had herbs. What small stores the medicine woman had carried in her work bag when she'd been forced from her home had long since been used.

I approached the gates, and shading my eyes, looked up at the soldiers who guarded the entrance. "Please, sir," I called, using my politest tones. "My father is ill."

A blue-uniformed soldier leaned over the wall and stared down at me. "So? What do you expect me to do about it?"

"He needs fresh water and medicine," I called. When he didn't respond, but only stared, I continued, "If you don't have any herbs, I could gather them. I know what to look for."

He laughed, a harsh guffaw that grated on my already raw nerves. "What? You expect me to let you out so you can go berry picking in the forest? Not bloody likely, girlie."

I bit my lip to keep from crying. "Water, then," I called. "We need more water. Please!"

He shook his head. "Food and water will be distributed at the appointed time." With that he moved to the other side of the tower and disappeared from view.

I returned to our little camp determined to help Mother cope. We would do our best for Father. Other women, hearing our plight, scrounged what water and rags they could and gave them to us. Mother tried to shield me from the worst, both for my father's dignity and for my own peace of mind, but it wasn't possible. We had no privacy and little ability even to keep him clean.

The indignities he suffered as he lost all control of his bodily functions...I was relieved when he ceased to recognize us. The terrible sights, disgusting smells, and hellacious sounds of those horrific days will never leave me.

In the end, the very soldiers who would not help us dragged my beloved father's corpse away to be burned with the other poor souls who perished in that awful place.

CHAPTER FOUR

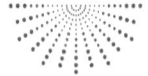

I shook myself from the despair of my memories and tried to see beauty in the day. I paused on the road, longing to sit down and rest my blistered feet, but knew I didn't dare. Mounted soldiers patrolled our march and I'd seen more than one straggler whipped into line.

Laughter reached my ears and I glanced toward the welcome sound. No one laughed on our miserable trail.

Four young whites, close to my age, raced toward us. Two boys and two girls, their pockets and aprons bulging.

I watched them warily. I no longer expected anything good from white American hands. I was not disappointed. Both the boys and one of the girls began pelting my people with rotten fruit.

We were so world-weary that those affected didn't even pause in their shuffling gait. Heads bowed under the weight of their hopelessness, they simply endured, wiping the mess from dirty faces and tattered clothing as they moved beyond their tormentors' range.

The second girl had clearly intended to join the fun, but she'd run up so close to me that our eyes met, and in that instant something changed. A shadow crossed her face and she lowered the rotten plum that was staining her fingers with blood-red ooze.

She dropped the corners of her apron and other nasty fruit splattered to the ground at her leather-booted feet. Her gaze never leaving my face, she reached into her pocket, pulled out a windfall apple, and offered it to me.

I glanced from her to the apple and back again, not sure what to do. In my experience, white hands didn't offer gifts freely.

"Go ahead," she said. "You can have it."

I took it from her hand, careful not to touch her sticky fingers, and raised it to my nose. Closing my eyes, I inhaled deeply ... and relaxed. The sweet, tangy fragrance took me home. For a moment I was back in the orchard near our village, my little sister high in the branches of an ancient apple tree, laughing and tossing glossy red fruit into my waiting hands.

A small smile curved my lips and I opened my eyes. Whatever else the white men had stolen from me, my memories remained. My family lived as long as I could recall those precious moments.

I reached into the cotton bag slung over my shoulder and drew out the corn dollie Yellow Bird had carried from our home. It was all I had left of her. All but my memories.

"It's all I have to trade," I said, holding it out to the girl. "It was my little sister's."

Her eyes widened and she took a step back from me, hiding her hands behind her back.

"That's all right," she said. "I don't need no trade. Enjoy the apple."

Her words surprised me, and I lowered my head to hide the tears that threatened to fall. "Thank you," I whispered.

Clutching that apple to my chest, a talisman of both memory and unexpected kindness, I resumed my endless journey along the trail stained by the grief and hopelessness of my people. But my back was a little straighter and my step a little lighter than before.

CHAPTER FIVE

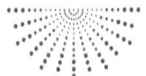

We arrived in the Indian Territory on a wind-swept day in early March, at a place the elders had named Tahlequah.

I sank into the dry and brittle grass, well trodden by the weary feet of my people, and cried. When my tears were spent, I raised my eyes and gazed at my new land.

I did not see mountains and valleys carved by the wings of the Great Buzzard or rocks marked by the frightful claws of Uktena, the horned serpent, but I did see rolling hills, vast plains, and shining lakes. These were not the lands where the Creator had set the first man and first woman of the Tsalagi, but He had allowed the white Americans to drive us to this place, and we had survived.

I had survived.

Though still a girl in years, hardship had molded me into a woman. I was not yet ready to take my place in the council of mothers, but The Removal had shaped and strengthened me. As I looked upon the strange land the white men had forced my people to accept, I knew that when my time came, I would work tirelessly to rebuild our nation. The Tsalagi would rise again, and though we were weak now, our numbers decimated, we would remain.

This would be our home, and Tahlequah would be the heart of our nation.

PART IV
SISTERS IN SUFFRAGE

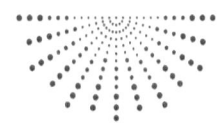

DEBBIE MUMFORD

SISTERS IN
SUFFRAGE

SPUN YARNS
A Short Story

PROLOGUE

I was nineteen years old that cold November night in 1917. Even though the world was at war, a pretty girl of good family such as myself should have been attending dances and being wooed by handsome young men. I should have been accepting my place in society as a wealthy man's decorative bride. Never should I have been subjected to the humiliations of prison nor beatings at the hands of brutal guards.

Never should I have had the audacity to stand sentinel to my beliefs with a banner in hand in front of the White House.

I had made my choices and they had led me to a night of terror.

CHAPTER ONE

Though my heart pounded with excitement and my mind buzzed with nervous questions, I strode confidently along the street, my navy skirt and linen petticoats swishing around my ankles, the lace of my starched white mutton-sleeved blouse brushed my chin, and a little feathered hat perched jauntily on my upswept dark hair. The air was redolent with flowers from Lafayette Park and birdsong lilted in the breeze. In short, it was a beautiful summer day in Washington, D.C.

I stopped before the stately three-story home that housed my destination, Alice Paul's newly formed National Women's Party. Had I done the right thing in coming here? I'd defied my father, who was even now assiduously seeking an advantageous marriage for his only daughter. I'd left his home and protection without permission. Had I made a wise choice? My heart hammered in my chest and my throat constricted. Panic near to choked me.

I closed my eyes and willed myself to calm. Too late for misgivings now. I had arrived. Opening my eyes and breathing in the sweet summer air, I studied the women who moved purposefully across the lawn and porch, who threaded in and out the ornately carved front door. Young women barely old enough to be out of short skirts, matrons who would look at home with children round their knees, and dignified matriarchs who might be holding court over large family gatherings. A full range of the feminine spectrum. My panic eased. This was where I belonged, these were my equals, my sex, but more than that, my sisters in suffrage. For we were all here for one purpose: to join Alice Paul in demanding that our government, as represented by the man who resided across the park in the White House, hear and respect our voices.

I settled my face in what I hoped was a pleasant expression, lifted the latch on the front gate, and stepped onto the stone pavers that led to the porch. A young woman separated herself from a group gathered around a long table and approached, her golden hair shining in the afternoon sun.

"Hello," she said with a smile. "Are you new? I don't believe I've seen you here before."

I licked my lips and straightened my shoulders. "Yes, I've only just arrived from New York." I glanced again at the women who chatted and laughed as they worked around me. "Is this the NWP?"

Her beautiful, liquid-brown eyes widened and filled with a fervent light. "Oh, yes. Have you come to join us?"

I held out my gloved hand, which she immediately clasped with paint-stained fingers. "I have. My name is Emily Tuttle, and I've come to stand sentinel with Alice Paul."

"Welcome, Emily. I'm Tilly Armbruster. If you've only just arrived, you'll need a place to stay." She bit her lip, then leaned forward and whispered conspiratorially, "I've a room here at headquarters, which you'd be most welcome to share. Did you leave your bags at the station?"

I nodded, and Tilly led me inside.

As easily as that I became a suffragist, and Tilly Armbruster became my fast friend.

CHAPTER TWO

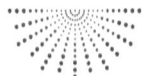

Father was right. I was naïve in the extreme.

I joined the NWP alight with patriotic fervor. Father had always espoused the belief that government derived its power from the consent of the governed, but somehow he failed to see that Mother and I also factored into that equation. He believed wholeheartedly that he had the right to voice his opinions and be heard, that he had the right to vote, to send representatives to Washington to enact laws on his behalf. But he overlooked his wife and daughter. As head of the household, he spoke for us. His voice, his vote, should be sufficient for us.

I disagreed, and so I journeyed to Washington and joined the Silent Sentinels of the NWP.

Somehow I'd imagined that once President Wilson read our banners and saw us standing there, women of all ages, all from good families, all discreetly clad, he would honor our request and champion our cause. The rights of mothers and grandmothers, sisters and aunts, daughters and nieces. Such was not the case.

At first he tipped his hat to the sentinels as he walked by, exhibiting a bemused confusion, as though uncertain why my sisters in suffrage were there. Later he ignored them. By the time I arrived and took my place, the mood had changed. America had entered the Great War and the men who passed us on the streets cast evil glances our way, calling us unpatriotic. How dare we picket a sitting president when the nation was at war?

When I first heard these sentiments, my belly shriveled and writhed and I cast my eyes down, afraid to meet their censure. What if they were right? What if we were wrong? Was I being disloyal to my country, to the young men fighting abroad, by standing in front of the White House holding a banner?

But as the days and weeks wore on, my resolve stiffened. How dare my government send soldiers overseas to defend the very rights which were denied to me and my sisters at home? How dare those men look at me with disdain? Was I not also a child of God? Was I not an intelligent being capable of informed and rational thought? Was I not also governed? How dare those men take it upon themselves to decide for me what I could and could not think?

And so I took my place on the sidewalk of Pennsylvania Avenue and proudly held my banner high.

And then, everything changed. The men's patience had grown thin. Tired of humoring the little women, of waiting for us to come to our senses and go home, the men in authority decided to act.

We were arrested.

My heart jumped to my throat as police surrounded us and bystanders gawked and jeered, but we had been trained for this eventuality. Pulse hammering in my temple and mouth dry as sand, I walked quietly to the paddy wagon, stepped inside and took my place on the bench beside Tilly.

She reached for my hand and squeezed tight as the motor van lurched toward the police station.

We were escorted inside amid cat-calls and laughter and stood huddled on the well-worn boards of the station floor. One of our number, an older woman possessed of a serene dignity stepped to the high wooden desk of the sergeant on duty.

"May I enquire as to the charges?" she asked. "I do not believe it is against the law to stand on a public sidewalk."

The sergeant frowned and glanced at the officer in charge of our arrest. "What are the charges, Sergeant Davis?"

The man's cheeks reddened. He opened his mouth, closed it, then strode past a little swinging gate to a nearby office. Knocking, he waited to be admitted before disappearing inside.

Tilly and I and the other four sentinels settled ourselves on benches that lined the walls of the holding area and waited. We observed men rushing from one office to another and back again, before Sergeant Davis returned.

He spoke to the desk sergeant. "They are to be charged with obstructing traffic on Pennsylvania Avenue."

I glanced at Tilly with raised eyebrows. Her dark eyes were wide with surprise, but none of us made a sound, honoring the *silent* of our self-chosen title: Silent Sentinels.

CHAPTER THREE

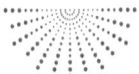

$\mathcal{W}$e were only detained for a few hours that first time, but as our arrests became more frequent, our time behind bars lengthened until at last the local constabulary could no longer accommodate us.

Tilly and I were among the first to be convicted and deported to Occoquan Workhouse in Virginia. Tired of our recalcitrance, the authorities determined to break our spirits.

Shoved into a small, dark cell, Tilly and I stood firm while the guards remained, but once they had gone, we clung to each other and surveyed our surroundings. A metal-framed bed with a bare, stained mattress occupied most of the floor space, barely leaving us room to stand. A bucket in the corner was to be our only toilet. The air was fetid and dank and a scurrying at the edge of the room informed us we were not the only inhabitants. Little as we wanted to touch the dirty mattress, we sank onto it and pulled up our feet, leaving the rats clear title to the floor.

During a walk around an enclosed yard for air and exercise, we learned that Alice Paul was also at Occoquan. She called for a hunger strike to protest the abysmal conditions we were being held in.

"Well," Tilly said, with a hint of a smile, "that won't be a hardship."

Indeed, neither of us had taken more than a mouthful of the slop we'd been given the evening before. The thin gruel had wriggled with worms.

I grimaced. "I hope the rats enjoyed our meal. I certainly didn't."

Tilly and I took comfort from each other, bolstering our courage in our shared discomfort. Our stomachs growled continuously and we grew too weak to stand, but we held to our principles and refused the wormy food.

After several days, we were dragged from our cell, stuffed into another paddy wagon and taken to an asylum. If we would not eat, clearly we were mentally deficient and should be locked away for our own protection.

Separated from Tilly, I waited in a stark white room, so bright after my days in that dark, dank cell that my eyes watered.

The doctor entered, his white coat flapping around his knees, and took a seat in a chair opposite mine. Two guards from Occoquan stood beside the door. I smiled to myself to think they considered me, weak with hunger as I was, a potential threat to the life and health of the good doctor.

"You are Miss Emily Tuttle?" the doctor asked, his gaze on the papers attached to his clipboard.

"I am," I replied.

"Do you know why you are here, Miss Tuttle?"

"I haven't been informed, but I would guess it is because I have refused to eat."

At this point the doctor looked up and met my gaze. A small frown creased his brow.

"Your eyes are clear and I see from your history that you are well-educated," he said. "Why would you endanger your health by refusing to eat?"

I smiled and his frown deepened. "Tell me, doctor, would you willingly eat thin gruel laced with live worms?"

Amazement registered on his face and he glanced at the guards, neither of whom betrayed by the slightest movement that he had heard a word I had spoken.

Our interview lasted a few more minutes, at which time the doctor excused himself. When he returned, the Occoquan superintendent accompanied him.

"I find no reason to commit any of the women you have brought here today, Superintendent Whittaker. I suggest you take them back to Occoquan and offer them decent food."

The superintendent looked stunned. "But doctor, they've been picketing for months, have been arrested over and over, and have now undertaken a hunger strike. Surely these woman are insane."

The doctor shook his head. "I find them of sound mind and exceptional bravery. Courage in women is too often mistaken for insanity." And with that he left the room.

Superintendent Whittaker was not best-pleased. When we returned to our cells, far from being offered decent food, we were taken one by one to a dismal room and strapped to a chair.

My heart pounded so hard I could barely hear, fear blurred the edges of my vision, but I bit my lip, determined to exhibit the bravery the good doctor had credited me with.

Superintendent Whittaker entered the room followed by a thin, weasely man carrying a rubber tube and a bowl whose contents I could not see.

"If you will not eat," the superintendent said, "I have no alternative but to force feed you. Carry on, Mr. Jenkins."

The weasely man stepped forward and, with the help of a guard, forced my mouth open and the rubber tube down my throat. He then proceeded to force feed me raw eggs.

I gagged and spluttered, felt like I might drown on the concoction. My eyes watered and I gripped the arms of the wooden chair so tightly my fingernails broke, but still Jenkins continued. When he finished at last and the tube was removed, my throat ached and burned and my stomach roiled.

I tried to relax, tried to close my eyes and tell myself it was over, I had survived, but was given no time to even catch my breath. Rough hands unstrapped me and I was dragged back to my cell and flung inside.

Tilly was absent.

As I dragged myself onto the foul bed and curled into a ball around my aching stomach, I could only imagine that my friend was enduring a similar fate. Tears slid down my face and I prayed for her fortitude.

CHAPTER FOUR

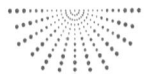

*I*f the authorities thoughts the abysmal treatment we had received at Occoquan would end our vigil before the White House, they were disappointed. When we were released, we returned to Washington, licked our wounds and healed for a few days, and then resumed our stance on the sidewalks of Pennsylvania Avenue. The Silent Sentinels refused to be intimidated.

Our incarceration at Occoquan with its attendant hunger strike and forced feedings had awakened the public to our plight. More and more women swelled our ranks, and letters to the editors of prominent newspapers began to appear. People questioned the rightness of sending women to workhouses for no worse crime than standing on a public sidewalk holding a banner.

We were making progress. Our cause was being noticed. We were embarrassing the White House.

We were elated.

We shouldn't have been. Such progress always carries a price, and our bill — which I naively believed had already been paid — was about to come due.

CHAPTER FIVE

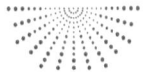

*I*n mid-November thirty-three Silent Sentinels were rounded up and shipped off to Occoquan, including myself and my fast friend, Tilly Armbruster. We were not unduly alarmed. All of us were veterans of incarceration.

What could happen?

We had already decided that hunger strikes were not worth the forced feedings and were not to be repeated. We'd already been sent to the asylum and judged sane. No. Occoquan held no further horrors. We would spend a few miserable weeks in the workhouse eating stale bread and wormy gruel. We had long since come to terms with our fellow inmates, the rats.

So it was with an air of resignation, but not trepidation that we entered the entry hall to find Superintendent Whittaker and forty guards awaiting our arrival. Once the papers had been signed remanding us to Whittaker's custody, the Washington policemen left us to our fate.

We stood quietly, waiting for Whittaker to direct his men to accompany us to our cells.

He did not. Instead, he called his men to attention, and we saw that each guard carried a club.

Too late, we recognized our peril. But what could we do? We were thirty-three unarmed women faced with forty burly men armed with clubs. As Whittaker set his men on us with the order to teach us our place in this world, we strove to circle, to move our weakest members —the dear little seventy-year-old woman who stood with us resolutely despite a weak hip and knee—as far from the men as we could.

I liked to believe that I was brave, that I owned the courage the good doctor at the asylum had ascribed to me, but I am not ashamed to say that within minutes of being beaten by a full-grown man with a club I was groveling on the ground, attempting to shield my head, my face, my belly with its access to my tender inner organs from a brutality I had never imagined.

The room descended into hell itself. Women's screams and sobs tore the air accompanied by men's grunts as they waded into their work with heartless ferocity. The stink of blood and feces gagged me as genteel ladies' bowels voided from fear and injury. Terror reigned led by an unholy battle lust.

The sights and sounds and smells of that awful night will haunt my dreams unto death.

At last Whittaker judged our punishment complete. He yelled and whistled until the last man stepped back and drew shirtsleeve across sweating brow.

"Take them to their cells," he commanded.

Rough hands grabbed me by the hair and yanked me upright. My legs shook so that I could barely stand, but I held myself together as I was pushed and shoved through the corridors to my cell.

It's over, I told myself. *Just a few more steps and Tilly and I will be able to rest, to bind up our wounds. It's over.* I stumbled drunkenly to the door of my cell and leaned bonelessly against the wall while my guard opened it.

He shoved me inside so that I landed on the floor beside the bed, and then kicked me so hard in the belly that all breath flew from my body. My muscles seized. I couldn't breathe. He might as well have been holding my head under water for all the nourishing oxygen I could pull in.

Laughing, he stood aside as his comrade hurled Tilly into the cell.

I lay on the floor unable to move, unable to draw breath, and watched as Tilly's golden head cracked against the corner of the iron bedstead. She slid to the ground beside me, still. Too still.

The guards grunted, slammed the door and locked it, their booted feet echoing as they walked away.

And Tilly remained still, except for the red stain blossoming on the floor beside her head.

Gradually, my muscles relaxed and I drew breath. All up and down the corridor, women moaned and cried and sobbed in agony.

But not in our cell. In our cell the fetid air was quiet. Even the rats kept to their crevices.

I gained my hands and knees and crawled to my Tilly.

Still. So very still.

With tender fingers I explored her wound. They came away bloody, but what was worse was the feel of her skull. Not smooth and hard, but ragged and spongy. My stomach revolted, and I turned away from her to be sick on the floor.

I stumbled to the cell door and beat my hands bloody upon it's unflinching surface. Someone had to come! Tilly would die! A doctor, we had to have a doctor!

No one came.

But a voice from another cell asked me to describe Tilly's injuries. My response was met with silence. Finally, the voice came again. "Tear strips from your petticoats. Bind up her wounds as best you can. If you have the strength, make her comfortable on the bed."

I heard the resignation in her voice, heard the hopelessness, but I refused to allow it space in my mind. I had a task. I would do for my friend all that could be done.

CHAPTER SIX

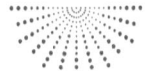

Four days after that terrible night, we were released from Occoquan, never to return. A judge had ruled that we had been unlawfully detained. No mention was ever made in any official document of the beatings we had endured.

The husbands of some of our number waited outside the prison gates for our release. Solemnly, they conveyed us home. Tilly was taken immediately to the hospital. She was not the only one to have suffered grievously from lack of medical attention, but she was the only one who never woke up.

My fast friend, my bright-eyed, happy-spirited Tilly died in hospital at the age of nineteen. Her only crime having been to stand on a sidewalk with a banner asking for the right to have her voice heard, her vote counted.

No history book records Tilly's sacrifice, but I remember.

I remember that less than two months after that horrible night, President Wilson relented and called upon congress to enact legislation to give women the right to vote and hold office.

I'll never know whether he was shamed by the brutality he had allowed to fester on his very doorstep, or whether he truly believed it was a matter of wartime necessity as he proclaimed to the nation. I do know that the vote failed in 1918 by two votes, and yet again in 1919 by the vote of a single senator. But in 1920 the Nineteenth Amendment to the Constitution of the United States passed, securing for women the right to vote.

I celebrated by taking flowers to Tilly's grave and telling her she had not died in vain.

PART V
A WARM TALE FOR A COLD NIGHT

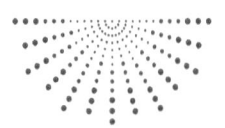

DEBBIE MUMFORD

BESTSELLING AUTHOR OF *SORCHA'S HEART*

A Warm Tale for a Cold Night

SPUN YARNS
A Thrilling Short Story

PROLOGUE

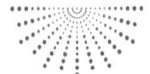

a cold winter wind blew through the narrow lane, cutting through my heavy woolen cloak as though I'd ventured forth in the nude. I pulled the hood closer around my ears and hurried across the frozen muck that made traversing the lane a challenge to even the most skilled warrior's balance. The painted wooden sign of the Black Destrier Inn swung wildly, making the warhorse appear to leap and kick.

I slipped on the ice and fell heavily against the Inn's arch topped door. Catching my balance, I opened the door and stepped into the welcome warmth of the Inn's smoky tavern. I surveyed the familiar room as I stamped my booted feet and shook the melting snow from my cloak. A cheery fire leapt and crackled on the hearth while an aproned serving girl wove among the tables with a tray of mugs and platters of meat balanced precariously above her head.

Men of all ages and descriptions crowded the dark wood bar and sat at scarred wooden tables. I spied one table in the far corner that was occupied by a lone man, a scruffy looking fellow with long dark hair, matted from lack of grooming, and a patch over his left eye. Nodding to myself I pushed through the crowded room, grabbed an empty chair, and joined him.

He straightened and glared at me with his one good eye, but I spoke before he had the chance to object.

"Seating's tight," I said. "If you wanted privacy, you should've kept to your room."

He glanced around the room, shrugged, and settled back in his chair. "If you're looking for company, find someone else to annoy."

I nodded and signaled the serving girl. A mug of mead and a plate of whatever passed for meat that night was all the companionship I required.

When I was fully warmed by the consumption of mead, beef and tubers, I turned again to the man who shared my table.

"You look like a man with a load of woe gnawing on him."

Another glare met my gaze.

"So what if I am?"

I shrugged and leaned back in my chair. "You might do well to give your cares voice," I said, "and I've a willing ear."

He studied me with that single, shrewd eye, before nodding.

"Aye, it might ease the burden to tell the tale."

I nodded encouragingly. "And you've no concern with me hearing it as I'll be on my way as soon as the current storm blows over."

He clasped his hands on the dark, scarred table top and fixed his gaze on them. "I've a brother," he said quietly. "An identical twin brother," he paused and drew a shuddering breath, "and at times … well, at times we share each others' thoughts. See through the others' eyes."

He raised his head and stabbed me with the intensity of his gaze. "This is his tale."

THE BROTHER'S TALE

A mixture of terror and elation spur me down the steep, rocky slope. The harsh, cold wind buffets me, making it had to keep my leather-booted feet beneath me.

I can't slow down. Can't fall. If I so much as pause … she might come back, might realize what I've done. If she catches me on this unprotected slope, she'll roast me alive.

The backpack bounces against my shoulders, its warm, reassuring weight throwing off my balance. I've done it! I slipped into her lair, stole an egg, and made it back to the cold, fresh air of the mountainside.

I've got to keep moving, got to make it to the forest. She won't be able to find me once I reach the trees' thick canopy.

I pant, cold air numbing nose and cheeks and making my lungs ache. But the precious egg in my pack, the one I risked everything to steal, is safe and warm, protected by a nest of soft woolen blankets.

The ground beneath my feet levels, turning from rock to coarse, low grass and sedge. Tree line is within sight, its stunted larch and fir trees twisted by the constant fierce, cold wind that whistles past my ears and makes my eyes water.

I'm going to make it. Those scraggly trees aren't much, but they're my only hope. The first cover on this wind-swept mountainside. Just a little way beyond the tree line, the proper forest begins. Tall spruce, firs, and aspen with sufficient canopy to shield a fleeing man from even a dragon's sharp vision.

The worst is behind me. Once I gain the forest, I'll be safe.

Terror loosens its grip on my heart and exultation bubbles through my core. A near-hysterical giggle forces its way past my chapped lips. Truly, I've done it. The jade-green egg with dark blue mottling is mine. A prize beyond measure. And not just because of the gold I will demand. My reputation will be made once I return to the city with a dragon egg in my pack.

I savor the fruits of my stealth. All that remains is to reach the safety of the forest.

A shadow passes overhead, and I stumble, my foot snagging on a tangled mass of sedge. I catch my balance and glance up at the clear blue, cloudless sky. My breath seizes and my heart plummets.

A dragon wheels in the sky.

She has returned. She had recognized her loss and hunted me.

My pulse thunders, beating twice its normal tattoo. Blood sings in my veins, throbs at my temples, tingles in my fingertips. A burst of energy propels me down the slope. I must reach those trees.

With a screech of indignation, the dragon plummets to earth, landing between me and the trees. The backwash from her wings knocks me off my feet. I twist as I fall, keeping the packed egg safe, but sustaining a nasty jolt to my shoulder and wrenching a knee.

I gain my feet and crouch, ready to run, but where?

The dragon, a solid mass of muscle and anger, easily as big as my two-room hut, unfurls her wings and hisses. Her long, snake-like tongue lashes the air between us.

Dragon stink fills my nostrils, a noxious mix of sulfur, rotting meat and blood that solidifies the terror freezing my heart and paralyzing my thoughts. Pain throbs in shoulder and knee, darkening the edges of my vision. Bitter, poisonous bile gags me.

All is lost.

No way forward. Not past a hulking beast whose wings blot out the scraggly trees beyond.

No way back. Not across a barren slope of alpine tundra.

Death stares at me with malignant satisfaction.

The inevitability of my demise calms me, thawing my terror and freeing my mind. I still have a card to play. I still hold the egg.

She can't crush me for fear of harming the egg. Nor can she use flame against me.

While I hold her egg, we are at an impasse. I stare into her yellow, cat-slit eyes and know that she understands our stalemate as well.

I hunker down to think while the dragon studies me with narrowed eyes. She furls her wings and settles, the barbed tip of her tail tapping restlessly.

The elation of a few moments before has shriveled. I wish wholeheartedly I'd never imagined this foolhardy scheme. Why did I gamble my life on the insane possibility of stealing a dragon's egg?

For unimaginable wealth and everlasting glory.

To be the first man to climb the dragon's mountain and return with an unblemished egg.

To be the man who made it possible for the High King to take his place among the gods. To provide the key ingredient to the fabled elixir of immortality: the heart of an unborn dragon.

And all I have to do to make those dreams a reality is steal past a massive, angry dragon and make my way back to the city with my prize.

Before any scrap of a plan can present itself to my fevered mind, the dragon's tail ceases its tapping and a soft, low coo swirls upon the wind.

I frown. Do dragons coo?

The coo sounds again, soft, melodious, remarkably like the call of a mourning dove. The dragon closes her eyes and lowers her head.

Is this my moment? Can I steal past her while she's not looking? Could I reach the cover of the trees?

I lean forward, gathering my legs beneath me, ready to spring.

The egg in my pack jumps, pulling against the straps on my shoulders, ruining my balance. I stumble forward a step or two, catch myself and scramble back, away from the dragon's cruel talons.

Sweat beads my forehead and drips down my nose. The egg jumps again, hard enough to pull me onto my rump.

The dragon waits quietly, eyes closed, cooing, the sound oddly welcoming.

Another jump nearly unseats me.

I wriggle out of the pack, pull it into my lap, and swipe my shirtsleeve across my sweaty brow. Opening the pack, I shove layers of soft wool aside to expose the precious egg. A crack mars its perfection.

My heart sinks. I've waited too long. The egg is hatching.

Even if I survive the dragon, there will be no elixir of immortality. Not without the heart of an unborn dragon.

A louder coo burbles from the mother dragon. I glance up. Her eyes remain closed, her wings furled. If I didn't know better, I'd think she was asleep.

On a gut level, I understand: she is focused on the hatching egg.

Now is my moment. I must leave the pack with its now useless egg and run for cover. She won't follow. She's not interested in me. All she wants is to see her offspring safely hatched.

I glance back up the mountain. Are the other eggs hatching? Could I leave this one and grab another? If I did, would I be able to get it down the mountain before it hatched?

Slowly, carefully, I slide back from the nested egg.

The dragon ignores me, continuing to coo.

I stand, paralyzed with indecision. Escape past the dragon and return to the city, empty-handed, but alive, or seize this opportunity to return to the lair, grab another egg, and escape down a different path while she is focused on this hatchling's birth?

The voice of caution, my mother's voice, screams at me to run for the trees. To save myself. To live to scheme another day.

But another voice, my twin brother's more daring voice, tells me what I want to hear. *When will you ever have such a chance again? You know where the dragon is and she doesn't care about you. A little peril could earn you riches and eternal glory. Seize the moment, or spend the rest of your life regretting its loss.*

I take a few cautious steps upslope, half expecting the dragon to pounce on me. She doesn't even open an eye. My injured knee aches, but does not give way. I turn and race full tilt back to the dragon's lair.

A few minutes later I step out of the howling wind, into the shelter of the cave. Leaning against cold rock, I stand on my good leg, resting my aching knee, and wait for my labored breathing to ease, for my eyes to become accustomed to the dark.

The air is fetid with dragon stink, the floor littered with broken bones and bits of moldering pelts, remnants of long-forgotten meals.

I push myself upright and limp into the gloom. At the rear of the cavern, the eggs huddle in a nest of stout limbs lined with the pelts of bears and wolves. Climbing into the nest was easier last time. Now my shoulder throbs with every heartbeat and my leg trembles with the strain of my injured knee. But I make it.

Exhausted, I collapse onto the warm, coarse furs and crawl to the mound of eggs. I only need one. One egg and fame and fortune will be mine.

I reach toward the mound of deeper darkness that is the pile of eggs, and encounter not a smooth, hard shell, but soft, leathery skin.

Disappointment floods my soul and I jerk my hand back. At least one of the eggs has hatched, but perhaps there is still hope. Perhaps a late bloomer languishes beneath its more advanced siblings.

I inch sideways and reach into the pile again.

Immediately glowing eyes pop open and soft, gurgling cries sound. Small bodies scurry in the dark, accompanied by snaps and cracks as shells are trodden upon. I soon find myself surrounded by blinking, luminous eyes.

By their pale light I see that all the eggs have hatched. Nothing remains on the furs but infant dragons and splintered shells.

My whole enterprise has been too late. I never had a chance of getting an unblemished egg back to the city.

My hopes dashed, I crawl back across the pelts. I still have to climb out of the nest and escape this accursed mountain. The task seems insurmountable now that no reward awaits me.

Disappointment makes me stupid. I've forgotten I'm in a dragon's lair. Forgotten that despite their small size, I am surrounded by dragons.

I am reminded forcibly when a hatchling bites into the calf of my injured leg and tears away both fabric and meat. I scream in agony, kick out with my good leg, my leather boot connecting firmly with a small body.

But it is too late. Blood pumps from my wound, exciting the hatchlings, turning their newborn hunger into a feeding frenzy.

I curl into a tight ball, hoping to protect my tender belly from sharp talons and teeth. My last sight before my vision darkens is of the mother dragon's arrival, bearing her final hatchling to the feast.

EPILOGUE

*B*ack in the tavern of the Black Destrier Inn, I stared at the one-eyed man, my mouth agape, my breathing shallow and light. My hands itched to grasp my sword, to defend myself against a dragon I'd never seen.

"And he died?" I managed to gasp. "The dragon and her hatchlings devoured him?"

The tale-teller nodded. "I felt the life leach from my brother. Felt his pain and revulsion at the manner of his passing."

He leaned back in his chair and wiped his face with shaking hands. "He died thinking he should have listened to Mother's voice." He swallowed and licked his lips. "He died cursing me."

After a moment's reverie, I rose and bowed to my companion.

"You have my sympathy for your loss … and my thanks for a warm tale on a cold night." I pulled a silver coin from my purse and laid it on the table. "For the drink you'll be needing to drown those memories."

I turned and strode into the jaws of the winter storm, thankful to all the gods that I knew nothing of dragons or their eggs.

PART VI
WISE WOMAN

DEBBIE MUMFORD

BESTSELLING AUTHOR OF *SORCHA'S HEART*

Wise Woman

A Story of Lastalrig

CHAPTER ONE

*M*oira wiped the damp from her face with the tail of her plaid before wrapping the tightly woven cloth more closely about her head and shoulders. The day had been soft and fine when she'd left her home in Lastalrig village to wander the gorse covered hills in search of herbs and wild berries for her mother's pantry, but the weather had turned. At first the fine drizzle hadn't concerned her—born and bred in the lowlands of Scotland, Moira was accustomed to changeable weather—but now thunder sounded in the distance and she feared she was about to be caught in a drenching downpour.

Time to return to Lastalrig.

Hiking up her skirts and clutching her gathering basket in one hand while holding her plaid about her head with the other, she pelted toward home. The path beneath her bare feet soon turned to rivulets of mud interspersed with slippery rocks, but she found her way with the ease of long practice.

She'd just rounded the bend that should have brought the village into view when her reality shifted.

Instead of the thatched cottages and winding lanes of Lastalrig, she saw a misty vale of white-barked trees whose leaves glistened silver in the clear light of a blue-white sky. The edges of this unexpected vision shimmered with an incandescent light so bright she dropped her plaid to shade her eyes…

…and in so doing discovered yet another profound oddity.

Rain no longer poured from the sky in her natural world. Individual drops hung suspended in the air all around her. They sparkled like jewels caught in the hair of some high-born lady, but they did not fall. Neither did the wind blow nor the rivulets run about her bare feet. Nothing moved, save Moira…

…and a tall, stately being who approached her from the vale within the circle of shimmering light.

Moira dropped her basket, preparing to gather her skirts and flee from the approaching stranger. But her feet refused to obey her command to run. Instead, they remained firmly rooted to the wet ground, surrounded by beads of rain that should have long since washed over them. Heart hammering and ears awash in a deafening roar like the waves of the firth on a stormy day, Moira sent a silent plea for protection to the goddess and awaited her fate.

The being stopped just inside the circle of light and raised a hand in greeting.

He was close enough now for Moira to recognize him as male, but not a man such as the Scotsmen she had grown to young womanhood among. No. This was no mortal man, but one of the Fair Ones. She cast her gaze to the ground lest her frightened stare give offense, all the while memorizing every detail of his appearance.

Tall and lithe with an impossibly handsome face, the man's long, white-gold hair was held in place by a slender band of shining gold. His garments were like nothing she had ever seen. A finely woven robe of a material so white and clean it seemed to radiate light

114

covered a soft tunic of sky blue belted with a filigree of skillfully wrought gold and precious gems. His trousers were the deep green of a forest glade and his feet were clad in boots of supple leather.

She glanced at her own bare feet, streaked with dirt, and the rough homespun wool of her skirts and plaid and felt shame to even be seen by such a fine laird.

"Well met, Moira, daughter of Senga, granddaughter of Flora, kin of the wise woman Fiona. I greet you, Beloved of the Cailleach, in the name of the Seelie Queen."

Moira's heart hammered so hard she thought it might burst from her chest. He had called her by name! More astounding still, his greeting implied she was known to the Seelie Queen. And what had he meant by calling her *beloved of the Cailleach*? What would the goddess who had created the mountains and hills of Moira's homeland know of a simple village girl?

She should answer. Courtesy demanded she find her tongue.

But what could she say when she didn't even dare raise her eyes to glance at his face?

"Th-thank you, Laird," she finally managed to stammer.

"Come, Beloved of the Cailleach," he said, stepping through the glowing circle and waving away the rain. As soon as he stepped fully into Moira's world, the vision of his own shimmered out of existence. He smiled and held out his hand to her.

Startled that he should invite her touch, she scrubbed her hand on her skirt before placing her fingers in his.

He nodded. "You are brave. The Cailleach has chosen well." Holding her hand firmly in his, he stepped forward, away from the village... and her home.

She licked her lips, unsure whether or not she dared to question him, but the words leapt from her throat. "Where are we going?"

He cocked his head and waited until she met his gaze. "We go to Fiona, your kin. She who has served your people as wise woman for so long that most have forgotten her name."

Moira's mouth dropped open. The wise woman was named Fiona? Moira had never heard her called anything but *Mother*, usually in hushed and reverent tones. The wise woman lived in a cave in the hills above the village. The ancient woman helped any who asked a boon of her, and in return the villagers ensured she had everything she needed.

The wise woman was healer, mid-wife, and seer. She brought new life into the world and guided the spirits of the departed to the Summerland. She cared for the village, healing their hurts and warning them of coming danger. She was the heart and soul of their community; the mother of them all.

And she was kin to Moira?

The man of the Fair Folk led Moira so quickly and by such a direct path that she wasn't sure her feet even touched the ground. Sooner than she, who knew this land like the lanes of her own village, would have thought possible they stood before the opening to the wise woman's cave. The warm orange glow of a hearth fire welcomed them, and the man of the Fair ones raised his hand in blessing.

"Fiona," he called, his voice clear and strong. "Bréanainn the Fair greets you in the name of the Seelie Queen. May we enter?"

Moira started. The Fair One's name sounded like a breeze whispering through the silver leaves of the white-barked trees of the vale from which he'd come. She knew she'd never be able to teach her vulgar mortal tongue to say such a fair and fearful name, and she stared at him in wonder. Tall. Lithe. Inhumanly beautiful. And yet, this awesome being, this Fair One, asked permission to enter a humble cave.

"Brendan the Fair," came the response, in a voice that wavered and creaked. "Long have I awaited your return. Enter and be welcome."

Moira breathed a sigh of relief. Brendan was a name her lips could form.

The Fair One ducked and stepped into the cave, drawing Moira along behind him.

CHAPTER TWO

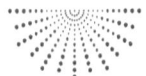

The interior of the wise woman's cave was not dank and gloomy as Moira had expected, but warm and cheerful. The floor of hard-packed dirt had been swept clean of leaves and other wind-blown detritus, and a well-tended fire crackled at the back of the cave, its smoke drawn upward through a crevice in the rock. A sturdy bedframe of lashed wood stood to one side, its wool-stuffed mattress covered by a finely woven plaid blanket. Shelves of dried herbs and beans made up the pantry and a large barrel of water rested between a neat stack of firewood and the hearth.

The ancient wise woman made to rise from a beautifully carved rocking chair beside the fire when Brendan and Moira entered, but the Fair One waved her down.

"Be at ease, Fiona," he said. "You need not trouble yourself for me." He turned to Moira and beckoned her forward. "I have brought you a companion. This is Moira. She is the daughter of Senga, granddaughter of Flora."

The old woman's eyes sparkled and she held out her hand. "Come closer, dearie. Mah eyes be no longer keen and I would see ye clearly."

Moira stepped forward, took the woman's gnarled hand, and knelt beside her knees.

"Aye," the old woman said, nodding. "I ken ye now. Ye've the look of Flora about ye, though it's long since I've seen mah twin."

Twin! Moira inhaled sharply. She'd never heard that Grannie Flora had so much as a sister, let alone a twin.

The wise woman pushed the plaid from Moira's head and stroked her hair before grabbing her chin and turning her head from one side to the other.

"Aye," she said again, her voice wavering, though whether from emotion or age, Moira couldn't have said. "Ye've the same bonny red hair and yer eyes tilt just so. Do ye have a wee dimple when ye smile?" she asked, touching the spot on Moira's cheek where just such a dimple was wont to appear.

Brendan laughed. "I imagine the girl is too over-awed to smile for you just now, Fiona. Get to it. Tell her why she's here."

Fiona patted Moira's cheek before turning a frown on the Fair One.

"Th' choice is hers," she said. "Ye canna force her. She main decide o' her own free will."

Brendan held up a hand. "Peace, woman. I know the rules, but she cannot make a choice if she doesn't know her options. Tell her why she's here."

Fiona turned her rheumy gaze on Moira, sighed, and said, "Ye are of my blood, lass, and we've a compact with the Fair Ones. If she so chooses, a woman of our line can be gifted by th' likes o' Brendan wi' th' *Sight* and wi' th' healing touch. The Cailleach has chosen ye. If ye wish, ye can take up the mantle o' wise woman when I leave this land."

"Me?" Moira squeaked. "Be the new wise woman? What would my parents say?"

"They willna' know," Fiona said quietly. "'Tis one price o' the gift. All who ha' known ye will forget ye."

Moira swallowed. So that was why she'd never known the wise woman was her kin. Fiona's family... even her own twin sister... had forgotten her existence.

"And that's no th' only price," Fiona continued. "If ye choose this path, ye will never know love, never wed, never birth bairns o' yer own. Ye will bring other women's babes into the world, but that joy will be denied to ye."

Moira sat back, landing on the hard packed dirt with a thump. Her family would forget her? She'd never wed? She thought of Conor, of his merry eyes, lovely dark curls, and the trim body which had drawn her eye more and more often as she matured. She'd expected to wed him, knew that he merely bided his time until she reached the proper age. He'd ask her father for her hand on her next birthday. Next week, in fact.

And suddenly the timing of the Fair One's visit made sense. Brendan had to issue the call before she was pledged to wed.

Moira raised her head, met the wise woman's gaze, and saw her own sorrow reflected in Fiona's eyes.

Brendan cleared his throat, and Fiona nodded.

"O' course, 'tis not all loss and sorrow," she said. "Yer name may be forgotten, but yer people will love ye. They'll come to ye with their burdens, and ye will make them light. Ye'll bring healthy babes into the world, babes who might have perished, an' their mothers wi' them, were it not for yer healing touch. Ye'll see beyond the veil, and bring warning o' fire and flood. Yer people will thrive because o' ye, and when they die, ye'll guide them frae this land wi' calm, giving them a peaceful passage to the Summerland. Ye will be a boon to yer people, and they will bless ye an' care for ye." She gestured around the comfortable cave, her other hand caressing the arm of the beautifully carved rocker.

"Of course," Brendan said, "you must never ask for payment for your aid. Gifts you may accept, but those gifts must come from an outpouring of love and gratitude, never by your request."

"Aye," Fiona agreed. "Only a witch would demand payment, and ye will never be a witch. Ye will be a wise woman, the Cailleach's gift to her people."

Brendan stepped forward to stand beside Fiona and his gaze sought Moira's. "What say you, lass? Will you accept this destiny?"

CHAPTER THREE

*T*he wise woman sat alone in the comfort of her hillside cave, stroking the gleaming surface of a small, finely wrought, silver box. She smiled as she settled more comfortably in her rocking chair beside the dancing flames of her hearth fire. The silver casket had been a gift from the laird of Lastalrig Castle. The good laird was unaware of how important his gift would be, but her *Sight* had shown her its value. At some as yet unknown time in the future, she would place a powerful spell upon this casket, and the outcome of that working would forever change the fate of the heirs of Lastalrig.

Life was good.

She had made the right choice.

Certainly, she had shed more than her share of tears in the early years, but time had mellowed the pain of the price she had paid for the power to heal and protect her people. Resting her head against the carved wood of her rocker, she recalled those early experiences. They had been traumatic in the moment, but time had encased them— like an insect caught in amber— turning them into precious jewels; fragments of a life no longer hers.

She remembered the first time her sister had come to her for a boon; the shock of seeing no recognition in her sibling's clear blue eyes.

The night she had been called to the home of the man she'd once thought to wed to usher his first-born son safely into this world; the exquisite pain of holding a babe who, had she made a different choice, might have been hers.

The evening she sat beside her father's bed and guarded his soul as it left his body and began its journey to the Summerland; the mixture of intense sorrow and joy she had experienced when he had looked into her eyes for the last time… and recognized her for who she really was.

Closing her eyes, she whispered aloud the words that sustained her, that kept her identity whole, her destiny grounded.

"I am Moira, daughter of Senga, granddaughter of Flora, and, by the grace of the Cailleach and the gift of the Fair Ones, the Wise Woman of Lastalrig."

PART VII
HER HIGHLAND LAIRD

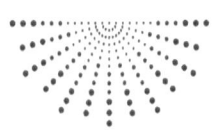

DEBBIE MUMFORD

BESTSELLING AUTHOR OF *SORCHA'S HEART*

HER
HIGHLAND
LAIRD

A Logans of Lastalrig
Time Travel Novella

CHAPTER ONE

*C*at Logan wandered through Edinburgh in a dreamy glow. The musical lilt of the inhabitants' speech delighted her almost as much as the easy juxtaposition of ancient and contemporary architecture. Everywhere she turned, she discovered new reference points for her recently acquired degree in medieval literature, as well as her clan heritage. The Logans of Lasterrick had left an indelible mark on Edinburgh.

Each day brought new revelations, and she blessed Gran Da for his extravagant graduation gift. Life had been hard for both of them since her father's death, but Gran Da had been determined to celebrate Cat's achievement in style.

"I'm so proud of you, Cat," he had said, draping an arm around her shoulders. "I only wish your mother and father could be here to share this day."

"Me, too, Gran Da." Cat nestled into her grandfather's embrace and blessed the fates who had given her into this dear old man's care. Gran Da had welcomed her father and his infant daughter home after Cat's mother had died. Complications from Cat's entrance into the world had robbed her father of his wife and Cat of her mother, but she'd never felt any stigma of blame. Gran Da had been there for them. He had provided warmth and stability in Cat's life while her father had pursued his military career.

But David Logan, a high-ranking air force pilot, had died in a training accident last year. Cat and Gran Da had both been devastated by his loss.

As if to punctuate Cat's need for a European vacation, her ex-fiancé Brent Myers had chosen the night before graduation to announce he'd fallen out of love with Cat and into bed with Ariana Davidson.

She'd given that scumball four years of her life. Why had he asked her to marry him if he hadn't been certain she was the woman he wanted to spend his life with? Why had she accepted? How could she have missed a character flaw that allowed such blatant disloyalty and unfaithfulness? Obviously, her judgment sucked when it came to good-looking men.

Gran Da had taken the defection in stride.

"I'm sorry, love," he said quietly when Cat informed him of the broken engagement. "I won't discuss it further, if that's yer wish, but ye need tae ken I'm nae surprised. I've a bit o' the sight, an' I've always known ye were destined for an unexpected path. Nothin' about Brent was unexpected.

"Go tae Scotland, darlin' girl, an' if opportunity arises, ne'er look back. I've a feelin' in me bones ... Scotland holds yer future."

———

On her third day in Edinburgh, a previously undiscovered lane beckoned. She hesitated. If the most ancient byways were also the narrowest, allowing the least penetration of the summer sun, this one qualified as the oldest of the old. The narrow passage drew her, the near-compulsion reminding her of Gran Da's remarks about second sight. Curiosity won out over caution, and she followed her instincts to a shabby, little establishment near the midpoint of the narrow lane.

Cat studied the grimy window of the ancient thrift shop. The interior appeared as black as the tarnished silver door knocker. Did she really want to push past the door and breach the musty interior? She'd passed a reputable-looking antique shop two blocks back; perhaps she should browse there.

Yet, the same indescribable *something* that had pulled her past the clean, well- kept shop and into this narrow lane prompted her to linger.

Follow your heart, her grandsire's voice whispered in her mind. But why would her heart lead her to a second-hand junk shop in a forgotten district of Edinburgh?

She'd never learn the answer if she was too cowardly to cross the threshold. Expelling a sigh, she straightened her shoulders, grasped the doorknob, and turned.

An old-fashioned bell tinkled, and she stepped into the little store. A single bulb dangled from the ceiling, barely lighting the dark recesses of the room. Shelves towered against the walls, and stacks of shabby furniture obscured the floor. Cat wended a careful path between tottering stacks of rubbish.

She lingered over a yellowing baptismal gown for an infant, fingering the fine lace and admiring the tiny, precise stitches of the hand-sewn seams. Hard to imagine that all clothing had once been sewn by dedi- cated women. And men. Mustn't forget the tailors of the world.

"May I help ye fin' somethin', miss?"

Cat gasped and dropped the gown. She hadn't noticed anyone in the gloom of the shop. An elderly man with stringy, grey hair and stubbly jaw stood behind a sturdy wood counter — the only flat surface in the shop not covered with a jumble of knick- knacks.

"No thank you," she said with a little smile. "I'm just looking."

"Nae many Americans stop to browse in my wee shop."

"My accent gave me away?"

"Aye, lassie. Nae a body will mistake ye for a Scot."

She sighed and turned back to the baptismal gown. "That's too bad because my roots are here."

"Ahh," he breathed. "Sae you're one o' those. Searchin' for yer ancestry, are ye? What's yer surname?"

"Logan. I've traced my family back to Sir Robert of Lasterrick."

"Well, then," he said, smug satisfaction lighting his homely face, "Ye've come tae th' right shop. I happen tae hae a relic of Sir Robert's only son, Sir Eideard Logan. We'd name him Edward today."

He rounded the counter and scuttled between rows of merchandise to a tall shelf at the back. Opening a ladder, he climbed to the top with surprising agility and poked his hand behind a grimy vase. Carefully, he withdrew his prize and returned to the floor of the shop.

Cat sidled over to join him, her heart beating a quick tattoo against her chest. "What is it?" she asked, breathless with anticipation.

"A silver casket," he replied, revealing a tarnished silver box roughly the size of a ream of paper.

Cat stretched out her hand to stroke the embossed lid.

"'Tis rumored tae contain Sir Eddie's heart."

"Eww!" She snatched her hand back and buried it in her pocket.

The shopkeeper laughed, a full, rich sound that bounced off the ceiling and skittered among the piles of rubble.

She smiled wanly. "Don't you know what's in the box?"

"Nay, miss. 'Twould take a braver man than me tae open this box. 'Tis cursed, ye

see."

Now it was Cat's turn to laugh. "Cursed? You believe in such nonsense?"

The man nodded gravely. "Aye, lassie, I dae, an' sae should ye if ye ken what's good for ye." He turned back to the ladder and started to climb.

Cat's heart leapt. Her instincts screamed that the silver casket held a secret — that its contents had drawn her to this dusty little shop.

"Wait," she cried. "Please."

The man paused. He studied her face with narrowed eyes, glanced at the casket, and then nodded. Stepping back to the ground, he led the way to his counter and gently placed the casket upon it.

Cat followed him, and this time her hands ignored her brain. They cradled the tarnished box, stroking the ornamented surface of the lid.

"Here now, miss. Ye're gettin' filthy. Let me clean 'at up."

Gently, he disengaged the casket from her reluctant fingers and wiped it with a soft cloth. The more he rubbed, the more Cat itched to hold the casket again. Finally, when she could bear the separation no longer, she pulled the box back and stared at the now gleaming lid.

"Are those words?"

The shopkeeper adjusted his glasses and cocked his head. "Aye. There's an inscription."

"Can you read it?"

"Probably. But nae if ye clutch it sae."

A nervous giggle escaped her lips. "I'm sorry. I don't know what's gotten into me." She shoved the casket across the counter to him.

He turned the lid to the light and read in a halting voice, "Catriona, return to me my heart. Lastalrig Castle. By the bright of the moon. Eideard."

Apprehension seized Cat's throat and squeezed. Her vision swam, and her fingers tingled. She clung to consciousness by sheer force of will.

"What ...." Her voice croaked and died. She moistened her dry lips, cleared her throat, and spoke again. "What was that name?"

He stared at her with open curiosity. "Catriona. It's th' auld form of Katherine."

"I know. My name is Catriona Logan."

CHAPTER TWO

*C*at sat hunched in the middle of her bed at the inn. The silver casket taunted her with its nearness ... with its supernatural connection to her soul.

She'd paid several times its value, but once she'd heard the translated inscription, she knew the casket held her destiny.

Three times she'd reached to open the casket, and three times her courage had failed. The casket was cursed. Generations of the shop-keeper's family had held the box in trust, and not one person had been able to lift the lid.

Still, if its contents were meant for her, she had to open it.

But what if it held the desiccated remains of a human heart?

What if it did? What could dried tissue from a long dead ancestor do to her?

She reached for the casket. Her fingers connected, and a wave of welcome washed over her. With utmost care, she released the delicate latch and raised the lid a millimeter at a time. The hinge groaned its displeasure, but the lid rose smoothly.

Cat leaned forward and peered inside. Relief flooded her. No blackened, dehydrated heart. Only a roll of vellum, neatly tied with crumbling ribbon. She reached inside and removed the scroll. The ribbon disintegrated into a fine powder, leaving a pale smudge. Hoping the vellum would withstand the stress, Cat unrolled the paper-thin hide while cataloguing anyone who might be willing to translate the missive.

Her breath caught, and she stifled a scream. Translation would be the least of her worries. The unfurled vellum revealed a meticulously drawn rendition of Cat's own face, but the artist had captured a thoroughly unfamiliar emotion. Cat had never had occasion to wear such a soft, dreamy-eyed expression of love.

A sudden pang of envy pierced her heart. What wouldn't she give to meet the man who could inspire such obvious love? A rueful, little laugh erupted from her throat. Jealous of a woman dead these many centuries. How sad. Almost as sad as her dismal love life. She thrust the thought of love away and concentrated on the familiar face.

"How bizarre," she whispered. "You look just like me. How is that possible? How can we have the same face?"

But the similarities were undeniable. The artist had detailed the slight upward tilt of her nose, the heart-shaped face accentuated by a firm chin and a riot of short, dark curls...and the eyes. She'd never seen that expression in her eyes, but the shape and the generous fringe of dark lashes beneath bold brows...The similarity was uncanny.

And what about the inscription? *Catriona, return to me my heart. Lastalrig Castle. By the bright of the moon. Eideard.*

If the silver box had actually held the man's heart, perhaps she could have understood his request to have it returned to his ancestral home. But the casket held a portrait... of a woman in love, a woman who looked remarkably like her.

Cat shook her head, returned the portrait to the casket, and closed the lid. She slipped from the bed, stretched, and moved to stand before the window overlooking the city. Of course, she'd intended to visit the ruin — it had once been the stronghold of her clan, but not in the dead of the night.

And certainly not *by the bright of the moon.*

Cat rummaged in her bag, found a cable-knit sweater, and pulled it on over her *Scotland Rocks* T-shirt. She'd leave the mystery to simmer while she joined the throng in the street in search of a pub and supper.

————

I'M a complete and utter idiot, Cat thought as she struggled up the slope to the ruins of Lastalrig Castle by the light of the full moon and a wavering flashlight. The silver casket, encased in her backpack, thunked uncomfortably against the middle of her back with every step.

At the top, the ghostly outline of broken towers against the moonlit sky beckoned her forward. She lowered her backpack to the ground, retrieved her water bottle, and straightened to admire the view. When she'd drunk her fill of both water and view, Cat stowed her bottle and retrieved her flashlight. Walking slowly and carefully, she paced the inside perimeter of the remains of the castle walls. Low, stone barriers marked the occasional interior wall.

Lastalrig wasn't a true castle, not the way Americans imagined them. The Logan stronghold had been a Pele Tower, a fortified defensive structure that housed the laird's family and provided emergency shelter for the larger clan. She stood within the ruin and savored a moment of clan pride, fancying herself a part of that history. Lord Eideard had requested the return of his casket by the light of the full moon, and centuries later, she had granted his wish. Only ... now what?

In answer to her unspoken question, the clouds shifted, and a soft glow of moonlight illuminated a particular stack of stones. Cat rummaged in her backpack, pulled the casket free, and slung the nearly empty pack over her shoulder. With deliberate steps, she approached the moonlit stones and deposited the silver casket upon them, as if they were an altar.

"Welcome home," she whispered, stroking the casket with loving fingers. A sudden desire bloomed to see the portrait one last time. Foreboding followed. She needed to open the casket — but knew her life would change forever if she touched the box again.

The logical side of her nature scoffed, but the superstitious Celt at her core screamed that she wasn't in modern Edinburgh anymore. This was Lastalrig. She stood in the ruins of her ancestral home by the bright of the moon. Magic was afoot.

Logic overrode ancient wisdom. She stretched out her hand, flicked open the latch, and lifted the casket's lid. Moonlight and human flesh caressed the rolled vellum in the same instant ... and Cat's reasonable world ceased to exist.

Sudden, intense pain elicited a scream, but no sound escaped. Cat's body elongated and compressed — she felt as if she were being squeezed through a narrow pipe — and her quick panting breaths ceased. Her lungs burned with the need for oxygen, and the saliva in her mouth frothed. Unimaginable pressure; implosion or explosion, surely one was imminent. And then, pain faded to background noise as her brain sheltered her conscious mind by blacking out.

CHAPTER THREE

ool stone vibrated beneath her cheek, leaching the warmth from her unprotected face. By the time she identified the faint tremor as footfalls, a buzz of quiet voices had filtered through her dazed mind. People. Help. Whatever had happened, she needed help.

Gathering her strength, she stood and leaned heavily against the wall. Her eyes flew open as sense registered. The wall! It no longer ended at waist height; she leaned against a fully constructed wall in an enclosed corridor!

Her stomach roiled, and she fell to hands and knees, spewing vomit over the stone floor. Disoriented, shaking, and drenched in cold sweat, Cat huddled against the wall.

The owners of the voices arrived. Words swirled around her, bounced off the walls, and pounded her aching head. Men spoke rapidly in an archaic form of Scots-Gaelic that she recognized, but couldn't follow. Sweat-stench mingled with the acid tang of her sick. She panted through her mouth to lessen the impact of the odor on her queasy stomach. Too tired to do more than lift her head, she glanced around the corridor. Flickering light revealed four broad, shadowy figures.

God! Where was she? And how had she gotten here? Her shaking arms gave way, and she collapsed in an exhausted heap on the cold stone. Shock pushed her over the edge of the abyss, and she fell back into unconsciousness.

———

CAT WOKE with a throbbing headache and jangled nerves from a terrifying dream: she'd been compressed, unable to breathe. She pushed the thought away and huddled deeper under the covers, pulling the scratchy sheet over her aching head and adjusting her hips to avoid an offending lump in the mattress. She frowned and opened her eyes a slit. Dim light filtered through a coarsely woven, yellowed sheet. Panic stricken, she threw the sheet aside and, ignoring the sharp pain in her skull, scrambled from the bed. Bare feet connected with cold stone, and memory returned in a rush.

Frigid morning air brushed her skin, and she shivered. She stood in the middle of a stone chamber naked as the day of her birth. Yanking the sheet from the bed, she wrapped herself in its rough, but warm, folds and surveyed the room.

Stone walls and floor, rough-hewn beams supported what could only be a thatch roof. Narrow arrow loops served as windows spilling both sunlight and frosty air into a chamber furnished with a low, wooden bed, a chamber pot, and a rickety table with ewer and basin. A single, crudely fashioned chair stood beside the table.

The door creaked open, and she flattened herself against the wall, hugging the sheet tightly to her breast. The most dangerous-looking man she'd ever seen stood poised on the threshold. Tall, muscular, with long, dark auburn hair, he looked like a warrior prince from a Scottish fairy tale.

Heat suffused her face — and every other part of her body — as his gaze raked her from tousled hair to bare feet. Oh, God! To meet a man like this ... wrapped in a sheet!

CHAPTER FOUR

*E*ideard stared at the woman who'd given his household such a fright. A wee slip of a lass with dark curly hair cut shorter than a lad's, but with a woman's curves beneath the sheet she clutched so tightly. Yet her appearance last night had so unnerved the men who discovered her that they'd sent a rider to fetch him home from Edinburgh.

What was it about this lassie that had unsettled seasoned warriors? He'd not find the answer gawking at her pretty face.

"I pray you are well this morning, lady," he said in the courtly English his father had insisted Eideard learn to speak fluently. The wily, old laird had never trusted Scotland's neighbor to the south and had insisted his son be prepared.

The tightness around the lassie's eyes relaxed, and her shoulders lost their rigidity.

"Oh! Thank heavens. You speak English. I didn't understand a word those guys said last night. Of course, I was really sick, so maybe my brain wasn't fully functional. Where am I, and what happened to my clothes?"

Eideard fought to keep pace with her words, but the strange accent robbed the bright sounds of meaning.

He latched onto the last word and concentrated on guessing the question her rising tone indicated.

"Truly, lady, we have no idea what happened to your garments. The maids tell me you were most unsuitably attired. Were you ravished? For surely no well-bred lady such as ye would appear in such dishabille."

Her lovely face underwent a transformation during this speech. Her brows drew together in the most beguiling frown, and then shot to her hairline in undisguised surprise.

"You found my clothes unsuitable?" she asked.

"Not I, gentle lady," he hastened to explain. "I have only just returned from Edinburgh. The ladies who undressed you reported the strangeness of your garments."

"I see." A fascinating, little pout marred her features. She pulled the sheet higher and straightened against the wall. "And what makes you think I'm a well-bred lady?"

He crossed the room in two quick strides and pulled one of her hands free of the sheet. He examined the fine, long-fingered hand, "Not a callous to be seen. Ye have done no hard labor with these dainty hands."

She jerked her hand away and put a little distance between them. "Well, unsuitable or not, I'd like my clothes back, please. I'm getting tired of dragging this sheet around."

Heat flushed his face and neck. He stepped away from her and averted his eyes.

"Of course," he said to the arrow loop. "Forgive my churlishness. I'll send a maid to help ye dress at once." He strode to the door before glancing over his shoulder. "Would ye honor me with your name, lady?"

"Excuse me?"

"Your name," he repeated, wondering if a fall had addled her brains. "Ye do have a name and a clan, do ye not?"

"Cat," she said, and then shook her head and reconsidered, "Catriona Logan."

He whipped around to face her fully. "The hell ye say!"

———

Now what? Cat wondered. The handsome hunk had been on the verge of telling some flunky to get her clothes when he whirled around and skewered her with those damnably gorgeous hazel eyes.

"What is your problem?" she asked in exasperation, tired of standing there barely covered.

"Ye are no Logan," he said, narrowing his eyes and studying her closely. "I am Eideard Logan, clan chieftain. I know every Logan in these lands, and ye are nae one o' them. Who is your sire?"

"Wh-what?" Cat's brain stumbled over his words. This man, this gorgeous hunk of a Scot who spoke with a totally foreign formality had just named himself Eideard Logan.

Catriona, return to me my heart. Lastalrig Castle. By the bright of the moon. Eideard.

Cat's vision blurred, and an ocean sounded in her ears. She leaned heavily against the wall and slid to sitting, heedless of the sheet's skimpy coverage.

CHAPTER FIVE

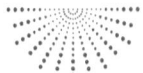

*E*ideard scowled at the lass, unaccustomed to not receiving an immediate response. She had paled when he asked for her lineage, as well she should, the lying, little vixen. Why, he'd have her flogged! Though, in truth 'twould be a mortal sin to mar the perfection of her skin, and he could see rather more of her delicate flesh than 'twas right and proper for a man not her betrothed.

He pulled his thoughts from her body as he realized why she was so exposed. The foolish woman had fainted. Puddled on the floor at the base of the wall, she lay with the sheet askew, revealing a firm, round bosom. Eideard swallowed, frozen in indecision. Should he approach the lady and risk touching that smooth, enticing flesh? No. He should call the headwoman. A female in distress was Mistress MacLennan's domain. But he was here, and she was not, and he'd not have it said that this wee lassie had frightened him into scampering around in his own castle.

Decision made, Eideard lifted his chin and strode to the young woman's side. He stroked the hair from her forehead and found it damp with sweat. Was she feverish? Could that account for her muddled speech? He settled himself on the floor beside her and carefully pulled her into his arms. The sheet slipped yet further, providing him with a heart-stopping view, but when her alluring, young bum settled into his lap, he groaned aloud.

"Sweet Mary, Mother of God! I should have run when I had the chance," he whispered through clenched teeth.

He shifted her limp body into a more ... appropriate position and was reaching to pull the sheet across her luscious curves when a stifled yelp sounded from the doorway.

"Laird Eideard! What are ye doin' tae that puir, wee lassie?"

"Och, I'm that glad tae see you, Mistress Mac," he said, yanking the sheet over Catriona's bare skin.

"Aye, I am certain of it." A gimlet gleam lit Mistress MacLennan's eye, and she hurried over and hauled the lassie from his possession. "I hadnae thought it o' ye, Eideard. Gropin' a puir, defenseless lassie. Ye might have waited until she was awake!"

"She was awake," Eideard roared.

"Holy Mother of God!" cried Mistress MacLennan. "'Tis worse than I thought. Have ye done this puir child violence?"

She made to drag Cat to the bed, but Eideard had endured enough. He scooped the unconscious woman from the headwoman's grasp and deposited her neatly on the bed.

"I havenae touched a hair on her head," he began, but Mistress MacLennan's steely gaze shriveled his words. "Well, I havenae harmed her. She fainted, and I went tae her aid."

Mistress MacLennan clicked her tongue and set to arranging the lass comfortably. She stroked the hair from Cat's forehead and checked for fever. "She isnae ill. Whatever has befallen this puir wee'un, she's safe now. Ye'll be handfast tonight, o' course."

"What?"

She whirled on him, hands clenching into fists and settling on her hips. "Eideard Logan, your da may be dead, God rest his soul, an' ye may be clan chief now, but I raised ye better than this. Ye cannae compromise an innocent an' then nae dae right by her. I saw what I saw, an' the Lord God knows ye had this lassie in a grasp nae man but a husband has th' right to. Ye will announce your betrothal tae th' clan tonight, or I will be speaking tae th' priest on the morrow."

Eideard stared from his kinswoman to the sleeping beauty on the bed and discovered he had nothing with which to refute his foster mother's words.

CHAPTER SIX

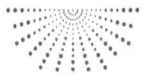

*C*at snuggled into the warm nest of covers and tried to hold onto her rapidly fading dream. A powerfully built, darkly handsome man with rich auburn hair towered over her, smiling. Her heart leapt to her throat and thudded in rapid staccato, her core heated to nuclear melt-down temperatures, and the nexus of her legs tingled with anticipation. No man had ever gazed at her with such evident admiration and desire. Not even Brent.

She writhed on the bed, seeking new comfort and banishing Brent from her delicious dream. If such a gorgeous hunk existed, she'd never seen him ... or had she?

Eideard Logan, Lord of Lastalrig.

Cat's eyelids popped open. She stared wildly around the room. Stone walls with arrow loop windows, a middle-aged woman in medieval dress, and skulking at the threshold looking like a guilty child, her dream man.

"Oh my God," she cried. "It wasn't a dream! Where the hell am I, and who are you people?"

Dream guy straightened, and the lost puppy expression disappeared. He scowled at her across the woman's head as she bustled to Cat's side.

The woman glanced over her shoulder at Dreamy. "Be gone, Eideard. Ye've arrangements tae make, nae doobt. Send Lizzie up when ye pass the great hall."

Dreamy's brow furrowed in a deeper scowl, but he turned to go.

"Eideard," Cat said, tasting the name on her tongue.

He turned to face her, and his expression cleared. "Aye?"

"Is it true?" she asked, surprised by the timidity of her tone. "Are you really Eideard Logan?"

He nodded, his gaze never leaving hers. "Aye. Have ye heard of me, lass?"

She shivered and drew the covers closer to her chin. "Yes. Once." The question she'd been longing to ask burst from her lips. "What year is it?"

A quizzical expression crossed his face. "'Tis the year of our Lord Fourteen Hundred and Fifty-Two."

Tears sprang to her eyes, and she fought to stem their flow. If she cried, she might well drown in a lake of her own making. 1452. Oh, God! Why was she here? Alone. A stranger among people who had no concept of the world she'd left behind. How could she return to her own time when she had no idea how she'd come to this one?

A gentle hand stroked Cat's hair, and she stiffened.

"He's gone, lassie," said the woman. "I can see ye have had a rough time o' it, but never fear. Ravished or nae, ye will be safe in Lastalrig. Lord Eideard will dae right by ye."

Cat refused to open her eyes. Now that she understood, she didn't want to face the truth of her precarious position, didn't want to see the rough stone walls or the woman's old-fashioned dress. Neither did she want to feel the lumpy, straw mattress beneath her curled body, or the roughness of the homespun sheet. She especially didn't want to smell the pungent farmyard odor wafting through the arrow loop.

1452!

"Are ye able tae stand, wee'un?"

"What?" Cat said, startled from her morose thoughts. She opened her eyes and studied the middle-aged woman whose steely grey hair was tightly knotted at the nape of her neck and demurely covered by a linen cap. The Logan tartan wrapped around her ample waist, one end pinned to the left shoulder of a dark green vest laced with a black cord. The linen sleeves of a loose peasant blouse blossomed from beneath the vest. Firm, capable, in control, but her expression was sympathetic, as if she understood Cat's unusual circumstances.

"I asked, are ye able tae stand?"

"Yes, of course."

"Well, then, rise, lassie. I must take the measure o' ye."

"Measure?" Cat's brain felt thick. The woman's odd speech cadence and word choices weren't quite registering.

"For clothes, lass. I'll send Lizzie tae the storeroom tae fetch ye an arisaid, corsage, and plaid, but I need tae estimate your girth."

"Okay." Cat unfolded and slid from the bed. She dragged the sheet with her, less for modesty than because the rough fabric had become a talisman.

"There's a good lassie. I'm Mistress MacLennan. How are ye called?"

"Cat," she said automatically, and then amended it to, "Catriona."

"Well, Catriona, 'tis pleased I am tae make your acquaintance. Call me Mistress Mac. All the wee'uns dae."

"Excuse me, Mistress Mac, but what happened to my clothes? My backpack?"

The woman clicked her tongue, her eyes widening. "Those odd undergarments? They are in my apartment. How did ye come tae be wearing such odd garb? Were ye attacked?"

"I...well, I had an accident."

"Aye? I've heard tell the Sassenach wear trousers, but only the men." Mistress Mac narrowed her eyes and stared shrewdly at Cat's short hair. "Ye have an odd accent, an' the men said ye dinnae understand the Gaelic, an' your hair. What woman allows her crowning glory tae be shorn save for fear o' life an' limb? Have ye run away, lass? Have ye cut your hair an' donned men's garb tae escape some horrible fate?"

Cat struggled to hide a smile. Her crowning glory? She lowered her gaze to avoid rolling her eyes at the old-fashioned attitude. Old-fashioned? Oh, God! She'd have to guard her tongue. She considered for a moment, and a cover story swirled into her mind. "Yes, that's it exactly. I've run away. My father's enemy overran our manor and vowed to make me his whore. Father couldn't rescue me, so I cut my hair and disguised myself. I thought he'd never dare to follow me to Scotland."

Mistress Mac's eyes widened and sparkled with tears. "Och, well, the good Lord has brought ye tae safety an' given ye into the care o' a good man. Lizzie! What has taken ye sae long?"

Cat puzzled over Mistress Mac's comment while the headwoman instructed a girl with flaming red hair regarding the garments she wished brought from storage. The young woman gave a startled cry, bobbed her head in apology to Mistress Mac, and slid a furtive glance at Cat. The moment the older woman stopped speaking, Lizzie hurried from the room.

"Well now, tae work. Sit ye down, Catriona, an' I'll see what is tae be done aboot your hair. I cannae grow it back o' course, but I will brush it until it shines like moonlight on the Firth of Forth." She pulled a stiff-bristled brush from a copious pouch suspended from her belt.

By the time Lizzie returned laden with woolens and linen, Mistress Mac had finished brushing and instructed Cat in the most efficient method to wash with a ewer and basin of ice cold water.

"Let me see what ye found, Lizzie," said Mistress Mac, pulling a linen gown from the girl's arms. She held it up to Cat and clicked her tongue. "Aye, we can make this work."

She urged Cat to stand, yanked the sheet from her hands, and dropped the gown over her head before Cat had time to squeal.

"I'll set Eibhlinn tae work on a new arisaid — she has a braw hand wi' a needle has our Eibhlinn — but this one will dae for now."

The linen arisaid, soft as down, fell to mid-calf on Cat. Lizzie tightened the ribbons around Cat's wrists as Mistress Mac adjusted the drawstring at the neck.

"There now," said the headwoman, "that is better than huggin' a sheit tae your bosom, isnae it?"

Cat smiled her agreement.

"Hand me the corsage, Lizzie."

The girl raced to the bed and plucked a deep blue velvet garment from the heap.

Cat had no opportunity to examine the corset before the women began lacing her into it. The corsage acted as a foundation garment despite being worn on top of the gown. Cat glanced down and gasped in surprise. Since when did she have cleavage?

Finally, Mistress Mac arranged the clan tartan into a skirt, belted it in place with a thick leather thong, drew the trailing end over Cat's shoulder, and fastened it to the blue velvet corsage with a silver brooch.

Mistress Mac clapped her hands in delight and exclaimed, "Och, lassie! Ye will make a bonny bride."

"Bride? What do you mean, bride?"

"Never ye mind. Ye are a bonny wee thing, 'tis all I meant." Mistress Mac shooed Lizzie from the room and, turning in the doorway, held out her hand to Cat. "Come along, lass. Come along. We dinnae want tae keep the laird waiting."

CHAPTER SEVEN

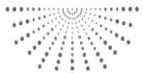

*E*ideard paced the great hall, avoiding the servants as they laid the evening meal and tended the fire in the oversized hearth. He'd be handfast before the night was out, and to a young woman of unknown parentage. Holy Mother of God! Why hadn't he called for Mistress Mac?

His fingers tingled with the memory of her soft, creamy skin. He'd known a few women, clan widows happy to school the young laird in the ways of the flesh, but none with skin as smooth and fine as the sassenach lass. He wheeled around and paced back to the head table, unsettled by the memory of her fresh young face.

She'd claimed his name, even before he'd touched her. He paused and stared unseeing at patterned tiles on the hearth. Could she be a witch? Had she befuddled his mind so that his actions were not his own? He scowled at the thought and resumed pacing.

No. He'd not lay blame for his decisions on an innocent lass.

His pacing carried him to the entrance of the great hall just as Mistress Mac chivvied her charge inside. He stopped short, mouth open in amazement. He'd known the lass was fair, but he'd not accounted for angelic beauty.

"Mistress Mac," he breathed. "Is this ... Are ye the same wee'un I met in yon chamber?"

"Close your mouth, Laird. Ye will catch flies. Of course, 'tis the same maid, though I wouldnae call her a wee'un."

"Nor would I," agreed Eideard.

Arrayed in his clan tartan with a corsage of royal blue, the lass outshone every woman he'd ever known. Her unnaturally short hair curled softly around her face and urged his gaze to follow her slender neck to an enticing bosom. The creamy linen enhanced the delicate whiteness of her skin.

He swallowed and forced his gaze from her alluring breasts. Instead, he looked into her eyes and smiled.

"'Tis pleased I am tae welcome ye tae Castle Lastalrig."

She blushed and lowered her gaze. "Thank you, Lord Eideard. I'm pleased to be here."

He held out his arm, and she laid her hand lightly upon it. Proudly, he escorted her to the head table and seated her on his left. Mistress Mac settled on Catriona's other side.

The hall filled rapidly with his kinsmen and women. Most had heard tales of the sassanach wench. They craned their necks to get a better view, and a few hardy souls approached the head table and engaged Eideard in conversation. More, he was sure, to study Catriona than from a desire to learn his views. He smiled indulgently on one and all.

When the last dishes had been cleared away, Eideard stood and rapped his sgain dhu upon the table. "Clansmen," he called, "'tis glad I am to see sae many of ye in the hall tonight, for I have auspicious news tae share."

An ocean swell of sound greeted these words.

Eideard held up his hands for quiet before continuing. "Few have had the opportunity tae speak tae our newest clan member, but ye shall come tae know her well in the years tae come."

He held out his hand to Catriona, and Mistress Mac urged her to rise. The lass blushed prettily, but rose with grace and dignity and laid her hand in his outstretched one. He grinned in triumph,

"Logans of Lastalrig, I give ye Catriona, my handfast wife!"

His kinsmen roared their delight, stamping feet, clapping hands, and thumping furniture.

Eideard held Catriona's hand tightly when she would have jerked it back. One glance at her livid face told him he was lucky the room was too raucous to allow her words to carry.

———

CAT GLARED at the man who held her hand in an iron grip. Her heart had lodged in her throat at the words *handfast wife*; she couldn't seem to get an intelligible word past. Try as she might, all she managed was an appalled splutter.

The noise in the great hall assaulted her ears and isolated her from Eideard. She was familiar with handfasting, having run across it in her studies. Every soul in the great hall had seen her place her hand willingly in Eideard's, and since he was the clan chieftain, disputing his claim of their betrothal would be impossible.

Her mind raced, and her body shook with impotent rage. She glowered at Eideard. What had possessed the man to claim her as his betrothed? He had seemed genuinely angry before she fainted.

At last, the thunder of the clan's celebration died away, and Eideard allowed her to resume her seat. He leaned close and whispered in her ear, "I promise tae explain all in our chamber."

He squeezed her hand, released her, and turned to join the man on his right in conversation.

Our chamber, she thought. *What does he mean, our chamber?* But she knew. A handfast betrothal became a true marriage when the couple engaged in sex. This medieval warlord intended to move from betrothal to marriage in a single night!

Dream on, buddy, fumed Cat. *I'm a twenty-first century American woman, not some starry-eyed medieval maiden honored by the great lord's interest. I won't be forced into marriage.*

As if reading her thoughts, Eideard turned a worried, hazel-eyed gaze upon her. His mouth twisted in a wry half-smile, and he shrugged his shoulders.

Damn him! She barely knew the man, but he could already wriggle around her defenses. Why did he have to have hazel eyes? She'd always had a thing for hazel eyes, and his with their unusually long, deep auburn lashes, were the most intriguing she'd ever seen.

She frowned, shook her head, and studied the scarred wooden table before her. She didn't belong here. She certainly didn't belong with this man. She belonged in the twenty-first century with Gran Da and all her friends. The only question was: how had she gotten from there to here, and how could she reverse the process?

CHAPTER EIGHT

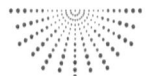

he interminable evening finally ended. Eideard stood and extended his hand to Catriona. The woman hesitated, wariness narrowing her eyes and tightening her soft lips, but she placed her hand in his and rose from her seat. Eideard smiled encouragingly, before turning his attention to Mistress MacLennan.

"I trust our room has been properly prepared?"

"Aye, milord. Your lady will find all she needs within your chamber." Mistress Mac reached for Catriona's unoccupied hand, squeezed it, and said quietly, "Did I nae tell ye the Lord God had given ye into the care o' a good man? Ye are a bonny, wee thing, and Lord Eideard is an honorable and true man. I should know; I helped raise him. Trust the good Lord's wisdom, Catriona. Eideard will dae right by ye."

The lass looked mutinous, but held her tongue, accepting Mistress Mac's kiss with good grace. Eideard led her from the high table. His clansmen clapped him on the back, cheering and calling ribald comments in the Gaelic as they passed. Unmarried lasses vied to touch Catriona's hair or gown.

"What are they doing?" Catriona asked, her hand tensing in his, skittish as a new colt.

"Why, they are nae but borrowing some of your luck," he said, surprised at her lack of understanding. "Dae the unmarried maidens nae desire to be brides in your country?"

"Oh, yes. Of course they do," she murmured. "I just ... well, I didn't expect to be touched."

When they reached the corridor beyond the great hall, Catriona balked.

"Look," she said. "I'm sure you're a very nice man and everything, but I have no intention of sleeping with you. So could you please show me back to my own room?"

Eideard stared at her. Was the lass daft? Did she truly expect him to ruin both their reputations by sending her to a solitary bed after announcing her as his handfast wife?

"Where you sleep is of no consequence, as long as I am there. Come, my lady. We will discuss our future in the privacy of our chamber." He stepped forward.

She refused to budge. "I won't sleep with you, so get that out of your head."

The doors to the great hall opened, and Eideard's clansmen spilled into the corridor in a wave of cheerful voices and pungent odor. When they spied their lord and his lady, they stopped. A hush as thick as fog on the Forth descended.

Eideard glanced from Catriona to his men and took immediate action. He swept the woman from her feet, tossed her over his shoulder, and ignoring her complaints, saluted his warriors.

"Rest well, kinsmen," he said with a grin. "I intend tae!" And he strode down the corridor to cheers from his men and a tattoo of blows from his handfast wife's tiny fists.

"I dinnae know where ye come from, woman, that ye dinnae ken these things, but ye must learn what is expected o' a laird's wife." He opened the door to his chamber, their chamber, strode across the floor, and tossed the lassie on the bed. "Arguing in front o' the men is nae acceptable. What were ye thinking tae hold me in the corridor and unman me in front o' men who must follow me in battle?"

He turned from her, re-crossed the room, and slammed and bolted the door. "Ye must come from a verra soft place, if your men can afford tae have their women question their judgment publicly."

She righted herself and sprang from the bed, a spasm of anger contorting her comely face.

"Well, now. That's just it, isn't it?" she hissed, advancing to the middle of the room, fists on curvaceous hips. "I don't know anything about you or your judgment, do I? All I know is that you claimed me as your wife and tried to carry me off to your bed. You're lucky I didn't deck you right in front of your men. I waited until we were alone, didn't I?"

He stared at her in open-mouthed amazement. "I am lucky you dinnae ... what?"

"Deck you. Knock you on your ass. Beat you to a bloody pulp, you arrogant bastard!"

Eideard's gaze traveled the length of the diminutive woman, and a slow smile spread across his features. She had spunk. Her eyes blazed, and she sparkled with misplaced confidence. He could see she believed herself capable of fending him off. No matter. He might have to prove his prowess eventually, but not tonight. He had taken advantage of the lass, and then announced their betrothal without explanation. The time had come to call a truce with his affianced bride.

"Aye, well, 'tis glad I am ye forbore tae embarrass me before my clan," he said, pitching his voice low and soothing, as he would to an untamed mare. "I was wrong nae tae tell ye my intentions, and ye were wrong tae question me in a public corridor. Now 'tis just the two of us. Let us make a new start."

Her stance relaxed, fists slipping from her hips, and her face lost its fierce intensity, but she retained a wary cast to her eyes. "Why?" she asked. "Why did you trick me into taking your hand so that I seemed to consent to the handfasting? For that matter, why would you want to be handfast to me?"

His eyebrows shot up, and his eyes widened. "Are ye truly upset that the Laird o' Lastalrig, the clan chief o' the Logans, would take ye as his bride?"

She raised her hands and turned in a slow circle as if appealing to an imaginary crowd. "Are all men this arrogant?"

Retreating a few steps, she perched on the bench that ran the length of the foot of the bed, scrubbed her face with her hand, and then glanced up at him.

"I don't care if you're Jesus Christ incarnate. I don't know you, so why would I want to marry you?"

Her flippant blasphemy hit him like a physical blow.

"Who are ye?" he asked in a wary tone. "Are ye a witch, tae use the Lord's name with such disrespect?"

She closed her eyes and slumped forward. "I'm sorry," she said, her voice heavy with exhaustion. "I didn't mean to shock you. I'm just confused." Raising her head, she met his gaze full on. "I'm not a witch, but I don't belong here. I can't marry you. I have to find my way home."

He searched her gaze as he considered her words and finally nodded. "How can I help?"

"I don't know because I don't know how I got here."

"Tell me where ye are from, and I will take ye home."

Her laugh made his skin crawl.

"You won't understand."

"I willnae if ye dinnae tell me," he agreed. He sat beside her on the bench. "Ye are right. Ye dinnae know me, and I havenae given ye reason tae trust me tonight, surprisin' ye with the handfasting."

She tensed, but he squeezed her shoulder and continued, "But even that 'twas for your own good. Ye must trust someone, Catriona. Trust me."

She sagged against his side and rested her head on his shoulder. "How was the handfasting for my own good?"

His face heated, and his heart raced. He wanted to change the subject, but he'd asked her to trust him. She deserved an answer.

"Ye, uh, fainted," he said. "Earlier. I asked ye about your father, and ye fainted."

"So?"

"Well, I, uh, I tried tae help," he said, and then in a rush, "Ye werenae wearing anything, only that blasted sheit. When I tried tae rouse ye the sheit shifted, and my hand touched your... well, my hand touched a place it shouldnae, and then Mistress Mac arrived and accused me o' seducing ye, and..."

His words trailed off, and he waited for her cry of shock. Instead, her body shook.

Alarmed, he moved to kneel in front of her and held her by the shoulders at arm's length. Her eyes danced with mirth. The woman was laughing!

"Let me get this straight," she said when she caught her breath. "You claimed me as your handfast wife because Mistress Mac caught you copping a feel?"

"I ... what?"

"Copped a feel. You know, touched my boobs, uh, breasts."

"Yes," he gritted his teeth and spat out the words, "I touched your breasts."

"Okay."

"Okay? What does that mean?"

"I forgive you. You don't have to marry me. You go your way, and I'll go mine."

He released her shoulders as if her touch burned him and rocked back to sit cross-legged on the floor. This was no ordinary lass. Her strange speech was nothing compared to the alien nature of her thoughts. She seemed completely at ease with the fact of his inappropriate touch.

"Are ye a whore, then?"

The rapidity of the blow startled him. The woman possessed snake-like reflexes.

"No," she seethed, "I am not a whore."

He touched his stinging cheek gingerly and said, "I'll ask again: Where are ye from?"

She sighed and settled back on the bench. "Fine, I'll tell you, but first you must promise you won't try to lock me up."

He narrowed his eyes and studied her face. She was spirited and quick, but she posed no danger. "I promise."

"I was visiting Edinburgh. I hiked up to the ruins of Lastalrig Castle and found myself here."

A river of ice flowed through Eideard's heart at her words. He didn't want to hear the answer, but asked anyway, "What dae you mean, the ruins o' Lastalrig Castle?"

She slipped from the bench and knelt before him. "Eideard, in my time this castle has been in ruins for hundreds of years."

"In your time?"

"In the year of our Lord two thousand twelve."

Eideard crossed himself, scrambled to his feet, and gaped at the creature he had just claimed as his wife.

————

EIDEARD STARED AT HER, his eyes so wide they threatened to pop from his head.

Great, she thought. *Now he thinks I belong in some freak show. I knew I should have kept my mouth shut.*

"Remember your promise," she said, her voice low and steady.

He opened his mouth, closed it, opened it again, and croaked, "Ye are a witch."

"Oh, for heaven's sake! I am not. I'm a perfectly normal twenty-first century girl. In fact, compared to most of my friends, I'm so normal I'm boring."

He scowled at her and edged closer to the door.

"Don't be like that," she cried. "You asked a question, and I answered. And besides, this is as much your fault as it is mine."

Eideard stopped his stealthy retreat, straightened, and glared at her. "My fault? And just how do ye find fault in me? Ye are the unnatural being!"

Cat sucked in her breath and blasted the arrogant bastard. "I'd still be in Edinburgh in my own time if it weren't for you!"

"How is it my fault? I have nae magic tae call a shade from the future."

"I'm not a shade. I'm not a witch. I'm a twenty-two year old woman, who just happens to be out of her own time." Cat sat on the bench.

"And I'd still be in my time if I hadn't bought that God-forsaken silver casket and followed your instructions."

"*My* instructions?" He strode forward and knelt before her. "Tell me what happened."

"I was in this junk shop — where they sell old things that aren't really valuable," she explained. "Anyway, a silver box caught my attention. Filthy thing. Hadn't been dusted in ages. The shopkeeper told me to leave it alone, said it was cursed, but it drew me. Like it was meant for me."

She paused, rubbed her hands on her skirts, and frowned. The woolen fabric felt alien beneath her fingers. She should be wearing jeans and a tee-shirt.

"What happened next?" He knelt on one knee, his kilt brushing the stone floor. The linen shirt stretched across his broad chest, the full sleeves dripping from muscular arms, which were braced against the bench on either side of her body. Dark auburn hair shone in the fire-light, neatly bound in a single braid, pulled back from a commanding face. Strong brow, intelligent eyes, high, even cheekbones, and firm jaw. But the lips captured her attention. Rough, wind-chapped lips; not too full, but sensuous. She longed to kiss those lips; they drew her, much as the silver casket had done so many centuries in his future. Those lips had spoken the enigmatic words....

"*Catriona, return to me my heart. Lastalrig Castle. By the bright of the moon. Eideard.*" She forced her gaze away from his lips only to be captured by his hazel eyes. "That was embossed on the casket's lid."

Eideard paled and pulled away. He stood and paced to the hearth where the firelight outlined him in molten gold. "What was inside?"

Cat shook off the spell of his virility and stared at her hands. "The shopkeeper said it was rumored to hold your heart, but no one had ever been able to open it to find out. When I took it back to my room, it opened without difficulty. I suppose that should have worried me."

"What did you find?"

"Not a heart, that's for sure." She laughed at her own expectations. "A roll of vellum. It was a pen and ink portrait of a woman ... of me."

He glanced at her, a dagger of piercing speculation. "And ye obeyed the inscription. Ye took the casket and its contents tae Lastalrig by moonlight."

"I did," she agreed. "And was pulled through ... something ... and found myself here. With you."

He turned from the fire, his face unreadable. Crossing to her side, he cupped her cheek in his large, calloused hand. "Gae tae bed, Catriona. I willnae bother ye. Ye need rest, and I need tae think." He bent to kiss her forehead, and then turned and strode to the door. "I remember my promise," he assured her. "I will see ye on the morrow."

He left her to a restless night's dream of hazel-eyed men and molten kisses.

CHAPTER NINE

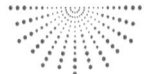

*T*he next day, Cat's first as a fully functional fifteenth-century woman, passed without incident. She managed to dress herself, though the lacings on the corsage required her full attention. But when Mistress Mac caught sight of her, the older woman hurried her into an unused pantry, stripped the tartan skirt from her waist and provided an impromptu lesson in the intricacies of folding a proper plaid.

"What are your specialties, dearie?" Mistress Mac asked as the two women toured the castle.

"My specialties?" Cat repeated.

"Aye. Which household tasks dae ye excel at?" When Cat continued to stare blankly, the headwoman prompted, "Are ye a seamstress? Dae ye make a good cheese? Nae? Perhaps ye have a deft hand at brewing beer?"

Cat closed her mouth with an effort and shook her head.

"Come now, lassie, dinnae be modest. Ye cannae have reached maturity without *some* special skills."

Cat racked her brain for something this woman would consider a useful skill. "Yes," she cried in relief. "I know herb-lore ... which plants are safe for dyes and simples."

"Aye, well, that is braw, dear." Mistress Mac's expression and tone announced her disappointment.

"Isn't that good?" Cat asked.

"Tae be sure, herb-lore is valuable. 'Tis just that every wee lassie above the age o' seven knows herb-lore. Have ye nae other wifely art?"

She bit her lip and shook her head.

"Aye, well. Ye are a bright lassie, tae be sure. 'Tis certain I am that ye will learn quick enough. Let me see your hands."

Mistress Mac took Cat's soft hands in her calloused ones.

"Well, ye are nae suited tae spinning. 'Twould take too long tae build up a proper callous. And Eideard wouldnae thank me for ruining your fine skin with tanning or dying. Come along. Fiona will have ye weaving fine cloth in nae time."

Fiona kept Cat so busy warping the loom and threading heddles that she didn't realize she hadn't yet seen Eideard.

"Well, now, ye have made a good beginning, Mistress Catriona," Fiona said as she inspected the warp Cat had meticulously threaded through the loom. "Tomorrow I will teach ye tae weave. In a month, ye will be able tae produce a fine kilt for your husband."

Cat bristled at the word husband, but held her tongue, choosing instead to thank Fiona for her patience.

"Come, lass. I will accompany ye tae the great hall for supper."

Cat glanced at the high table searching for Eideard's dark auburn head. She discovered many shades of red among the clansmen, but found no sign of the laird. Reluctantly, she settled at a table with

Fiona and tried not to think of a thick, juicy hamburger while she ate the unrecognizable meat set before her.

She ended her meal by licking her fingers clean — napkins being conspicuous by their absence. The sound of benches scraped near the entrance, and she turned to see what caused the commotion. A large, bushy-bearded Scot entered the room, and nearby men leapt to their feet to greet him. The newcomer roared with laughter, slapping men on their backs and women on their rumps. The former beamed, and the latter scattered.

Cat grimaced. A clan chieftain, she guessed. Below Eideard on the social scale, but anxious not to be overlooked. She'd met the type a million times in her life as a military brat. Officers in the lower echelon who waltzed into social gatherings with only one aim: get noticed. The social niceties were often lost on such posers.

She prodded Fiona in the ribs and pointed to the man. "Who's the big guy?"

A small frown flickered across Fiona's features. "Yon clansman is Donal. Cousin tae yer own Eideard. Ye will be safe, o' course, boot the rest o' us wimmen stay beyond his reach."

Cat lifted an eyebrow. "He's a danger to you?"

"Danger? Och, nay. There's nae harm in him, but his hands dae roam. Nae one is safe from his pats an' pinches."

"Someone should put him in his place. Teach him to respect women."

Fiona laughed aloud, pulling the big man's attention to them. "Put Donal in his place? Aye, I wouldnae mind seein' 'at, but ye main remember, his place is secure. Bein' th' laird's cousin."

Donal crossed the distance to Cat and Fiona and stopped, fists on hips.

"Fiona, ye hae found a new friend. A bonny lass wi' hair like a laddie."

Before Fiona could warn Donal off, Cat rose and faced her husband's cousin.

"I don't believe we've met. I'm Catriona. I've only recently arrived at Lastalrig."

"Weel, I am glad tae make yer acquaintance, Catriona," he said with a devilish glint in his eye. "In fact, I woold like tae get t' know ye much better."

With a wink, he reached around her and squeezed her buttock hard enough to elicit a gasp.

Cat spun out of the man's grasp and assumed a fighting stance. "Touch me again, and you'll be sorry," she spat.

"Och, now," he drawled. "thar is nae reason tae be afeerd. I am big, tae be sure, but I weel be gentle wi' ye darlin'."

He glanced around to be sure of his audience, a smug smile on his face, and then lunged for her. But this time Cat was ready. In a move her sensei would have applauded, Cat used the man's weight and momentum against him and flipped him deftly onto his back. She followed him down and knelt on his chest, her right knee cutting off his wind.

"I warned you not to touch me," she snarled. "You won't need to be gentle because you won't be touching me. Ever."

"Catriona!"

She glanced up and met Eideard's dark gaze.

"Release my kinsman."

"Tell him — and every other arrogant jerk in this place — to keep his filthy hands to himself."

"No man who owes fealty to clan Logan shall touch this woman without her consent," he said, and his words rang from the rafters, and then, more quietly, "Release my kinsman, Catriona."

She rose from the clansman's chest, kicked him once in the ribs, and stepped to Eideard's side. "I will not be fondled in public by any man," she whispered. "I don't care what your customs are."

Eideard nodded and turned his attention to her would-be attacker.

"Donal," he said, watching the man struggle to his feet while rubbing his bruised neck. "Were ye nae at supper last night?"

"Nae, laird. I have only now returned frae Edinburgh."

"Ahh. That explains your lack of courtesy tae my handfast wife."

Donal, whose face had been beet-red with angry embarrassment, went whiter than Eideard's linen shirt. "Laird?"

Eideard reached for Cat's hand, and she accepted his touch. He brought her fingers to his lips and brushed them with a kiss before turning a cold, hazel glare on his liegeman.

"Catriona, may I present my cousin, Donal, my second-in-command? Donal, this is the Lady Catriona. We were handfast last night."

Donal fell to one knee, head bowed. "Felicitations, my lord, and my apologies, lady."

Eideard motioned for him to rise, and the man obeyed. But as he hugged Eideard, Cat heard him whisper, "God bless ye, Eideard, but are ye sure ye want tae take 'at wee fiend tae yer bed?"

Eideard cuffed him playfully, turned, and held out his arm to Cat. "If ye have finished with your meal, I would have a word."

Cat placed her hand upon his arm and inclined her head. "As you wish, my lord."

Eideard ushered her from the great hall.

CHAPTER TEN

*T*hey walked in silence through the corridors of Castle Lastalrig. Catriona's warm fingers rested lightly on his arm. He covered her small-boned hand with his own much larger one and marveled at the strength she had displayed.

If he hadn't witnessed the event ... if one of his men had tried to tell him this diminutive beauty had knocked Donal on his rump and nearly throttled him ... well, he'd have said the man was too far in his cups to know what he'd seen.

He opened the door to their chamber and ushered her inside. When he'd secured the door, he turned to find her leaning against the arrow-loop gazing into the night sky. Sadness permeated her expression, and her shoulders sagged under an invisible weight. He hated to see her so dejected.

"Are all of the lassies in your time sae formidable?" he asked, crossing the room to sit on the bench at the end of the bed.

Her eyebrows quirked, and she straightened away from the window. "In my time? Does that mean you believe me?"

He shrugged and patted the bench beside him. "It means I had a long talk with Mistress Mac. Fiona reports that ye made a fine start tae weaving today. She expects ye tae be deft within the month, but ye cannae spin, nor brew, nor make cheese? Ye are a mystery tae the womenfolk o' the castle, Catriona."

She wandered closer as he spoke and sat on the edge of the bench. "And what does that tell you? That I'm a spoiled daughter who paid little attention to her lessons?"

He smiled, and then laughed aloud. "Nae, lass. Coupled with the demonstration ye gave with Donal, it tells me ye have nae place in this world. Ye were nae raised by any man now living." The thought sobered him. "Are ye very unhappy here, Catriona?"

She shrugged her shoulders and leaned back against the end of the bed. "It's very strange here," she admitted. "In my own time, I'm smart, well-educated, a capable woman. Here, the very young girls know more than I do about womanly duties."

She picked at the wool of her skirt absently, noticed what she was doing, and turned an embarrassed grin on him. "I couldn't even dress myself without help this morning. I mean, I thought I'd done it right, but when Mistress Mac saw me...."

The chagrined look in her eye melted the last of his reluctance to believe. He had no idea how this woman had come to be in his castle, but he knew beyond doubt she'd told him a true tale. Somehow, through unimaginable magic, he had called Catriona from her time to his. She was his destiny ... and he was hers.

He leaned close, inhaling the fragrance of her skin, and kissed her forehead. "Tomorrow, I'll help ye," he whispered, kissing each eyelid in turn. "If ye will allow me to stay tonight." He kissed the tip of her pert, little upturned nose.

She angled her head, gazed deep into his eyes, and, closing her own eyes, nuzzled his lips with her own.

Eideard's heart raced, and lightning sizzled through his veins. He pulled Catriona into a firm embrace and accepted the offered kiss. Full and softer than oriental silk, her lips enchanted him and heated his blood. He wanted more, so much more, but he forced himself to hold back. She must be wooed and won, not ravished against her will.

"Stay with me, Eideard," she whispered, unbinding his hair. "Show me why I've come through time to find you."

She kissed him again, this time parting those sensuous lips and inviting him inside.

His tongue delved the moist sweetness of her mouth, and his manhood leapt to attention.

Her warm, deft-fingered hand slid beneath the folds of his kilt, found his erection, and grasped it firmly. "I knew I liked kilts," she said before returning to yet another soul-scorching kiss.

Eideard groaned in delicious agony as she fondled him with short, firm strokes.

"Gods, woman." He yanked her hand from his loins. "Ye will make me spill me seed if ye dinnae stop."

She pulled back from him, an odd expression on her face. "You want me to stop?"

His heart hammered, his erection ached, and he could barely think past the red haze filling his vision. "Great God Almighty! No! I want ye on your back with your skirts around your ears. What I don't want is me seed spilt upon the floor."

He jumped to his feet, held out his hand, and smiled at her. At least, he hoped it was a smile; he'd never felt more predatory.

"Will ye come tae bed wi' me, Catriona, and properly consummate our marriage?"

She paled, licked her lips, and nodded. "I will ... but you should know, I'd have sex with you without marriage."

He scooped her from the bench and deposited her in the middle of his bed.

"Ye are an odd one, Catriona Logan," he said, untying the laces of her corsage and freeing her breasts from the neck of her arisaid. "Ye slap me for asking if ye are a whore, and then offer tae spread your legs for me without benefit o' marriage."

He leaned forward, suckled one tight, rosy nipple, and jerked her skirt above her waist. When satisfied by the moans issuing from his lady, he raised his head and gazed into her lust-crazed eyes. "The men in your time must be sore confused."

She reached down between their overheated bodies, grasped his erect manhood, and guided it to her cleft. "Let me clarify the issue," she murmured. "I want you inside me."

"Aye?"

"Oh, aye!"

With a shuddering thrust, Eideard fulfilled her desire.

CHAPTER ELEVEN

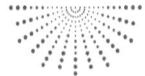

*C*at woke the next morning to find herself twined around a warm, hard-bodied man, both of them completely bare. Though the air in the room was cold, Cat was snug and comfy in the nest of linen sheets and woolen blankets she shared with Eideard. But then, she suspected the handsome Scot could keep her warm in a blizzard. She might be an ultra-modern woman, but memories of the night before brought a blush to her cheeks. The man had stamina — and talk about a quick study.

A shiver of delight raced down her spine, and she curled closer to her new husband. Husband! Who would've thought she'd find herself in a medieval handfast marriage? She'd known from the moment he announced their status that sexual relations would be required to complete the marriage; she'd just never considered they would fall into bed so fast. Or so thoroughly. But then, neither had she realized it was possible for a man to get it up that many times in a single night.

She smiled and hugged him around the middle. Without warning, a memory of the portrait in the silver casket swam to the surface of her thoughts. She was probably wearing that dewy-eyed expression right now.

Eideard stirred in his sleep, pulled her close, nuzzled her hair, and sighed.

Oh, God, she thought, *I could die of happiness, but I'm too greedy. I want this man for the rest of my life.* She melted in his arms, more content than she'd thought possible.

A cold hand squeezed her heart. What if whatever had brought her here sent her back? How could she protect herself when she didn't have a clue what had caused her time travel? Hadn't Eideard's inscription begged her to return? What if she'd been ripped away from him after their first night of passion?

She buried her face against his chest, unwilling to think about losing him now that she'd found him. Hot tears seeped from beneath tightly closed lids and splashed against her lover's well-tanned skin.

Eideard stirred again.

"Catriona?" he said in a groggy voice. "Are ye well, lass? Have I harmed ye in some way?"

"What?" she asked, gulping back a sob.

"Those are tears," he said, sitting up and pulling her with him. "I have hurt ye!"

"Of course, you haven't." She dashed tears from her eyes and straightened away from him.

Get a grip, she told herself. *You don't love this man; you don't even know him. You're just terrified because you're somewhere you don't belong. You're not some simple medieval girl. You know the difference between love and lust.*

But did she? Her experience with Brent had taught her she was a complete idiot where men were concerned.

"Then why are ye crying?"

Eideard's voice yanked her back to the present — or the past as the case might be — and she smiled at him through her tears. The man had given her the most exquisite night she'd ever known; she couldn't have him thinking he'd hurt her. "Don't worry about it. It's nothing."

He looked at her askance, his expression clearly voicing his disbelief.

A hiccough of near-hysterical laughter bubbled to the surface as Cat considered her dilemma. She barely knew this man, and her understanding of his culture was dismal. She'd behaved badly last night. First, she'd decked his best friend, something no woman of this time would even attempt, and then she'd acted like ... well, to his mind, she'd acted like a whore. What had possessed her to tell him she'd sleep with him without marriage? And why in God's name had she suggested some of the more unusual sexual positions during their incredible night? What must he think of her?

"You didn't do anything wrong, Eideard. I'm not crying because I'm hurt. I-I'm just scared." She lowered her gaze to the woolen blanket and traced a blue thread through the sett. "I don't understand how I got here, and I don't know whether or not it's permanent."

Eideard lifted her chin with a finger and met her gaze with a determined, if guarded, expression. "Dinnae fash yourself, Catriona. Ye are my wife now, and I will keep ye safe for as long as ye choose to stay."

She gaped at him. Choose? Did the man imagine she had control over the time fluctuation that had brought her here?

"Eideard..."

"Hush," he said, pulling her into an embrace. "Dinnae worry about it. We must get up soon and gae about our business. Let us enjoy these last moments in our bed." He kissed her thoroughly, and all the blood deserted her whirling mind to concentrate on more involved portions of her anatomy.

CHAPTER TWELVE

*T*he ease with which she fell into life at Castle Lastalrig amazed Cat. The challenge of mastering new and surprisingly fascinating skills filled her days, while passionate, enthusiastic sex occupied her nights.

Eideard's lovemaking continued to delight her, but his cool nonchalance in public irritated her sense of self-worth. She was woman, and the casual dismissal of her thoughts and ideas by the male establishment made her want to roar.

I'm in the fourteen-hundreds, she reminded herself a hundred times a day. *I'm lucky Eideard doesn't beat me for my lack of instant obedience. Women are possessions here. He's very indulgent.*

And he was. She'd seen the looks his men traded when Eideard ordered her to bring more wine or sit quietly and not interrupt, and she responded with a mutinous glare. They thought he should beat her into submission.

"Eideard, ye must control yer woman," Donal had said in the corridor outside their bedchamber the night before. "The men find her behavior unbecoming. She stares at them when she should lower her gaze, and she speaks aboot things she shouldnae."

"Catriona is my problem," Eideard answered, his voice hard. "Nae one will lay a finger on her. Dae ye hear me, Donal? Neither ye, nor any man in this clan will sae much as speak tae her in a less than civil manner."

"Then deal wi' her, cousin," Donal snapped. "They all saw what she did tae me that night. Her lack o' modesty makes them wonder if she has whipped ye as well." Cat winced at the dull thud of Eideard's fist contacting flesh, and she covered her mouth with her hand to keep from crying out. "Keep a civil tongue in your head, Donal. Ye may be my close kin, but I am still your liege lord. Dinnae be forgetting your place."

"Aye, *Lord*," Donal replied, his voice newly nasal. "See that ye remember what is due the clan."

Cat scampered across the room as Donal's footsteps rang down the corridor. Settling herself in the chair Eideard had placed near the hearth for her, she pulled a mangled embroidery into her lap. It was hard to stifle her thoughts and bite her tongue. And how was she supposed to remember that a proper woman didn't look a man in the eye?

Eideard stormed into the room, his expression black, but he stopped at the bench and took three deep breaths. When he turned to face her, his face was calm and composed.

Cat's breath caught, and her heart swelled. Even under Donal's provocation, Eideard had no word of condemnation for her. What had she ever done to deserve such a man?

She threw the embroidery to the floor and ran to her husband. "I'm sorry," she whispered. "I'll do better tomorrow. I'm sorry."

His arms tightened around her and he rested his cheek on the top of her head. "No need for apologies, my heart. I know 'tis hard for you."

They nestled on the bench together, taking comfort from each other. At last, Eideard broke the silence. "I have found a wise woman. She lives in the cliffs above the Forth. Seamus has brought her down to meet with us."

"A wise woman? I don't understand."

"Some would call her a witch. If anyone knows about magic such as pulled you intae this time, 'twould be one such as her."

"I see." A knot of ice formed in Cat's heart. Eideard wanted her to go back. Honorable man that he was, he wouldn't set her aside, but she was a liability to his leadership. He wanted to send her back to her own time.

"Come, let us tae bed," he said, not meeting her eyes. "We will visit the wise woman on the morrow."

CHAPTER THIRTEEN

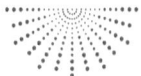

*E*ideard led Catriona through the narrow streets of Lastalrig village to the stone hut. He bent low to enter the doorway and pulled her through behind him. She had been unusually quiet this morning, and their lovemaking last night had possessed an odd, solemn quality. He had given her hope that she might leave this place, might return to her own time, but she didn't know how to say good-bye.

He had no doubt she cared for him. How could a woman give herself as freely as Catriona had done and not care for the man? But he knew she didn't belong here. He wasn't a fool. He could see how hard she worked to fit in, but the very light of her soul proclaimed her *sassenach* ... foreigner.

He loved her for the daily struggle. Loved her spirit, her intelligence, her willingness to stand up to him in private, while trying to appear submissive in public. And God only knew how much he loved the wanton way she used her body to drive him into fiery passion every night. He loved her ... and because he loved her, he sought to return her to her own time.

Her absence would leave a hole in his heart that would never heal, but he would cut her out and return her to her own time if he could. He would not grasp the jewel of her so tightly that she lost her luster and forgot how to shine.

"Good day, Mother." He bowed to the wrinkled, old woman who knelt on the hard dirt floor beside the fire. "I am Eideard, and this is my wife, Catriona."

"Aye," said the wise woman. "I ken ye both. The sight ha' shown ye tae me. I ha' a marriage gift for t' lady."

"For me?" Catriona squeaked. "Is it not a wedding gift for us both?" She moved closer to Eideard and put her hand in his.

The wise woman nodded her gnarled head of wispy white hair. "It main be, but th' decision lies wi' ye, lady. Ye main decide whether or nae tae undertake th' journey. Ye came frae afar tae find this man, but only ye ken if he is enough tae hold ye in his time."

Eideard's pulse pounded in his ears at the woman's words, nearly drowning out Catriona's reply.

"What do you know of my journey?" she asked.

"I ken all. 'Twas mah magic which brooght ye here."

His wife shivered in reaction to the crone's revelation, and Eideard drew her close.

The old woman struggled to her feet, moved into a dim corner of the hut, and rummaged through a pile of rags. At length, she turned and hobbled to Catriona.

"Do ye know this casket?" She held out a small casket similar to one Eideard's mother had treasured. Lady Agnes had kept her jewels in the small, wooden box. The one the crone held was more ornate. The finely wrought silver shone like new fallen snow.

"That's it," cried Catriona. "Eideard, that's the casket I found in the junk shop." She accepted the box and frowned. "But it's different. The lid isn't inscribed."

"Aye, lady, as I said, 'at is fer ye tae decide."

"How does it work?"

"Who can explain th' workings o' th' gods?"

"No, you misunderstand," said Catriona, her voice eager with anticipation. "What do I do to make my decision?"

Eideard's heart plummeted to his boots. How anxious she sounded to be gone.

"Th' magic o' th' casket is strong, lady. Ye are th' only body who can open it, noo an' fer eternity. When th' decision is made, put an object inside 'at belongs tae th' life ye wish tae inhabit. After 'at, ye hae only tae allow th' beams o' th' bright moon tae fall upon it."

"Once I've made my choice, no one else can mess it up?" Catriona asked.

Confusion lit the old woman's eyes, but she studied the girl's eager face. Understanding dawned, and the wise woman cackled. "Nae, lassie. Yer choice will be safe. Th' casket awaits yer pleasure."

The old woman cocked her head as Eideard placed a silver coin in her gnarled hand.

"Thank ye, Mother."

She studied his face and nodded. "'Tis her choice, Laird."

"I understand."

"If ye wish an inscription on th' lid, ye can take th' casket tae any silversmith," she said, watching Catriona with a canny eye. "Scribing willnae harm th' working."

"Thank you," said Catriona, kissing the old woman on the cheek. "Whatever the outcome, you have blessed my life."

CHAPTER FOURTEEN

*T*he next week passed like a mouse slogging through molasses. Indecision plagued Cat's every waking moment. She knew she should dig her cell phone from the backpack she'd shoved beneath the bed and place it in the silver casket, but couldn't bring herself to do it. She didn't want to leave Eideard, not even knowing he wanted her gone.

Instead, she placed the silver casket on the table beside their ewer and basin and tried to pretend it was an ordinary jewelry box.

Her lack of action plagued Eideard, too. He eyed the box every time he entered the room, and Cat noted his gaze slip to it even as orgasm spasmed through his body. The night before the bright of the moon, tension filled the great hall. Eideard barked orders at Mistress Mac and cuffed one of the younger clansmen for inattention.

Donal sulked in surly silence and glowered at Cat whenever she caught his gaze.

"What?" she snapped at last.

"Gie on wi' it, woman," Donal growled. "Whatever it is ye main dae, dae it! Ye are drivin' him tae insanity."

"I don't know what you're talking about."

"Aye, ye dae. Ye are unwillin' tae make some choice, an' all his kith an' kin are payin' fer it. He willnae tell me th' crux o' th' matter, only 'at th' choice is yours ... an' by God, woman, ye main decide!"

"Donal!"

Cat froze in the midst of framing a retort. She'd never heard Eideard speak with such deadly authority. All eyes near the head table fastened on the threesome as Eideard approached his seat between Donal and Catriona.

"Leave my hall, Donal Logan. Dae nae return until I send for ye personally."

"Eideard, ye dinnae..."

"Dinnae presume tae tell me what I dae and dae nae mean, clansman. I am nae a woman tae be bullied by your words. Leave my hall. Now!"

Donal jumped to his feet, overturning his chair. He glared at Eideard, but turned his wrath on Cat.

"This is yer daein', woman! Ye hae brooght naught but strife intae this hall. By th' Lord God, I wish ye had ne'er come tae this place!"

Eideard drew his sgian dhu, leapt at Donal, and had the small, sharp knife at his cousin's throat before Cat realized what was happening.

She lunged to her feet, caught Eideard's right arm, and threw all her weight into holding the knife away from Donal's throat.

"Eideard, my lord! No!"

His arm was like steel beneath her fingers, and she knew that should he decide to slit Donal's throat, she wouldn't have the leverage to stop him. She also knew no man in the hall would lift a finger against his liege lord.

"Eideard, please," she begged. "Please, my love. For my sake, release him."

His arm relaxed beneath her fingers, and she breathed a little easier. Eideard threw Donal from him. "Because my lady wife desires it, ye shall live. Leave my hall, Donal. Ye are nae longer my kin."

Donal rose and glanced around the hall. All eyes avoided his gaze. Wherever he looked, heads turned from him. Only Cat met his gaze. The pain she saw in the big man's eyes broke her heart. Donal stumbled from the hall.

My fault, thought Cat. *All my fault. Eideard has lost his best lieutenant, and for what? Because I haven't the courage to leave him. Donal was right. The whole clan is paying for my indecision, and Eideard most of all.*

She drew herself up to her full height, held her chin high, and strode from the hall. As soon as she reached the anonymity of the corridor, she ran to her bedchamber. Her refuge. The one room in the castle where she had been free to be herself and where she had enjoyed romance and passion and the lustful appreciation of the only man she would ever love.

For she could no longer hide from the fact that she did indeed love Eideard Logan. If she didn't, she would have sealed her cell phone in the casket at once. She would have been waiting with high anticipation for tomorrow night and her opportunity to return to the twenty-first century, to her old life, to Gran Da ... whose second sight had sent her to Scotland and ultimately to Eideard.

Instead, she dreaded what she knew she must do. She ran to the washstand, opened the casket, dropped to her knees, and searched beneath the bed for her backpack. She had to find that cell phone, had to seal it in the box now, while she still felt the stigma of Eideard's anger. Donal was right. She never should have come here. Eideard would forget her. He would marry a dutiful, little clan wife and father a dozen sons … but first she had to leave, had to set the timeline to rights.

Where was that blasted backpack? Tears blurred her vision, and her breath came in heaving sobs. She couldn't even do a right and noble thing without making a mess of it.

"What are ye searching for, Catriona?"

Between her hammering heart and wracking sobs, she hadn't heard the door open. Cat sat back on her heels and stared up at Eideard.

"My backpack," she wailed. "I need my backpack, and I can't find it."

"I have hidden it," he said, his voice quiet but menacing. "Tae prevent ye making your choice without giving me my say."

He strode across the room, grabbed Cat by the arm, and hauled her from the floor and into his embrace.

"Did ye truly mean tae decide without at least asking my leave?"

She struggled against the iron of his arms. "I don't need your leave," she cried, despair transmuting to anger in the space of a single heart-beat. "The decision is mine. Mine!"

Eideard's mouth captured hers, and the force of his kiss swept the breath from her body and replaced it with liquid fire. She stopped struggling against him and threw her whole soul into the scorching blaze of that kiss.

He growled low in his throat, picked her up, and stumbled to the bed, never once breaking contact with her lips. They fought their way out of clothes and savaged each other in their need to meld their flesh into a single fiery organism.

One last night, she thought, agony blistering her soul. *I will hold him inside me this one last night. It must be enough; the blaze must burn hot enough to warm me for the rest of my empty life.*

Their sexual encounter resembled war more than love. The two combatants fought, each attempting to emblazon their memory on the other's soul. When the hard-won orgasm shuddered through the pair, both were traumatized and shattered.

Cat's tears flowed freely as Eideard dragged himself from atop her. She felt bereft, though he lay but a handspan away.

"Gae then," he said, his tone defeated and dead. "I will get yer wee pack, and when the moon rises, ye can gae back tae yer own world."

He rolled on his side and drew his knees to his chest, his dark auburn hair curtaining his face.

A spasm of sobs wracked her body, and she fought for control. "I'm sorry, Eideard." She whimpered as a fresh wave of emotional pain swamped her. "I'm so sorry I couldn't be what you wanted, that I couldn't fit in. I'll go quietly, but I'll love you forever."

She closed her eyes, rolled into a tight fetal position, and sobbed.

Eideard's hand gripped her shoulder. He pulled her toward him and yanked her hands from her face.

"What did ye say?"

"I-I said I'd go, like you want me to," she whispered.

"Nay, th' last part. Th' part aboot lovin' me forever."

She nodded and wiped the tears from her eyes so she could see his handsome face. "I will," she promised. "No one will ever take your place."

He stared at her in shock, his whole body stilled. "Ye dinnae want tae leave?"

"No!" she cried, and a convulsive shudder wracked her body. "What w-would I do without you?"

His chest expanded, and he scowled down at her. "Then why in God's Holy Name are ye tryin' tae return tae th' future?"

"B-because you want me to go," she wailed. "Because I'm too much of a problem for you."

"Great God Almighty, woman!" he cried. "Ye are th' most tryin' female th' Lord God ever saw fit tae give th' breath o' life." He swooped down upon her, scooped her into his arms, and hugged her so tightly she could barely breathe. "Ye unman me in front o' my men, 'tis true. Ye vex me wi' yer unholy thoughts an' ideas, aye." He paused to kiss the tears from her eyes. "But ye are th' greatest gift th' Lord ha' bestowed upon me, an' my life will be without joy or color or song if ye go." He kissed her gently, a hint of passion brewing in the depths. "Stay with me, Catriona," he whispered. "Stay an' bear my bairns. Dinnae cut my heart frae within me."

"Oh, Eideard!" Fresh tears blurred her vision. "Of course, I'll stay. I've only avoided a decision because I didn't know you wanted me."

He sighed and rested his forehead against hers. "Ye are a trial, Catriona. How could ye doubt my love? Have I nae forborne tae beat ye when all my kinsmen hae counseled me that ye needed naught but a good lashing tae learn your place?"

She giggled incoherently, but managed to say, "That's not exactly a testament of love where I come from."

"Aye, well, since ye dinnae understand my actions — or my restraint, let me tell ye clearly: I love ye, Catriona Logan. Ye are my heart and my destiny, and there will be nae other love beside ye." He paused and a huge grin lit his face. "What say ye? Shall we seal th' bargain now?"

Without waiting for an answer, he tossed her onto her back and pounced. She wriggled happily, savoring the kisses he rained over her body.

"Eideard," she sighed after their lovemaking climaxed yet again.

"Aye?"

"Will you call Donal back?"

He opened one eye and peered at her through deep auburn lashes. "Why?"

"Because he was right." She snuggled closer and kissed his throat. "Don't punish him for speaking the truth and forcing us to face our fears."

"Mmmph." He stroked her hair for a moment, and then asked, "Will ye make your peace with him? I willnae have him causing strife in my hall."

"We'll share a private meal, just you and me and Donal. He and I both love you, Eideard. We'll find a way to accept each other."

"Mmmph."

Contented silence reigned for a few moments before Eideard spoke again. "What will ye put in yon casket?"

She straddled him, licked her lips, and smiled. "First, we'll have it inscribed... *Catriona, return to me my heart. Lastalrig Castle. By the bright of the moon. Eideard.*"

His hazel eyes sparkled with triumph. "Aye, that we will."

"And then," she bent forward, nipped his ear lobe, and whispered, "we'll put the necessary part inside." She rotated her hips, and his manhood hardened. "A portrait of me."

Eideard groaned, grabbed her hips, and thrust his necessary part deep inside.

Cat gasped with pleasure and whispered, "Home ... where I belong!"

PART VIII
HER HIGHLAND YULE

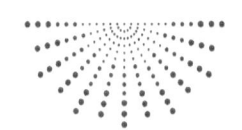

DEBBIE MUMFORD

HER
HIGHLAND
YULE

A Logans of Lastalrig
Short Story

CHAPTER ONE

*L*ady Catriona Logan swept into the great hall of Lastalrig Castle, her tartan skirt swishing around her ankles and her corsage laced so tightly she could feel her every breath. Hands fisted on hips, she paused to admire the decorations. The huge stone hearth at the far end of the room was swept clean, ready for the lighting of the Yule log when the men returned from procuring the traditional birch tree. The brass candle sconces fairly shone, having been polished for the festivities. Once the wicks were lit, the beeswax candles would cast a pearly glow on the rough stone walls. Fresh rushes were strewn across the flagstone floor, and the tables and walls were bedecked with holly, ivy, and mistletoe. In pride of place hung a beautifully woven kissing branch. The large spherical ornament was suspended from the rafters above a spot right in front of the head table where Cat and her highland laird Eideard would be seated.

Christmas at Lastalrig was like nothing Cat had ever experienced.

In the six months since she'd fallen through time to land in Eideard's life, she'd grown accustomed to the Scotland of 1452, but Christmas … well, Christmas was a time for family and friends, for beloved traditions like twinkling lights on a decorated tree, caroling in the snow, and lazy Christmas mornings with hot chocolate, cinnamon rolls, and beautifully wrapped presents under the tree.

At least, that was what every other Christmas of her life had been. But this wasn't 2012 and she wasn't in North Carolina with Gran Da. No, this year she was the Lady of Lastalrig Castle in the year of our Lord fourteen hundred and fifty-two. And it wasn't even Christmas they'd be celebrating tonight. It was Yule, and the festivities would last twelve days, with the biggest celebration occurring on Twelfth Night, January 5th, the Eve of Epiphany.

Eideard had explained it all to her, making sure she understood her role for the various saints' days that fell between Christmas and Epiphany, and she was somewhat familiar from her university studies of medieval literature, but reading about something that happened hundreds of years ago and experiencing it first hand were vastly different beasts. At least she knew she could rely on Eideard to guide her through the intricacies of the season.

Eideard. Her highland laird. The love of her life and the reason she was here, in a castle that was little more than a moldering ruin in the time she'd been born to. Eideard. He'd loved her enough to discover a way for her to choose her fate, and once she'd recognized his forbearance as love, she'd followed her heart and chosen to stay.

She smiled, remembering his declaration of love, "Ye are a trial, Catriona. How could ye doubt my love? Have I nae forborne tae beat ye when all my kinsmen hae counseled me that ye needed naught but a good lashing tae learn your place?"

A giggle escaped her lips and she glanced around to be sure she was still alone. She'd actually had to explain to the poor man that not beating her didn't equal love in a 21st century woman's mind!

But regardless of their vastly different communication styles, not to mention world views, Eideard did love Catriona, and Cat loved him so deeply, so completely, that she'd given up the opportunity to return to her own time, and instead worked daily to settle into her new life as the laird's wife, the Lady of Lastalrig.

And even though it was Yule, not Christmas, and gifts would not be exchanged for centuries yet to come, Cat would hold to her own traditions. Her hands relaxed from their fists and slid across the folds of her tartan skirt to rest protectively over the slight swell of her belly. Tonight, in the seclusion of their bedchamber, she would give Eideard the most precious gift she'd ever held: the knowledge that she carried his child.

CHAPTER TWO

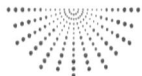

A few hours later, Cat sat beside Eideard at the high table enjoying a meal of roast goose and mince pies. The Yule log crackled merrily on the hearth providing both warmth and a rosy glow to the crowded room. Many of the members of Clan Logan had come to Lastalrig for the Yule celebration, and the castle teemed with life. Every room, except the bedchamber Cat shared with Eideard, boasted extra inhabitants, and the kitchens scurried to keep everyone fed.

Cat glanced at Eideard and her heart did a familiar little flip, raising her pulse. Her husband was easily the most handsome man in the room. Powerfully built with broad shoulders and a narrow waist, his dark auburn hair glistened in the firelight. He'd clubbed it at the back of his neck for the night's festivities, though Cat loved it best when it hung loose around his shoulders. As though feeling her gaze upon him, Eideard turned his head and smiled, his hazel eyes sparkling.

"Are ye enjoying the meal, love?" he asked, his English lilting with the Scots brogue she loved.

She nodded, heat suffusing her cheeks as she thought of how his accent thickened when they made love in the private paradise of their marriage bed.

He grinned, and grabbing her hand, lifted it to his lips. "Ye are especially lovely tonight, Catriona. That new gown suits ye."

"Thank you, Eideard," she said, lowering her eyes demurely. "I'm glad my appearance pleases you."

Eideard chuckled, squeezed her hand, and, leaning close, whispered for her ear alone, "That was well said, my love. Ye'll have the clan believing ye are a well-bred lass yet." He kissed her cheek before continuing, "but 'tis a lucky man who knows the truth of who and what ye are … and that man is me."

Heat rose throughout her body, and she knew that her cheeks flamed to match the red of her new gown. She widened her eyes, met his gaze more boldly than any fifteenth century woman would dream of, and said with a very good imitation of innocence, "Why, my lord, I cannot imagine what you mean. I can assure you, my breeding is excellent."

Eideard guffawed. When his mirth had settled, he raised his goblet to her. "To yer health, wife."

Cat lifted her own cup and said with a smile, "And to yours as well, husband," and took a sip. Alone of all the revelers in the great hall, Catriona drank water. Boiled water. Though the castle's supply of drinking water came from a pristine spring, Cat had given Mistress Mac, the castle's headwoman, instructions that any water she and Eideard consumed was to be boiled first. As soon as she suspected her pregnancy, Cat had stopped drinking the ale that was served with every meal and insisted on water. Mistress Mac might think her strange, but the headwoman had long since accepted that the laird's wife held some distinctly odd notions.

After the remains of the meal had been whisked away to the kitchens, several of the clansmen pushed the large trestle tables away from the center of the room, clearing a wide area before the high table.

"What's happening, Eideard?" Cat asked, leaning close to her husband.

Eideard's eyes widened and his brows lifted in surprise. "Did ye no tell me that folk still carol in yer time?" he asked in a whisper.

"Well, yes," she said, watching in fascination as several pipers prepared their bagpipes, "but everyone could just as easily sit at table and sing. Why is so much open space needed?"

"Sit at table and sing? I can see we've verra different ideas of caroling," he said with a wry smile. "Watch and learn, wife. Clan Logan will show you what it is to carol."

With that, Eideard rose from the table and clapped his hands. The room quieted except for the residual hum of a pipe as it continued to bleed air. The laird left the table and strode to the center of the cleared space.

"As Laird o' Lastalrig, I claim the first carol. Who will join me?"

Cat watched in wonder as men and women rushed to the open area and formed a large circle around their laird. Those who didn't join the circle climbed onto the tables at the edges of the room and settled to watch. When all were in place, Eideard nodded to the pipers and began to sing in a rich baritone. The bagpipes caught his melody and the folk in the circle moved to the intricate rhythms of the carol.

The song was like nothing Cat had ever experienced. Eideard sang in Scots Gaelic, and while her grasp of the language had vastly improved over the last six months, she had trouble following the words, buried as they were in unexpected rhythms, the shuffle of dancing feet, and the screel of bagpipes. Cat sighed. If she'd expected to find comfort in the familiarity of *traditional* Christmas carols, she would obviously be sorely disappointed. Instead, she straightened in her seat and chose to enjoy the spectacle. Gran Da would never believe this!

When his carol finished, Eideard bowed to the dancers and left the circle. Another singer took his place, a woman this time, and for a few moments the circle blurred as some left to sit on the tables and others took their places. Then, at a nod from the singer, the next carol began.

Eideard made his way back to Cat's side, dropped into his chair and drank deeply from his goblet. Wiping his mouth on his sleeve, he nodded to the circle. "That is how we carol at Lastalrig."

Cat smiled. "In my time, people walk about their neighborhoods in groups of five or six and sing Christmas carols. Or, if you're having a holiday party, everyone might sit around after dinner and sing. I've never seen carols accompanied by bagpipes and a circle dance."

Eideard shook his head, a small frown creasing his brow. "Everyone sings? How would they all agree on the melody?"

His words stunned her. "Agree on the melody? You mean it isn't standardized?"

He puzzled over her question for a moment before answering. "Standardized? Do ye mean everyone knows the carol? It doesna change with the singer?"

"That's right," she said with a nod. "The words and music are written down so everyone sings the carol the same way."

He stared at her. "How verra strange. Is it no boring to know exactly how it will sound?"

"Well, no. It's very comforting. You can relax into the music and remember other times, other places." Her eyes suddenly filled with tears as longing for her family and friends overwhelmed her.

Eideared picked up her hand and lifted it to his lips. "Dinna cry, lassie," he murmured. "Ye've home and family here now, and I'm verra glad ye chose to stay with me."

She wiped her eyes with her other hand and smiled at him. "So am I, my love." She drew a shuddering breath and turned to watch the carolers. "But it is so very different here."

When the next carol ended, Donal, Eideard's cousin and second in command, moved to stand before the high table. "Will the Lady o' Lastalrig not honor us wi' a carol?"

Cat's heart thundered so loudly that she almost missed Eideard's response when he rose to address the room. "My lady's customs are different," he said, his voice smooth as silk. "She is no accustomed to the dancing and the pipes."

She rose to stand beside him, squeezed his hand and said, "I'll gladly share one of my carols, and you're welcome to dance if you wish," she turned to the pipers and bowed her head, "but if you wouldn't mind, I'd ask you not to play."

The lead piper removed the blowstick from his mouth, bowed to her, and said, "We would be honored to listen to yer song, Lady."

Cat's thoughts raced. Which carol should she choose? Which would these people find most familiar? Which would make her seem least alien?

Eideard released her hand and seated himself beside her. The clan moved quietly out of the circle of dancers, waiting for her to begin.

When she sang the first note, the hall stilled. She hadn't realized she'd chosen until the words and melody emerged.

"Silent Night."

Her heart had chosen for her, and the choice was perfect. She sang the simple melody with all the warmth and longing in her soul. She sang for Gran Da and all the friends she would never see again. She sang for Eideard and the child growing within; for the future and the family they would build. She sang for Lastalrig Castle and the clan that had welcomed her, despite her odd ways. She sang for herself, for the woman she had been, and the one she was becoming.

When the last note faded away, Cat came to herself, suddenly embarrassed by the many eyes watching her. Then Donal began to clap and the hall filled with applause.

Eideard rose, pulled her into his arms, and whispered, "That was verra well done, Catriona. My people … *your* people were moved."

When the hall quieted again, Donal bowed to her and said, "Thank you for sharing a carol, mi'lady." He turned to the hall and beckoned the people to gather. "Form a circle," he cried. "My own carol is burstin' to be sung!" And the hall filled again with what Cat was coming to recognize as Gaelic gaiety.

CHAPTER THREE

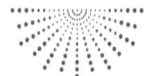

*T*he party, or *ceilidh* as Eideard called it, was still going strong a few hours later. The music had become more boisterous and the dancing more frenetic, but the energy in the hall remained cheerful and full of good spirits. Unfortunately, Cat's energy was flagging.

Though her pregnancy was still in the early stages, she tired more easily and found herself seeking solitude more frequently. Peace and quiet restored her soul, and this evening's feast and festivities had been anything but tranquil.

She turned away from Eideard and tried to stifle a yawn, but her husband was too aware of her to be fooled.

"Are ye tired, lass? Do ye wish to retire?"

She smiled wearily. "I'm fine," she said, another yawn spoiling her attempt to deflect his concern. "I don't want to spoil your fun. You stay. I can see myself to our chamber."

"Nay, my love. We'll go together. None in this hall would knowingly cause ye harm, but some men are too far in their cups to notice who ye are." He stood and offered her his hand. "Come."

She took his hand and stood, appreciating his steady strength as fatigue weighted her limbs. Together they left the hall, stopping here and there along the way to wish the joy of the season on various members of the clan.

When they reached their bedchamber, Cat sank into a chair before the hearth, blessing Mistress Mac for her foresight in seeing that the fire burned brightly.

Eideard knelt beside her chair and gazed earnestly into her eyes. "Are ye well, Catriona?" he asked, surprising her with his question.

"Of course," she said. "I'm just tired. It's been a long day."

He nodded, but his eyes continued to search her face. "Aye, it has, but ye seem to tire more easily these days. If there's aught amiss, ye'd tell me, would ye not?"

Her heart did a little backflip and she knew the moment had come. How she loved this man! She was out of her time and often out of her element, but he believed her, accepted her though she was so often not what the world expected of a woman in this time and place, and loved her wholeheartedly. The fates had blessed her when they had brought her to Eideard.

She smiled, joy flooding her soul. "Nothing is wrong, Eideard. In fact, something is very, very right." She took his hand and guided it to rest on her abdomen, the folds of her new red gown soft beneath their fingers. "I'm carrying your child," she said very softly, her voice husky with emotion.

Eideard's eyes had followed the movement of their hands, but now his gaze jumped to lock on hers and his hand spasmed on her belly.

"Truly?" he whispered. When she nodded, he asked, "Are ye certain?"

She laughed. "Well, if I were at home, I'd run down to the pharmacy and buy a pregnancy test, but since I can't pee on a stick here …" She stopped, seeing the bewilderment in his eyes. "Yes, Eideard," she said simply. "I'm sure."

He bounced to his feet, pulled her from the chair, and swung her into his arms. Holding her as easily as if she were a child, he spun in a circle before depositing her on the bed. "I'm to be a father!"

Landing beside her, he wrapped her in his arms and kissed her thoroughly. When they broke apart, he stroked her hair and asked, "When?"

"Uhm, given that I've never been pregnant before, I'm just guessing," she said, grinning at the impatient growl she both heard and felt. "But by my calculations, I think mid-July."

"Ye've made me verra happy, my love," he said, nuzzling her neck, "but ye are wearin' too many layers for me to properly appreciate the wonder o' the moment."

Later, as they lay spooned beneath the blankets, Eideard's hand splayed protectively across her belly, Cat spoke into the peaceful quiet. "You know, in my time, it's traditional to give presents at Christmas." She squirmed around in his arms until they were nose to nose. "I think this," she pressed his hand to her belly again, "is the best Christmas present either of us is ever likely to receive."

He kissed her tenderly, and then rested his forehead against hers. "I know 'tis one I'm no likely to forget."

She laughed and said, "I can't wait to meet this baby. I wonder if it will be a boy or a girl?"

He kissed her forehead lightly. "I dinna know, but whichever it is, I will love it until the day I die … just as I will its mother."

Lady Catriona Logan sighed happily, all nostalgia over Christmases past lost in the wonder of her first Highland Yule.

PART IX
INCIDENT ON THE HIGH LINE

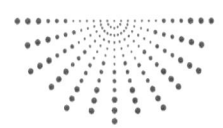

DEBBIE MUMFORD

BESTSELLING AUTHOR OF *SORCHA'S HEART*

INCIDENT
ON THE
HIGH LINE

SPUN YARNS
A Short Story

CHAPTER ONE

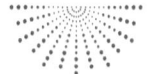

Tom Easton patrolled the weathered boards of the Breckenridge railway station platform. Tall pines and whispering aspens rose behind the narrow gauge steam engine, the whole scene framed by craggy mountains capped in glacial snow. The blazing blue of the Rocky Mountain sky put such a shine on the white caps, Tom's eyes watered just glancing at them. Despite the acrid tang of the steam engine, the late summer day smelled fresh and clean.

It was good to get away from the stink of Leadville. Too many unwashed miners crowded that booming town. Breckenridge was a thriving community, but for all its recent growth this end of the High Line was still wholesome as a newborn lamb in comparison to Leadville. Ever since that lone metallurgist had realized the heavy, black sand that had defeated the gold panners was actually a tell for silver, the mountains around Leadville had exploded with prospectors. And fortunately for Tom and the Pinkerton Detective Agency, where opportunity thrived, grift and greed followed.

The Pinkerton Agency had been good to Tom. His personal moral code closely aligned with that of the company, making his work deeply satisfying. His current assignment, guarding the High Line railroad, was light duty. He hadn't had to deal with more than a few drunk and disorderlies in the five months he'd been riding these rails. The crisp mountain air and spectacular scenery made up for the lack of excitement, but Tom was counting the days until his six-month tour was up. His next assignment promised a raise in pay and a return to civilized society. With that advancement, he'd finally be in a position to offer for Emily. Delight tugged a curve to his lips at the thought of changing Miss Emily Langstrom's name to Mrs. Thomas Easton. Gentle, sweet-tempered Emily, the lovely lady who owned his heart.

Putting away his tender feelings for his sweetheart, Tom studied the narrow gauge train with a practiced eye. Smaller than the standard gauge trains that had tamed the continent, the narrow gauge was well suited to the tight twists and hairpin curves that threaded these Rocky Mountains. The sturdy little locomotives did an excellent job of hauling ore to smelting centers and workers to the mines. Today they'd be hauling three empty ore cars back to Leadville, along with a single passenger car and, as it was the end of the month, an express car carrying gold for the payroll of the Matchless Mine.

Tom glanced at the hulking expanse of the windowless express car. Nothing for him to worry about there, the rolling fortress was already locked up tight. An expressman and two hired toughs hunkered inside to guard the gold. A glance forward elicited a satisfied grunt. The engineer and fireman were already building a head of steam that would pull them out of Breckenridge and carry them through to Leadville. Empty ore cars could tempt those who'd like a free ride up the mountain, but that wasn't Tom's concern. The railway's station men would ensure that the open-topped ore cars stayed empty. All Tom had to do was keep an eye on the fare-paying passengers.

The Pinkerton man continued his restless prowl, boot heels ringing against the silvered boards, while passengers bustled around, calling to each other, hefting trunks and other baggage, and finally clambering up the wrought iron steps to settle in their seats. Mostly working class men, hair slicked back, beards and mustaches freshly trimmed from their time away from the mines. A few families boarded. Bonneted and aproned women herding youngsters up the steps and into the car, their men loaded with carpetbags and much needed supplies.

A handsome young woman caught Tom's eye as she crossed the platform to be handed aboard by the conductor. Thinking of his Emily, he noted the propriety of her dress: voluminous gray skirts with a matching short cape buttoned to just beneath her chin. She presented a fine figure of a woman — firm jaw line, delicate features, golden hair upswept beneath a little alpine hat decorated with a pheasant's feather. But where was her escort? Why would a refined lady be traveling alone? He shook his head. An unescorted female heading to a rough mining town was asking for trouble. Of course, she might be a new fancy lady for the saloon, but he didn't think so. She reminded him too much of Emily to entertain that possibility. Her dress was too fine, her carriage too proper. Surely a father or husband waited for her at the Leadville station. Until then, Tom would keep an eye on her; make sure she came to no harm.

A cloud of steam belched from the engine's stack, and the conductor bellowed, "All aboard!"

Tom saluted the engineer, nodded to the stationmaster, and climbed onto the narrow iron deck at the rear of the passenger car. The conductor grabbed the brass handrail and followed him up. "That's everyone," he said, giving Tom a satisfied smile. "Should be a nice quiet run."

Tom nodded, sweeping the Breckenridge platform with a final gaze as the train lurched forward, its pistons working to break free of their resting inertia. "Nothing suspicious caught my eye." He paused before asking his question. "Do you know the lady? The pretty one without a man?"

"Wondered about her myself. Fine clothes. Nice manners. Looked to be alone." The conductor shrugged. "Hope she knows what she's about."

"That makes two of us." Tom grasped the door handle, twisted, and stepped into the passenger car. The conductor trailed just behind and, after securing the door, began checking tickets. Tom moved down the aisle, adapting his pace to the slight sway and buckle of the train's movement. He made note of each seat's occupant as he passed, finally taking his place on a bench at the front of the car facing the passengers.

CHAPTER TWO

The train chugged through a valley following the flow of Tenmile Creek when the man seated behind the unescorted female leaned forward, tapped her shoulder, and then grabbed her arm and jerked her upright.

The other women gasped and clutched squealing youngsters close as their men spread protective arms across their own. Tom surged to his feet, only to stop dead. The man had his captive in a neck lock with a pistol shoved into her side.

"Sit back down, Pinkerton man. Slide your six-shooter to my partner, real easy like." The outlaw dragged the young woman into the narrow aisle as another man rose from a seat a few paces from Tom. "Do it, or watch this pretty lady die."

Tom swore; he knew that unescorted female would be trouble. Moving slowly, deliberately, he pulled his revolver from his holster with two fingers, set it gently on the vibrating floor, and pushed it toward the accomplice with his foot.

The first outlaw glanced around. "Don't any of the rest of you get no ideas neither," he growled to the other passengers. "I got me an itchy trigger finger and plenty of ammo."

The second man grabbed Tom's gun. "Got it, Coal Creek," he crowed, shoving Tom's revolver into his belt with his left hand while he drew his own weapon with his right.

The first man grimaced. "Ain't you got the sense God gave a hog? We ain't usin' names here." The second man reddened, but trained his six-shooter on Tom.

Coal Creek. Coal Creek. Tom searched his memory and dredged up the name from a recent watch list. Coal Creek Davis. Wanted for cattle rustling up Wyoming way, general thievery in several territories, and horse stealing on the plains east of Denver. He'd escalated some if he thought he could rob a payroll train.

Tom ignored the man pointing a gun at him and concentrated on the young woman. "Try to stay calm, ma'am," he said, voice cool and confident. "I don't aim to give old Coal Creek there any cause to harm you."

"That's right, Pinkerton," Coal Creek said with a nasty laugh. "You just mind your Ps and Qs and nobody gets hurt. Little Miss Bradford here is gonna get us just what we want."

Tom's gaze snapped to Coal Creek and back to the young woman. "Bradford?" he asked. "Josephine Bradford?"

Eyes bright with fear, she managed a tiny nod before her captor tightened his hold.

"That's right. The boss's daughter, Pinkerton man, so make sure you don't get her killed."

James Bradford was a major stockholder in the High Line and part owner of the Matchless Mine. What in the name of all that was holy was his only daughter doing on this train? Why hadn't Tom been notified she was expected? Why in hell was she traveling alone, unprotected? Good God! If Bradford's daughter came to harm on his watch, Tom's career would be over. He'd never be able to offer for his Emily.

Tom was still trying to wrap his brain around this new development when he felt the train slow. The door at the front of the passenger car opened and the conductor stepped in followed by yet another man with a gun.

"Sorry, Tom," the conductor muttered. "They were waiting for me on the ore car cat-walk. There's two more up watching the engineer and the fireman."

The train rolled to a stop beside Tenmile Creek, and Tom felt his stomach knot. It would be another hour or so before the stationmaster in Leadville realized they were late. Nightfall would be on them before the Leadville sheriff could round up a posse and follow the rails back to their position. He was on his own. Disarmed, with innocents to protect and the payroll to guard. At least there were three armed men locked in the express car; they'd be getting antsy what with the train stopping unexpectedly. Honeycutt was a good man. He'd be on guard and have his hired men ready for whatever these outlaws had in mind. Five bandits against three express guards and a Pinkerton man. The knot eased a bit. Law and order could still prevail.

If only he didn't have to worry about Bradford's daughter.

"Everybody out." Coal Creek Davis' gruff voice snapped Tom back to attention. He stood and stepped forward, hoping to place himself between the outlaws' guns and the families pushing for the door.

"Not you, Pinkerton," said Coal Creek. "You stay put." He motioned to the man holding a gun on the conductor. "You two, out. Keep the passengers together and out of trouble. The boys from the engine will back you up."

"You got it, boss." The outlaw grabbed the conductor's shoulder and pulled him back out the door they'd just come through. They clattered down the iron steps and into the meadow beside the stream.

An odd sense of unreality assaulted Tom. This couldn't be happening. The sun shone brightly above snow-capped peaks, meadow grass waved in a light breeze, and now that the train's noise was hushed, Tom could hear the gurgle of Tenmile Creek, the high sweet song of meadowlarks. Yet here he stood, one of four people on a train car, with a cocked pistol aimed straight at his racing heart. Clamping down on his fear, Tom studied his companions: Josephine Bradford, her outward calm belied by a tiny line of sweat beading her brow; Coal Creek Davis, the gleam in his eye proclaiming his satisfaction with the day's events; and Tom's guard, an overly excited accomplice with loose lips.

Coal Creek released his neck lock on Josephine and pushed her onto a seat, keeping one hand on her shoulder. "Here's the way this is gonna be," he said, pointing the gun at her head. "The little lady and me are gonna go visit the expressman. She's gonna tell him who she is and what I've got pressed to her head, and he's gonna unlock that door."

"What if he doesn't?"

"Then she's gonna get real dead. I don't think her daddy would like that very much, do you?"

Josephine's face paled and her lip quivered. A small whimper escaped, but she bit her lip and remained still, posture erect.

Anger laced with impotence burned in Tom's belly. She shouldn't be in this position. She was holding up well, but she shouldn't be facing a gunman. He'd failed to protect her. Her *father* had failed to protect her. "What do you want from me?"

"You? I don't want nothin' from you, Pinkerton." Coal Creek leaned down, rubbed his whiskers against Miss Bradford's pale cheek. She flinched slightly and closed her eyes. A single tear slid from beneath delicate lashes. Coal Creek straightened. "I'm gonna get everything I want with no help, nor hindrance, from you. You just stay here and think about what'll happen to her if you cause me any trouble."

Pulling Miss Bradford to her feet, the outlaw moved toward the door at the back of the car. "Keep a close eye on him," he said to his accomplice. "I'll send one of the boys to get you when the time comes."

Tom's captor nodded and slipped into the seat directly in front of Tom as Coal Creek and the young woman exited the car. "Might as well take a load off. This could take a while."

Sinking back onto his bench, Tom studied the other man. He'd noticed him when he boarded the train, but hadn't been concerned. Just one of the less-well-groomed workingmen. Dark hair slicked back from an unshaven face. Eyes set too close together. Clothes fairly clean but hard-worn. Hands calloused, Tom had assumed from wielding a pick ax. Now that he had time for a closer inspection, he noted crooked teeth and a squint to the eyes that might indicate poor eyesight. Of course, he could hardly miss a target sitting this close even if he were half blind.

"How did you know?"

"How'd I know what?"

"How did you know Miss Bradford would be on this train?"

The man shifted in his seat, but kept his gun trained on Tom. "Heck, that weren't nothin' special. Thought you'd be more interested in the payroll."

Tom shrugged. "The express car's easy to spot, but one lone skirt? That's different. Was she just a lucky break?" But Tom knew that couldn't be right. Coal Creek had known her identity when Tom had not.

"Yeah. Luck. That'll do." The man shifted again, clearly uncomfortable with Tom's question. This time, however, his aim faltered as he glanced out the window.

Tom took advantage of the momentary lapse. He lashed out, knocking the gun-hand aside. The outlaw flailed. The gun skittered across the floor. Heads knocked as both men scrambled for the weapon. Tom's fist caught the outlaw's temple, stunning him. Another blow and the man lay unconscious on the scuffed wooden floor.

Wiping blood from the corner of his mouth, Tom rested for a moment. When he'd caught his breath, he pulled handcuffs from his pocket, cuffed the outlaw to a seat support, and reclaimed his revolver. Moving low and as quietly as boots on wooden floorboards allowed, he positioned himself beside the door nearest the express car. He chanced a quick peek out the door's window and saw Coal Creek and Miss Bradford framed in the open door of the express car. Honeycutt and his hired guns had their weapons drawn and aimed, but Coal Creek had the upper hand. He held a gun to Josephine's temple.

With Coal Creek's attention firmly fixed on the three, armed men, Tom straightened and caught Honeycutt's eye. He mimed his intentions, and the big expressman shifted slightly to one side in acknowledgement.

Tom drew a deep breath, holstered his weapon, and eased the passenger car door open. He crept onto the iron deck, steadied himself, and when Coal Creek gestured, moving the gun momentarily from its target, Tom launched himself against the outlaw.

Coal Creek staggered forward. Honeycutt grabbed his gun hand while the guards wrestled the outlaw down. Tom caught his balance, threw an arm around Miss Bradford's waist and dragged her down the steps and around the corner of the express car. Once out of the line of fire, he pushed her against the side of the car and flattened himself at the corner, between her and where the outlaw might reappear.

Drawing his weapon, Tom waited, tense but controlled. "Don't you worry, Miss Bradford. I'll keep you safe. Honeycutt and his men should have Coal Creek subdued by now."

He'd pulled her down the closest steps, and had ended up on the opposite side of the train from where the rest of the gang held the remaining passengers. He wished he could see them. Wished he knew whether or not the other three members of the gang had noticed the scuffle. It had been quick and fairly quiet, but he and Honeycutt needed to disarm those men, ensure the safety of the engineer and the other passengers.

With his attention on their plight, Tom ignored Miss Bradford...until he felt the circle of cold steel press against the nape of his neck. A tingle of fear raced along his spine, heavily spiced with confusion.

"Be still, Mr. Easton," the woman said. "This may only be a derringer, but I assure you, I'm not afraid to use it. Now, hand over your gun."

Tom closed his eyes, defeat washing over him. He'd been taken in, seen too much of his guileless Emily in this unknown woman. She hadn't been a hostage. She'd been a decoy. He should've listened to his instincts when Coal Creek called her by name. How would the outlaw recognize Josephine Bradford, know the lady's itinerary when he, Tom Easton, a Pinkerton detective, didn't?

He uncocked his pistol and handed it over his shoulder, making no attempt to turn toward his second captor of the day. "You know my name."

"I checked the schedule. I needed to know who would be on the train, how many would be guarding the gold."

"Are you really Josephine Bradford?"

She snorted softly, a sound he was sure his lady-like Emily would never produce. "Yes. As a matter of fact, I am."

"Why?"

"You'll have to excuse me, but I haven't time for conversation right now."

And with that, she screamed, an ear-splitting, banshee wail that had Tom jerking away despite the derringer barrel at the base of his skull.

"Honeycutt!" she screamed, panic rife in her voice. "Honeycutt, please help me. It's Tom! I don't know what to do."

Footsteps pounded on the iron deck and steps and Honeycutt jumped from the train, his weapon at the ready.

The big man stopped, took in the scene before him, and cocked his revolver.

"Thank you, Mr. Honeycutt," she said, her tones smooth as cream. "Now, if you'll just have your assistants release Mr. Davis and hand over the gold, we'll finish our transaction with no further delay."

Honeycutt glanced at Tom, then narrowed his eyes at the woman behind him. "I don't think so," was his only reply.

The barrel of the little derringer dug deeper into Tom's flesh.

"Well I do, unless you want Mr. Easton's blood on your hands."

Honeycutt caught Tom's gaze and a look of understanding passed between the men. The expressman nodded once, and, eyes locked on Tom's, opened his mouth and shouted, "Lock 'er up, boys, and don't open up again until you hear the sheriff's voice in Leadville."

Josephine screamed again, but this time the sound was pure fury. The hammer on the derringer clicked back, a soft sound, but one that could mean the end for her captive.

Tom closed his eyes and pictured Emily, his heart thudding as if to accomplish all the beats it wouldn't have time to complete if the derringer served its purpose.

The gun barrel eased back a fraction and Tom took his chance. He dropped to his knees and rolled away from the tracks. Leaping to his feet, he saw that Honeycutt had disarmed Miss Bradford and had her restrained. The young woman was red-faced and furious, eyes flashing, hat askew and hair flying free from its upswept 'do.

"Thanks, Honeycutt," Tom said with a grin, his heart expanding with appreciation for life. "I owe you."

"Nah. We were both taken in by this little skirt. What's next? How many more are there?"

"They've got three more guarding everyone else on the other side of the tracks." He glanced toward the aspen grove at the foot of the mountain behind him. He could just make out the opening to a narrow canyon. "No telling if there are more waiting in the trees. I'd guess they have horses stashed somewhere nearby."

He glanced at Josephine, but the thin line of her lips told him he'd be wasting time trying to get answers from her. Movement in his peripheral vision caught his attention. When he turned to study the aspen grove, a stirring beneath their branches told him that whoever had waited with the horses had chosen to cut their losses.

"Got any rope?" Tom asked, nodding to Honeycutt's prisoner.

The big man grinned and pulled a pair of handcuffs from his pocket.

"Even better," Tom said as Honeycutt cuffed her to the brass handrail on the side of the express car.

With the lady subdued, the men climbed the steps, crossed the small deck and peered into the meadow beside Tenmile Creek. The unexpected sight caused them to raise a cheer. Nobody in that meadow needed rescuing, except maybe the last three members of Coal Creek's outlaw band.

Tom and Honeycutt jumped down from the express car and loped over to join the conductor and the engineer. "What happened here?" Tom asked once they'd exchanged grins and back-slaps.

"Well, we heard the little lady scream like the hounds of hell were after her," said the conductor, "and it surprised the gunmen so that us menfolk were able to make our move."

The engineer nodded and took up the tale. "Denny, my fireman, and I took that one," he said, pointing to an unconscious outlaw, "while Johnson here tackled another."

"One of the miners helped," added Johnson. "Conducting doesn't usually require scrapping, so I was glad of the aid."

"The last feller went down under a pile of men. Not sure who was who, but they got the job done."

"Is the lady all right?" asked the conductor.

Tom's face pinked a bit, but he nodded. "She's fine, but she was in on it."

The slack-jawed expressions on the other men's faces told Tom he hadn't been the only man on the train to be taken in by a pretty face and lady-like manners.

By the time they got everyone loaded back in the passenger car, Tom and Honeycutt had filled the others in on their part in the adventure. By mutual consent the male outlaws were bound and placed in one of the empty ore cars with Honeycutt on guard. Tom handcuffed Miss Bradford to the first seat in the passenger car and resumed his place on the bench facing her.

He shook his head as the engineer and fireman got the locomotive moving again. "You never told me why," he said by way of conversation.

She turned and stared out the window. "You wouldn't understand," she murmured. "You've never been a woman."

"That I haven't," he replied, and tipping his head back, closed his eyes.

CHAPTER THREE

*W*hen the train pulled into Leadville station, the sheriff waited with the stationmaster. "We were getting worried," he said to Tom when the Pinkerton man stepped down from the train.

Tom nodded. "Good that you were. We had a bit of trouble."

When he'd given the sheriff a run-down of the attempted robbery, the man shook his head. "Bradford's own daughter. That'll be a hard blow to weather."

They walked to the ore car and watched as the outlaws were hauled out. "I'll put these men in the jail. The district judge is due in a few days. But I don't know what to say about the woman. Can't rightly see housing her in the jail."

They wandered back along the station platform and watched her through the passenger car window. Handcuffed as she was, she hadn't moved from her seat.

"What would you think about taking her back to Breckenridge and handing her over to her father?"

Tom blew out his cheeks. "Well, I can't say as how I'm anxious for the duty, but I see your point about the jail here in Leadville."

They checked with the stationmaster and decided to do just that, arranging for seats on the next day's train. The sheriff took charge of her, locking her in a room at the boarding house and putting a guard outside her door with another watching her window. Tom took the precaution of sending a telegram to James Bradford, to ensure the man would meet the train and take custody of his wayward daughter.

The ride down the mountain the next day was uneventful. An empty express car, loaded ore cars, and very few passengers, with Josephine securely handcuffed, quiet and subdued. Just the way Tom liked it. He hoped he'd seen all the adventure the High Line had in store, at least until his tour was finished and the next man rode the rails.

He recognized James Bradford immediately when the train rolled into the Breckenridge station. The meticulously dressed gentleman strode across the platform as if he owned it, which in a very real sense he did. His calf-length black coat was woven of fine wool and sported fur lapels and collar. Highly polished boots and a tall stovepipe hat spoke of wealth and refinement, especially when pitted against the frontier homespun of the platform's other occupants. Tom noted the similarity between Mr. Bradford's finely chiseled features, highlighted as they were with neat mustache and pointed goatee, and his daughter's more delicate chin and cheekbones.

Josephine glanced out the window, espied her father, and squared her shoulders. She rose with quiet elegance when Tom released her after the train had come to a complete stop. He waited for the other passengers to exit before offering her his arm and leading her from the car. To the casual observer, it would appear that the young lady descending the steps to the platform was in the company of an admirer rather than a jailer. However, the glacial cold of the glance she exchanged with her father could hardly be misconstrued.

"Mr. Easton." James Bradford nodded to Tom, hands resting on the carved top of a walking stick. "My thanks for escorting my daughter home. I trust that she afforded you no further difficulty today."

"No, sir. Our journey was uneventful." Tom touched the brim of his bowler hat in a gesture of respect.

James Bradford reached for his daughter's hand, but she avoided his touch. Dark blue eyes flashing, he stepped closer to her and said in an angry whisper, "I can't imagine what you were thinking. Allying yourself with such vulgar men. I shall have the devil's own time keeping you from prison."

Her own blue eyes, so like her father's, mirrored his expression. "Can't you? Well let me see if I can explain. I was thinking of my extremely wealthy father divorcing my invalid mother and leaving her very nearly destitute. All to be free to wed a woman younger than myself." She sniffed and raised her chin. "As far as I'm concerned, the only true criminal here is you."

Turning her back on him, she extended a slim hand to Tom. "My apologies, Mr. Easton, for any inconvenience my actions may have caused you." And with that, she sailed across the station platform and disappeared into her father's carriage.

James Bradford blustered for a moment before saluting Tom and following his daughter, with what was like to be a permanent scowl etched across his face.

Tom shook his head and strode across the platform thanking God and all the saints in heaven that Miss Emily Langstrom had nothing in common with James Bradford's daughter.

PART X
TREASURES

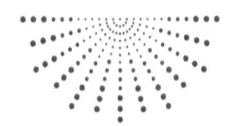

DEBBIE MUMFORD

BESTSELLING AUTHOR OF *SORCHA'S HEART*

Treasures

SPUN YARNS
A CONTEMPORAY SHORT STORY

CHAPTER ONE

$\mathcal{M}$amma has always had a love for other people's possessions. I've known this my whole life, so I hovered over her like a hawk eyeing a prairie dog.

"Oh, Mother Lange," I exclaimed. "What a wonderful piece of Lladro." I deftly removed my mother-in-law's prized porcelain statuette from Mamma's greedy fingers, and placed the little figurine back on the mantle. Taking a firm grasp of Mamma's elbow, I guided her to the center of Mother Lange's sofa. The most appropriate seat I could find for a kleptomaniac: nothing in arm's reach save a throw pillow.

"I'm so glad you like it, dear," said Roger's mother. I smiled up into her elegant face without relaxing my grip on my own mother's arm.

Roger, my husband of six months, had no idea how lucky he was to have been raised by this genteel and guileless woman. Mamma suffered by comparison. Of course, Mamma suffered by comparison to a baboon… whose females make remarkably good mothers.

"And you, Mrs. Wilson," said Mother Lange, "do you enjoy art?"

"Oh, aye," said Mamma, her gaze straying back to the little figurine. "I do love a well-made knick-knack."

Mother Lange looked startled. Doubtless she'd never heard a piece of her expensive collection referred to as a 'knick-knack' before. She recovered quickly, and leaned forward to begin the process of pouring tea.

"I'm so glad you could come today. I've regretted that we didn't meet before the children wed."

"Well," said Mamma, "I'm sure you remember how urgent young love can seem."

In truth, there'd been nothing urgent about Roger's and my courtship. Our mothers hadn't met for the simple reason that mine had been locked up in Attica until a month ago. They wouldn't have met today if I'd been able to think of any way around it. Though I had to admit, Mamma had cleaned up nicely for the occasion.

My mother, Senga Wilson, might have been a beautiful woman once, but her face showed signs of hard wear. Too much sun and wind in the prison exercise yard resulted in deep wrinkles around the eyes and mouth, and her once auburn hair had lost its luster to gray. Still, she'd made the effort to find a dark blue business suit that gave her the austere look of one of the prison matrons rather than an inmate. She'd even managed a bit of powder and lip gloss.

I released my grip on her arm, gave her a pat, and relaxed against the sofa's blue chintz cushions. Roger and I were happily married. Mamma couldn't hurt me, not this time.

"Elizabeth tells me you've been away for your health," said Mother Lange. "I do hope you're feeling better."

I felt Mamma's gaze bore into the side of my head, but refused to blush. Instead, I accepted a cup of tea from Mother Lange with a quiet, "Thank you."

"I've had cause to be away, aye," Mamma said. "In fact, I missed most of Lizzie's growing years."

"Lizzie?" Mother Lange set her own cup on the table and clapped her hands. "Is that what your family calls you, dear? But how charming! I don't remember ever hearing you referred to as anything but Elizabeth."

My face heated to scarlet as I wiped away the tea I'd just dribbled down my chin.

"Oh, she'll no want you to call her that," Mamma said hastily. "She's always put on airs, has my Lizzie. She'll want to be called 'Elizabeth,' to be sure."

Stung, I glared at her, before turning my attention to Roger's mother. "I'm not putting on airs, as Mamma so quaintly puts it," I told her, "but I do prefer Elizabeth."

In the tense silence that followed, Mamma rose and moved across the plush cream carpet to stand before a small oil painting, gilt-framed with its own recessed spotlight.

Mother Lange turned in her wingback chair to see what had captured Mamma's interest.

"That's my husband's pride and joy," she said, her voice conveying her own unmistakable pride, "the crown of his collection: an original Monet."

"Oh," said Mamma, examining the painting closely, "it's a bonnie wee picture, aye, but no an original. Whoever told you that should be tied to a post and whipped."

The effect of these words was utter chaos. Mother Lange jumped from her chair like she'd been shot from a cannon, while I managed to drop my cup on the mahogany table where it shattered, spilling the staining liquid into the carpet's deep pile.

"Whatever makes you say such a thing?" Mother Lange demanded, reaching Mamma's side.

"Mamma," I cried, "don't. Whatever you're scheming, just don't!"

Both women turned to stare at me, and I knew I looked a fright. My heart pounded, assuring my cheeks a hot flush, and I shook all over. My eyes had to be flashing, because anger boiled in my system.

"You can't ruin this for me," I yelled, holding up my ring finger for both to see. "We're already married; you can't hurt me this time!"

Color drained from Mamma's face and she stepped back as if I'd struck her. "Is that what you think, Lizzie? That I'm trying to harm you and yours?"

Mother Lange reeled away from Mamma, and perched unsteadily on a nearby chair, the painting forgotten.

"When haven't you hurt me, Mamma?" I dashed tears from my cheeks with stiff-fingered stabs.

"When were you ever there for me? When I started my menses, and thought I was dying? No. Daddy explained about the wonders of the female body. You were in prison for stealing Mrs. Davidson's emerald brooch. What about when I wanted to go to camp? I couldn't. We needed every penny to pay for your appeal."

Mamma stepped back with each accusation, until she pushed against the wall, as if willing it to absorb her. But that didn't stop me. I still had more to say.

Glaring at her, I continued. "What about when Daddy died of cancer? Were you there to ease him from this world and into the next? Or to comfort me in my grief? No. You've never been there for me."

I paused, took a deep breath, and finished my exorcism. "Other people's possessions have always been more important to you than me or Daddy."

Grabbing a linen napkin from the table, I blew my nose with such force that my ears rang.

"Well, I have my own family now, and it doesn't include you. Roger loves me, and I hope Mother Lange will still accept me after meeting you, but even if she doesn't, well, Roger loves me!"

I ran from the room without a backward glance, stopping only when I reached the safety of Roger's childhood room. I slammed the door, locked it, and collapsed on his bed amid ample evidence of his normal and well-loved childhood.

CHAPTER TWO

*W*hen I woke, having cried myself to sleep, I found Roger sitting beside me, stroking my back.

"How did you get in here?" I asked, sure I'd locked the door in my desire to lick my wounds in private.

He dangled a key before my eyes. "Used to be my room, remember? I know all its secrets." He leaned close and kissed my swollen eyelids. "Come downstairs, love. Our mothers have something to tell you."

I groaned and tried to bury my head in the pillow. "Just take me home," I whimpered. "I can't face them. Not today. Maybe not ever."

He picked up my hand and lifted it to his lips. "Yes you can. You're the strongest person I've ever known." He stood, pulling me up with him. "You were right, you know."

"About what?"

"I do love you, and we are a family, no matter what."

I took refuge in his arms and he held me tightly while I struggled to breathe. When I calmed, I lifted my head and gazed into his dark brown eyes.

"Do we really have to go downstairs?"

"We do." He kissed me tenderly and led me to the door.

Mother Lange met us at the living room threshold and squeezed my hand before walking us to the sofa.

"Senga and I have had a long talk," she said with a glance at Mamma. "I want you to know, Elizabeth that nothing that happened here today has caused me to think less of either you or your mother. In fact, I'm more honored than you can know to have you in my family, and your mother has done us a great service."

I must have looked skeptical, because she hurried to explain.

"It's true. Your mother explained her reasons for believing the painting to be a fraud, and I must bow to her expertise. I phoned Howard, and he agrees. We're having the painting examined and its provenance authenticated."

She stood and reached for Roger's hand. "Now, we're going to leave you and Senga alone for a few minutes." She caressed my cheek with her free hand and, cupping my chin, raised my eyes to meet her own. "You might want to rethink your decision to ban Senga from your family."

I sat in miserable silence until Mamma came to kneel in front of me.

"I'm that sorry, Lizzie," she said quietly. "I can't change what's been, and you're right about me never being there, but I hope you'll let me try to make a wee spot for myself in your future." She rose to sit carefully on the edge of the wingback chair opposite me.

I raised my eyes then, and gazed at her worn face. Thief she might be, but she'd never lied to me, never claimed to be anything but what she was.

And she was my mother.

"I'm sorry, too, Mamma. Sorry for everything we've missed." I sighed and managed a weak smile.

"As to the painting," Mamma paused and clicked her tongue reproachfully. "You should have known better, child. When have I ever stolen from family?"

I gazed at her with a calmness that astounded me.

"Really, Mamma? You've never stolen from family? What about Daddy's peace of mind?"

I rose and walked to the door, ready to join my husband; ready to leave the past in the past. I paused on the threshold and glanced at her over my shoulder.

"What about my childhood, Mamma?"

CHAPTER THREE

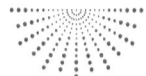

hree years to the day later, Mamma and I once again joined Mother Lange in her comfortable living room. The changes in the room and its occupants were understated, but significant. The fake Monet had been replaced by a Renoir of impeccable provenance, thanks in large part to Mamma.

Who knew that a life of crime could have marketable value in the world of art?

Certainly not me, but my father-in-law's insurance company had been quick to offer Mamma a job. She had recently reached a milestone: two-and-a-half years of diligent service. A few more and she'd be bonded in her own right—able to work without a supervising partner.

More important to me than her gainful employment was her new outlook on life. Mamma could now play with other people's treasures with impunity. The life suited her. She looked younger and healthier than I'd ever seen her, and radiated a quiet calm when we were together, which was often these days.

The most significant change in our lives raced across the room and threw himself into Mamma's arms.

"Choo-choo?" my son asked.

Mamma pulled the sturdy two-year-old onto her knee before rummaging in her capacious purse. To his delight, she pulled a little train engine from its depths and presented it to him.

"Run along with ye now, and don't be marring yer granny's table."

He slid from her lap and moved to the stone-floored entryway to play with his prize.

"He's such a good boy," Mother Lange said. "So like his father at that age."

"Aye, he's a bonny lad," agreed Mamma, turning a proud gaze on me. "And verra lucky in the parents who brought him into this world."

I smiled at the compliment. Mamma and I would never regain the lost years, but I was content. My son had two loving grandmothers in his life, and true to her word, my mamma no longer stole from family.

knew without a doubt that we were more important than other people's possessions... and that knowledge was balm to my healing heart.

PART XI
ICE HOUSE

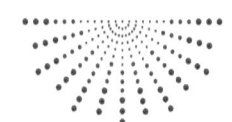

ICE HOUSE

SPUN YARNS
A Mystery Short Story

CHAPTER ONE

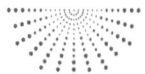

*J*immie and Trey trudged across the ice crusted snow toward the beach house on Lake Ontario's eastern shore. Both men's cheeks and noses were red with cold despite being bundled in down jackets several seasons out of date, ratty looking knitted scarves, and thick woolen mittens that could stand to be washed. Every few steps, one of their booted feet would break through the thick crust of ice, allowing the snow beneath to swallow the foot or even the calf. Consequently, the legs of their well-worn jeans were getting soggier by the minute, and it was cold enough in the wind off the lake without adding damp denim to the mix.

"We'd better find a good haul," Trey muttered after pulling his left foot free of yet another snow hole. "This weather is a bitch."

Jimmie stuck his mittened hands in his armpits while he waited for his partner to extricate himself. "Yeah, well, it's also why we have a chance at this beach house. Nobody in their right mind's gonna to be out in this weather."

"You got that right," Trey answered, brushing snow from his pants leg. "I shoulda known better than to let you talk me into this."

"Hey! You were anxious enough to come when I told you about it. Besides, we're already wet and cold. Might as well finish what we started."

Jimmie glanced across the white landscape. Everything kind of blended together—the gray of the lake, the dirty white of the snow and ice covered beach, even the sky was overcast and colorless—but he'd done his homework. He knew where the house was, knew that the late February storm that had blown in off the lake had covered the isolated beach house in freezing water, that the west side of the house was encased in thick white ice, along with everything else on the property.

It was a nasty day; nobody was around for miles.

He shaded his eyes, and then pointed to a featureless mass a little further along the beach. "Grab your stuff," he said, pointing. "There it is."

Trey mumbled a few words Jimmie didn't catch and picked up the expandable black duffle he'd dropped while extricating his boot. Both men wore empty backpacks as well, hoping to fill them with valuable loot from the isolated house.

"I sure hope you're right about the ice being thin on the street side," Trey said as they approached the single story dwelling. "I'd hate to've come out on this miserable day for nothin'."

"Just shut up and grab your pick," Jimmie answered. "The street side doesn't face the lake. The ice is bound to be thinner." He stood back and surveyed their target. The house was completely encased in white. No way to tell what color it was when it wasn't marooned in a sea of gray-white sky, water, and beach. Icicles the size of small stalactites hung off the roof, and windows and doors were visible only as indentations in the ice. Every detail of the house was sculpted in white, like it had been dipped in thick frosting and left to harden.

Jimmie grabbed a crowbar from the duffle and went to work chipping ice from what he hoped was the front door. By the time he and Trey had uncovered the frame all the way around, they'd worked up a sweat. Mittens were stuffed in pockets, and unwound scarves hung limply from their necks.

Trey dropped his pick, wiped his face on the sleeve of his jacket, and stared at the door.

"No sense trying to pick the lock," he said after a moment's study. "The mechanism will be frozen solid. Let's just break it down."

Jimmie nodded. "Yep. You want the crowbar, or should I do it?"

"Go for it," Trey said, stepping back a couple of paces.

Jimmie hefted the black steel crowbar and wedged the curved, flattened end into the seam between the door and frame right above the deadbolt. Applying pressure to the handle, he worked the blade back and forth until the frame splintered. The frozen hinges creaked as he levered the door open. The sound was ominous in the frozen silence of the cold, bleak day.

"All right," said Trey, slapping Jimmie on the back. "Let's get looting!"

Jimmie followed Trey into the entry and immediately felt a shiver run down his spine. The place was creepy quiet and the light filtering through the white-iced windows made him feel like he was walking into a tomb. He shook his head, trying to rid himself of the heebie-jeebies and studied the layout. The faster they looted, the faster they could leave this bizarre place.

He had three choices: walk straight down a hallway lined with family photos, enter what looked like a formal dining room on his left, or turn right into a living room.

"Bet that dining room has some good stuff," Trey said, breaking the eerie silence. "I'll check it out. You see if there's anything in the living room, then we can both head down the hall and see what else we can find."

Jimmie nodded, not willing to trust his voice. He was spooked enough that it might come out in a squeak, and if it did, Trey would never let him live it down. Instead, he took a deep breath and stepped into the living room.

It was a nice enough room, hardwood floors, walls painted the color of sand, a comfortable couch and two wing-backed chairs done up with soft blue upholstery, but it was clearly used for visitors or reading. There were small side tables with knick-knacks and one wall held an overflowing bookshelf, but nothing of value to Jimmie. No electronics. No silver. Just breakables and books. What a waste of space.

He moved back into the entry and watched Trey ransacking the dining room. "Anything?" he asked as Trey yanked a bunch of linens from behind a door in the lower half of a fancy built-in cabinet.

"Naw," Trey answered. "Just dishes and napkins and crap. If they have silver, it's not in here." He stood up and glanced at Jimmie. "You have any luck?"

Jimmie shook his head. "Not in there. Let's check out the rest of the house. They've got to at least have a TV and stereo somewhere."

"I sure as hell hope so. Everybody's got electronics, right?"

Jimmie led the way down the hall, past framed photos on the walls, some new, some in black and white with the people dressed in old-timey get-ups. "Right. There'll be a family room back here. That's where the good stuff'll be."

Just as he'd expected, the hall emptied into a comfortable family room. Off to the left was a kitchen, kind of behind the dining room. Straight ahead was a little eating area, his mom would probably call it a breakfast nook. The main space held a wrap-around couch, a couple of slouchy bean-bag chairs and a big stone fireplace with a digital TV suspended above the mantle. There were glass-fronted cabinets on both sides of the fireplace, and Jimmie could see game sets and video players and other electronics peeking out through the glass. Jackpot!

There was also another hallway at the back of the room, probably leading to bedrooms. If there was any jewelry to be had, it would be back there.

Trey made a beeline for the electronics. "This is more like it!"

But Jimmie heard something, and the sound rooted him to the spot.

"Did you hear that?"

"What?" Trey was busily unhooking cords from a high-end game set. He didn't even glance in Jimmie's direction.

"I heard something … like a snuffle."

"Maybe they left a dog closed up in a bathroom."

"Naw. Didn't sound like an animal. Besides, who'd leave a dog in a closed up beach house in winter?"

"Who cares?" Trey asked as he packed stuff into the duffle.

Jimmie stood for another moment, listening intently. He should be helping Trey, but he just couldn't quite...

There! He heard it again.

Without really thinking about what he was doing, he followed the sound down the back hall. Sure enough, he found one bedroom, and then another. The noise stopped, but when he stepped into the furthest room, he discovered he wasn't alone.

A baby sat in the middle of the floor. Probably a little girl seeing as how she was all bundled up in a pink snowsuit that made her look like a puffy Easter Bunny. Her wide blue eyes were red from crying and her little button nose dripped snot. Even so, she was cute sitting there in her pink snowsuit on the pale blue plush carpeting at the foot of a four-poster bed.

What in hell was a baby doing alone in a deserted house?

She wasn't. Alone, that is. That was the only answer. Only, where was her mother, or whoever?

The baby girl hiccoughed and quieted, watching him as he stepped carefully past her into the attached bath. He found his answer. A young woman lay sprawled on the bathroom floor, her head beside the tub. A smear of bright red blood stained the edge and down the outside wall of the tub, ending in a pool that dyed her blonde hair pink.

She'd been pretty. Now she was dead.

Jimmie froze. He and Trey were thieves, sure, but they didn't go in for violent crime. He'd never seen a body before. He didn't know what to do, except…

He filled his lungs and bellowed, "Trey! Get in here, man."

He listened as Trey stomped down the hall. Heard him say, "What the fuck?" when he saw the baby. Felt his familiar presence as he stopped dead behind Jimmie.

They stared at the body, as frozen as the ice encasing the house. Then Trey broke the spell. He backed out of the bathroom, past the staring baby, and ran, yelling over his shoulder, "Grab whatever you found. We gotta get outta here!"

Jimmie glanced once more at the body, turned to follow Trey, but stopped when he saw the little girl.

"Come on, bro," Trey yelled. "We gotta split. Now!"

Jimmie strode to the bedroom door, his head swiveling between Trey and the baby. He wanted to follow Trey. He really did. But what about the baby? It was damn cold in this house.

"We can't just leave that baby alone," he said, taking a step toward his friend.

"What are you talking about? We don't know nuthin' about kids. What are we gonna do with it?"

The baby snuffled and started to wail, and Jimmie turned back to the bedroom. He saw the little girl in her pink snowsuit, and knew for sure he couldn't leave her. She was probably only nine or ten months old. His sister had one that size. What if it was Jenny? What if his sister was the one dead on the bathroom floor? Wouldn't she want someone to rescue Jason?

"Jimmie," Trey called from the other room. "Come on, man! We gotta get outta here before someone comes to check on that woman."

But Jimmie knew he couldn't do it. He was stuck. He couldn't leave this little girl alone in a freezing house. He grabbed a tissue from a bedside table and knelt before the baby. "How ya doin' there, kid?" he asked softly, wiping her snotty nose with the tissue. "I know you're scared, I would be too, but everything's gonna be okay. I promise."

Picking her up, he walked to the family room to join his partner in crime.

Trey's eyes widened. "What're you doin', bro? We can't take her with us."

"I know," Jimmie said calmly. "But I can't just walk away. Here's what we're gonna do."

CHAPTER TWO

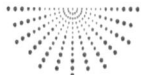

*J*immie sat on the pretty floral couch in the living room with the baby asleep in his arms. Muted red and blue lights played across the white coated windows and sirens blared outside. The police had arrived.

Two uniformed officers stomped onto the porch and swung through the ruined door, guns swinging in an arc until they aimed at Jimmie.

"It's okay," Jimmie said quietly. "I'm unarmed … and she just fell asleep."

The first officer, a dark haired woman, holstered her weapon and moved to kneel beside Jimmie and the baby. Two more officers joined her partner, who said, "Take his statement, Officer Lewis. We'll check the rest of the house."

She nodded, her gaze never leaving Jimmie. "Are you the one who called 9-1-1?"

"Yes."

She pulled out a notebook, opened it to a blank page, and asked for his name and contact information. Once that was taken care of, she glanced up and said, "Tell me what happened."

"I was out for a walk on the beach," he said, and noticed how her eyebrow quirked in question. He smiled. "I like wild weather," he explained. "Besides, I heard about how beach houses can get coated with ice; I wanted to see one."

She nodded and a made a note. "Go on."

"Anyway, I was out for a walk when I saw a guy runnin' away from this house. I walked over, saw the door was busted and figured I'd call the police."

He paused, adjusted the baby's weight in his arms, and continued, "I'd just pulled out my cell phone when I heard something." He glanced at the little girl. "She was crying. So I came in. I found her. Found her mother too. Figured the best thing was to call for help and try to keep her warm until you got here."

Officer Lewis jotted down a few more notes. "Did you put her in the snowsuit?"

"No. She was all bundled up sitting on the floor in the bedroom when I found her." He shrugged. "Guess her mom was getting ready to leave when it happened."

"Did you know the mother?"

He shook his head. "Never seen her before."

"Any idea what happened? How she got dead?"

"Nope. I just know that once I saw this baby, I couldn't leave her alone in an ice house. I had to wait with her. Make sure she was safe until you showed up."

Officer Lewis nodded. "Can you give me a description of the man you saw running away?"

Jimmie frowned, as if thinking. "Naw. I was too far away. I just know he was runnin' … oh, and he had a backpack and a duffle bag."

The second policeman came back into the room. "Everything's just like the 9-1-1 call said." He glanced at Jimmie. "Anything else I should know?"

Officer Lewis shook her head. She rose and the two of them moved back to the front door. "Looks like a good Samaritan," Jimmie heard her say. "We'll check out his story back at the station, but so far it rings true."

She stepped back to Jimmie. "We'll call for the coroner … and for social services." She glanced at the baby. "Little one seems content with you, if you wouldn't mind sticking until the social worker arrives, it'll make my job easier."

Jimmie nodded. "I don't mind. I've got no place in particular to be."

EPILOGUE

An hour or so later Jimmie handed the baby girl over to a young woman with a freckled complexion and red curls sticking out from under a navy blue knit cap. His arms felt a little empty once the baby's weight was gone, but his heart was light. He'd done a good thing, and it didn't look like anyone suspected him of breaking into the ice house.

He shook hands with Officer Lewis, turned down her offer of a ride back to his apartment, and said he'd be happy to answer any further questions, but he couldn't imagine what else he could say.

And then he walked back toward the beach, retracing his earlier steps. The snow was just as crunchy as earlier and he still broke through the icy crust every few steps, but it didn't bother him nearly as much this time. He smiled and, putting his unmittened hand in his jacket pocket, stroked the edges of the diamond earrings he'd found in the safe in the master bedroom.

A nice reward for a job well done … and for saving a baby girl's life.

PART XII
DELIA'S DECISION

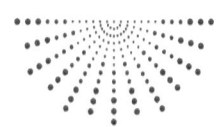

Delia's Decision

A Short Delia Laubhan Mystery

DEBBIE MUMFORD

CHAPTER ONE

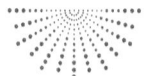

My name is Delia Laubhan. I'm a no-nonsense kind of person dedicated to the facts. Opinions are nice, but they're open to discussion. Facts are facts.

These are the facts about me. I'm female, twenty-nine years of age, single, and currently between jobs. I served my country as active duty military police for eight years overseas. The job was both tougher and easier than I imagined when I signed on the dotted line with my recruitment officer. I learned a lot in the military, not the least of which involved police procedure and investigative technique.

When my tour of active duty ended, I mustered out and headed home to Denver, Colorado a wiser and somewhat more jaded woman. I'd seen the worst of human behavior, but I'd also witnessed acts of self-sacrifice that could only be described as heroic.

Now that I was home in Colorado and retired from military life, I had options, but those options called for decisions, and after taking orders for eight years, I was unaccustomed to making my own choices. But life is all about change, and those who can't—or won't—change wither and die.

I had no intention of rolling over and playing dead, so I needed to pull myself together and make a decision: what did I want to do with my life?

With my background, I was probably best suited for police work. The boys and girls in blue would undoubtedly welcome me with open arms, but did I really want to join the force as a rookie after the years of investigative experience I'd accumulated?

I could go back to school. I had an undergrad degree thanks to the military, but I could use my G.I. educational benefits to get a law degree or train in one of the many branches of forensic science. But returning to the sedentary existence of classroom lectures and study groups after leading an active life as a military investigator didn't really appeal.

While I was pondering those weighty choices—and trying to convince myself that I was qualified to make such a decision—a challenge fell into my lap. One that would allow me to procrastinate on the decision making, while telling myself I was doing a good deed.

My mother's Honda Accord was stolen.

She reported the theft immediately, but the police held out little hope of finding the car. Honda Accords were the most frequently stolen vehicle on the Front Range. When I heard Mom's plight, I knew what I had to do: find her car.

Great! A legitimate excuse to set aside the uncertainties of my future and concentrate on a mission. One I was uniquely qualified to undertake.

"No worries, Mom. I'll have your car back in the carport in no time."

Famous last words.

CHAPTER TWO

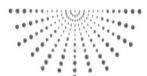

racking down a car thief in the civilian world was harder than I'd anticipated. I no longer had a badge, a gun, or investigative resources at my fingertips. Nor did I have the military chain of command to bolster my authority. I couldn't just order civilians into interrogation. I had to be friendly, chat up the neighbors, and hope they unwittingly dropped a clue I could follow up on.

What a waste of time and energy!

On the second day of my attempted investigation, I loitered in the downstairs hallway of Mom's apartment building, hoping to encounter a neighbor willing to talk. The front door opened and a middle-aged woman I'd known since childhood entered the building.

"Hey, Mrs. Malloy. How ya doin' today?" I asked brightly.

"Why, Delia! I had no idea you were back in Denver. Are you on leave?" The slightly frowsy little woman beamed up at me. Now, I'm not exactly an Amazon, but it doesn't take much to tower over Mrs. Malloy's five-feet-nothing.

"No, ma'am," I answered. "I finished my tour and mustered out. I'm home for good, though I gotta say, being a civilian feels a bit strange."

"Oh, your mother must be so happy to have you home. Are you staying with her?"

"No, ma'am. I've got my own apartment. It's in another complex, but it's only a few miles away. Mom will get sick of seeing me, I'm sure."

Mrs. Malloy laughed. "I doubt that. She's spoken of you often during your deployment." She stepped past me down the hall to her first floor apartment, which faced the back of the building and the covered parking that was reserved for tenants. "Would you like to come in for a cup of coffee?" she asked. "Or are you on your way up to visit your mother?"

"Actually, I'd love some coffee and a chat."

"Wonderful. Come right in."

Gesturing for me to follow, she unlocked the door and stepped into her living room. Mrs. Malloy's apartment was laid out just like Mom's. The hall door opened into a decent sized living room with a sliding glass door opening onto a small concrete patio—Mom's, being on the fourth floor, opened onto a minuscule deck—across the way, a breakfast bar separated the living room from a compact kitchen. Next to the kitchen was a short hallway leading to a bathroom and two small bedrooms.

Mrs. Malloy's living room put me in mind of a tropical forest. She had plants everywhere. African violets and gloxinia covered the end tables on either side of a deep burgundy sofa. A huge rubber tree stood in the corner beside the patio door, and philodendron runners crept along shelves and bookcases. She'd even arranged some of the runners to drape across the ceiling between the living room and kitchen. And then there were the hanging pots! English ivy, spider plants, ferns, and some sort of succulent with little round leaves dripped from macrame hangers.

"Have a seat, dear," the woman called as she pulled off her jacket and stowed it and her purse in the closet near the front door. "It won't take but a minute to fix that coffee. I have one of those new-fangled machines that brews it by the cup. Do you take cream or sugar?"

"Black is fine, ma'am," I said. "The military cured me of the fancy stuff."

She trundled off to the kitchen, chuckling. "I'll just bet it did."

A few minutes later we were settled with good-sized mugs of coffee, Mrs. Malloy in a well-used wooden rocker and me on the sofa. The mug was warm in my hands and I inhaled the bittersweet aroma of the brew. Closing my eyes, I appreciated the fresh scent. I'd downed too many cups of stale coffee during my stint in the service. Finally, I lifted the mug to my lips and sipped. Delicious!

"So what are you doing with yourself, now that you're home?" Mrs. Malloy asked.

I opened my eyes and met her gaze. "I'm still getting my bearings," I said. "Haven't made any concrete decisions about the future yet." I took another sip, then found a place for my mug among the pots of flowers on the end table. "Right now, I'm helping Mom out with a problem."

"Oh?" she asked. "And what might that be?"

I grinned. "I'm glad you asked, 'cause I wanted to ask you a couple of questions."

She lifted a questioning brow, and I continued.

"Someone stole her car late Tuesday night or early Wednesday morning, and I was wondering if you might've seen or heard anything unusual that night?"

Her eyebrows drew together in a frown of concentration. "I'm sorry to hear that. Tuesday night, you say? I don't think so, but then I go to bed as soon as the news is over."

I sighed. "I was hoping… since your patio looks out over her parking spot, but…"

She clicked her tongue, and I glanced up again.

"It's not that unusual, but Greg Jennings and a group of his friends were hanging out in the parking area that night. Just talking and smoking, you understand, but they would've still been there after I went to bed. You might check with them."

"Thanks, Mrs. Malloy. I'll do that."

I picked up my mug and enjoyed another swallow of coffee while Mrs. Malloy caught me up on her son and his wife, and their three boys. I might not be living up to Mom's expectation in the progeny department, but it sounded like Stan Malloy was doing just fine.

CHAPTER THREE

*G*reg Jennings lived in the next building over from Mom's. I was aware of his family, but didn't know them well. They'd moved into the complex about a year before I left for college in Boulder. If I remembered right, Greg had been about nine at the time, which would make him in his late teens now.

The perfect age for the male of the species to start causing trouble. Not that they all did, of course, but enough did to raise my suspicions.

How to approach my quarry?

I could use the direct approach. Simply knock on his parents' front door and ask to speak to him, but that would put him on his guard. Better to arrange a *chance* encounter somewhere. I decided to stake out his apartment and follow him. Surely he'd end up in some public place where I could approach him casually.

As I hung around the Jennings' building, I had a moment of deja vu, realizing I was back to loitering in an apartment building. Fortunately, I'd spent enough time with Mrs. Malloy that even a teenage boy would be up and about on a warm summer's day like this one. I'd barely taken up a post standing at the top of the third floor staircase when the door to the Jennings apartment opened and Greg stepped out. Since I didn't want to call attention to myself, I started up the stairs to the fourth floor while Greg sauntered down the hallway and headed to the first floor. When he reached the landing, I turned and followed him down and out of the building.

Three blocks later, I ducked into a convenience store and pretended to study a revolving rack of sunglasses. The mirrors on the rack allowed me to keep an eye on Greg as he moved along the snack aisle. When he neared where I stood, I *accidentally* bumped into him.

"Hey! Watch it," he said in a slightly belligerent tone, scrambling to keep hold of the bags of chips and cookies he held.

"Sorry about that," I said. Turning to face him I feigned surprise, widening my eyes and raising my eyebrows. "Greg?" I asked. "Aren't you Greg Jennings? Wow. It's been, like, forever!"

A frown creased his forehead. I stuck out my hand and when he freed one of his and took it, shook his vigorously. "Delia Laubhan. My mom lives in the building next to yours. I've been overseas for several years." I looked him up and down. "You've really grown up."

"Uhm, yeah," he said. "Nice to meet you."

"What say I buy you a cola and then we can walk back together?"

He didn't exactly jump at the offer, but shrugged his shoulders and muttered, "Sure."

After a couple of blocks, I said, "So, I hear you were hanging out in the parking area of Mom's building Tuesday night. Did you see anything unusual?"

He gave me the side-eye and said, "Depends on what you call unusual." He took a sip of cola, then asked, "Why? What's it to you how I spend my time?"

I shrugged and winked. "Couldn't care less... unless of course you were in on the theft of my mom's car."

He stopped dead, and I turned to face him.

"That was your mom's Honda?"

I nodded. "What do you know about it?"

He bit his lip and a trickle of sweat ran down his temple as he studied me. After a moment's pause he seemed to make up his mind.

"Nothing really. The guys had just left and I was about to head home when this guy hopped out of a car and ran over to this silver Honda Accord. I was out past curfew, so I kind of hunkered down so he wouldn't notice me.

"The car drove away and I thought he was just picking up his own ride. But I did think it was kinda strange that he was dressed all in black... I mean black jeans and a black hoodie with the hood up even though it was a warm night. Then I realized he didn't have a key; he was jimmying the lock on the driver's door."

He shrugged, chugged his cola, and started walking again.

"Once he had the door open, he hot-wired it, slid into the seat, and took off."

"Did you recognize the guy?" I asked

Again with the side-eye. Another swig of cola and he lobbed the empty can into a trash bin. "Yeah. I saw his face when the door light came on."

"And..." I prompted.

"It was Mrs. Malloy's grandson, Mark. Mark Malloy."

My turn to stop dead. "Wait a minute. You're telling me Mark Malloy is old enough to boost a car?"

Greg shook his head sorrowfully and gave me a look that said I was too stupid for words. "He's the same age I am, and I've had my license for a year."

Not that you needed a license to steal a car.

I stood there feeling old and tired. Mrs. Malloy was going to be so disappointed to learn one of her beloved grandsons was a car thief. At least, I sure hoped it was only one... I didn't have a clue who'd dropped Mark off at the parking area.

"Shame," I said. "I really like Mrs. Malloy." I started walking again and Greg and I continued to his building. "You willing to tell the police what you saw?"

He grimaced, but nodded. "Sure. I guess since I told you I don't really have a choice."

"Appreciate it," I said. "It'll sure make it easier for Mom to get her car back. Come on, I'll drive you down to the precinct."

CHAPTER FOUR

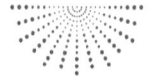

A week later, I watched the local news while I ate my version of dinner: a frozen chicken pot pie fresh out of the microwave. Mom wouldn't consider it a meal—she still believed the evening meal consisted of meat, vegetables, some form of potato, and a side salad... and if you ate all your veggies... dessert—but it worked for me.

The news show flashed mug shots of Mark Malloy and his cousin Devon Harris. I sighed as the reporter droned out the story of the teens' arrest for stealing cars. Evidently the pair had been at it for a while. When the police arrested them at the Harris's auto body shop, they discovered a dozen stolen vehicles.

I'd kept my promise to Mom. She had her car back, but she was not happy about the circumstances. Comforting sweet little Mrs. Malloy wasn't a pleasant task. Not when I'd been the cause of her grandson's downfall.

Never mind that the real reason for Mark's trouble were his own poor choices.

Decisions could be a bear at any age.

I hit the button on the remote, turning the television off, and leaned back in my chair. Past time to face some decisions of my own. Hopefully with a better outcome than Mark Malloy and Devon Harris had seen.

Apply to the police force and be a rookie again?

Go back to college and train for a new career with another degree?

Weren't there any other choices?

I pulled my laptop from the table beside my chair and looked up the qualifications for a Colorado private investigator's license. Studying through the website, I discovered I more than qualified. I could apply for a license and open my own business next week!

But what did I know about investigating in the civilian world or running a small business?

Not as much as I should if I wanted my business to succeed.

I did a search on private investigators in the Denver area and made a list of the ones that struck me as professional and having solid standards. Surely one of them would be willing to take on apprentice and teach her the ropes.

I closed my laptop and relaxed. Decision made. I was on the way to becoming *Delia Laubhan, P.I.*

And the choice felt good.

PART XIII
QUILTS

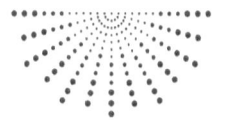

Quilts

A Short Kristi Lundrigan Mystery

DEBBIE MUMFORD

CHAPTER ONE

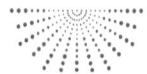

*K*risti paused on the front step of the pretty little white bungalow and breathed a sigh of contentment. The Daphne shrubs to either side of the door were filled with small, pinkish white blooms, lending a friendly aura to the entry and sweetening the late spring morning with their delicious fragrance. She turned an exuberant pirouette on the step, her long patchwork skirt swirling around her ankles. What a perfect day in Garnet Gateway, Montana. Cerulean blue sky, fluffy white clouds, majestic mountains, and the key to her very own quilt shop in her hand!

Nearly giddy with joy, Kristi turned back to the door, slipped the key into the lock and twisted. The lock snicked its release, and she pushed the door open. Delectable Mountain Quilting was officially hers.

Hers. Not her father's. Not her ex-husband's. Not even a partnership's.

Hers.

At long last, all the small business loans had been negotiated and the contracts signed. The inheritance her maternal grandmother had left her had given her the necessary leverage to swing the deal. Grannie

Olesen would be proud to know she'd helped Kristi with this dream. And it was a fitting use of the money, considering Grannie was the one who had infected her with the quilting bug.

Kristi smiled, savoring the knowledge that this quaint little quilt shop was her very own. She, Kristiana Lundrigan, was the proud owner of the land, the building, and the inventory.

And, oh, what an inventory!

Kristi stepped inside, flicked on the lights, and inhaled the enticing aroma of quilting cottons. High quality greige goods and premium dye. There was nothing else like that aroma in the universe. A rainbow of color winked at her from every shelf ... and the little shop was filled to overflowing with shelves.

The previous owner had over-stocked, allowing the shop to become crowded. She'd purchased high-quality cottons, but hadn't understood how to display them to their best effect. Kristi squeezed through the too narrow aisles while she planned her attack. A good third of the inventory would need to be moved to the storeroom. Customers needed room to browse without running into each other, space to lay out bolts and consider color choices, see how the patterns blended. They needed a leisurely experience that encouraged thinking and dreaming ... and buying *just one more* fat quarter.

Currently, the bolts of fabric were too crowded to allow quilters to fully appreciate the glory of their meticulously woven or stamped designs.

Pulling a small notebook from her embroidered denim shoulder bag, Kristi began to sketch. The shelves lining the walls were fine, but the interior displays would need to be thinned. Some would need to be rebuilt. And the notions were totally misplaced. Thread, pins, needles, rotary cutters and mats. All the necessary but unglamorous items would need to be moved into a small room at the back of the store.

She tapped her pen against her lips as she thought. Yes. A pass-through window would need to be cut in that wall, allowing customers to see the notions, but separating them from the color and almost hypnotic appeal of the quilting cottons themselves.

She wandered the store, checking the storeroom, the soon-to-be notions room, the toilet— that would need to be spruced up— and making notes on where to hang various quilts from her personal collection. She was pleased that in addition to the small kitchen, which would function as a lunch room for her employees, there was also a nice-sized room that could be transformed into a classroom. Quilt shops needed a place to teach the fine art of quilting, whether by hand or machine. A place to pass on the legacy, and to entice beginners to try a new craft.

Something thumped against the exterior kitchen door, causing her to jump. She'd been so lost in dreams of a shop filled with eager quilters of all ages that she'd forgotten the outside world existed. She moved to stand beside the door to the alley and was reaching for the deadbolt above the locked doorknob when she heard the unmistakable *crack* of a gunshot. She pulled her hand back and stumbled away from the door.

Was she in danger?

She glanced around the deserted quilt shop. She was alone. No one knew she was here. Except for the real estate agent who had processed the paperwork at closing and given her the keys, no one even knew the building was officially hers.

Taking a shaky breath, she pulled her cell phone from her shoulder bag and called Jason's private number. Her ex-husband might be the last person she wanted to talk to, but he was also Garnet Gateway's chief of police.

———

KRISTI SAT on the front steps of her new quilt shop, as far from the back alley as she could get and remain available to answer questions. The sky was still a beautiful blue and the Daphne blooms were still fragrant, but the day had lost its luster.

A man had been killed right outside the back door of her shop. She'd heard him stumble into the door as he tried to get away from his assailant. She'd also heard the shot that had killed him. And after Jason and his deputy had arrived, she'd seen his dead body.

She'd never seen a body before, at least not one that a mortuary hadn't prettied up and made as presentable as possible. Certainly not one that had died violently. She wasn't sure she'd ever manage to scrub that image from her mind.

And right outside the kitchen door of her new business. How long would it be before she could open that door and not shiver?

She frowned and gave herself a good shake. What was she doing? Worrying about how she felt about the quilt shop when a man had lost his life? What kind of person was she?

A shadow fell across the step and she glanced up to find Jason looming over her.

"Mind if I join you?" he asked.

She shrugged. "Whatever." Then realizing how flip, maybe even surly that sounded, she sighed. "Sorry. Please, sit."

Jason dropped to the step beside her, removing his official felt Stetson hat and running his fingers around the brim. "I'm glad you were comfortable enough to call," he said, not looking at her. "You were wise not to go out and investigate on your own. Whoever did this might have still been around."

She nodded, staring at the pavement between her feet. "I appreciate you coming so quickly. Once the shop is up and running, I won't be so skittish, but today…"

He glanced at her and then away again. "I didn't realize you'd bought the place."

She smiled, a bit ruefully. "Just took possession today. I was doing a walk though, imagining the changes I want to make, when … well, when it happened."

"That's too bad."

They lapsed into an awkward silence. Kristi wondered how things could ever be anything *but* awkward between them. She closed her eyes, but could still see his face. High forehead, strong jaw, steely gray eyes that could go all soft and almost blue with emotion.

Stop. She had to stop thinking about him that way. Had to forget how his wavy chestnut hair felt like silk between her fingers, or the delights of his scratchy unshaven chin against her skin first thing in the morning. He wasn't her lover anymore. They were divorced. Hell, they weren't even friends now. He'd seen to that.

Jason's voice brought her back to their current situation.

"We've identified the body as Gary Stebbings," he said. "I don't suppose…"

"Wait," she interrupted, meeting his eyes and holding his gaze for the first time. "Did you say *Stebbings*? Any relation to Mattie Stebbings?"

His dark brows drew together in a slight frown as he checked his hand-held tablet. "Says here his wife's name is Matilda." He looked up into her eyes. "Suppose she goes by Mattie?"

Kristi nodded.

"How do you know?"

"I've seen her full name about a hundred times today. I just bought Delectable Mountain Quilting from Mattie Stebbings."

CHAPTER TWO

Since she knew Mrs. Stebbings, Jason asked Kristi to accompany him when he notified the woman of her husband's death.

"I'm still not sure this is a good idea," Kristi said as Jason parked his police issue Trail Blazer in front the Stebbings home. "I bought a business from her, I don't know her socially. It's not like we're friends."

Jason turned to face her, his left forearm resting on the steering wheel. "I appreciate you coming," he said, his gray eyes meeting her blue ones. "Garnet Gateway doesn't see a lot of murder. This isn't a common notification I'm about to make. You may not know her well, but you're a familiar face and you're a woman. Your presence will help. I'm sure of it."

She nodded and glanced at the home. Gary and Mattie kept a tidy property. The grass was neatly trimmed and flowers were beginning to peek through the soil in freshly turned beds. The single story house was well kept too, painted blue siding, navy shutters, the front door a bold red. Kristi shuddered. She and Jason were about to shatter the life of the woman inside that pretty little house.

"Okay. Let's get this over with." She opened the car door and climbed out. Jason joined her and they approached the red door.

Mattie opened the door after only a moment's delay. She was a petite woman, a few inches shorter than Kristi's five foot six, with short curly dark hair and wide brown eyes. She wore a plum colored tunic top and floral leggings. Her feet were bare.

When she saw who stood on the other side of her front door, her eyebrows rose. "Sheriff Reynolds. Kristi. What brings you here?" A little frown creased her brow. "There hasn't been a glitch in the sale? I thought everything was signed and sealed."

"It's not about the quilt shop, Mrs. Stebbings," Jason said. "May we come in?"

She stepped back, opening the door wide, her free hand fluttering like a butterfly in a net. "Of course. I'm sorry, I didn't mean to leave you standing on the step. I was just so surprised, that's all. Please, come in."

Jason tugged off his hat and ran a hand through his hair as he followed Kristi into the house. Mattie Stebbings closed the door, stepped around them, and directed them from the small entryway to a formal living room. Where the entry had been floored with hardwood, this room was carpeted with beige plush carpet. The matching sofa and overstuffed chairs were covered in a deep rose and blue and forest green floral upholstery fabric, and the light blue walls were decorated with several of Mattie's stunning quilts.

A vintage double wedding ring hung on the end wall, away from the direct sunlight spilling through the wide front window, but Kristi's eyes were drawn to the Delectable Mountain quilt that hung above the sofa. The wide outer border was a rich chocolate brown, while the two-inch inner border was a vivid tone-on-tone scarlet. The blocks themselves were done in lush fabrics that matched the colors of the upholstery. Mattie had obviously designed this quilt to hang in this room ... in the pattern that announced the name of her quilt shop to anyone familiar with the craft.

Kristi smiled with silent approval. Nothing like subliminal advertising ... aimed at the people most likely to be customers. She'd have to make sure her own Delectable Mountain quilt was prominently displayed in the shop.

"You have a lovely home, Mattie." She nodded toward the vintage quilt. "Is that from the twenties?"

Mattie shook her head. "1890s. My great-great grandmother made it, in Kansas before they made the journey to Montana. My family has been in Garnet Gateway ever since."

Kristi stepped closer to the double wedding ring. "It's in beautiful condition," she said, letting her admiration show in her voice.

"Thank you," Mattie replied. "But I don't think you brought the sheriff by to admire my quilts."

"No, ma'am," Jason said. "We're here on official business. I asked Kristi to join me since she's familiar with the case ... and you two are acquainted."

Jason's comment seemed to unnerve Mattie. Her hand trembled as she gestured them to the sofa, and her voice quivered slightly when she said, "Please, have a seat. Would ... would you like a cup of tea, or water, or..."

Jason interrupted. "We're fine, Mrs. Stebbings. If you'd take a seat."

Mattie perched on the edge of one of the overstuffed chairs, while Jason and Kristi settled on the sofa.

Jason placed his hat on the floor at his feet, cleared his throat, and looked directly at Mattie. "There's no easy way to say this, ma'am, so I'm just going to come right out with it. Your husband, Gary Stebbings, was shot to death this morning."

All color leached from Mattie's face, leaving her lips pale and outlined in white. Her hands shook visibly as she raised them to her mouth. Her eyes were wide and glazed, and a vein throbbed at her temple. If she hadn't been sitting, Kristi was certain the woman would have fallen.

"I'm so sorry for your loss," Kristi said, feeling the total inadequacy of the words. She glanced at Jason, who gave an almost imperceptible nod, and then moved to kneel before the stricken woman. "Can I get you anything?"

Mattie didn't respond, even when Kristi laid a sympathetic hand on her knee.

"Is there someone we can call for you, Mrs. Stebbings?" Jason asked. "A relative or friend who can stay with you?"

"M-my mother," Mattie whispered. "Please call Mother."

Jason opened his mouth, but Kristi spoke first. "Is her number programmed into your cell phone?"

Mattie nodded.

"Where is it?" Kristi asked quietly.

"In my purse. On the desk in the kitchen."

"I'll get it," Jason said and left the room. A few moments later he reappeared carrying a black leather shoulder bag.

Mattie accepted the purse, but was shaking so badly she nearly dumped the contents.

"Here, let me," Kristi said. She reached inside and quickly extracted a slim cell phone. Handing it to Jason, she closed the bag and placed it on the floor beside Mattie's chair. She bit her lip, wondering if she should say anything about the cool metal her fingers had brushed as she sought the phone.

No. Not yet. Mattie was obviously distraught. Jason was calling for someone to assist her. Kristi's incidental information could wait until she and Jason were back in the Trail Blazer.

Jason waited until Mattie's mother, Velma Carson, arrived before asking any questions. Once Velma had settled Mattie with a lap robe and a cup of tea, Jason and Kristi resumed their places on the sofa.

"I know this isn't a good time," he said gently, "but I need to ask: can you think of anyone who'd've wanted to harm Gary?"

Velma pursed her lips, but kept quiet.

Mattie shook her head. "We've had some financial trouble." She glanced at Kristi. "it's why I sold the shop. But nothing that we couldn't handle."

Jason nodded. "We'll leave you to rest, Mrs. Stebbings. I'm sorry to have brought you such terrible news." He picked up his hat, stood, and on his way past, pressed a business card into Mattie's hand. "If you think of anything else, call me."

He gave Velma a significant glance. "Mrs. Carson, if you'd walk us out?"

She stood, glanced at her daughter, and nodded. "Of course."

The three stepped through the red front door, and Jason pulled it closed.

"What didn't you want to say in front of your daughter?" he asked.

Velma glanced down the street, pursed her lips again, then sighed. "I don't like to speak ill of the dead, and this is Mattie's business, not mine…"

"But," prompted Jason.

"But Gary liked to gamble," she said, her voice taking on a hard edge, "and he wasn't good at it. Mattie tried to get him to stop, but, well, she liked to think of it as an addiction."

"She sold the shop to cover his debts?" Kristi asked, her heart racing with shock and sympathy. She suddenly felt as though she'd taken advantage of the woman's distress.

Velma nodded. "Mattie loved that place. I know the money from the sale will put things right … for now, but how is giving up her income going to help the next time he loses?"

Her eyes widened and her hands flew to cover her mouth.

Jason nodded. "I guess that won't be a concern now, will it?"

Velma's eyes filled with tears. "Oh, my lord." She glanced at the living room window, beyond which her daughter sat huddled in her chair. "Gary wasn't the best husband to my daughter, but she loved him." She turned back to Jason. "I'm sorry he's dead, but not that he's out of Mattie's life."

"Thank you for your time, Mrs. Carson," Jason said, touching the brim of his hat in salute. He nodded to Kristi and the two of them walked to his vehicle.

Once they were safely inside the Trail Blazer, Kristi said, "Mattie has a gun."

"What?" Jason turned to her, surprise tinged with anger lining his face. "Why didn't you say something?"

"I'm saying it now," she snapped. Closing her eyes, she took a deep, calming breath before continuing. "When I reached into her purse to get the cell phone I felt something metal. I'm sure it was a revolver."

Jason nodded, his jaw clenching and unclenching.

"I didn't see the point in saying anything in there. She was clearly upset, I didn't want to make things worse. I'm telling you now, before we leave, in case you feel the need to go back in and get it."

He stared at the house. "No. The moment's passed. If you had pulled it out of her purse, I could've taken it as evidence. You had her tacit permission to have your hand in her bag." He turned to stare at her, and his gray eyes had that steely glint that she'd always thought of as his *cop's eyes*. "Now I'd need probable cause and a warrant to search her purse."

Kristi swallowed. "I'm sorry. I should've handled this differently."

His gaze softened and he sighed. "No. I'm sorry. You're not law enforcement. It's not your job to investigate. Thanks for telling me."

She nodded and lowered her eyes. They drove to the police station in silence.

CHAPTER THREE

*J*ason offered to drop Kristi off at home, but she declined. She didn't want to spend the day cooped up in her apartment, and since her new quilt shop was now adjacent to a crime scene, she wasn't anxious to go there either. Instead, she tagged along with her ex-husband, figuring if he didn't want her around, he'd tell her to go away.

When they were seated in his office— a dingy little room with pale green walls, a beat up old-fashioned school teacher's desk, an ancient rolling desk chair, two uncomfortable looking visitor chairs, an overflowing bookshelf, and a gray metal four-drawer upright file cabinet — Jason clasped his hands on the desk top and studied Kristi.

"So you thought Mattie was genuinely surprised and upset by the news."

Her eyes widened in surprise. "Didn't you?"

"Hard to tell," he said, leaning back in his chair. "I'd say she was nervous before I told her. 'Course that could've just been having the sheriff in her living room."

She nodded. "Yes, I noticed a tremor in her hands when she asked us to sit, but the way the color drained from her face…"

He shook his head. "Not a clear indication either way. She could've been shocked to hear her husband had been murdered, or she could've been caught by surprise that we'd already found the body."

Kristi tilted her head and gazed past Jason's shoulder out the none-too-clean window. "No, if she already knew he was dead, the fact that you were there told her you'd found the body." Her eyes snapped to Jason's face. "Besides, why would she have sold Delectable Mountain Quilting to me if she was going to kill him? Surely the insurance money would've covered his debts and she'd still have her store."

He frowned. "You're assuming Gary was insured."

"True, but the timing still seems off. What about whoever he owed money to? Maybe they got tired of waiting."

"Doubt it. Dead men don't pay debts."

"But maybe their estates do."

"I'll check into it." He stood up and grabbed his hat from the hook where he'd hung it. "Listen, I want you to go home. I'll let you know how this turns out, but I don't want you involved any further." Pushing the hat firmly on his head, he took her by the shoulders and turned her toward the door.

"Hey," she said, pulling away, "you're the one who insisted I go with you to break the news to Mattie. I didn't volunteer for any of this."

"I know." He opened the office door and gestured her to the hallway. "I'm starting to regret that decision."

She glared at him, raised her chin and strode out of the office. "I regret a lot of things."

He winced, but kept quiet, following her to the door.

"Sure you don't want a lift home?" he asked once they were outside on the sidewalk that edged Garnet Gateway's Main Street.

"I'll walk," she said, her words short and clipped. "I've had enough of you."

She turned and walked away, leaving him staring after her.

God! Why did it have to be him? Why did she have to call Jason when she needed the police? Worse yet, why did she have to care what he thought?

She slowed her pace and considered. She cared because she still loved him. Would probably always love him. Her eyes teared up and she bit her lip to keep them from spilling. She was stronger than this. The man had broken his vows, had cheated on her with some unknown woman he'd picked up in a bar in Butte. Divorce was a given; Kristi wasn't a woman who'd allow herself to be disrespected that way.

She might love him, but since he'd thrown their relationship away on a one night stand, he obviously didn't love her. At least, not enough. She'd taken back her maiden name and moved on. The purchase of Delectable Mountain Quilting was part of her renewal.

Kristi was almost home when it occurred to her to wonder why Gary had been in the alley behind Delectable Mountain? Coincidence that he'd died behind what had been his wife's store only the day before? Not likely.

If he was running from someone, why run there? Why not escape into an inhabited space? Somewhere he might find safety in witnesses. Garnet Gateway wasn't exactly a hotbed of crime. If he'd stayed in plain sight, he might have stayed alive.

Without even thinking about it, she turned away from home and toward the quilt shop.

Did Gary even know the date of the closing? Would he have known that ownership had passed from Mattie to Kristi? Possibly not. His name hadn't been on any of the legal documents, so his signature hadn't been required.

Her steps quickened as she pulled her cell phone from her denim bag and called Jason.

"Did you find Gary's keys in the alley?" she asked as soon as she heard Jason's voice.

"Well *hello* to you too," he responded. "Why do you care about his keys?"

"Just answer the question, did you find his keys?"

"Let me check."

Silence.

"No keys are listed."

"Doesn't that seem odd to you? That a grown man would be out without any keys?"

"A bit," he admitted. "Again, why do you care about a dead man's keys?"

"Because he died at the back door to my quilt shop." Kristi paused for a beat. "My newly acquired quilt shop." She gave that a moment to sink in. "He might've had keys to his wife's building, and I haven't had time to change the locks."

His change in attitude telegraphed itself over the air waves; Kristi felt it immediately.

"Where are you?" he asked, words clipped and no nonsense.

"The front door of Delectable Mountain Quilting."

"Don't go in."

"Sorry. You lost the right to give me orders."

"Damn it, Kristi, I'm on my way to the casino. It'll take me a few minutes to get back to you. Don't go in."

She straightened her spine and clenched her teeth. "No promises," she ground out and clicked the phone off.

Walking into the alley, she noted that the body was gone. The area was wreathed in yellow crime scene tape, but no one was about. Returning to the front, she breathed in the sweet scent of the Daphne and steeled herself to go in. She should wait for Jason; she knew she should, but she also knew that she was a woman alone in the world, that she couldn't afford to wait around for someone else to deal with her problems.

This was her life. Her quilt shop. She refused to be afraid to live the one or enter the other.

Turning the key in the lock, she opened the door and stepped inside.

She wasn't alone. The lights were on in the back, and rattled though she'd been earlier, she knew she'd turned everything off. Leaving the door open, she crept through the crowded aisles until she had a clear view of the storage room.

Velma Carson stood on a stepstool with her hand on a cloth bag resting on the very top shelf.

Kristi relaxed and stepped into the room. "Velma," she called. "What are you doing here?"

The older woman nearly fell off the stool, but she caught her balance and, pulling the cloth bag into her arms, turned to face Kristi.

"I'm sorry, Kristi. Mattie just told me your transaction had been completed, so I raced over to retrieve one of my grandmother's quilts."

Kristi frowned. "One of your grandmother's quilts? Why didn't Mattie remove it earlier? I bought the inventory as well as the property, you know."

The woman blushed and climbed down to the floor. "Mattie told me. She didn't take it home because she didn't know it was here. I suppose technically I'm stealing, but, well, it shouldn't have been included in the sale. After all, it's mine. It wasn't Mattie's to dispose of."

"I see," Velma's logic made sense, but there was something else in play. Something didn't feel right. And then it clicked. "How did you get in?"

"Mattie gave me her keys."

Kristi shook her head. "No. She didn't. She turned all of her keys over to the agent for closing. *I* have Mattie's keys."

Velma clutched the cloth bag tightly, which Kristi could now see was a simple white pillowcase used to store a folded quilt, and reached into the supple burgundy leather purse she wore strapped across her body. When her hand emerged, she aimed a revolver at Kristi.

"Velma! What are you doing? There's no need for that."

"I'm sorry, Kristi. I didn't mean for you to be involved in this. It's a family matter after all. I need to protect my family, my heritage."

Kristi swallowed and tried to remember exactly what was around her. Could she dive out of sight before Velma could pull the trigger? If she did, what could she hide behind? How fast could she get to the front door?

"This is just a misunderstanding, Velma. If your grandmother made that quilt, of course you should have it. I was just surprised to find you in what I thought was a secure building."

Velma took a step closer, and Kristi recognized an unhealthy gleam in her eyes … and knew whose keys she'd used. Her stomach sank. For whatever reason, Velma had already killed once today, and that had been her daughter's husband. She might not have liked Gary, but he was family. Kristi was not.

"I'm sorry you asked about the keys, Kristi. This is nothing personal. I'm just protecting what's mine."

It was now or never.

Kristi dropped to the floor. Velma pulled the trigger.

The shot reverberated through the building as Kristi scrambled behind a wall of quilting cottons. An all too insubstantial barrier.

Suddenly the lights in the main shop flicked on, and Jason's voice rang out. "Drop the gun! This is Sheriff Reynolds, Mrs. Carson, and I'm armed."

Velma screamed and pulled the trigger again. The noise deafened Kristi as she huddled behind the colorful bolts of fabric. Another shot, this one from the front of the shop, followed by a scream of pain.

Heavy footsteps ran from the front door to the storage room and Kristi heard the low rumble of Jason's voice through the noise-induced fog in her ears. Then he was looming over her, and she'd never been so glad to see anyone in her life.

He knelt beside her and taking her chin in his hands turned her head to face him. "Are you all right?" She saw the words as much as heard them, and nodded her head.

Instantly he wrapped her in his arms and hugged her so tightly she could barely breathe. He said something, but she couldn't quite make it out, though she felt the words reverberate through his chest.

He might have said, "Thank God! I thought I'd lost you." But that couldn't be right. He didn't love her anymore. They were divorced.

Whatever. Right at that moment, she didn't care. Right then all that mattered was that no one was shooting at them … and she was safe in Jason's arms … where she belonged.

CHAPTER FOUR

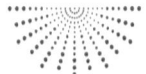

*J*ason shook his head. "Seriously? She killed a man over a quilt?"

Kristi leaned her head against the high back of the booth in her favorite Italian restaurant. Okay, Garnet Gateway's *only* Italian restaurant, but even if there'd been fifty, this one would've been her favorite. Lots of memories lived in this place, with its red-checked tablecloths, its raffia covered wine bottle candle holders, its soft recorded music, and its comfortable quasi-private booths.

Jason had ordered a glass of wine for her though it wasn't yet five o'clock, and she sipped it as they talked.

"It was an heirloom and a valuable piece," she said in Velma's defense, "and she knew he was going to sell it with no thought to its significance to the family."

"Still, a man's dead, you were almost shot, and Velma's going to prison … over a quilt?" He stared at her with such a dumbfounded expression that she smiled.

"Never underestimate the value of a quilt," she said. "Besides, I bet if you talk to big city investigators you'd find people had been killed over less."

The waitress arrived with plates of spaghetti, and Kristi's mouth watered. Getting shot at was hungry work.

"I'm sure you're right," Jason admitted, "but I don't live in a big city, and here in Garnet Gateway, killing over anything short of self defense is just … well, not done."

She nodded and silence reigned as they devoured their early dinner.

When their plates were as clean as they were going to get, Jason reached across the table and took Kristi's hand. She stiffened, but didn't pull away.

"You know," he said quietly, looking at their clasped hands rather than meeting her gaze, "when I saw her pointing a gun at you and knew I couldn't get there in time to save you…" He stopped, swallowed, and looked deep into her eyes. "Well, everything kind of snapped into focus."

He looked away again. "I've been a fool. You were right to divorce me; I drove you away." He met her gaze and held it. "But if there's any way that you could give me another chance, I swear I'd never take you for granted again."

"Jason…"

"I can't promise I'd never disappoint you," he said quickly. "That would be impossible, but I'd sure like a chance to earn your love and trust again."

She squeezed her eyes shut to hold back the tears, and then squeezed his fingers. "I'd like that, too, Jason."

When she opened her eyes, she saw that his gray eyes had gone blue with emotion, and his smile lit her world.

PART XIV
FOOL'S PUZZLE

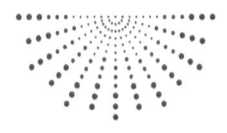

Fool's Puzzle

A Short Kristi Lundrigan Mystery

DEBBIE MUMFORD

CHAPTER ONE

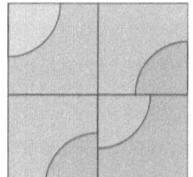

Kristi Lundrigan sailed into Delectable Mountain Quilting, her ankle length patchwork skirt swirling around her legs. She grinned at Mattie Stebbings, her best and most experienced employee. Mattie nodded in acknowledgment as her hands were busy measuring a length of gorgeous deep purple batik print for a customer who stood with her hand resting possessively on a stack of at least six additional bolts of fabric.

Business was good. Barely past their 9:30 a.m. opening and Mattie was already preparing to cut a good-sized sale.

Kristi smiled and said. "Good morning, Mattie." She turned her attention to the customer. "Thanks for coming in, Eleanor. Did you find everything you need?"

Eleanor beamed at her, running her fingers lovingly over the stack of bolts. "Oh, Kristi, I just love these new batiks. I've got a Double Nine Patch planned and with these…" she paused, sighing happily, "it's just going to sparkle."

"How wonderful. Be sure to bring the top in when you get it pieced. We'd love to see it."

"Oh, don't wait that long," Mattie added with mock concern. "Bring the blocks in as soon as you have enough to lay out the design!"

Kristi laughed, waved, and moved to the kitchen to put away her purse, acknowledging several other customers as she passed. What a great way to start her day! She was so lucky that Mattie had agreed to come to work for her.

The petite, dark-haired woman had owned the shop until last spring when she'd been forced to sell in order to cover her husband's gambling debts. Kristi had been fortunate enough to buy the whole package: building, land, and inventory. Of course, she hadn't known the reason for the sale at the time. That had come out later, when Mattie's husband, Gary, had been murdered just outside the shop's back door.

But all of that was behind them now. The grand opening of Kristi's new and updated Delectable Mountain Quilting had taken place nearly six months ago, and thanks to her marketing savvy and skillful redesign of the shop's floor plan, the business was doing better than anyone had dared to hope. After three months of employing only one sales clerk, Kristi had approached Mattie about coming back. The former owner had jumped at the chance. She was still mourning the loss of her husband—not to mention her mother's betrayal—and was glad to have a reason to get out of the house and interact with people who loved quilts and fabric as much as she did.

Back out on the sales floor, Kristi re-shelved bolts of quilting cottons as Mattie finished cutting, chatted with customers, and offered suggestions as to which fabrics might blend well in blocks.

She was straightening books in the notions room when Anna Marsten approached her. "Excuse me, Kristi."

Kristi turned to the heavy-set woman. Blonde and blue-eyed with a florid complexion, Anna had been a beauty in her youth. Now the rancher's wife and mother of six could best be described as warm-hearted and sturdy. "Anna, how nice to see you. How can I be of help?"

Anna clutched a bolt of white-on-white backing fabric to her ample bosom, licked her lips, and asked, "Have you ever done any appraisals? Quilt appraisals, I mean."

Kristi cocked her head to one side, considering the question. After a moment's hesitation, she said, "Well, yes. I'm certified by the American Quilter's Society, but it's been several years since I've done any. Do you need an appraisal for insurance purposes?"

Anna shook her head. "No, not me. I don't need anything." She bit her lip and glanced at the rack of books Kristi had been straightening, her demeanor tense and uncertain. Finally, she blurted, "It's Carl's mother. A man has contacted her about quite a few of the items in her estate. He's making all sorts of wild claims about the money she could have if she follows his advice. Carl is convinced it's a scam."

Kristi's brow furrowed. "That's awful, but I'm not sure how I can help."

"Well, part of his advice concerns her quilts. He's suggesting that they're worth thousands of dollars ... each. Now, you know that I love quilts, and I value them, but I'm pretty sure the market value is nothing like what he's quoting. Carl and I, we just don't know how to counter his hold on Momma Marsten. But I thought if we could bring in a quilt expert and disprove what he's saying about her quilts, maybe she'd be less likely to fall for his lies about all her other things."

"I see. Well, as I said, my market information is out of date, but I'd be happy to inspect her collection, document the designs, types of the fabrics, the stitching, the binding... the general condition of the quilts, and then do the market research to give her an accurate appraisal."

Anna's expression cleared and her grip on the bolt of fabric eased. "Oh, thank you, Kristi. What would you charge?"

"Let me give you my email address. If you can tell me approximately how many quilts you'd like appraised, I'll work up an estimate for you. Then you and Carl can decide whether or not you want to proceed."

She paused for a moment, and added, "But I have to warn you, depending on the number and types of quilts, this may not be a quick project."

Anna nodded, relief evident around her eyes and the set of her jaw. "I understand. I'll get the information to you this evening, and thank you so much. Just to be able to tell Carl we might have this option means a lot to me."

CHAPTER TWO

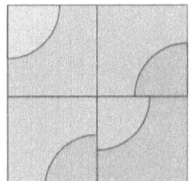

*L*ater that evening, Kristi sat across the table from her ex-husband, Jason Reynolds, at Rizzoli's Fine Italian Restaurant. Rizzoli's was also Garnet Gateway's *only* Italian restaurant, but since it was a favorite of Kristi's, the couple ate there often.

Recorded violin music wafted dreamily through air spiced with the aroma of roasted tomatoes, garlic, oregano, and beeswax from the candle flickering on their red and white checked tablecloth. Kristi gazed contentedly at Jason. He was focused on trapping the last bite of linguini between a bit of crusty bread and his fork and didn't notice her fond expression. After their divorce a year ago she'd never have believed that they could even be friends, and yet, here they were, dating again.

She'd had a brush with death during the investigation into Gary Stebbings' murder, and Jason, Garnet Gateway's sheriff, had reacted by declaring his continued love for her and asking for a second chance.

Kristi had been glad to grant his request, and now, six months later … she was even more at ease with her decision. The repairs to their relationship would take time, but Jason was worth the effort.

The object of her concentration, looked up, noticed her gaze, and the undoubtedly sappy little smile on her lips, and reached for her hand.

"You look happy," he said, his gray eyes twinkling in the candlelight. "Did you have a good day?"

"I did," she said, squeezing his fingers. "And I had an unexpected request. Actually, it was a bit odd."

"Oh? Tell me about it."

When she finished explaining the conversation with Anna Marsten, Jason frowned.

"I'd appreciate it if you'd keep me informed about this," he said, his tone more serious than she'd expected. "If someone is preying on our elderly citizens, I want to put a stop to it."

"Preying? That seems like an odd word choice."

He released her hand and leaned back against the cushioned booth. "It may be nothing, but the fact that Carl and Anna are concerned enough to ask for your help raises a red flag for me."

She nodded. "Yes, I agree their agitation is concerning. But I can't see what this man stands to gain. So far, he seems to be promising Carl's mother *more* than her things are worth."

Jason clenched his jaw, then relaxed. "Yes. That's part of the problem. It sounds like he's running a con on her, but I can't see what it is with the information we currently have."

"Maybe I'll discover more when I inspect the quilts." She shook her head and amended, "If I inspect her quilts. I haven't been hired yet."

She glanced at the time on her cell phone and sighed. "Speaking of which, I need to get home so I can work up that estimate." She smiled at Jason as she scooted to the edge of the booth and stood. "Thanks for dinner, Jason. Sorry I have to cut our evening short."

He stood as well, nodded to the waitress, and said, "I'll be right back, Jenny." Then to Kristi, "Let me walk you to the door." When they stood outside in the evening shadows, he pulled her into his arms. "I like having dinner with you, Ms. Lundrigan." He kissed her gently, sweetly, not invoking heat, but promising so much. "Maybe someday soon, we'll decide that we should have dinner together every night... for the rest of our lives."

She couldn't see his eye color in the soft light, but she imagined his gray eyes were edging toward the blue they wore when emotion was high. She kissed his cheek, a little scratchy this late in the day, and stepped out of his embrace. "Maybe someday," she agreed, and turned to unlock her bright red Subaru Outback.

As she settled into the driver's seat and fastened her seat belt, she heard the jingle of the restaurant door as Jason returned to settle their bill. It wouldn't do for the sheriff of Garnet Gateway, Montana to fail to pay for his meal.

CHAPTER THREE

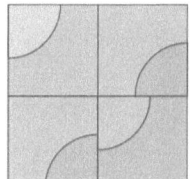

*K*risti guided her bright red Subaru Outback over the rutted dirt road that led from the paved county road to the Broken M Ranch. The mid-September day was fine, the weather not yet cold enough to require a full down coat, but the high overcast of the sky spoke of snow in the near future. She'd been on enough ranches to know this was a busy time of year as the cattle were brought down from the high meadows and preparations were made for the coming winter.

The fact that Carl and Anna were taking time to meet with her about a quilt appraisal now spoke volumes about their level of concern. Events like this were usually saved for dreary winter days.

Pulling into the ranch's main compound, Kristi parked in front of a two-story home that probably dated back to the mid-1800s. White with black shutters and door, the front steps led to a wide porch. Bare now, she imagined it furnished with wooden rockers and small tables in the summer months. Across the way stood a younger version of the home, this one painted yellow with white shutters. Anna and Carl and their children lived there, but this one, the original ranch house, was the domain of Momma Marsten. This was where she and her late husband had raised Carl and his siblings.

Kristi had just stepped onto the front porch when someone called her name. She turned to see Anna crossing the yard to greet her.

"Welcome, Kristi," she said as she reached the steps to her mother-in-law's home. "Glad to see you found the place."

Kristi waited until Anna joined her on the porch to extend her hand. "Your directions were easy to follow. Thanks."

"Carl's out with the cattle," the rancher's wife said, "but he should be back by noon."

Kristi's eyes widened in surprise. "Whatever for? I mean, he's welcome of course, but we won't need his help to lay out and measure quilts."

Anna grimaced and glanced at the still closed front door. "I certainly hope not, but…" She stopped herself, drew a deep breath, and waved the thought away. "No sense borrowing trouble. Let's go in and get started."

She knocked on the door before pushing it open and calling, "Momma Marsten? It's Anna and I've brought the appraiser for the quilts."

Kristi followed Anna past a stairway leading to the upper floor and into a long hallway, its walls lined with framed photographs, many of them going sepia with age. There were pictures of this house in various stages of its existence: a lone building with an indistinct man and woman standing before it; the same house with a sturdy barn with a high-pitched roof in the background; other views as the out-buildings multiplied; and finally a color photo of the current ranch compound with its two homes and multiple out-building in sharp focus.

There were family photos as well. Many featuring long-dead ancestors, but there were also relatively current photos of Carl's family and the families of his siblings. Kristi smiled, appreciating the history of the place, the lives these walls had known and sheltered. Too many Montana ranches had been broken up for development; it was good to see this one alive and well and prepared to move forward into the future.

Doors opened off the hallway into several spacious rooms. Formal living room. Sitting room—Mrs. Marsten probably still thought of it as a parlor. A library that doubled as an office, and a dining room where the lady of the house waited.

"Momma Marsten," Anna said, stepping to where the older woman sat at the head of a beautifully polished walnut table with clawed feet, "this is Kristi Lundrigan. She bought Delectable Mountain Quilting last spring and she's an AQS quilt appraiser."

Mrs. Marsten nodded and held out a hand that Kristi hurried to shake. "Pleased to meet you, Kristi, though I'm not quite sure why Anna dragged you out here."

Kristi gave her a winning smile and released her hand. "Anna's told me about your quilt collection. I'm thrilled to be able to help you document the pieces. You know how important it is to record vintage quilts. They're part of our heritage, a history of Montana's women written in fabrics of their day and tiny stitches."

Mrs. Marsten smiled and nodded. "I hadn't thought of it that way, but you're right. They're so much more than just bed coverings."

Anna's expression expressed her gratitude for Kristi's quick explanation, but she only said, "Shall I bring down the first set, Momma Marsten?"

The older woman nodded her permission and rose to clear the table to provide a work surface. "Do we need to put a leaf in?" she asked.

Kristi eyed the table, which was easily six feet long without the leaf. "Let's start with this. We can add the leaf later if needed. If you'll excuse me, I'll go get my tools."

When she returned, Kristi found the table clear with all the chairs pulled back to the walls, and a stack of six or eight quilts folded neatly on the walnut sideboard.

Anna took the cardboard from Kristi and covered the table's gleaming surface—it wouldn't do to accidentally mar that polish with pin scrapes—while Kristi laid out three sets of white cotton gloves, her digital camera, measuring tape, magnifying glass, and the tablet she'd use to record the data. Anna had indicated Mrs. Marsten had at least two dozen quilts to be appraised. They had a full day's work ahead of them.

The women were working on the third quilt of the morning, a beautifully executed crazy quilt, when a knock sounded at the front door.

"Shall I get that, Momma Marsten?" Anna asked.

"Don't bother. I'll take care of it. You girls keep working."

When her footsteps had receded down the hall, Anna caught Kristi's eye. "I didn't have a chance to thank you," she said. "She was all set to send us packing, but your answer smoothed her feathers and made everything work." She studied Kristi's face and nodded. "You know a thing or two about people, don't you?"

Kristi cocked an eyebrow and said with a sly smile, "I can't imagine what you mean, Anna. I simply stated the truth."

Anna laughed. "The right truth at the right moment. You're good, Kristi, and you're a fine appraiser too."

Footsteps on hardwood and a murmur of voices announced Mrs. Marsten's return. A moment later she entered the dining room followed by a well-dressed man in his late forties. Clean shaven, with neatly groomed dark hair and light brown eyes, the man was not much taller than Kristi's five foot six.

"This is my son's wife, Anna," Mrs. Marsten told the man, gesturing to her daughter-in-law, "and this is Kristi Lundrigan, a quilt appraiser who's helping me document my collection. Ladies, this is Mr. Benedict Peters."

Peters shook hands with each of them. "A pleasure to meet you, Anna. I've heard such wonderful things about you. Ms. Lundrigan, how nice of you to help Emma with this project."

A sidelong glance at Anna's face told Kristi that the man's use of Mrs. Marsten's Christian name had shocked her as well. Kristi hadn't even known what the older woman's given name was until she needed to enter the information into the appraisal form... and then Mrs. Marsten had seemed reluctant to give it.

"It's always a pleasure to be allowed to examine quilt collections," Kristi said.

He nodded, leaning over the table to study the embroidery stitches on the Crazy quilt. "The history of these quilts is important," he said, "but I hope you're not bothering to do an appraisal." He straightened and met her gaze. "I've already done that."

"I see," she said with an easy smile. "I didn't realize you were a quilt appraiser. We have something in common."

"Not officially," he said, stepping away from the table and waving airily. "I'm an antiques dealer... from New York." He added this detail as if it gave him all the credentials he needed. "I've worked with enough estates to know what's of value and what isn't."

"How fascinating," Kristi said, widening her eyes. "And what brought you all the way to Garnet Gateway, Montana?"

His gaze slid away from Kristi's and he moved to Mrs. Marsten's side. "A friend of a friend mentioned Emma's wonderful antiques to me," he said with a shrug. "Six degrees of separation. You know how it is."

Kristi was beginning to believe she knew exactly how it was. Jason was right. This man was running some kind of scam on Mrs. Marsten and he didn't want a certified appraisal to be completed. The quilts were unlikely his main focus, but if she could prove he was lying about the quilts, she could cast doubt on the rest of his patter.

Benedict Peters was a con artist. She was sure of it, but what was his end goal? What did he hope to accomplish?

Peters tried, very suavely Kristi thought, to dismiss her when Carl came home and the work stopped for lunch, but by that time Emma Marsten was invested in documenting her foremothers' work for posterity.

Anna and Carl went to their home for lunch, but Kristi was invited to join Mrs. Marsten and Peters for a bowl of fresh vegetable soup and a ham sandwich. Their conversation was light, consisting mainly of observations about the quilts they'd worked with that morning.

Peters tried to draw Kristi out about her background, but desisted when she mentioned her relationship to Garnet Gateway's sheriff.

"You were married to Sheriff Reynolds?" Mrs. Marsten asked in impressed tones. "I absolutely adore that young man. He's been out here several times. Always so helpful, and so dedicated." She eyed Kristi thoughtfully. "I'd've thought he was a keeper."

Kristi felt her cheeks flame. "Well, we had some difficulties," she said quietly. "But we're trying to make amends. I have hope that this time…"

Mrs. Marsten patted her hand. "I'm sorry, dear. I didn't mean to pry."

When the last quilt had been documented, Kristi packed up her supplies while Anna and Mrs. Marsten put the room back in order.

They said their good-byes and Anna, who was heading home herself, walked Kristi to her car.

"You'll let me know what you turn up about the value?"

"You can be sure of it. I'll give you a complete report and a print out of the historical information that you can share with Mrs. Marsten. You can decide whether or not to share the results of the appraisal itself."

"Perfect," agreed Anna. "And again, thank you for everything, Kristi. I'm not sure we could've accomplished this without your deft handling of the situation."

"You're very welcome. I'll be in touch."

Kristi had a lot to think about during the drive back into Garnet Gateway. As she neared town, she called Jason. "Are you at the office?"

"I am," he responded. His deep voice soothed away the day's concerns.

"Great. I'll be there in just a few minutes."

"Okay," she heard the wariness creep into his tone. "Is there a problem I should be aware of?"

"Not exactly," she said, "but I want to discuss the situation at the Broken M with you."

"What did you find out?"

"I'll tell you when I get there."

CHAPTER FOUR

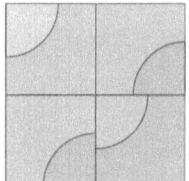

ifteen minutes later she sat in one of the uncomfortable visitor's chairs across the scarred wooden desk from the man she loved, though she was still hesitant to admit that, even to herself.

Jason Reynolds wore his uniform well, looking every bit the capable law enforcement officer that he was. His gray eyes were clear and cool, his forehead high and his jaw firm. He radiated calm assurance; this wasn't a man to tolerate outsiders preying on those in his care.

"Have you ever heard of a man named Benedict Peters?" Kristi asked.

"No," he said, scribbling the name in a notebook, "but I'll run a background check. What does he do?"

"He claims to be a New York antiques dealer."

"Claims?"

She squirmed on the hard wooden seat. "I don't know. Something about him rubbed me wrong." She frowned, trying to pinpoint exactly what had made her suspicious. And then it hit her. "He called her *Emma*," she said quietly.

"Excuse me?"

She glanced up and met his confused gaze. "Sorry. I just realized that was what did it. He called Mrs. Marsten by her given name. It was too familiar... and she didn't object." She stood and paced across the room. "I don't know what he's up to, but he's got her mesmerized, and she's a strong-minded woman." She stopped and rested her hands on the back of the chair she'd just vacated. "I think he expected to be able to dismiss me, but we'd connected— Mrs. Marsten and I. We'd established a bond over the history of those quilts, so he wasn't able to get rid of me."

Jason nodded. "As you said, she's strong-minded, which makes it even more concerning that he's managed to worm his way into her confidence. What else?"

Kristi detailed the day's events, trying to remember every word Peters had spoken, his every gesture and tone of voice.

"Wait a minute," she exclaimed as Jason finished writing his notes. "I've got a picture of him. Just a second."

She dashed out of the station and returned a few minutes later with her digital camera and a USB cable. Jason fired up his computer while she found the picture she was looking for. Once it was downloaded onto the sheriff's computer, they studied the image.

"I knew he wasn't from around here even before the introductions. Look at that suit. I bet it's hand tailored. You won't find anything like that even in Billings. And his hands. You can't see them in the picture, but they were soft, his nails manicured. Definitely not a rancher's hands, and I bet even the lawyers and accountants around here have more calluses than he does."

Jason studied the picture, but glanced at her with admiration. "You do notice details, Kristi. And good job getting this picture. If Benedict Peters is an alias, this photo will go a long way in figuring out who he really is."

She blushed. "Thanks. If he's a legitimate business man, I'll eat my Fool's Puzzle quilt!"

He laughed. "I'm betting on your instincts; I think the Fool's Puzzle is safe, but I'm not so sure about the fool who calls himself Benedict Peters."

CHAPTER FIVE

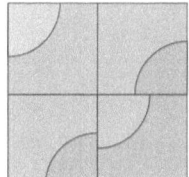

*J*ason called Kristi bright and early two days later. Glancing out the window as she answered her cell phone, she saw that the day was anything but bright. Gray clouds obscured her view of the majestic Absaroka Mountains; the snow wouldn't hold off much longer.

"Have you given that report to Anna and Carl yet?" Jason asked.

"Of course not," she answered, mildly irritated. "I'm barely awake and not even dressed yet."

"Great," he said. "I'm coming over."

"What?" But he'd already disconnected.

Kristi stared at the phone in her hand. What was he up to? She glanced around the mess that was her living room. She'd been up late last night researching quilt values and finishing her appraisal of the Marsten quilts. The coffee table was littered with books and print-outs, and her clothes were scattered across the floor. She'd been too tired to be neat. Plus, she lived alone...if she didn't count her two moggy cats, Stitches and Between, and when it came to messy rooms, who counted cats? They didn't care if the sink was piled high with dirty dishes.

But Jason? He was an entirely different matter.

Unless she got her butt in gear, got dressed, and met him outside.

Properly motivated, Kristen accomplished the feat. When Jason's Trail Blazer pull into the drive, she was out the front door, carefully locking it behind herself, and across the lawn before he had a chance to climb out.

He reached across the seat, opened the door for her, and leaned back while she settled into the passenger seat and fastened her seat belt.

"Where are we going?" she asked.

"I would've come in," he said.

"I know. I repeat, where are we going so early in the morning?"

He put the vehicle in gear and backed out of her driveway. "The Garnet Gateway Inn. I want to catch Peters before he has a chance to leave his room."

"Ah. I take it you found something."

He glanced sideways at her. "I found a lot, mainly thanks to that picture you took."

"Well?" she asked. "What's he up to? Tell me."

He shook his head. "You'll hear it all when we get there."

"Uh-huh. And why am I tagging along?"

"Oh, I just thought you'd enjoy watching me put the fear of God into a no-good hustler." He smiled. Kristi thought he looked like a shark. "And when we finish with him, we're heading out to the Broken M. I need to apprise Mrs. Marsten of the situation and you need to deliver your report."

"I can hardly wait," she said drily.

Jason parked in front of the Inn, and Kristi followed him inside. Definitely not a hardship; he had a fine butt and his determined stride showed off his physique nicely.

She jerked her thoughts back to their mission as he reached the front desk and spoke to the clerk on duty.

"Hey, Dave," he said, leaning on the counter. "I need the room number for Benedict Peters."

"Hey yourself, Jason," Dave responded. "You know I'm not allowed to give out that information."

"You are when the sheriff asks," Jason said, a hint of steel edging his voice. "This isn't a social call, Dave. Police business. Now, what room is he in?"

"He's up top," Dave answered, looking a little shaken. "The penthouse suite. What's he done?"

"Nothing that concerns you or the Inn, Dave."

Dave nodded, his expression somber.

The Garnet Gateway Inn was an historic building. Built at the turn of the last century, it was five stories high with a vintage elevator, all gilded ironwork and polished glass. The Inn's owners hadn't updated because the elevator was part of the Inn's charm, but it was inspected regularly and kept in peak working order. Everything else in the place was up to date, including in-room microwaves, refrigerators, and Wi-Fi connections.

"The penthouse," Kristi said as Jason pulled the elevator grill closed behind them. "He must have some excellent backing."

Jason grunted his agreement and they rode up in silence.

Kristi stood a little behind Jason when he knocked on the penthouse door. After all, he was law enforcement; she was just along for the ride.

The man she knew as Benedict Peters opened the door and frowned at Jason. He was casually dressed in khakis and a light blue polo, but he still appeared polished.

"I'm sorry. Do I know you?" he asked, frowning at Jason.

"I'm Sheriff Jason Reynolds. I believe you've met Ms. Lundrigan."

He peered past Jason and nodded at me. "Of course, Kristi isn't it? But that still doesn't explain why you're here."

"May we come in?" Jason asked, and his expression said that the answer should be "yes."

Peters opened the door completely and stepped out of the way. "Be my guest."

They moved into the sitting room of the penthouse, a spacious room tastefully decorated with fresh flowers, beautifully upholstered sofa and chairs, and plush carpeting in a deep plum. A certain tension in the air kept everyone standing.

"You are Benedict Peters," Jason stated. He pulled out a small notebook, flipped it open, and, after a glance, continued. "Also known as Reginald Lewis, Maximilian Davenport, and Xavier James?"

Kristi watched in fascinated silence as the color drained from Peters' face. Then his eyes flashed, color returned to his cheeks, and he straightened his shoulders.

"I don't know what you're talking about," he said, his tone waspish and full of disdain. "Certainly I'm Benedict Peters. I have no idea who those other men are."

"Uh-huh," said Jason, watching Peters with those cool cop's eyes of his. "Well, they're all aliases for Jimmie Fredricks, a smooth talking hustler out of Denver. Now I can add Benedict Peters to the list."

"I assure you, you can't. I have no idea where you got your information, but your little backwater connections are mistaken. I am a prestigious antiques dealer from New York." He glared at Jason and moved toward the door. "Now, if you'll kindly leave, I have business to attend to."

Jason sat down on the pretty little sofa with its muted lavender and green floral pattern. Kristi raised an eyebrow, and at his nod, followed suit.

"I'm sure you think you have business, Fredricks, but you don't. Not in my jurisdiction. My *backwater* connections include the FBI database, and the photo Ms. Lundrigan took when you met the other day was a positive match for all the names I've stated."

Peters, or Fredricks, or whoever he was, folded into a chair. The man seemed to shrink in on himself.

"Now, before I give you your options, I need to know, do you have any documents signed by Mrs. Emma Marsten?"

Kristi's brow creased, but she sat still, certain that the con was about to be revealed.

Peters shook his head. "I'd intended to have her sign a contract the other day," he said, glaring at Kristi, "but events didn't unfold as planned." He shook himself and straightened in the chair. "But you have nothing to hold me on. The contract was simply an agency agreement giving me permission to arrange for the sale of her possessions after her death. I have better contacts and can get better prices than a local dealer."

"Yes," Jason said. "I'm sure that's what you told her, and that's what the document would've said when she read it."

Peters expression cleared and some of his bravado returned. "Of course. I can let you see the contract if you like."

Jason nodded. "I'd like a copy for my files." He smiled that shark smile again. "And I'm sure I'll find that the signature page is separate from the rest of the document... as it was in all the other contracts you've negotiated with wealthy ranchers in this state. Easily removed from one document and attached to another." Jason shrugged and leaned back into the sofa. "Not the best business practice for a legal document," he continued, "but what can you expect from these *backwater* lawyers?"

"Now see here, Sheriff," Peters blustered. "You can't just make accusations like that. You have no proof that I've done anything illegal."

Jason straightened. "You're right. I don't have any proof. If I did, you'd be in cuffs right now. And you haven't done anything illegal in my territory yet... and you're not going to. Because when I leave this room, you're going to pack and leave town. Immediately. No need to contact Mrs. Marsten. I'll be paying her a visit to explain things as soon as we finish our business here."

Jason stood, and Kristi jumped up as well. She followed him to the door, where he turned back to Peters and said, "I'd leave the state, if I were you, and I'd find new associates. I've sent out a statewide alert with your picture attached. I think several rural districts are interested in what you can tell them about ranches being unexpectedly left to development conglomerates instead of their expected beneficiaries. I've also sent a report to the state attorney general's office."

Jason opened the door and Kristi stepped through. "Get out of my town," he growled. "Now. Before I *discover* something to charge you with."

Kristi didn't say a word until they were out of the Inn and safely ensconced in the Trail Blazer. "That's really what he was doing?" she asked. "Trying to get Mrs. Marsten's signature on a legal document that he could then switch out?"

Jason turned to face her. "He's done it at least three times in other parts of the state. He's working with some shady developers, essentially stealing ranches. In a couple of the cases, there wasn't anyone close enough to the victim to protest; no one contested the false documents."

He turned back to the dashboard and started the car. "That's not the worst of it. In at least one case, the victim seemed to be living too long. It looks like these people may have gotten impatient and arranged for her to have a fatal accident. The sheriff I spoke to last night will be reopening that case and reexamining the evidence."

Kristi shivered as big fluffy snowflakes began to drift onto the car's windshield. "How awful. Emma Marsten has had a close call. She's lucky you're here to protect her."

He smiled grimly. "She's lucky Carl and Anna are careful… and that you had the good sense to snap a picture of Peters. And I'm going to make sure she appreciates what all three of you did for her."

Kristi settled back for the ride to the Broken M Ranch. The first snowfall of the season was always lovely. This early in the fall, when the weather was still fairly warm, the flakes were large and drifted lazily, making it easy to enjoy their beauty. Later when the temperatures dropped and the blizzards raged, the flakes would be tiny and driven… and they'd pile high, burying the countryside.

Quilts were a great comfort during a Montana winter.

"You know," Kristi said when they turned off the pavement onto the packed dirt road. "We make a hell of a good team."

Jason kept his eyes on the road, but reached for her hand and clasped it tightly. "We do, indeed," he said quietly. "And I hope we always will."

PART XV
WILDFIRE!

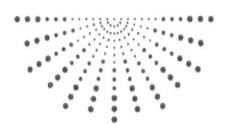

Wildfire!

A Short Kristi Lundrigan Mystery

DEBBIE MUMFORD

CHAPTER ONE

Kristi Lundrigan sat at her scrubbed oak breakfast table and stared out the window at what was usually a serene view of Montana's Absaroka Mountain range. But this morning, the scene was anything but calm; it was downright worrisome. A storm overnight had produced lightning, which had kindled a fire in Garnet Canyon, which led straight down Garnet Creek and into the Paradise Valley town of Garnet Gateway... and Kristi's home.

Situated as her home was on the eastern edge of town, Kristi had a clear view of the black clouds billowing up from the canyon. The only good news was that the smoke continued to hover above the rocky, tree-lined slopes. The wind had died down as the storm passed, so the smoke and flames weren't being pushed toward town. Yet.

Dragging her gaze away from the ominous scene, Kristi forced herself to finish her breakfast. Usually the creamy blend of rolled oats, honey yogurt, and apricot nectar delighted her, but this morning she ate her refrigerated overnight oats mechanically, concerned only with finishing as quickly as possible. She knew she'd need the fuel for what was likely to be an uncomfortable and harrowing day, but she begrudged the time.

Not being in the habit of watching early morning news shows, she'd been blissfully unaware of the fire as she showered and dressed for the day in her favorite long patchwork skirt and a white cotton shell, but Stitches and Between, her moggy cats, had been uneasy, pacing the bedroom and bumping up against her legs repeatedly as she dressed, applied her usual minimal make-up, and pulled her long blonde hair into a high ponytail.

She'd scolded them for their insistence, thinking they were simply anxious for breakfast, but the moment she stepped into the breakfast room and saw the cloud of smoke hanging over the canyon she'd known her cats were more attuned to Mother Nature than she was. Trouble was brewing… and it had chosen a dangerous form: wildfire!

Now, as she carried her bowl to the sink, she wondered if her house would still be standing at the end of the day. Glancing down at her cats, she noted they'd barely touched their own breakfast.

"Too worried to eat, huh, kids," she said as she rinsed out her bowl and placed it in the dishwasher. "Well, it won't matter. You're in for an adventure today. How'd you like to come to the shop with me? I'll set you up in the back with a basket, a blanket, and your food bowls. You'll be quilt shop cats for the day."

As she chatted to the cats in what she hoped was a normal voice, she found their cat carrier, packed a bag of their favorite toys and blankets, and grabbed bags of kibble and litter. Once their things were safely tucked into a box, she packed a small suitcase of her own. After stashing the luggage in her bright red Subaru Outback, Kristi sat down in the middle of the living room floor and opened the door to the cat carrier. To her amazement, Stitches, the older of the pair, took the lead and stepped regally into the carrier and curled into a gray tabby ball, hiding all four white paws beneath her tail and nose. Between (who'd been named because his claws reminded Kristi of the tiny, sharp needles used in hand quilting) followed without even a *meow* of comment. The little tuxedo male curled up beside his best friend and stared at Kristi as if to say, "Well? What are your waiting for? Close us in and get us out of here!"

Kristi did just that, hefting the carrier and settling it safely on the floor of the Subaru's backseat. "All right, kids, we're off to *Delectable Mountain Quilting*." As she pulled out of the garage, she couldn't help glancing at her neat, one story home with its freshly mown front lawn and wondering if she'd ever see it again.

She really hoped so.

She'd been happy in this little house. Her first real home. Not her parents' where she'd lived as a child, or her husband's where she'd lived as a spouse, but her very own, purchased after the divorce that had nearly broken her heart. Her home, and her kitty-kids, had seen her through a tough couple of years, but things were better now. She now owned *Delectable Mountain Quilting*, and after more than a year of hard work, business was thriving, and best of all, her relationship with Jason was healing.

Her ex was not only the sheriff of Garnet County, Montana, he was also her personal hero. He'd saved her life when a murdering mad woman had decided Kristi had to die… and that close call with death had opened both their eyes. They might be divorced, but there was still a lot of love between them. They'd started dating again, but were taking things slow and easy as they worked to rebuild the trust his infidelity had destroyed.

She was just pulling into the parking area behind the shop when her cell phone rang. She finished parking, then pulled the cell from the pocket of her embroidered denim shoulder bag and glanced at the display. Jason. Of course.

She answered with a smile. "Hi, Jason. What's up?"

"Are you still at home?" he asked, his voice gruff and official sounding.

"No, the cats and I just parked behind the shop."

"Good, the cats are with you. Then you're aware of the fire."

She nodded, though he couldn't see her. "It was pretty obvious from my place. How bad is it?"

"Bad enough that we're going to be evacuating the homes on the east side of town, yours included. I'm glad to know you and the cats are already in town."

"Yep, and I packed a bag. I figured I wouldn't be going home again until things settle down."

He sighed and when he spoke again, his voice had mellowed and lost its official edge. "Good to know you're safe, Kristi. I'll stop by the shop later and check in with you, but for now, I have emergency crews to mobilize."

"Stay safe, Jason," she said quietly.

"Always," he responded, and disconnected the call.

CHAPTER TWO

*B*usiness at *Delectable Mountain Quilting* was beyond slow. It was non-existent. Kristi and her sales clerks, Ruby Andrews and Mattie Stebbings, busied themselves by checking the inventory of quilting cottons, moving new bolts to the sales floor to replace ones that had sold out, and cutting a new supply of fat quarters to replenish the shop's stash of the popular 18x22 inch rectangles. Ruby hadn't been scheduled to work that day, but she lived alone on the east side of Garnet Gateway and when the sheriff's department called with the evacuation order she'd decided she'd rather spend her day at the quilt shop than in one of the town's emergency shelters.

Each of the town's four churches had opened their fellowship halls for those who'd been displaced, and the community center on the town square was also taking in refugees. Knowing those sites were likely to be overloaded, Kristi had contacted her employees, including DeAnna Waters (the shop's bookkeeper), who worked from home, and told them they were welcome to shelter at *Delectable Mountain Quilting*. The accommodations wouldn't be luxurious, but they'd have a nice bathroom and a fully functional kitchen... and Jason had volunteered to supply them with cots and blankets if those items became necessary.

Kristi really hoped they wouldn't need to shelter overnight.

After all, the Incident Management Team for the Northern Rockies had arrived mid-morning and firefighters were pouring into Garnet Gateway from all across the state. The IM team had set up a helipad near where Garnet Creek emptied into the rolling Yellowstone River. Kristi and Ruby had taken a break and stepped outside to watch the helicopters dip their buckets into the river like so many giant dragon-flies before zooming off to drop their loads on the flames raging out of the 'Sorkees.

Later in the afternoon, the IM team expected bombers to lend their efforts to dousing the wildfire, but Kristi had no idea where the massive planes would land or how they'd refill their tanks. However they accomplished the task, Garnet County would be grateful for their help.

Around 11:00 a.m., Ruby and Mattie left to take a shift at the community center, volunteering to distribute box lunches to the firefighters. They promised to bring lunch to Kristi when they finished their shift. Alone in the shop, Kristi was surprised to hear the front door open. Glancing up, she discovered a young woman wearing jeans and a T-shirt, with a baby wrapped against her chest and clutching a toddler's hand.

"Hello, I'm Kristi. How can I help you?"

The young woman licked her lips and glanced over her shoulder nervously. "W-would it be all right if we... uhm... if we took shelter here?" She pulled the toddler further into the store and glanced again at the front door, or maybe the street beyond. "I mean, I know this isn't a designated shelter, but..." The baby squirmed in its wrap and the young woman patted its back and shifted her weight from side to side, murmuring soothing sounds.

"Of course," Kristi said quickly, moving around the cutting table to the young woman's side. Odd that she'd chosen the quilt shop. Kristi didn't recognize her as a customer, nor as a relative of one of her students. "You're welcome to wait here, but are you sure you wouldn't be more comfortable at one of the churches? They have nurseries and toys for your little ones."

The young mother shook her head, and now that she was closer, Kristi noticed a bruise on her left temple. She looked a bit unkempt, as did the toddler, neither of them looking as if their dark hair had been combed recently. They must have left home in a hurry. Of course, nearly everyone who'd been forced to evacuate had done so hurriedly, and getting two little ones ready to leave couldn't have eased this woman's process. Still, she seemed unusually nervous, glancing over her shoulder repeatedly.

Almost as if she were hiding from someone.

Kneeling down, Kristi spoke to the toddler. If she had to guess, she'd say the child was a boy, though at this age and with that wildly curly head of dark hair, it was impossible to tell for sure. "Hi there. I'm Kristi. What's your name?"

The little one's eyes widened, and he stepped behind his mother, hiding his face against her jeans. She released his hand and stroked his hair.

"His name is Jesse. He's a little shy."

Straightening to standing, Kristi smiled at the mother. "He's a fine boy, and you're welcome to stay."

The woman glanced at the door again, and Kristi decided they might be more comfortable deeper in the store. "Why don't you come with me," she said, leading the way to the back. "The restroom is over there, and this is our kitchen / breakroom. I don't have any kind of playpen, but I can get you a box and one of my quilts for the baby, if you want to unwrap her and put her down? Is she a girl, or another little boy?"

The moment the door closed behind them and they could no longer be seen from the front door or display windows, the young woman's shoulders relaxed and her hand went to her forehead. She looked exhausted. Kristi gestured toward a chair, and the mother sank into it.

"Girl," she said. "Jill. I call her my little Jelly Bean." When his mother sat down, Jesse scrambled under the table and leaned against her legs.

"And you are?" Kristi asked.

"Charlene Jenkins," the woman replied. "But everyone calls me Char."

"Well, Char, you and Jesse and Jill are safe here. Shall I set up that makeshift cradle for you?"

"Yes, please." Char said with a weary smile. "It'd be a relief to put her down."

Kristi scoured the storage room for a box, the end of a roll of batting, and two of her early quilts that she sometimes used in classes as examples of how *not* to piece. Once Jill was nestled safely in her makeshift bed, and Kristi had folded the other quilt into a pallet on the floor for Jesse, she checked the kitchen cabinets.

"Ah-ha! I thought I still had some granola bars in here." She pulled a box off the shelf and offered it to Char. "You and Jesse are welcome to share these, and there's bottled water in the refrigerator."

"You're very kind," Char murmured and unwrapped a bar, broke off a piece and offered it to Jesse. The little boy didn't hesitate, but grabbed it and stuffed it in his mouth.

"I'm sorry I don't have any toys, Jesse," Kristi said with a smile, "but my cats are visiting the shop today. Maybe Stitches and Between will come out of hiding now that we're all settled in."

Jesse's eyes widened and he looked around the kitchen while he chewed.

"If you sit very still, they might come out for a visit. Stitches is gray with four white feet, and Between is black with white markings. Do you like cats?"

The little boy nodded, still searching the room with his gaze.

Kristi beckoned to Char, and the two women stepped to the door to the sales floor.

"Are you in trouble, Char?" Kristi asked quietly. "You seem frightened."

Char glanced at her son, but Stitches had decided to put in an appearance, and the little boy was absorbed in watching her. His mother glanced at Kristi before lowering her gaze and nodding. "It's my husband. He's abusive. He's always knocked me around, but the other day, he hit Jesse." Glancing again at her son, she continued, "I've put up with it for myself, but I won't let him hurt my kids. So, when the order came to evacuate, I decided…"

She paused, took a deep breath, and continued quietly. "I decided to take a chance. I've never been in this shop before, so he shouldn't think to look for me here. I know he'll check the community center and the churches, but…"

She stopped, licked her lips, and met Kristi's gaze. "I don't know what to do now. Even if he doesn't find us here, what do I do next? I don't have a car… or money… or family to call for help." She bit her lip and her eyes filled with tears. "This was a mistake. I shouldn't have bothered you with this. There's no way out for us."

Kristi placed a gentle hand on the woman's arm. "Yes. There is. You may have picked my shop at random, but it was a good choice. I know Sheriff Reynolds. He's a good man and he'll see that you get to a shelter in Billings. You and Jesse and your little Jelly Bean are going to be fine."

Char's eyes widened and she drew in a sharp breath. "Really? You'll help us?"

"Of course I will." Kristi smiled and nodded to where Jesse sat on his pallet with Stitches stretched out beside him and Between curled in his lap. "And so will they."

CHAPTER THREE

*K*risti left Char and her little ones in the kitchen and returned to the sales floor. She'd just pulled her cell phone from the pocket of her long patchwork skirt when the door opened and a man strode in, an unusual occurrence on any day for *Delectable Mountain Quilting*, but ominous after Char's confidences. A large, overblown man with a full head of unruly dark hair and a belly barely contained by his chambray shirt and blue jeans, he stopped just inside the door and surveyed the sales floor.

"You alone in here?" he asked, his voice deep, his manner brusque.

Kristi moved away from him, behind the cutting table. "I don't see that that's any of your business," she said, though she tried to keep her voice pleasant. "Did you want to buy some quilting cottons?"

He glared at her and drew himself up to his full, and substantial, height. "No. I'm looking for my wife and kids. Are they here?"

Kristi feigned innocence and glanced around the shop. "Do you see any children here?"

He turned, as though to leave, but two things happened to prevent that. The front door opened and Ruby and Mattie came in carrying four box lunches, and…

…a baby cried.

Char's little Jelly Bean had chosen the wrong moment to wake up in a strange place.

"They *are* here," the man bellowed, and charged toward the door to the kitchen.

Kristi threw herself into his path, yelling to her friends, "Get help!"

Mattie dropped the box lunches on a counter and ran to help Kristi as she struggled to keep the big man away from the kitchen door. Not that the petite sales clerk carried much weight to throw around!

Ruby screamed, "Stop!"

And amazingly, the man turned to stare at her.

She glared at him. "I don't know what's going on here, but the sheriff is joining us for lunch, so I suggest you leave." Stepping away from the door, Ruby pointed at the man, then at the door. "Go. Now!"

He glared at Ruby, then turned to Kristi and growled, "You won't get away with this. You can't keep a man from his kids."

The front door opened again, and Sheriff Jason Reynolds stepped into the quilt shop. He took a quick look around, his gaze resting on Kristi's flushed face for a moment, before nodding to the man and saying, "Jenkins. Didn't know you were a quilter."

"I'm not," Jenkins answered. "This bitch is hiding my wife and kids and I want them back. Right now."

"I see," Jason said, walking into the shop and stepping between Jenkins and Kristi. "Well, you should know that this *bitch* is *my* wife and I don't appreciate you bullying her." He glanced at Ruby and Mattie, then returned his gaze to Jenkins. "I suggest you leave now. I'll look into your claims and let you know what I find."

Jenkins straightened his back and stared into Jason's eyes. "You'll find my whore of a wife and her brats," he said in a surly tone, "and you'll bring them back to me."

"That's enough, Jenkins," Jason said, his voice soft, but with a deadly edge. "Leave. Now. Or face arrest for menacing."

"Fine," Jenkins snarled. "I'm leaving." He stepped to the side so that he could make eye contact with Kristi. "But I'll be back."

CHAPTER FOUR

*W*hen the front door slammed behind him, everyone turned to Kristi.

"What was that all about?" Jason asked.

"Come with me." Kristi turned and led them all to the kitchen where they found Char huddled on the floor beside the exterior door, cradling Jesse and Jill.

Kristi moved to crouch before the frightened woman. "Char, this is Sheriff Reynolds, the man I was telling you about."

Then she pivoted to face Jason and her clerks. "This is Char Jenkins and she's trying to escape an abusive marriage."

Jason took off his official Stetson, laid it on the kitchen table, and turned to Mattie and Ruby. "I think we're going to need a couple more box lunches."

The women took the hint and left the kitchen.

"Mrs. Jenkins," Jason said, "why don't you join me at the table and tell me your story. Kristi and the others will watch your little ones, won't you, sweetheart?"

Kristi smiled and held out her hands to take Jelly Bean. "I'd be delighted. Come on, Jesse, let's go find Stitches and Between."

She could relax now. The Incident Management Team would bring the wildfire under control, and Jason would protect Char and her children. All was right with Kristi's world.

CHAPTER FIVE

A week later, Kristi and Jason sat at their favorite table near the window of *Rizzoli's Fine Italian Restaurant* enjoying steaming plates of flavorful lasagna and generous tossed salads. Kristi felt truly relaxed and at ease for the first time in days, and Jason's presence had everything to do with her state of mind. Of course, the perfectly spiced beef, rich tomato sauce, and generous layers of gooey cheese in her lasagna didn't hurt. Neither did the bottle of Chianti wine Jason had ordered for them. The red wine's tart cherry flavor, along with its alcohol content, made Kristi want to purr with satisfaction.

Jason smiled at her across his wine glass. "It's been a week, hasn't it?"

"It sure has," she nodded. "And not one I'm anxious to repeat."

The Incident Management Team had declared the wildfire under control and had packed up and left three days ago. Since then, Jason and the Garnet County fire chief had been busy mopping up the aftermath, while keeping a watch on the canyon to make sure no hot spots erupted into flames.

Everyone had returned to their homes, which were all still standing, and cattle herds that had been moved from the ranches in peril to the safety of those on the west side of the Yellowstone were in the process of being returned to their home ranges.

"I'm sure glad Garnet Gateway escaped without loss," he said, placing his glass on the table and reaching for his fork.

"So am I," Kristi agreed. "Stitches and Between were really glad to get home again. Cats aren't fond of upheaval."

Jason smiled and his eyes softened. "Neither are people." He reached for her hand. "You were great with Char Jenkins and her kids, by the way. Protecting her from her thug of a husband took courage."

She squeezed his hand. "Well, I didn't do it alone. Mattie and Ruby were there to back me up, and we were all relieved when you arrived."

"Good thing I'd planned to have lunch with my favorite quilters."

Kristi took a bite of lasagna and closed her eyes, savoring the blend of flavors. When she opened her eyes again, she met Jason's gaze and asked, "So what happened with Char and her little ones? Were you able to get them to safety?"

He swallowed, wiped his lips with his red checked napkin, and said, "Yes. They're safely settled in a shelter in Billings. I introduced Char to the district attorney, and between the two of us, we convinced her to press charges. The DA's also going to help her find a divorce attorney." He took another sip of wine. "And he had a doctor examine Char and the children, and the DA thinks between the doctor's testimony and mine he'll be able to get a conviction." He ate another forkful of lasagna and swallowed before continuing. "At the very least Char will be able to get a restraining order against the man."

"But they're safe right now?" Kristi asked.

"They are. The shelter doesn't give out names of its residents and it has a great security system. Plus, no one in Garnet Gateway knows where I took them." He paused, his eyes taking on that expression Kristi so often thought of as his *cop's eyes*. "Not even you."

She nodded, satisfied. They finished their dinner in companionable silence.

It had been a long week, but ultimately a good one. The wildfire was in the past, Char and her little ones were safe, and Kristi and her kitty-kids were back in their snug little home.

Plus, her relationship with Jason was becoming more solid and trusting by the day.

She smiled and reached for her wine glass. All was right in Kristi's world.

PART XVI
SILVER-TIPPED DEATH

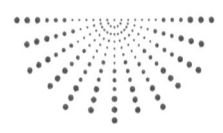

DEBBIE MUMFORD
BESTSELLING AUTHOR OF *SORCHA'S HEART*

SILVER-TIPPED DEATH

SPUN YARNS
A Short Story

CHAPTER ONE

*M*y cousin Evan threw a parachute at my head. I dodged, caught the pack and shrugged it on, fastening heavy buckles with awkward fingers. Crap! I was barely awake. I didn't need this shit. I needed answers.

Where the hell were we? What was happening? Why did I need a parachute?

"No time for questions," Evan yelled. "Just secure the chute and get to the door."

I obeyed. My heart pounded, accelerated by a surge of adrenaline. A couple of minutes ago I'd been sound asleep, exhausted from the week of twelve-hour workdays I'd put in to prepare for this trip—a man could only take so much abuse before he crashed. Next thing I knew, Evan was shaking me awake, shouting that we had to jump, and lobbing a parachute in my face.

"Have you ever jumped?" Evan shouted over the roar of wind and the sputtering engine of Uncle Ben's four-seat prop plane.

"Once. In college. With an instructor."

"Sorry." He shook his head. "No time for a refresher." He patted a ring on his own shoulder. "This is the ripcord. Don't pull it until you're clear of the plane."

With that, he turned and jumped.

Fear clutched my throat and choked me. That was it? That was all I got? I glanced wildly around the tiny cabin. A snow-capped mountain loomed beyond the windshield. Uncle Ben had locked the controls and was struggling into his own chute. "What are you waiting for?" he yelled. "Get the hell out of here!"

Words failed. I nodded. Edged closer to the door, clutched the parachute strap near the ripcord, closed my eyes, and stepped into the howling wind of the abyss.

Freezing air numbed exposed skin. Crap! No jacket. No gloves. I tried to pry my eyes open against the rush of wind. Double crap! Why didn't I have goggles?

Half-frozen fingers clutched the ripcord like a talisman.

Holy Mother of God! What had my jump instructor said? Why hadn't I taken actual lessons? Why in the name of God's Left Nostril had I agreed to fly with Uncle Ben and Evan? Everyone knew single-engine planes were death traps. Why wasn't I sleeping uncomfortably on some commercial flight?

Surely I was dreaming. Yeah. That was it. I was still asleep. Evan would wake me up any second now; laugh at my girly screams of terror. Just a dream. I relaxed as far as my ice-cold skin and chest- and leg-straps would allow.

Yeah. Right. A dream where if I didn't pull the cord soon, I'd splatter on the ground and never wake up.

Get a grip on yourself, man! You're not an idiot. You can do this. Force your eyes open, face reality, and pull that God-forsaken cord.

With stoic determination, I pulled the cord. The chute deployed—score one for my side!—and jerked me upright. Thank all that's holy, I'd managed to get it on right and tight. The rush of air eased, though it didn't warm any. I glanced up at the silk mushroom above my head, and then tried to make sense of my surroundings. Far to my right I could just make out the white circle of Evan's chute as it neared the earth. We wouldn't find each other anytime soon. My hesitation had cost me his companionship in this surreal event. To my left the mountain shone in the early morning light. My heart rate relaxed as I absorbed the stark beauty. When would I ever experience this again? Swaying in the arms of the wind while a hoary old-man mountain stood guard?

A flash of light and a distant roar of explosion jerked me back to reality. That mountain wasn't benign. It had just eaten our aircraft.

I glanced beneath my feet. The earth approached rapidly. Nothing beautiful about the vast expanse of nature below me; those heavily forested slopes were my enemy. I searched the tangle of evergreens for a town, a farmstead, a road winding through its depths. Nothing. No sign of man. The forest primeval prevailed. And it didn't look remotely inviting.

Cold clawed at fingers and face, but it was nothing to the icy fear clutching my heart. How would I survive down there? How would I find my out of that wilderness? Even if searchers found the wreckage, we were nowhere near it.

Crap! Why had I hesitated? If Evan and I were together, we might have a chance.

Wait a minute. What about Uncle Ben? He'd still been in the plane when I jumped. Did he make it out? Was he close to me? I glanced up and left. Another parachute floated on the wind. Close enough. We'd land close enough to find each other. A sliver of warmth beat back the icy fear: I wasn't alone.

Breathing a bit easier I turned my attention to landing. The spires of trees didn't look inviting. Pulling on the lines, I experimented with altering course. This chute didn't have a lot of maneuverability—and I was no expert, but anything could help. A gleam of silver alerted me to a river winding through the forest. I did my best to keep it in sight as I lost altitude.

Sweat prickled the back of my neck as I considered landing. What had my instructor said? Relax. Yeah. Right. Not likely in this situation. Keep your knees and ankles together. Keep some tension in your legs, but bend your knees. Roll to the side to distribute the shock. An image of Smoky the Bear popped into my mind. *Stop, drop, and roll.* I grimaced. The phrase took on a whole new meaning.

Praying for open space, I braced for impact. Prepared for the shock I was about to experience.

At the last instant a stretch of sandy shore appeared beside the river. I hit bare, rocky ground, stumbled, rolled, and stopped inches short of the water. Hopelessly tangled in the lines, the parachute billowed in and over the surface of a swift moving stream, threatening to drag me in for an impromptu dunking.

I scrambled around and managed to plant my feet against a good-sized rock. Slithering and squirming, I freed one arm from the rapidly tightening ropes, found what I hoped was the suspension line and yanked. The silk collapsed. Thank God for that one college jump!

The pressure on my bindings eased. I escaped the lines, unbuckled the harness, and stepped free. Dragging the silk to shore, I sprawled out on it and breathed deeply. Staring up through aspen and evergreen branches at the clear blue sky I'd just conquered, I grinned. I'd done it. I'd jumped out of a disabled plane, plummeted to earth, and defied the odds by landing in one piece with no broken bones. Laughter bubbled up and out. Hysteria? Very likely, but also sheer joy at finding myself alive and whole.

I had no idea where I was, nor any thought on how to find my way out of this wilderness, but for the moment, I was content to be alive with no greater injuries than scrapes and bruises. Once I'd caught my breath, I'd find Uncle Ben, but for now, it was enough that I still had breath to catch.

CHAPTER TWO

A couple of hours later, I found Uncle Ben.

After stowing the remains of my parachute, harness, and lines under a scraggly bush, I wandered over to the stream and gazed at the swirling water. I was thirstier than heck, but was savvy enough to know I'd be risking giardia or worse by drinking unfiltered water. On the other hand, what choice did I have? I'd jumped out of an airplane without even a jacket. I sure as heck wasn't prepared with all the crap I'd have carted along for a jaunt through the wilderness.

Stepping out onto a sizable rock, I'd cupped my hands into the frothy rush of ice-cold water and drank my fill. Satisfied, I straightened, stretched, chose a direction and strode into the tangle of undergrowth and low-hanging branches, calling for my uncle.

By the time I found the pool of blood, I was hot, tired, and more than a little cranky. Sweat dripped into my eyes, gnats and other hellish no-see-ums swarmed around my head, flew up my nostrils, buzzed in my ears, and tried to land in my eyes. My arms were covered in scratches and my loafer-clad feet were killing me. Miserable as I was, all physical complaints dissolved when I stepped in his blood.

The sickly sweet, faintly metallic odor assailed my senses. A sense of wrongness wrapped icy fingers around my mind and squeezed. I jerked to a stop, glanced at the ground beneath my feet, registered the dark sticky substance with its nightmare stench, and raised my gaze.

Uncle Ben hung fifteen feet above my head. His limbs loose, head lolling, parachute draped across several branches.

Stumbling back, partly from shock, partly for a better look, I called his name. He didn't answer. Head cocked, I studied the gruesome pose. The parachute lines fell loosely around him, so they weren't holding him in the tree. What was?

Cautiously, I moved to the base of the big spruce, found a foothold and climbed. Before I came close enough to touch him, I had my answer. Uncle Ben's corpse was impaled on a broken branch. The parachute must have snagged on an upper limb and slammed him into the trunk—right onto a natural stake.

I gagged. Closed my eyes, breathed through my nose, and rested my forehead on the rough bark of the spruce. When my heartbeat regulated and my breathing eased, I opened my eyes and continued to climb. The smell was indescribable, something I'd never forget. He wasn't decaying yet, but all his muscles had relaxed in death; he'd soiled himself. Between that and the blood and my own sweat, my queasy stomach was anxious to toss its contents. I fought to maintain and won—barely.

At last I reached him, and after a moment's hesitation, pushed my fingers against the cooling flesh of his neck to check for a pulse. I needn't have bothered. He stared glassy-eyed into eternity. No spark of life lingered behind those eyes. I closed them with trembling fingers.

We'd had a lot of good times, this youngest of my father's three brothers and I. Uncle Ben and Evan and I were good friends as well as family. Evan and I had been born the same year and so had always been thrown together at family functions. Ben was only seven years our senior, so when the three of us all settled in Seattle, hanging out had been a natural occurrence.

Now Uncle Ben was dead, I was lost in the wilderness, and Evan was undoubtedly just as bad off. I only prayed he hadn't ended up like Ben.

I swiped tears from my eyes and reached to unfasten Ben's harness—I couldn't just leave him hanging in a tree, when the rustle of undergrowth and a kind of snuffling snort alerted me to the presence of a large beast.

I froze, my gaze skimming the bushes beneath the spruce. What emerged to check out the blood pool at the base nearly caused my bowels to empty.

An enormous bear approached the soiled ground. Nostrils flaring, he whuffled and snorted, vacuuming the ground for all its scents. Coppery brown fur covered a massive, muscular body, shoulders as high as a man's chest, sloping down to powerful hindquarters. With his head lowered to sniff the ground, the hump between shoulders and neck was easily distinguishable. As were the silver tips of the fur on ears and hump.

Grizzly. A full-grown male in the prime of life. The claws on the front feet that scratched the bloodied ground were six inches long and razor sharp.

My heart thudded to a stop; my lungs froze; my brain ceased to function. I didn't need them. I was dead already. My mind just hadn't caught up to reality.

Only twenty-eight years old. I'd never thought much about how I would die. Who does, when life is stretching out before you in a shining road of unexplored possibilities? But even in morose moments in the dead of night, I'd never considered being mauled and eaten by a grizzly in the middle of God-only-knew-what wilderness.

I swallowed what little spittle remained in my mouth and my autonomic functions flared to life. My heart pounded so hard I felt sure the bear would hear. Air wheezed in and out of my lungs with a bellowing roar. When he raised his head and stared into the spruce, I knew he'd found me. Knew he'd heard my heart, felt my terrified breath ruffle his fur.

I'd forgotten the dead body of my uncle, blood still seeping from his wounds. But the bear hadn't; his keen senses had arrowed right in on Ben. The bear wasn't interested in me; he was after the source of those intoxicating odors. He shuffled back and forth, eyes on the prize, considering how best to reach his goal. A moment later, he reared back to stand on those powerful hind legs.

The monster was fucking huge!

Blood drained from my extremities to my core. The edges of my vision darkened and my fingers cooled. Crap! Not the time or place to faint with fear. I ground my teeth together, dug my fingers into the bark of the tree, and dredged up every curse word I'd ever heard or imagined. Silently, I hurled every last one of them into the universe.

Ben was dead. I wasn't. Fate, God—whatever!—could just go take a flying leap. I had no intention of buying it in a bear's gullet in the middle of a fucking wilderness.

The grizzly lunged against the spruce, and the trunk shuddered beneath my grasp. I scrambled up, across Ben's body, and onto a sturdy branch above my deceased uncle's head. Wedging myself into the crotch of the tree, I braced for the next assault.

The grizzly pounded the trunk again, but Ben's body stayed put—and so did I.

The silver-tipped monster stretched high and swiped a front paw at Ben's boots, missing by inches. He couldn't reach Ben. Not quite. I couldn't climb down while he waited below. We were at an impasse.

Dropping back to all fours, the monster paced beneath the tree.

Could he climb?

Possibly. I knew black bears climbed trees with no difficulty, but I didn't think grizzlies were as dexterous. Trouble was, I wasn't certain. I racked my brain for a plan.

Back and forth, he paced beneath the spruce, huge paws turned slightly inward, head held low, swinging side to side. Every now and then he paused to rest on haunches and stare up at his goal. I could almost see him planning.

How smart were grizzlies?

While he padded or sat, my brain raced. Fragments of ideas surfaced only to be swatted away like the no-see-ums that had annoyed me earlier. Finally, my subconscious thrust up a thought and refused to allow me to discard it. I didn't like it. Didn't want to consider it. Didn't think I could carry it out when I did allow it to fully form. Instead, I huddled deeper into the crotch of the tree, leaned my head back against the trunk and stared into the sky.

Last night the most important thing on my plate had been getting to the airport on time to join Uncle Ben and Evan on this jaunt across the mountains to Coeur d'Alene for a family reunion. This morning I'd been shaken awake, had a parachute thrust into my arms, and had forced myself to jump out of a plane. Sometime around noon, I'd found my uncle's dead body, and now, as the sun slowly slid down the sky, I contemplated the unthinkable.

Would I be able to live with myself if I did it?

I sighed and closed my eyes. I probably wouldn't have to worry about it if I didn't—I probably wouldn't live.

The grizzly continued to pace and growl his dissatisfaction while I stewed.

Look at it the other way. If I were the one impaled in a tree—already dead meat, would I mind if Uncle Ben used my carcass to buy his freedom?

How could I mind? I'd be dead.

I reached down and stroked Ben's hair. "I'm sorry," I whispered, unshed tears choking my words, "but if this works, you'll have saved my life."

I climbed down a branch and reached for the buckles securing him to the chute. Working quickly I stripped the harness from his lifeless body. Now all that held him in the tree was that damn impaling branch.

I rested my fingers on his cold cheek. "If this doesn't work, we'll both be on the menu," I said with a grim smile. "I hope I'll live to miss you, buddy."

Bracing myself against the trunk, I levered his body off the stake. It crashed to the ground, landing with a sickening thunk. The grizzly was on it before I could so much as look away.

Steeling myself to ignore the sounds of ripping fabric and worse, I climbed down the spruce, landing in a crouch on the far side from the feasting bear. I straightened. So did he, his jowls dripping gore. We stared into each other's eyes as I backed slowly away. I kept my eyes on his. I didn't want to see, didn't want to think about, what lay at his feet. What dripped from his jowls was bad enough.

After a moment he dipped his head and returned to his meal. I'd been dismissed. I turned and strode purposefully away, my thoughts bleak, my heart barren.

With effort I followed my earlier path back to the stream where I'd stowed the parachute. I yanked it from beneath its protective bush, bundled it into a makeshift pack and tied it to my back. I'd need its warmth when the sun went down. Breaking off a dead limb from a nearby tree—I avoided thinking what its fellow had cost me, I fashioned myself a walking stick and trudged along the bank of the stream. I'd follow it downstream until I either found my way out of this hellish forest or joined Ben in some carnivore's gut.

But no way was I going to sit down, bury my head in my hands, and wait for Death—who now wore the face of a silver-tipped grizzly—to find me. By God, he'd have to hunt me down and wrestle me into oblivion.

CHAPTER THREE

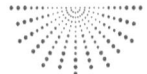

*T*hree days later, I emerged from the wilderness onto a paved road. Weak with hunger and dehydration, I sank to my knees, flattened my hands on the warm, hard surface of that symbol of civilization and wept. A passing motorist stopped, and while he kept his distance, used his cell phone to call the authorities.

By the time the sheriff and emergency medical team arrived, the guy had loosened up enough to toss a bottle of water to me. I didn't blame him for being cautious. I looked like I'd walked out of hell.

In a very real way, I had.

The grizzly had evidently found Ben a sufficient meal. He hadn't hunted me further. After facing him, no other denizen of the forest had worried me. I'd kept my wits about me, slept in trees, and put one foot in front of the other until the stream led me to the road. It hadn't been easy, but, hell, I was alive. Ben wasn't. Was I going to let hunger and a raging case of giardia defeat me? Absolutely not.

Evan survived as well. My cousin didn't have to face down a grizzly or sacrifice our uncle's remains, but his experience was no walk in the park either. Though we're both back in Seattle, we're neither one the same.

I had the skin of civilization scraped off me in that wilderness, and discovered a spine beneath. I'll never say I'm grateful for the experience, but I know myself better now. Know my essence, and that I can handle whatever comes my way.

I'll never forget Uncle Ben and all the good times we had together. Neither will I forget the way he died—nor that he saved me when silver-tipped death stalked beneath that tall spruce.

PART XVII
ICE STORM

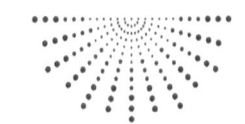

DEBBIE MUMFORD

BESTSELLING AUTHOR OF *SORCHA'S HEART*

ICE STORM

SPUN YARNS
A Short Story

CHAPTER ONE

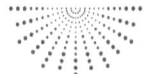

*K*ara slid across the ice on her butt. Not the most graceful mode of transport, but it got the job done. She slowed her forward progress by grabbing a handful of twigs stretched conveniently across the sidewalk from an overgrown rhododendron bush. Precarious anchor in hand, she inched her way onto her knees and across to the relative security of the sheltered concrete step in front of Lawrence's front door. She collapsed against the front door after reaching the safety of the porous step, one of the few surfaces not covered with an inch thick casing of ice. Every nerve ending in her body seemed to be firing at once. A trickle of sweat inched down her neck, while her arms and legs tingled from the exertion of maintaining balance on the skating rink that covered the City of Portland.

After a few deep breaths, she pushed herself to standing and dug the key out of her right front jeans pocket. Though an unnatural layer of ice covered her world, Kara was lightly dressed. Portlanders typically didn't own the down parkas and felt-lined boots that Kara had grown up with in harsh Montana winters. Her feet were clad in tennis shoes —she'd hoped the rubber soles would give her better traction than her typical leather-soled footwear—denim jeans clung to her long legs, and her torso sported a flannel shirt covered by a rain slicker. She hadn't managed to unearth her seldom-needed gloves, so her numb fingers trembled as she attempted to insert the key into the dead-bolt of Lawrence's mahogany front door. Who would've guessed the two-block walk between her apartment and his townhouse would be such an ordeal?

At last the key connected with the tumblers and Kara stepped inside, out of the unheard of cold and into the anticipated warmth of her invalid uncle's home. Warmth. Kara closed the door behind her and exhaled in relief. Even in the gloom of the unlit entry, she saw the cold gray cloud her exhalation produced. She frowned and looked around, as if the empty hallway could answer her unspoken question. The air was as cold, if not colder, in here than it was outside in the weak winter sun. Uncle Lawrence's electricity must be out.

Kara raced up the stairs to her uncle's bedroom.

"Lawrence! Uncle Lawrence? Where are you?" She ran down the upstairs hall, peeking around corners into obviously deserted rooms. She turned and sprinted back to the staircase. She leaned over the balcony railing and called in her loudest head-cheerleader tones, "Uncle Lawrence, where are you?"

Standing perfectly still, she concentrated all her energy on listening. All she heard was the rush of blood through her own veins. The silent house assaulted her psyche; a crypt interred in an ice-bound cemetery.

Kara fled down the stairs and searched the ground floor. Uncle Lawrence had to be here. An invalid, too weak even to maneuver through the halls of his own home, his live-in assistant, Gary, had put Lawrence to bed last night before crossing the Columbia River to visit his pregnant sister in Vancouver, Washington. The storm hit with sudden ferocity trapping Gary on the wrong side of the river. Both cities ground to a halt, motionless under a crushing weight of ice.

Galvanized by Gary's panic-stricken phone call, Kara had assured him she would spend the day with Uncle Lawrence. She could handle everything. Lawrence would be fine until the storm's grip lessened and Gary could return home safely.

Now she wasn't so sure. Where was Lawrence? How long had the power been out?

At last Kara's hurried search led to the large, oak appointed kitchen. A cursory glance told her this room was deserted as well, though Uncle Lawrence's walker stood abandoned near the stove, adding another layer of mystery to her search. Then she noticed that the basement door—hidden behind the massive refrigerator/freezer and opposite the ice-covered back door—stood ajar. A sliver of darker black showed between the white casement and the sunny yellow of the door's painted surface. Her heart stuttered. Lawrence couldn't be in the basement! He would've been hard pressed to make it to the kitchen. Descending the basement stairs would have completely depleted his resources.

She grabbed the flashlight from its place beside the refrigerator and dashed to the slightly open door. Pulling it wide, she swung the beam of light down the steps and screamed.

"Lawrence! Oh my God! Uncle Lawrence!"

CHAPTER TWO

*H*er uncle lay crumpled at the foot of the rickety stairs in a landslide of canned goods ... undoubtedly pulled from the shelves lining the steps when he attempted to break his fall.

Kara hurried to him, pulse hammering in her temple. When she reached his body, she hesitated, and then placed trembling fingers beneath his chin. Though his skin was cool to the touch, a strong, steady pulse met her questing fingers. She sank onto the floor beside him and tried to think what to do next.

9-1-1. That was it, she had to call 9-1-1. Decision made, Kara jumped to her feet and ran harried fingers through her slicker pocket. Cell phone in hand she made her way up two flights of stairs in search of blankets while the phone made the crucial connection.

"9-1-1. What is the nature of your emergency?" queried a calm, unruffled female voice.

"My uncle fell down a flight of stairs. He's unconscious. I don't know what to do," Kara said. Her voice sounded strange to her ears. It quivered and quavered, the pitch unusually high. She prayed the woman on the other end understood.

"Where are you now, miss?"

"I'm in the upstairs hallway, looking for blankets."

"Where, exactly, is your uncle?"

"At the bottom of the basement stairs. The power is off. He must've fallen trying to get to the breaker switches."

"Get back to him as soon as you can. I'm going to talk you through a cursory examination."

While Kara gathered blankets and hurried back to Lawrence's side, the emergency services operator questioned her about Lawrence's address, phone number and determined that Kara was not a resident of the house.

"I'm back. He's still unconscious. He looks awfully uncomfortable. Should I straighten his neck and arms?"

"No!" The operator's voice lost several degrees of cool. When she spoke again, she sounded calm and professional once more. "Without touching him," she said, "tell me exactly what you see."

Kara took a deep breath and began. "He's lying sprawled across the two bottom steps. His head is on his left arm, which is on the basement floor. His chest is also on the floor. His right arm is folded under his chest. His legs are on the steps, with most of his weight on the left side of his body." She paused for another deep breath. "Does that help? Oh, and there are canned goods scattered all around. Some of them are on his back and legs."

"Canned goods?"

"Yes, the walls of the basement stairs are lined with shelves. Uncle Lawrence uses them as a pantry. I think he must have tried to break his fall by grabbing for the shelves." Kara shuddered at the thought of her frail uncle being caught in that shower of canned soups and vegetables.

"All right. Here's what I want you to do ..."

"Is the ambulance on the way?" Kara interrupted.

"I'm sorry, Miss Davis. Our emergency services are spread very thin because of the ice storm. Half our drivers are stuck at home, and many of the others have been involved in accidents themselves. I can't guarantee you physical assistance." She paused to let that information sink in. When Kara didn't respond, she said, "Miss Davis, are you there?"

"Yes. Yes, of course, I'm here. What should I do?"

"First, cover your uncle with the blankets you brought down. Then check the breakers and see if you can restore power. My map shows that you're in a fringe area of the outage. You may have power available."

"Right." Kara heaped the blankets on her uncle's inert form, grabbed the flashlight and searched the basement walls for breaker switches.

"I found the box, but the switches aren't labeled."

"That's fine. Just flip them all. Since the power is out, you won't cause any damage. When you're finished, all of the switches should be laying to the left."

Kara methodically flipped each switch in turn. Most she flipped twice ... left to right to left again. A couple just went from right to left. It didn't seem to matter; nothing happened.

"Anything?" asked the voice in her ear.

"No. I've flipped every last one of them, and nothing happened."

"Okay," the operator paused; Kara could almost hear the wheels turning as the woman weighed her options. "Listen, this is highly irregular, but it's an unusual situation."

Kara's pulse jumped. "What? I'll do anything to help Uncle Lawrence!"

"Yes, I can tell," the operator paused again. "Hold the line, Miss Davis. I have a friend who's an EMT. He just lives a few blocks from you. I'm going to call him on another line and see if he's willing to try to get to you. He'll be able to assess the situation and assist you in moving your uncle, if that's advisable."

Kara's head felt suddenly light; she sat down on the step beside Lawrence's body. "Oh, that would be a God-send," she breathed.

Though she knew only a minute or two passed, it felt like hours before Kara heard the operator's voice again. She spent the time patting Lawrence's leg and praying for God to send help.

"Miss Davis?"

"Yes?" Kara's voice held a spike of fear.

"He's coming. He said it may take him a few minutes, but he'll be there soon. His name is Brad Keswick. He's tall, about 30, blond and blue-eyed. Ask for ID, but don't be afraid to let him in."

"Oh, thank you! You don't know what this means to me!"

Kara could feel the woman smiling. "Yes, Miss Davis, I do." She paused a moment, then added, "I'm going to have to sign off now, Miss Davis. We're overloaded with calls. If Brad isn't there in 30 minutes, call back and ask for Amy."

"I understand. Thank you, Amy."

"You're going to be just fine, Miss Davis. Good luck."

Kara heard the click and felt suddenly alone. She checked Uncle Lawrence's pulse again. Still steady. Unsure what to do while she waited, Kara climbed the steps out of the basement and went in search of more blankets. On her way through the kitchen, she noticed the stove. Gas, not electric. She wondered if it would be safe to use during a power outage. She hesitated, but decided to wait until Brad Keswick arrived. The EMT would be better versed in emergency preparedness than she was.

CHAPTER THREE

ara had amassed a small mountain of pillows, blankets and towels in front of the fireplace in the living room when a knock sounded at the door. She pulled her rain slicker tighter around her shivering body and approached the front door. Cautiously, she peered through the peep-hole. A tall, well-built man stood on the front step. He had a navy blue knit cap pulled over his hair, but she saw yellow tips feathering out from under. She opened the door a crack.

"Yes?"

"Miss Davis? I'm Brad Keswick."

As he spoke, the man pulled an ID badge out of his pocket and held it out for Kara's inspection. She noticed the singularly bad picture of the man's square-jawed, straight-nosed face, but focused on the name printed below the EMT logo. Yep, this was Brad Keswick, all right.

"Thank you for coming so quickly, Mr. Keswick. I was terrified when Amy said she couldn't send an ambulance."

Brad nodded. "I understand. It's hard to stand by helplessly when a loved one is injured." He stepped inside the front door and removed his gloves. "Let's see if he can be moved safely." He glanced around the dim room and nodded at the pile of bedding. "Then we'll see what we can do about getting you some heat and light."

Kara led the way to the basement stairs. Brad ran lightly down to Uncle Lawrence and began running careful hands over his body. Without looking up, he said, "Can you think of anything we can use for a back-board?"

"A back-board?" For a moment, Kara's brain froze over the unexpected question. Myriad episodes of TV emergency shows flooded her memory. "Yes, of course, I'll see what I can find."

She stood in the middle of the kitchen floor and scanned the room. Nothing in here to be pressed into service. She thought of the linen closet upstairs. Plenty of sheets to improvise a sling. She'd already thought of using them to drag her uncle up the stairs, but that wouldn't stabilize his back. A combination of linens and cookie sheets taped to his spine with duct tape? She shivered at the grotesque image the thought conjured.

She ran up the stairs to examine her uncle's bedroom. She was racing down the hall when she noticed the door to the laundry room. Quickly changing course, she pushed the door open and examined the room. Gary had been ironing shirts. There were several hanging on a rack near the ironing board. Wait a minute! The ironing board ... it wasn't as lightweight as a stretcher, but it was rigid, and when folded, the legs could be used as handles. She moved the iron to a table, collapsed the board and returned to the kitchen.

"Will this ironing board do?" she asked Brad as she reached the top of the basement stairs. The scene had changed. Brad had removed the blankets from Uncle Lawrence and straightened his body. He now lay flat on the floor, arms at his sides, head in line with his spine.

Brad glanced up at her. "That's a great idea, bring it down." He stopped to wipe his brow, then met her on the steps and took the board from her.

"I don't think anything's broken," he said, a smile lighting his features. "Once we get him warm and comfortable, I think he'll come around. His worst injury seems to be a bump on the temple, probably from that can of tomatoes." He nodded toward a large can which lay, dented, near Uncle Lawrence's head.

Relief washed over her and Kara sat down hard on the bottom step. "Oh, thank heaven!" Tears welled in her eyes, and she blinked rapidly, determined not to cry.

The EMT knelt in front of her and placed gentle fingers on her left wrist. After a moment, he said, "You're doing fine, Miss Davis."

"Kara. My name is Kara, and of course I'm doing fine." She wiped her eyes with trembling fingers.

"Nice to meet you, Kara. I'm Brad." He took her right hand in his and gave it a firm shake. "Now, let's get your uncle out of this basement."

The trip up the basement stairs with Uncle Lawrence strapped to the ironing board wasn't as bad as Kara had imagined. Brad took the lion's share of the weight, using Kara mainly for guidance and stabilization. Once they reached the kitchen, he co-opted Uncle Lawrence's discarded walker for wheels and Kara's job was reduced to making sure her end of the ironing board stayed balanced on the walker's handles. When they reached the living room, she helped Brad lift the board off its transport and onto the floor in front of the fireplace.

"All right," he said, "first things first. Does your uncle keep any firewood, or is this just for decoration?"

"There's kindling and small sections of pine just outside the kitchen door."

"Great, you get him covered and wrap yourself in a blanket while I get a fire started."

"Okay." She hesitated, then asked, "Do you know if it's safe to use a gas stove when the electricity is off?"

Brad turned to look at her. "It's a gas stove?"

She nodded. "I thought about it earlier, but was afraid to try it without asking someone." She felt her cheeks grow warm with the admission. "Uncle Lawrence was in bad enough shape without me blowing us both up."

Brad smiled. "The automatic ignition won't work, so you'll need a match, but it should be usable."

"Fabulous," she sighed. "I'll fix a pot of tea and some soup. That'll warm us up." She glanced back at her uncle. "Do you think he'll wake up, or will it take a hospital to revive him?"

Brad had turned to go, but he stopped and looked back at her. "I don't know. I don't think he has any broken bones, but I'm guessing he's got a concussion."

Kara was startled. "A concussion? From that can of tomatoes?"

"Yes." He moved back to her side and took her hand. "Try not to worry. We're doing everything possible under the circumstances." He pulled her gently toward the door. "Come on. The best thing we can do for him now is warm up this room and have some warm broth ready for him when he wakes up."

Kara shivered reflexively, nodded and followed him quietly to the kitchen.

Before long, the living room was well on its way to becoming an oasis of warmth in the cold house. Brad built up a roaring fire and carried in a stack of wood to keep it going. Kara drew the heavy, brocade drapes across Lawrence's wide front windows and pulled pocket doors closed across the entrance to the room.

"Nice." Brad nodded his approval as his cell phone rang. Checking the caller ID, he slid one of the doors aside and stepped through. "I need to take this."

Kara nodded and moved to her uncle's side. The elderly man hadn't wakened yet, but his pulse remained steady and his skin had warmed. She felt more confident of his recovery now that he'd been rescued from the basement.

Brad returned, glanced around the room in approval, and turned to Kara. "I'm going to have to leave you now," he said. "That was Amy on the phone and there's another family in need of assistance a few blocks away."

"I understand completely," Kara said, moving to stand beside him. "I can't thank you enough for your help."

"Glad I was in the neighborhood," he said, "and glad you were too. Your uncle would've been in bad shape if you hadn't braved the ice to come and check on him."

Kara's cheeks warmed. "Oh," she murmured, "that was nothing. It's just what families do."

He smiled a little sadly. "Not enough of them." As they walked to the front door, he continued, "Just keep him warm until he wakes, then help him get as much liquid down as possible. You'll want to call his primary care physician as soon as the weather stabilizes. He'll let you know what else needs to be done."

"I understand. We'll be fine now. Thank you for your help, Brad, and be careful getting to your next site."

He pulled on his gloves, opened the door and stepped onto the small landing. "Good luck to you, Miss Davis. Your uncle is a lucky man."

Kara waved and watched Brad Keswick disappear down the ice covered street. When he rounded the corner out of sight, she closed the door and returned to Uncle Lawrence. They were both incredibly lucky. She didn't like to think what might have happened if the emergency services operator hadn't been able to connect her with an off-duty EMT who just happened to live in the neighborhood.

She brushed the hair from Uncle Lawrence's forehead and smiled as his eyes blinked open. Yes. They were very lucky indeed.

PART XVIII
OPENING HER EYES

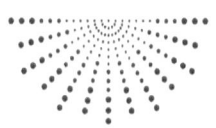

DEBBIE MUMFORD
BESTSELLING AUTHOR OF *SORCHA'S HEART*

*Opening
Her Eyes*
SPUN YARNS
A Sweet Romance Story

CHAPTER ONE

*E*mily Jane Williams chewed the nail of her right index finger and stared at her computer monitor. The glowing words mocked her with their blatant invitation to experience life beyond her small Rocky Mountain town.

<Crusader says: Join me in Shanghai. I'll make it my mission to show you a good time.>

The chat room friend she'd been fantasizing about for the past six months wanted to meet her... in a place as far from her normal life as she could imagine. Adventure. Desire. Danger. Those words belonged in novels, not in Emily's staid, placid life. A shiver tingled down her spine and she squirmed in her well-worn secretarial chair.

She ran trembling hands through her long brown hair and licked lips gone suddenly dry. This called for a witty remark, something that downplayed the rapid staccato of her heart. Unfortunately, her unsteady fingers moved with a life of their own.

<Sleeping Beauty says: Why now? Why Shanghai?>

Emily had lived her entire twenty-eight years in one place: Aspen Springs, Colorado. Her big adventure had been to spend her four years of college on the Front Range, at the University of Colorado's Boulder campus. She'd never been out of her home state, let alone out of the country. The thought of going to Shanghai, even to meet a man as fascinating as Crusader, filled her with terror.

<Crusader says: Why not now? A knight must meet his Lady, the one he's destined to adore.>

A frisson of delight spread through her core. Crusader always knew the right button to push. Knights and ladies, castles and dragons, these were images that made Emily's soul sing. Sometimes she felt like she'd known this mysterious man forever.

Mysterious. That was the operative word. She frowned and forced herself to think, to remember that she knew nothing about this man. Unwillingness to leave the United States aside, she had no business making plans to meet an Internet stranger. For all she knew, he could be a psychotic killer.

Or the love she'd waited for her whole life…

<Crusader says: What do you say? Are you up for an adventure?>

Her spine stiffened at the implied challenge.

<Sleeping Beauty says: Shanghai? No way! If I agree to meet you, it'll have to be here, on my home turf.>

That would put an end to his nonsense. Any man adventurous enough to choose Shanghai as a rendezvous would be totally uninterested in her little world.

<Crusader says: Name the time and the place. I'll be there.>

Emily's jaw dropped. She gasped like one of the brown trout she'd pulled from the clear, mountain stream last Saturday. He'd come *here*? He couldn't come here! What would a man like Crusader want in Aspen Springs?

The answer welled up like spring water, filling her with crystal coolness. Only one thing: her.

CHAPTER TWO

*E*very Monday morning since they'd returned to Aspen Springs from their respective colleges, Emily and Daria Roberts had met for breakfast at Katy's Kountry Kitchen. The ritual kept them close. Today, Emily wondered if that was a good thing.

"You told him where you live?" Daria stared at Emily, eyes wide, fingers drumming. "Have you lost your mind?"

Sunlight streamed across the freshly scrubbed oak of their favorite table as Emily considered her friend's words. Maybe she *had* stepped over the threshold of sanity. The diner's familiar scents of sizzling bacon, frying eggs, and black coffee clashed dangerously with the thought of an unknown man traveling from who knew where to meet her.

"It's not like I gave him my address. I just told him about Aspen Springs." Daria's expression told Emily that wasn't much of an improvement. "For heaven's sake, I'm not an idiot. I'll be careful."

"Not an idiot? Well, you're sure doing a great imitation of one." Daria huffed, clasped her hands to still their drumming, and attempted a smile. "At least tell me when and where you're meeting him. That way Tim and I can wander by, make sure you're safe."

Emily's rebellious side wanted to clam up, but her instinct for self-preservation won. "Sure. He's meeting me at O'Connor's at 7:00 Saturday night." She looked down at the sturdy ceramic coffee mug clasped in white-knuckled fingers. "But you don't have to worry. He won't be there."

Daria reached across the table, placed her hand on Emily's arm and squeezed. "Maybe not, but we will."

Emily heaved a sigh of relief and glanced gratefully into Daria's dark blue eyes. They were such opposites. Blue-eyed, blonde Daria, with her luscious curves and Germanic forthrightness, and dark-eyed, dark-haired Emily, slim and athletic, with a quiet, though stubborn personality. Maybe they'd become friends in preschool because of those differences. Emily didn't much care; Daria's steadfast support grounded her world.

With a wry grin, Emily changed the subject. "What's Chris up to these days?" Daria's little brother had been the bane of their existence growing up, but she hadn't seen the little monster since he earned his place as commanding officer of a SEAL team based out of California. Hard to imagine the perennial pest in a position of leadership.

Daria grimaced. "His career choice scares the blazes out of Mom, but he's doing fine. We never know where he is, of course, but he calls frequently, so we know he's okay."

"I can't imagine," Emily said, her voice thick with sarcasm. "Somebody actually gave him a gun. Heaven help us!"

Daria's grimace turned into a mischievous grin. "Right? He's a born trouble-maker. Remember that time he cut a notch out of your hair?"

Emily rolled her eyes. "As if I could forget! Mom had to cut my hair in a bob. I hated it."

"And his absolute obsession with that chocolate cake from Larson's Bakery?" Daria asked, her eyes glazing with the memory. "You know, the one with double fudge frosting."

Emily nodded, her expression softening. "It's a wonder he wasn't as round as he was tall. He bought that cake nearly every weekend once he started earning money mowing lawns in summer and shoveling snow in winter."

"Good times," Daria said, grabbing Emily's hand and interlocking their fingers. "And good friends. We're so lucky, Em!"

CHAPTER THREE

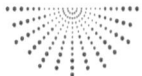

*D*aria pegged it, Emily thought. *My mind isn't just lost; it's fried.*

Saturday morning found her sitting in a beautician's chair having her hair styled and highlighted. She hadn't allowed anyone to touch her hair in years. But here she was, submitting her dignity and total lack of style to the hands of a teen-age girl with spiky purple hair.

"There you go, Ms. Williams." The girl smiled at Emily's reflection in the mirror. "You're now the hottest county planner in the state."

Emily's cheeks flamed a scorching red.

"Thanks," she said, scrutinizing her new do. The shoulder length brown hair swung freely, tips curling under in tidy conformity. Fresh, golden highlights hinted at days spent lazing in the sun.

"I feel like a new woman. You don't give advice on clothes, do you?"

The girl giggled, reminding Emily of the difference in their ages. "My style wouldn't suit you, but if you're serious, you should ask for Jean over at *Tres Chic*. She's my cousin, and she knows all the latest trends."

Emily thanked the girl, paid and walked out into the bright spring sunshine. The air was so clear she felt like she could see each individual needle on the pines covering the mountain slopes. And the scent! High country wildflowers bloomed in profusion in the meadows surrounding the town. What a glorious time to be alive.

Her heart sang, and then stuttered as thoughts of meeting Crusader clashed with her ebullient mood. She had just over eight hours before their appointed meeting, and she didn't even own a decent cocktail dress.

Ignoring the mountains' allure, she straightened her shoulders and headed to *Tres Chic*, hoping the spiky-haired teen-ager had given her good advice.

For the next couple of hours, Emily allowed Jean to supervise her wardrobe choices. The young hairdresser was right; Jean had superb taste.

Emily had been hoarding her salary for years, so money wasn't an issue, but she still felt her heart stutter when she noticed the price tags.

Quick to recognize sticker shock, Jean said, "Don't worry, we don't have to empty your closet and start over today." She led Emily to a dressing room, picking out a few classic pieces as she went. "We'll set you up with some basic coordinates. You can add to it a piece at a time."

With a sigh of relief, Emily allowed herself to be prodded down the path to a more stylish wardrobe.

CHAPTER FOUR

*S*aturday night found Emily seated at a table near O'Connor's dance floor. The establishment was an interesting mix of restaurant, bar, and dance club. Small enough to survive in a little mountain town, but big enough to give its patrons room to breathe on a Saturday night.

True to her word, Daria sat at the bar with her husband, Tim. Her fingers tapped a swizzle stick in rapid syncopation as she scrutinized her friend.

Emily sympathized with Daria's agitation – a combination of nerves about the coming rendezvous and shock over Emily's appearance. Emily hadn't looked this good since college, and even then she'd lacked the sense of style Jean had so carefully crafted.

So, here she sat, a beautifully groomed young woman resisting the urge to bite her newly manicured nails. Crusader had better show.

She heard a low whistle and turned to find Chris Peterson standing beside her chair. Daria's younger brother shared her Germanic solidity, but his eyes were a deep chocolate brown, his complexion was ruddier than his sister's, and his hair skimmed the border between blond and brown, seeming to shift from chestnut to golden. He had just arrived home from a tour of duty overseas and looked fit and tanned.

"Wow," he said, taking in every detail of her flirty red dress and freshly styled hair. "You're a knock-out, Emily."

She looked past him to the door, and then met his eyes. "Thanks, and welcome home, but... I'm meeting someone." Emily didn't want to be rude, but she didn't want him ruining her chances with Crusader, either.

"I know you are, and I must say, he's a lucky man." Chris pulled out the chair opposite her and deposited his lanky six-foot frame on it.

"Chris! Get up!" Irritation heated her cheeks. "I can't believe Daria told you about this, but I *am* expecting someone – and I don't want you butting in."

He smiled; a maddening, slow smile. The kind that had driven her nuts when they were kids. When Chris smiled like that, he was up to something. "Daria didn't tell me. *Crusader* did."

Her pulse skipped a beat. She focused on Chris, everything else blurring into the background. She hadn't told Daria Crusader's screen name.

"Where did you hear that name?" she asked, aware of every heartbeat, every breath that flowed through her lungs.

Chris reached across the table and took her hand. "Wake up, Sleeping Beauty. It's time to see the world as it really is." He stroked her fingers with his thumb. "*I'm* Crusader."

She snatched her hand away, jumped to her feet and turned to leave. Before she'd gone two steps, Chris blocked her path.

"Great idea," he said. "Let's dance."

He used Emily's own momentum to maneuver her onto the dance floor. With his strong arms encircling her, she had to force herself to think. Her body wanted to melt into his embrace.

She pushed back and peered up into his handsome face. "What are you up to, Chris? Why the big mystery? If you wanted a date, why didn't you just ask?"

He threw back his head and laughed until other patrons stared. When the fit passed, he dropped his head close to hers and said, "Emily, you're amazing, but you're totally clueless. I've been asking you out since high school. You've just never taken me seriously."

He tightened his embrace and rubbed his chin across her newly golden hair. "I had some leave coming; I wanted to see you. Crusader seemed like a good tactic." He shrugged and added, "Daria gave me your screen name."

For once in her life, Emily was speechless. She delighted in the thrill of her old nemesis's warm embrace and marveled that she'd been looking right through him her whole life. Daria's little brother had grown into quite a man.

"What would you have done if I'd agreed to meet you in Shanghai?"

"I'd have hopped a military transport," he said, his blue eyes sparkling, "but I knew you wouldn't." He guided her effortlessly across the dance floor. "I wanted Crusader to shake you up. Make you look at yourself and see what I see – a fascinating, sexy woman."

Emily blushed and lowered her gaze.

"But mostly, I wanted—"

She never found out what he'd wanted, because Daria chose that moment to tap Chris' shoulder and throw her arms around her brother's neck. "Chris! Why didn't you tell me you were coming to O'Connor's tonight?"

Emily didn't wait to hear his answer. She grabbed the opportunity to retreat, despite his best efforts to catch and hold her hand. Unsure what to think about the evening's unexpected turn of events, she grabbed her purse and practically ran home.

CHAPTER FIVE

*A*fter spending Sunday holed up in her home like a prospector protecting his claim, Emily awoke Monday morning with a fresh resolve. No more hiding in the house for this woman. She glared at her reflection in the bathroom mirror as she scrubbed her teeth.

"I've got no reason to be embarrassed," she stated, pointing her toothbrush at her foamy-mouthed reflection. She spit, rinsed, and continued her pep talk, "I didn't hide my identity and try to pull a fast one on anybody. Chris is the one who should be ashamed. We're too old to be playing stupid pranks."

She dressed quickly in her jogging outfit and pulled her hair into a pony tail while reminding herself again that Chris' only objective had been to embarrass her. He'd felt like a bit of mischief and had reverted to his childhood target of choice… his big sister's best friend, Emily.

Stepping onto the tiny front porch of her rustic-looking two-bedroom log cabin, she paused to lock the door and stow her key in the specially designed pouch in the laces of her left running shoe. She was still kneeling when she felt his presence. Straightening, she found herself looking up at Chris.

And damn, did he look good. Navy blue sweat pants, white tee pulled taut across a muscular chest and an unzipped hooded navy sweatshirt – the man fairly oozed testosterone. She raised her eyes to meet his gaze and concentrated on producing an icy glare. Not an easy task when her blood sizzled like liquid fire.

"I'm leaving for my morning jog, Chris." Her words dripped sleet. She congratulated herself on her poise in the face of raging attraction. "I don't have time for you."

"Fine," he said. "I'm not stopping you."

She turned away from him and began to run in easy rhythmic strides. He loped along beside her. She ignored him, reached the corner and turned toward the mountain trail that ran behind her subdivision. Chris turned with her.

"What do you think you're doing?" she asked, continuing to edge her words with ice.

"Jogging," he said. "I run five to ten miles every day. This is as good a trail as any."

"Choose another one," she snapped. "I don't want your company."

"It's a public trail, and I didn't start this conversation," he pointed out. "If you don't want to talk, don't."

Emily opened her mouth to reply, but changed her mind and clamped her lips together. Fine. If he wanted to play games, she was his match any day.

She stopped beside the bench at the base of the trail and ran through her usual set of stretches. He ran through his own routine beside her. She tried to keep her attention on the scenery, but her eyes betrayed her, stealing sideways peeks at the healthy male form striking poses beside her. Okay, so he wasn't actually posing, but those rippling muscle groups made a fine display. Daria's little brother made exceptional eye-candy.

Stop it, she told herself. *You're not interested in anything about this man.*

A self-satisfied smirk tugged at her lips as she ran lightly down the dirt trail. *Man? Yeah, right. This is Chris, remember? The pest who spied on you and Daria and followed you around like a stray dog; the insect who cut a notch out of your hair in fourth grade; the idiot who interrupted your first real make-out session with David Lang. This isn't a man; this is Chris... the closest thing you'll ever have to a brother. Thinking of him as eye-candy is, well, it's incestuous! Gross. Get a grip.*

Her resolve strengthened, Emily picked up the pace despite the path's increasing slope. She ran this trail daily. Her body knew every twist, every stray root and stone. Her breathing regulated and her brain kicked into its automatic pilot phase, leaving her free to contemplate the beauty of the mountain's early morning haze.

Chris loped along beside her when the path widened, dropped back where it narrowed. She felt his eyes on her derriere and stomped on the soaring elation that her butt was firm and perfectly packed into her spandex tights. He was vermin, not a man she wanted to entice.

She reached the high meadow where she always slowed to a walk, and Chris flew past her. Resolutely, she kept her eyes on the spring wild-flowers filling the meadow with riotous color. This walking portion of her morning routine gave her heart and other muscles a bit of a rest before she started the knee-pounding descent back into her ordinary world.

Emily loved this mountain. In point of fact, she loved the entire Rocky Mountain Range, though she'd only seen sections of its glory – the parts within her home state. She'd climbed all of Colorado's 'fourteen-ers' with her dad. They'd started with Long's Peak at the south end of Rocky Mountain National Park when she'd been fourteen. Dad thought it an auspicious start to her climbing career. She still found climbing fourteen-thousand foot peaks an exhilarating experience, but it wasn't one she could have on a regular basis. However, she jogged this trail daily, and hiked other nearby trails as often as she could. The season was just beginning, and she looked forward to revisiting all her favorite sites this spring and summer.

She picked up her pace and headed for home, congratulating herself on Chris' conspicuous absence. She'd done it. She'd outlasted the irritating man. The path turned around a thick stand of budding aspens and she caught sight of his navy blue sweats. Her pace faltered. Maybe she should walk the rest of the way down, avoid contact.

Hell, no. She wouldn't give him the satisfaction. Besides, if she changed her pace that much, it would throw her off schedule for the rest of the morning. She straightened her shoulders and resumed her normal rhythm.

Chris seemed to be waiting for her to catch up. He glanced back with a grin and then resumed his own long-legged stride.

Emily was left with an excellent view of his perfectly toned butt and legs. She groaned and thanked heaven that the mornings remained too cool for shorts; sweats showed her more than enough. She tried to distract herself with the scenery, but thick trees and undergrowth edged this part of the path. Her eyes kept moving forward and latching hungrily on Chris' very appealing anatomy.

CHAPTER SIX

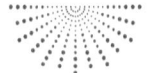

*C*hris jogged down the trail toward Emily's cabin. He'd thoroughly enjoyed the view on his way up. If anything, Emily was more attractive now than she'd been in high school. She'd ripened into a sexy, well-toned woman. According to Daria, Em still enjoyed hiking, backpacking, and fly fishing. All the things he was looking forward to doing when he retired from the SEALS and returned to civilian life.

He'd set his sights on Emily while they were still kids, and despite all the places his military career had taken him, he'd never found anyone to break that single-minded focus. Emily Jane Williams was the woman for him.

Now all he had to do was convince her that while he'd always be her best friend's brother, he was also an adult man with a mind of his own... and that he was singularly devoted to her.

Saturday night's mission hadn't gone exactly as planned, but he was a SEAL. He knew how to improvise in the field. He'd been disappointed by the delay caused by her determination not to leave her cabin yesterday, but he'd known she'd have to emerge this morning. She had a job, and she had a routine. And he was well aware of her habits, having casually turned his conversations with Daria to Emily on a fairly regular basis.

Daria was an excellent source of intel. Not that she'd known she was acting as such. She'd been genuinely surprised to see Chris dancing with Emily at O'Connor's on Saturday night. But she was clued-in now, and almost giddy with the prospect of claiming Emily as an honest-to-goodness sister. He'd have to remind is truthful-to-the-core, straightforward sister not to overplay her hand.

After all, Chris had to win Emily on his own merits, not just because she adored his family.

Chris frowned as he dodged a tree root. Em had been frosty this morning. She'd probably convinced herself that he was pulling a prank on her, making her the butt of a joke. A slow smile spread across his face. Hopefully his own well-muscled butt was gaining her attention at the moment. He'd certainly enjoyed watching hers earlier.

Yanking his thoughts away from her shapely posterior, he considered how to go about convincing her that his intentions were true, that he was honestly attracted to her... and had been since he was old enough to understand such things.

He reached the bench where they'd done their warm up stretches and turned to watch her jog her last few steps. He'd always thought the cliché that "women didn't sweat, they glowed" was malarkey, but, wow! Emily proved the sentiment. Even sweaty from a trail run, she was a knock-out.

He dropped into his cool down routine in order to stop himself from staring. She was skittish enough without him drooling on her running shoes.

Well, he'd done what he could for the morning. Now the ball was in Daria's court. He just hoped his sister's innate honesty wouldn't cause her to fumble the play.

CHAPTER SEVEN

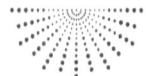

*E*mily joined Daria at their favorite table at Katy's, relieved that Chris hadn't followed her to breakfast. The man had dogged her steps all the way back to her front door. Fortunately, he'd been gone when she emerged again after showering and changing into her work clothes – a slim black pencil skirt, white silk blouse, and a lightweight charcoal gray sweater.

He'd rattled her enough that she was almost late meeting Daria.

"So," Daria said, a smile curving her lips, "how was your run this morning?"

Emily's eyes narrowed and she was about to accuse her best friend of colluding with the enemy when the waitress arrived with a steaming pot of coffee. Just breathing in that scent relaxed Emily's jaw and dissipated a bit of the morning's irritation.

"How are you ladies this morning?" the young woman asked as she poured coffee into white ceramic mugs. "Do you want the usual, or would you like to see the menu?"

"My usual, please," Emily said, picking up her coffee and blowing across the steaming surface.

"Got it. Two eggs over easy, a rasher of bacon, and whole wheat toast. No butter."

She turned expectantly to Daria.

"I'm feeling adventurous today," she said. "Bring me French toast and a side of bacon."

"Okey-dokey. I'll get that right up."

As she walked away, Emily turned a suspicious gaze on Daria. "What do you know about Chris turning up for my morning run?"

Daria avoided her gaze and stirred a packet of sugar into her coffee. Finally she looked up, expression as innocent as a puppy's, and said, "Chris joined you for your run? How nice."

"Nice?" The word exploded from Emily's lips. She leaned across the table and glared at her so-called best friend. "You think it's *nice* that he's trying to make a fool out of me?"

"What?" Daria yelped. "Is that what you think? Em, you've got it all wrong!"

"Did you know he was coming home to meet me? All that time I was telling you about the guy I'd met in that chat room... did you know it was Chris?"

"Of course not! Emily, I wouldn't do that to you, and no matter what you think, Chris is *not* pulling a prank."

Emily closed her eyes, took a deep breath, and forced herself to relax. When she felt a bit more grounded, she opened her eyes and studied Daria. Her lifelong friend was pale, her blue eyes wide and frightened. She extended her hand toward Emily, paused, and pulled it back. Her fingers shook.

"Emily," she whispered. "Please... say something."

The waitress arrived with their breakfast. She slid their plates in front of them with practiced ease, smiled, topped off their coffee, and bustled away.

Scents of bacon, fried eggs, and maple syrup wafted enticingly around the table, but neither woman touched her food. They sat as if turned to stone, staring into each other's eyes; one suspiciously, the other beseechingly.

After what felt like hours, Emily lowered her eyes. "We'd better eat," she said. "We don't want to be late to work."

Daria shook her head. "I'm not hungry. Call me later if you want to talk."

Emily grabbed Daria's hand before she could leave the table. "Don't go," she said quietly. "I'm sorry. I shouldn't have accused you of being in on this... whatever *this* is."

Daria twisted her hand in Emily's and locked their fingers together. "Chris might be my brother," she said, "but you've always been closer than a sister, Em. I'd never intentionally hurt you."

"I know," Emily said, squeezing her friend's fingers. They released each other's hands. "Shall we start over? Forget Chris exists?"

Daria laughed. "Easier said than done. Who knew he'd still be a pest at this age?"

The knots in Emily's stomach eased and she realized she actually was hungry. Suddenly the plate before her smelled fabulous and looked even better. She attacked her breakfast with gusto, pushing Chris to the back of her mind.

When her plate had been reduced to a smear of egg yolk and grease, she wiped her mouth and fingers on her napkin, glanced at her watch, and smiled at Daria. "Looks like we'll make it to work on time after all."

Daria smiled weakly, lowered her gaze, and played with her fork.

"What?" asked Emily, her suspicions aroused.

"Well, it's just…" Daria licked her lips, then met Emily's gaze and plunged in. "I don't want to upset you, but I promised."

Emily sighed. "Okay. I'm braced. What does Chris want you to do?"

"You're the best, Em," Daria said with a genuine smile, "and it's not just Chris, it's the whole family. We'd like you to come over tonight for a 'welcome home' barbeque. Chris will be there, of course, but so will Mom and Dad and Tim and I."

"Of course I'll come," Emily said after only a moment's hesitation. "Your house or your parents'?"

"Mom and Dad's." Relief glowed on Daria's face. "About 7:00, and Tim and I won't let Chris corner you. I promise."

Emily laughed. "That's okay. I'll be safe with your mom and dad there. Even Chris wouldn't dare get out of line with his mom watching!"

Daria grinned. "That's the truth. See you tonight."

CHAPTER EIGHT

*E*mily stopped at Larson's Bakery on her way home from work and bought Chris' favorite dessert: a chocolate layer cake with double fudge frosting. She told herself it was for the whole family, after all the Petersons were all chocolate fanatics, but she knew she was lying to herself. Chris had been crazy about that cake since he was a kid. She was buying it for him.

She stopped by her cabin just long enough to kick off her low heels, scramble out of her work clothes and pull on a comfortable forest green T-shirt and her favorite denim jeans. After lacing on her hiking boots, she grabbed the cake box and headed down the street and over a block to the Peterson's home.

Emily and Daria had grown up practically next door to each other, their respective homes being across the street and down one house from each other, but when Emily's parents retired last year, they'd moved down to Golden where the weather was a bit milder and the snow didn't pile up quite as high as it did in the mountains surrounding Aspen Springs. Just walking through the neighborhood stirred up childhood memories, but the Peterson home... well, that solid, two-story Craftsman house with its gable roof, spacious front porch, and creamy yellow board and batten siding was like a second home to her.

She followed the cement walk to the front porch and rang the doorbell. When the door swung open, Chris stood there looking even more delicious than he had that morning. He could've been a young god in black jeans and deep russet T-shirt.

"Hey, Em," he said, his baritone voice setting off harmonics that reverberated through her nervous system. "Glad you could come."

"Of course," she said, thrusting the cake box into his hands as she struggled not to ogle his stunningly muscled chest and arms. "I wouldn't dream of missing a barbeque with your folks."

A flicker of irritation crossed his features, but he smiled and waved her inside. "Come on in. Everyone's in the back yard."

Emily stepped past him, noting the spicy scent of his cologne – something citrusy with a hint of sandalwood – and continued down the hall, through the family room and out the sliding glass door to the patio.

Chris, right behind her, called, "Look who's here! And she came bearing gifts!"

Papa Peterson looked up from a grill laden with burgers and brats and waved a set of barbeque tongs at her. "Hey, Emily. Glad you're here. Wouldn't be a family party without you."

Mama Peterson bustled over from the picnic table, strategically located on the shadiest part of the flagstone patio, and pulled Emily into a motherly hug. "What have we here?" she asked, lifting the lid on the cake box in her son's hands.

Chris peered inside as well and whooped when he saw the cake. "Booyah! It's chocolate cake." He grinned at Emily and winked. "I knew I liked you!"

"Good thing he's holding that box," Daria said, coming to stand beside her friend, "or he'd be twirling you in a circle just now. You know how nuts he is about chocolate cake."

Emily laughed. "And not just any chocolate cake. It's from Larson's and that's double fudge frosting."

Chris moaned. "Can we forget dinner and move straight to dessert?" he asked his mom, his eyes pleading.

She laughed and swatted his arm. "Go put that cake on the table. And keep your fingers out of the frosting." She shook her head and followed him across the patio. "You'd think you were still ten instead of a grown man... and a military officer, at that."

Dinner at the Peterson's was delightful. Just like always. They gathered around the picnic table and ate Papa P's perfectly grilled burgers and brats, the meat so juicy the buns couldn't soak it all up. Emily's fingers were soon a sticky mess, but that didn't stop her from enjoying Mama P's homemade potato salad or Daria's contribution of fresh broccoli and bacon slaw. If Emily had been worried about being uncomfortable in Chris' presence, she shouldn't have. The family chattered and joked just as they always had.

After the meal was finished and the chocolate cake had been devoured, Daria and Emily cleared the table and put the leftovers in the fridge, while Tim and Chris cleaned the grill and gathered the trash. Mr. and Mrs. Peterson were relegated to lounge chairs in the backyard while the *youngsters* took care of what Chris termed *KP*.

When the chores were done, Chris approached Emily with an outstretched hand. "Would you walk with me, Em?"

Daria straightened, punched Tim in the ribs, and moved to join her best friend. But Emily smiled and shook her head. Instead, she accepted Chris' hand. "I'd like that."

She and Chris left the backyard by the gate and strolled along the side of the house to the front street. "What was that all about?" he asked.

Emily tucked her hand into the crook of his arm and gazed down the street. So many memories. Bicycle races. Sword fights with cardboard wrapping paper tubes. Sledding on the hill behind the Peterson home. And through good times and bad, her steadfast friend… Daria.

"Nothing. Just Daria being my friend."

"And I'm not?"

She laughed aloud. "No! You were the pesky the little brother." She stopped and looked up at him. "And for the last couple of days, I've been thinking of you as the enemy."

He quirked an eyebrow at her, but remained quiet.

"When Daria invited me to dinner tonight, she promised that she and Tim wouldn't let you corner me. She knew I was upset, but…"

He waited, the expression in his dark eyes intense. "But?" he encouraged.

She turned and walked forward, tugging gently on his arm. When they'd established an easy rhythm, she continued. "Dinner tonight reminded me who we all are. We're family, Chris, and whatever you're doing, you're not trying to hurt me. You're not my enemy. Never have been, never will be."

This time it was Chris who stopped. "I'm not your brother, either," he said, his voice quiet, but firm. "Never have been. Never wanted to be."

He took both of her hands in his and waited for her to meet his gaze. "I'm not teasing you, Emily. I outgrew the desire to tug your pigtails a long time ago. I love you and I'd like the chance to find out if you can love me, too."

Emily stared into the face of this man she'd known forever, and yet not known at all. A shiver of possibility ran down her spine, and she dropped her gaze.

"When Daria interrupted us Saturday night, I didn't get the chance to finish what I was saying, about why I used the Crusader persona," he paused, his fingers tightening around hers. "Like I said, I wanted Crusader to shake you up. Make you look at yourself and see what I see – a fascinating, sexy woman. But mostly, I wanted to throw you off balance so you'd have to open your eyes and really *see* me." He reached up and stroked her cheek with a single finger. "Not Daria's kid brother; not the boy who teased you in school." He placed that finger beneath her chin and, very gently, lifted. "I wanted you to see *me*... the man who's been crazy about you for years."

She lifted her face and their eyes met. A spark ignited and fire raced through her body.

"Can you see me yet, Emily?"

She swallowed, throat suddenly parched. "Yes, Chris." Her voice sounded husky, somehow raw. "I see you."

He roared with delight, scooped her off her feet, and lifted her into the air.

Emily gazed down at this man who'd been willing to cross the world to be with her... and wondered how she'd missed the love shining in his eyes.

PART XIX
A GROVE OF MOUNTAIN ASH

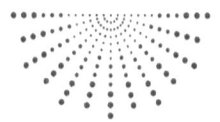

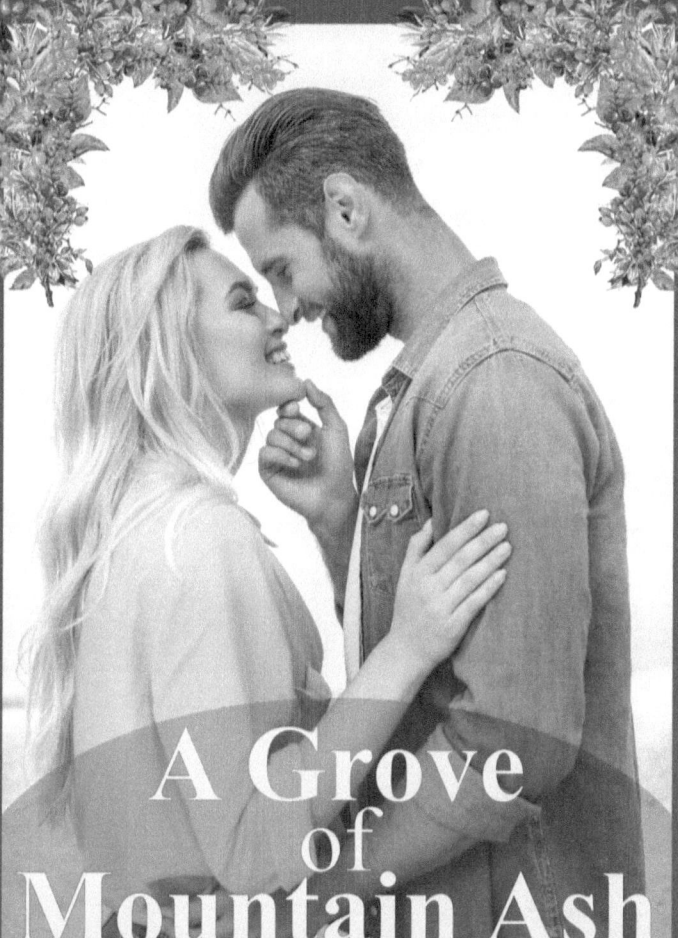

DEBBIE MUMFORD

BESTSELLING AUTHOR OF *SORCHA'S HEART*

A Grove
of
Mountain Ash

A Sweet Romance Story

CHAPTER ONE

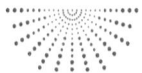

aul Freeman stood at the floor-to-ceiling window wall of his loft office, surveying what he thought of as his kingdom, the city skyline of Seattle. Described as a *Captain of Industry* by his admirers, and a *rapacious shark* by his detractors, Paul was a self-made man. He'd worked hard to amass the fortune that provided this stunning view, and he had every intention of accruing more.

At thirty-three, Paul was pleased with his life. Considered handsome by his social circle, with vivid blue eyes and wavy black hair, he worked out on a regular basis, determined not to let the desk and computer rob him of a lean body and healthy musculature.

A successful land developer, Paul's business savvy had also led him to conduct a number of hostile takeovers, earning him a reputation as a corporate raider. Not that he concerned himself with what others thought of him. He knew that if he hadn't used his vast wealth to intervene, those companies would have gone belly up, leaving their employees, and sometimes their communities, in financial ruin.

Yes, his business life gave him great satisfaction. If only the same could be said of his personal life. His wealth provided all the luxuries he could wish for, but it also robbed him of close relationships.

Nurturing friendships was exhausting. Determining who was genuinely interested in getting to know him as a person and who was simply currying favor was a skill he'd yet to acquire. Especially with women. He longed to find someone who wanted him for himself alone. So far he'd only met ones who coveted his possessions, what his position could give them.

Dismissing those unhappy thoughts, he turned from the window and ambled across the deep russet carpet to a mahogany credenza where a carafe of coffee awaited his pleasure. Pouring himself a cup of the fragrant brew, he allowed himself a moment to appreciate his surroundings. An impressive mahogany desk sat in front of the window's stunning view, its surface polished to a lustrous gleam. A few papers were stacked neatly to one side, and a matching computer desk sat at right angles to the main surface. Two mahogany client chairs sat across the desk from his own black leather executive chair. The carpet in this office was a deep, plush pile, in a rich russet tone. Not quite red, but with more character than plain, dirt brown. Artfully framed photographs of past projects adorned the warm beige walls.

He sipped his coffee, enjoying the full bodied flavor and pleasing aroma of the custom Kona blend. He'd come a long way from humble beginnings, and he intended to go a lot further. Friends and family could wait. He had an empire to build.

CHAPTER TWO

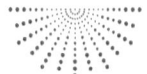

*R*owan Woodward breathed in the fresh autumn air. She loved this season, when the leaves turned from green to gold or red or deep burnt orange, and the air was tinged with a chill that hinted at the coming frost, but was not yet cold. Autumn was the time to enjoy crisp apples, fresh pressed cider, and carve fat, round pumpkins.

Dressed in her favorite red and black plaid flannel shirt, blue denim jeans, and well broken-in hiking boots, Rowan stood on a promontory overlooking a large meadow surrounding a lovely grove of mountain ash. Pushing a strand of dark blonde hair out of her eyes, she clambered off the rock and made her way down the hill to the meadow below.

Rowan loved this valley. She'd grown up visiting her grandfather's farm, had often played in that grove of mountain ash. If only Grandpa owned this meadow, but his land ended at the bottom of the hill.

The neighbor who did own it, Robert MacKay, had passed last year, and his son, who had left the farm for the sun and surf of California, had no interest in the land. Grandpa hadn't been surprised to learn that the younger man had sold the farm as soon as the law allowed.

Rowan had been dismayed by the sale, signaling as it did the close of a beloved chapter of her life, but hadn't been concerned until she'd discovered the identity of the buyer... none other than the despicable Paul Freeman. She felt certain nothing good would come of the billionaire developer's plans for this lovely place.

During those idyllic summers of her childhood, Grandpa's farm had seemed a world away from the bright lights and traffic clogged streets of Seattle. But no longer. Every year the city's suburbs crept closer and closer to this refuge of natural beauty.

And if Paul Freeman had his way, she was certain the city would soon creep into this very meadow.

Closer to the grove now, she noticed the clumps of bright red berries shining among the pale gold of the late October leaves. Beautiful! And if that weren't enough reason to leave the grove standing, what about all the birds and small animals that fed from its bounty?

Wandering through the grove, Rowan greeted each and every tree. Touching the bark of one, caressing a low-hanging leaf on another. These were the friends of her childhood. She'd climbed their trunks, swung from their branches, whiled away hours safely ensconced on a sturdy limb with her nose in a book.

When she stood in the center of the grove, she spoke her promise to the trees. "Don't worry. I won't let him hurt you. I'll find a way to fight whatever that demon, Paul Freeman, has in mind for this land."

CHAPTER THREE

When Paul Freeman arranged to meet the environmental engineer and the surveyor at the old MacKay place to discuss plans for the upscale subdivision he intended to build, he never expected to run into a protestor. But that's just what happened. The men had barely had time to park their four-wheel drive vehicle at the edge of the pretty little sheltered meadow and climb out when a young woman appeared from a clump of trees that stood in the center of the meadow.

A very pretty young woman, in an outdoorsy kind of way. And, as he soon discovered, a very opinionated young woman.

"Who are you and what are you doing in this meadow?" she demanded, eyes flashing and voice bold and … did he detect belligerence?

Paul frowned, glancing at the men who'd accompanied him. Both of them looked as surprised and puzzled as he felt. No help from either of them, then. All right, he'd solve the riddle on his own.

Pasting his best diplomatic smile firmly in place, he stepped forward to meet the young woman. "I might ask you the same question, since I own this land."

She stopped, crossed her arms across her chest, and glared at him. "You're Paul Freeman, then?"

Interesting.

A relative of old man MacKay, perhaps? Someone disgruntled by the sale? The younger MacKay hadn't mentioned any concerned parties, but Paul had learned long ago that 'full disclosure' was rarely complete. He studied her. Dark blonde hair swept up in an untidy ponytail. Casual clothes. No cosmetics or jewelry. Still, a pretty face—or he guessed she'd be pretty when she wasn't scowling quite so fiercely—with a pert little upturned nose, rosy cheeks, and hazel eyes that were flashing fire brands at him. Nice, trim figure, too. But it was her mouth that caught his attention, with its full lips and alluring bow.

He realized he was staring and dropped his gaze. What was he thinking? He never stared at women, not when they were aware he was looking at any rate. And he never lost his train of thought.

Giving himself a mental shake, he held out his hand. "I'm afraid you have the advantage. I'm Paul Freeman," he said pleasantly, "and you are?"

Looking as though she thought his hand might hide a poisonous snake, she touched his fingers. Something like an electric shock zinged from the point of contact through every portion of his anatomy.

His eyes widened.

Hers did too, and judging by the way she jerked her hand away, she'd felt the shock as well.

They stood as though turned to stone, her with those lovely lips slightly parted, showing just a hint of pearly white teeth.

After a moment, she said quietly, "Rowan Woodward." She shivered, rubbed her hand on her jeans, and repeated more firmly, "I'm Rowan Woodward. My grandfather owns the next farm over."

As if that explained everything.

"I see," he said, though he didn't. Not at all. What's more, his mind wasn't functioning in its normal clear, logical manner. His thoughts kept wandering to her lips, her eyes, her unadorned face. He kept wondering what her bustline was like beneath that oversized flannel shirt, wondering if her hands were soft or calloused from farm work?

He tightened his jaw and yanked his mind back to the present situation. This woman wasn't interested in flirting with him... which only made her more attractive.

Stop! This was neither the time nor place for romantic thoughts. He wasn't looking for love, he was planning a subdivision... and this woman might represent an obstacle.

And Paul Freeman was nothing if not good at overcoming obstacles.

"May I ask what you're doing on my land, Ms. Woodward?"

She straightened to her full height—a good head shorter than his six feet—and lifted her chin. "I'm protecting my friends."

Bewildered, Paul glanced around the meadow. Unless there were people hiding in those trees, the four of them were alone in this isolated place. He glanced at his associates. Both men looked as confused as Paul felt.

"Friends?" he asked the young woman. "What friends?"

She turned and gestured to the trees. "The grove of mountain ash." She turned back to face him squarely, hands fisted on hips. "I may not own this land, but I have no intention of allowing you to destroy a grove that has occupied this place for generations."

"Mountain ash," he repeated, sounding a bit dim even to his own ears. He stepped past her and stared at the trees. He hadn't known what kind they were, just that they stood in his way and held no commercial value. Now he looked at the trees themselves, a pretty sight clad as they were in autumn gold with generous clusters of cheerful red berries.

He frowned. Cheerful red berries? What was he thinking?

He glanced sideways at the woman and shook his head. She'd bewitched him. No matter what type they were, those trees meant nothing to him. Nothing except as an obstacle to the subdivision he planned to build. He couldn't afford to let this tree-hugging female upset his plans.

CHAPTER FOUR

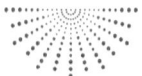

*R*owan watched as the man studied her beloved grove of mountain ash. Had she misjudged him? He seemed to be listening to her, taking her concerns seriously. Could Paul Freeman be a reasonable man, and not the monster she'd heard about?

He was certainly more attractive than she'd expected. Tall, easily six feet or more. Well-built, more athletically built than she'd have guessed for a man who spent his days in an office building. Wavy black hair, a little windblown at the moment, and sharp, intelligent blue eyes. The kind of eyes a woman could get caught in… and possibly drown if she didn't stay on guard!

Rowan bit her lip, remembering the electric shock she'd experienced when she'd shaken his hand. She longed to dismiss it as static electricity, but knew that wasn't true. Whatever the feeling was, it had nothing to do with the cool, crisp autumn air and everything to do with the strong attraction she felt building every moment she was in this man's presence.

Paul Freeman was charismatic and charming. And very dangerous to Rowan's sense of equilibrium.

Just then he turned to face his companions, glancing at her as he did so. She stifled a gasp at the glint in his eyes. She'd heard him referred to as a shark, and that predatory gleam definitely fit the label.

"Gentlemen," he said to his associates, "I'm sorry to have wasted your time today. I'll reschedule sometime next week. I'll join you at the car in a moment."

"Of course, Paul," said one.

"Not a problem," the other said, and both turned and walked back to the four-wheel drive vehicle they'd arrived in.

Paul Freeman turned to Rowan. "Do you live here in the valley, Ms. Woodward?"

Her eyes widened and her brows rose. She certainly hadn't expected such a personal question. But his gaze bored into her, demanding an answer... and she found herself giving it.

"No. I live in Seattle."

He nodded. "Are you returning to the city soon?"

She frowned. "Why do you ask?"

A slow smile crept across his lips, and Rowan shivered. Not in fear, but with anticipation.

Dangerous. This man was charming and dangerous.

"I thought we might have dinner," he said. "To discuss your concerns."

"D-d-dinner?" she stammered, and felt a blush heat her cheeks.

"You do eat, don't you, Ms. Woodward?"

Irritation flashed through her system, waking her from whatever spell he'd put on her. "Of course I eat," she snapped, "but not usually with people like you."

His eyebrows rose and he cocked his head. "People like me?"

"The rich and famous," she said, her tone more than a little snarly. "I'm nobody, Mr. Freeman. Why would you bother to take me to dinner?"

"You seem to be familiar with this," he said, gesturing to the meadow and her grove of mountain ash. "You can give me insight into the area. Call it research or... due diligence."

She narrowed her eyes and studied him, trying to find the lie, or the derision, behind his words, but found nothing to concern her. Nothing except a growing desire to spend time with him, to get to know him better.

She blinked. Why would she want to get to know Paul Freeman?

They had nothing in common. She wasn't some social butterfly out to snag the city's most eligible bachelor! She was a down-to-earth copy-writer for a respected Seattle news organization. She sat at a computer in a cubicle during the week and hiked or kayaked on the weekends. Her world hadn't a single intersection with Freeman's. She'd never have encountered him if it weren't for her beloved grove of mountain ash.

Still, she found herself nodding.

"All right. I'm spending the weekend with Grandpa, but I'll be back in the city on Monday."

He pulled a cell phone from his jacket pocket and opened a calendar app. "Monday night it is," he said, typing with quick, sure strokes. "Where shall I pick you up?"

She gave him her contact information, and he provided her with a business card he'd added a few lines to. Glancing at the neat hand-writing, she saw that he'd given her his personal cell and home address.

He flashed a smile at her before turning and striding to join his associates. "See you on Monday," he called as he stepped into the four-wheel drive vehicle.

Rowan lifted a hand in acknowledgment, but stood rooted to the spot as the vehicle drove away. What had she gotten herself into? She glanced over her shoulder at her grove, and prayed she had a chance at saving those precious trees.

Her breath caught at the memory of Freeman's touch and the almost predatory gleam in his eyes. Her knees buckled and she slid to the ground. Maybe she'd do better to pray she had a chance of saving herself!

CHAPTER FIVE

*P*aul stood by the granite fireplace mantel in the living room of his Mercer Island mansion. The late October night was cool enough to allow a fire, and he breathed in the scent of pine and ash and heat, savoring the way they mixed with the aromas wafting from the kitchen. He'd decided to entertain Rowan Woodward in his home instead of taking her to one of Seattle's famous restaurants. He hoped she'd appreciate the meal his chef was preparing: prime rib, roasted red potatoes, fresh steamed asparagus with lemon sauce, and a marionberry tart for dessert.

He hoped for a lot of things from this evening.

He'd spent the weekend re-envisioning his plans for the meadow where he'd met Rowan, and found himself as nervous as a teenage boy hoping for her approval.

How could the approval of a woman he barely knew be so important to him?

The doorbell rang and he heard his housekeeper, Mrs. Everett, greet his guest.

Stepping away from the fireplace, he checked his tie and straightened his dinner jacket just as Mrs. Everett ushered Rowan into the room.

His eyes widened and his jaw dropped. The young woman was stunning! Closing his mouth quickly, he stepped forward to greet her. He'd known she was pretty when they met in the meadow, but now, dressed in a shape-hugging emerald green dress and killer stiletto heels, she was enough to knock a man to his knees.

And Paul's knees felt the blow... solidly.

Her hair, which had been swept up in a windblown ponytail in the meadow, now flowed around her shoulders like rich, golden honey. It dripped across one cheek, while held back from the other by a clasp decorated with dark red berries. Mountain ash berries? Her lips wore that same alluring red.

She stood silently in the doorway, and he realized he needed to speak, but his mouth was parched, his tongue glued to the roof of his mouth. He closed his eyes to gather his wits, licked his lips, and exerted his will.

"Ms. Woodward, I'm so glad you could come."

"Thank you for inviting me, Mr. Freeman, though I was expecting a restaurant," she said, glancing around the room, "not your home."

"Please," he said, managing to move to her side and guide her into the room, "call me Paul. I have some plans I'd like to show you later, and that will be easier here."

She moved into the room and seated herself. As she did so, Paul looked at his living room, trying to see it through her eyes. The rock fireplace with its dancing flames and granite mantle dominated a space filled with dark leather furniture. A sofa and matching loveseat sat at an angle to each other, while a deeply cushioned armchair and matching ottoman rested near the fire. A large square hickory coffee table sat in the angle between the larger pieces, and a bookcase lined one wall. But the best feature of the room as far as Paul concerned was a picture window looking out on Lake Washington.

Tonight, moonlight sparkled on the water and the lights from the far shore twinkled like something out of a fairy tale.

"You have a beautiful home… Paul," she said quietly.

"Thank you," he said, wondering what he should say next.

Mrs. Everett saved him by announcing dinner.

Paul extended his hand to Rowan. She accepted, rising gracefully from her chair and allowing him to lead her from the room.

Mrs. Everett had set the table by a picture window in the library, the formal dining room being too large for a dinner for two. Paul approved the choice. A candlelit meal surrounded by books and leather suited him perfectly. Besides, the plans he wanted to show her waited on his desk on the other side of the room.

Dinner was a success. The prime rib was delicious, tender and succulent and seasoned to perfection. Rowan seemed especially pleased with the steamed asparagus with its tangy lemon sauce.

"Did you research me?" she asked with a smile. "Asparagus is a weakness of mine. I grew up hunting wild asparagus with my brothers. They didn't really like to eat it, but loved the hunt." She took a bite, chewed, and smiled. "I love everything about asparagus, and this sauce is wonderful."

The dinner conversation was companionable, not at all stilted. They chatted about their lives. Paul revealing that he'd grown up poor, the only child of a fisherman and a maid. His father had expected his son to follow him onto a fishing boat, but Paul's quick wit and impressive intelligence had earned him scholarships and a foot in the door with the business community. He'd intended to help his parents retire in comfort, but they'd been killed in a car accident before he could make that particular dream a reality.

Rowan had been moved by his tale, so much so that he'd quickly changed the subject to her family. She'd grown up middle-class, with one older and two younger brothers. They'd spent many summers at her grandfather's farm and knew the MacKay family well. She'd always considered the meadow with its mountain ash grove as her personal domain, though she admitted she had no legal claim to the land.

"Those trees are like family," she said. "I know that sounds ridiculous, but they've watched me grow up, sheltered me through my teenage years, and always been a source of peace for me. I can't bear the thought of them being cut down, their roots covered with concrete."

He reached across the table and took her hand. "I'm not sure why, Rowan, but I feel... connected to you." He paused, lowered his eyes, and breathed deeply. When he felt centered he met her gaze. "I don't know if you feel it too, but there's a definite attraction on my part. I've never met anyone quite like you."

She blushed a very becoming shade of pink and lowered her eyes. Her fingers trembled in his hand. "I feel it too," she admitted, so quietly he wondered if he'd heard her correctly. When she raised her eyes and met his gaze, he knew he hadn't misheard.

His heart raced and warmth filled him to the brim. He wasn't alone anymore. He'd found a woman interested in more than his bank account. Truth be told, she was interested in more than just his ownership of that grove of mountain ash, because he hadn't yet told her of his revised plans!

Grinning, he pulled her to standing. "Come with me. I want to show you what I'm thinking of for that meadow." He led her to the desk across the room. "I'd originally planned a subdivision, but after seeing how important those trees are to you..."

He unrolled the plans he'd spent the weekend designing and showed her a retreat and small conference center. One that sat beside, but did not disturb, her grove of mountain ash.

After she'd seen every detail and asked more questions than he'd anticipated, she turned to him, eyes shining with happiness. "Oh, Paul! It's perfect. The grove will survive and I'll still be able to visit it."

He nodded. "I discovered while I was working on the plans that you're every bit as important to me as those trees are to you." He took her hands, enjoying the warmth of her soft skin, and gazed into her eyes. "I hope you'll spend a lot of time overseeing the project... and getting to know me."

She leaned forward and kissed his cheek. "I can't think of anything I'd rather do."

Paul's heart soared. He pulled Rowan into his arms and kissed her. Gently at first, and then more thoroughly. As she snuggled into his embrace, he allowed his heart to anticipate a bright future... and to be thankful for a very special grove of mountain ash.

PART XX
BECAUSE OF THE
CHRISTMAS STROLL

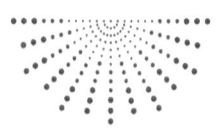

DEBBIE MUMFORD
BESTSELLING AUTHOR OF SORCHA'S HEART
Because of the Christmas Stroll
SPUN YARNS
A Sweet Romance Story

CHAPTER ONE

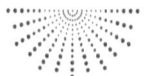

*J*ane Ann Kremetz experienced an interesting mix of exhaustion and exhilaration as she hurried along the snow packed street. The Christmas Stroll always had that effect on her. She worked herself until she could barely stand in the weeks leading up the annual holiday event—she was responsible for making sure everything ran smoothly, ensuring the community a memorable experience—but when the big day arrived, she received a jolt of energy from Main Street's festive atmosphere and the strollers' delighted chatter. That buzz always lasted until she fell into bed long after The Strolls lights dimmed and all the revelers returned home.

This year, like every other year, Main Street was closed to traffic for the free community event. Folks would turn out in droves to stroll the six block stretch this evening, singing carols, munching cookies and candy canes, and buying last minute Christmas gifts. There would even be horse-drawn sleigh rides available for those who tired of walking. Bright lights, festive decorations, and snow.

Lots of snow.

Jane Ann grinned. If there was one thing Bozeman, Montana could be counted on for, it was snow!

Pedestrian traffic was still light, but that would change soon. Jane Ann had only just finished supervising the gingerbread house decorating contest at the community center. Now a group of stalwart volunteers were moving the finished masterpieces to the Main Street bank lobby where strollers could marvel at the local children's ingenuity. Jane Ann was officially off duty for the rest of the evening. The Stroll would officially begin in a few minutes, and she intended to enjoy the event to the fullest.

Dressed in her warmest down jacket and ski pants, her fingers protected by warm woolen mittens knitted in a snowflake pattern, Jane Ann pulled her jacket's fur trimmed hood over her head, covering the matching knit cap. Her warm breath puffed out creating a tiny white cloud as it hit the cold late afternoon air. She patted her pocket, reassuring herself that her neck gaiter hadn't fallen out. She'd need it before the night was over; December in Montana was bitterly cold.

After her afternoon of kids and gingerbread, she craved a cup of steaming hot cider, and she knew just where to find it. She hurried past storefronts decorated in their holiday best—twinkling lights, plastic snowmen and reindeer, model trains circling ceramic villages, and of course Christmas trees, whether artificial or the real thing— aiming for her best friend's bookstore, *A Novel Experience*. Charity always had hot spiced cider and fresh baked snickerdoodle cookies available during The Stroll.

Jane Ann had almost reached the warmth and light of *A Novel Experience* when someone bumped into her, almost knocking her to the ground. A pair of strong hands in leather work gloves steadied her and she glanced up into the concerned face of a man.

A man she knew.

A man she hadn't seen since high school and had frankly never expected to see again.

"I'm so sorry," he said, releasing her as soon as she was stable on her feet. "I wasn't watching..." He stopped and peered into her face. "Janey? Is that you? I don't believe it."

"Hi, Chuck," she said. "What brings you back to Bozeman?"

CHAPTER TWO

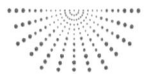

*T*he Christmas Stroll was in full swing, the street filling with happy crowds. Excited children dashed from display to display, while their parents alternately called out cautions and chatted with friends. Shops were packed so tightly customers could hardly move, but no one minded. Christmas spirit ruled, plus there were free brownies and cookies and cider for all.

The event was a huge success, but Jane Ann hardly noticed. She was in a daze. A Chuck Henzel induced daze. After nearly knocking her over, Chuck had accompanied her to Charity's bookstore where she'd watched fondly as Charity lost her mind. Chuck and Charity were twins, but the devilishly handsome man evidently hadn't warned his sister he was coming home for Christmas. When Charity had managed to stop bouncing and squealing, she'd composed herself and swatted Chuck on the shoulder.

"You know I can't leave the shop during The Stroll," she said with an accusatory glare. "You planned it this way."

Chuck laughed, a warm, deep rumble. "Maybe. But you couldn't expect me to miss The Stroll just because you have to work, could you?"

Charity rolled her eyes, but her expression showed nothing but delight. "I suppose not." Turning to Jane Ann, she said, "Keep an eye on him, will you, Janey? I don't want him disappearing before I get a chance to visit with him properly."

"Hey, now," Chuck protested. "I'm home for the holidays. Janey doesn't need to babysit me." Then he cocked his head and winked at Jane Ann. "Unless you *want* to babysit me, that is."

Jane Ann blushed, her fair skin turning even pinker than the frigid temperature outdoors had caused. She opened her mouth to respond, but nothing came out. Chuck's sudden appearance after so many years of absence had robbed her of witty banter. Needing something to do, she grabbed a cup of Charity's spiced cider and sipped. The warmth of the liquid soothed her, while the taste of tart apples combined with cinnamon, ginger, and cloves helped to clear her mind.

Ignoring Chuck's teasing comment, she turned to Charity. "He's not going anywhere, Char. Not without seeing your folks and Ed and the kids, but," she slid her gaze sideways to the man in question, "I'll be happy to stroll with him, if he'd like."

There. She'd lobbed the metaphorical ball straight back to him. Where it belonged.

Chuck laughed again, and Jane Ann thought she could get used to that distinctly masculine rumble. "Caught in my own net." He waved at his sister and held out a hand to Jane Ann. "Come on, Janey. Let's see what Bozeman has to offer these days."

An hour and a half later, after visiting every square inch of The Stroll and even indulging in a sleigh ride, Chuck and Jane Ann stood in front of the gingerbread house exhibit for the second time.

"I don't know," he said. "I know you like that Victorian with the frosted trees and the skating pond made out of blue sprinkles, but I'm partial to that little log cabin over there." He pointed to a very simple confection, constructed to look like stacked logs with icicles of white frosting dripping from a roof shingled with light gray wafer candies.

"Well, I may be biased since I supervised the contest and watched all of these houses being built." She smiled up at him, still surprised by how tall he'd gotten. He must have had a growth spurt after high school. "You wouldn't believe how hard these kids worked. Their concentration and attention to detail was impressive."

Chuck nodded. "I can see that. These are a lot better than the ones I remember making."

She laughed. "Yes, but you were always more interested in eating frosting than in building a house."

"Guilty as charged," he agreed, his eyes sparkling. "I don't know about you, but I'm about strolled out. Want to grab a pizza and warm up?"

She glanced at her watch. The Stroll still had an hour to go. As one of the organizers, she should really stay until the end. Then again, no one was expecting her to do anything further. The need to stay was just her over-developed sense of responsibility. Besides, pizza with Chuck sounded great. A perfect end to a perfect Stroll.

"Sure," she said with a nod. "Let's do it."

CHAPTER THREE

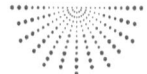

A surprisingly short time later, Jane Ann found herself seated across a table from Chuck at *The Pizza Parlour*, a favorite haunt from their high school days. Divested of her winter outerwear, she felt oddly exposed and vulnerable, as though her down jacket, mittens and cap had been armor, protecting her from... what? She glanced at Chuck as he studied the menu they'd both memorized back in the day and frowned. Why in the world would she be feeling shy and ill-at-ease around Chuck, of all people?

Why, he was practically her brother. She knew her best friend's twin as well as she knew her own father. At least she had before he left town.

The man sitting across the table from her was undoubtedly Chuck, but at the same time, he wasn't. The last time Jane Ann had seen Chuck, he'd still been a gawky teen, not yet grown into his full height. He'd still had that puppy-ish look of hands and feet too large for his body. But this Chuck... well, there was nothing gawky or immature about this man. This was a well-built, adult male in his prime who filled out his flannel shirt and jeans very nicely.

The man absolutely exuded masculinity.

Which confused and startled Jane Ann.

Chuck dropped the menu, met her gaze, and grinned. "What do you say? Shall we stick to an old favorite, or be adventurous and try something new?"

She froze, her mouth dry and her heart pounding. He was talking about pizza, she knew he was talking about pizza, but her traitorous hormones hijacked her brain and dragged it in an entirely different direction. Forget the old favorites, Jane Ann wanted nothing more than to have an adventure… an amorous adventure!... with this handsome, virile man.

With Chuck!

Her cheeks flamed and she dropped her gaze to the menu and shrugged. "Whatever," she managed to mumble. "You choose."

Chuck reached across the table and took her hand. "Janey? Are you okay?"

His use of her pet name broke her hormones' hold on her brain. This wasn't just some good-looking guy she could drool over. This was Chuck! She'd grown up with this guy. He was Charity's twin and the closest thing she'd ever had to a brother. She needed to get a grip. Forcing herself to calm, she raised her eyes, met his gaze, and smiled.

"I'm fine," she lied. "Long day. You're the returning prodigal; you choose the pizza."

He grinned and pulled his hand back. "Pepperoni with extra cheese, it is."

While they waited, a bit impatiently, for their pizza, Jane Ann drowned her inexplicable discomfort in conversation.

"So," she said, "where have you been all these years? What's up with you?"

"You know I joined the Marines right out of high school. That's kept me busy. Still does, as a matter of fact."

She eyed his red plaid flannel shirt and blue jeans. "You're still a Marine?"

He leaned back in his chair and studied her. "Sure am. Is that a problem?"

Her cheeks flamed, again. "Not at all, but you're not in uniform."

"I'm on leave," he said with a shrug. "Besides, I don't live in my uniform even on base."

She nodded and changed the subject. "I can't believe I haven't seen you since high school. How have I managed to miss your visits?"

"Well, let's see now, the first time I came home, you were in Seattle. I think Char said you'd followed a guy you met at university?"

She narrowed her eyes and hissed. "I did *not* follow him! I was just there for a visit."

"Ri-ight," he drawled, a knowing smirk on his handsome face. "The next time you were hiking in Yellowstone. With another guy." He grinned, but then his expression grew serious. "The next thing I heard, you were married. To the Yellowstone guy?"

Jane Ann sighed. Charity had obviously kept Chuck well informed. "Yes. Jeremy and I married just a few months after Charity married Ed. I was surprised you didn't come home for her wedding."

He shrugged. "Couldn't. My team was deployed."

A little frown creased her brow. "Really? Where?"

Wiggling his eyebrows and twirling a nonexistent mustache, he said, "I could tell you, but then I'd have to..."

She laughed and raised a hand. "Stop. I get the picture."

Just then their pizza arrived and Jane Ann breathed in the delicious aroma of Italian spices, tomato sauce, and crispy pepperoni. She and Chuck both pulled slices onto their plates. Conversation ceased while they enjoyed gooey cheese, greasy bread, and heavenly sauce.

With the edge removed from their appetite, Jane Ann restarted the conversation.

"So what about you?" she asked. "Married with kids like your sister?"

He paused with the remains of his third slice of pizza halfway to his mouth. "Seriously? You think I'd've showed up at the Christmas Stroll alone if I had a wife and kids?" He shook his head. "Just because you're an independent woman whose husband doesn't mind you wandering around without him doesn't mean I'd leave my wife alone while I came home to Bozeman."

Interesting. Chuck was still single… and Charity hadn't kept him up to date on everything.

"Jeremy and I divorced two years ago," she said quietly, then popped the last bite of pizza crust into her mouth. Chewing gave her an excuse not to elaborate.

Chuck dropped his pizza, wiped his fingers on a napkin, and reached for her hand. "Janey, I'm sorry. Char didn't tell me."

"No reason she should have," Jane Ann said, grabbing a slice of pizza she didn't really want so she could pull her hand from his. The sizzle of excitement his touch engendered had startled her so much she'd almost jumped. Taking a bite of the new slice, she slid her eyes toward his familiar, yet strangely unknown face. She'd have to be very careful around the man Chuck had become. He was entirely too sexy, and her body was not reacting to him as it should to a guy who was practically her brother!

CHAPTER FOUR

*T*he next week was torture for Jane Ann. Everywhere she went, she ran into Chuck. She'd expected to see him at *A Novel Experience*, and of course he'd show up at Charity and Ed's home, or the twins' parents' ranch. But the grocery store? The library? The Chamber of Commerce where she worked as a community organizer? Come on!

Yet it seemed like every time she turned around she came face to face with Chuck Henzel. And every time, her body reacted as if she were a dog in heat! It was embarrassing. Definitely embarrassing, and possibly even humiliating.

She reacted to Chuck like she hadn't to any man since she'd divorced Jeremy. Truth be told, her visceral reaction to Chuck was a magnitude greater than anything she'd ever felt for her ex-husband. She couldn't wait for Christmas to be over and for Chuck to disappear back to whatever faraway place he normally inhabited.

During their many—too many in her estimation!—encounters she'd learned that Chuck wasn't just a Marine, if there was such a thing a *just* a Marine. No, he was the Element Leader of a Tactical Element of

Marine Raiders, a special operations team of elite warriors. She couldn't imagine it. Chuck. The mischievous boy Jane Ann and Charity had spent so much time avoiding during their childhood was now the Marine equivalent of a Navy Seal!

And yet, Chuck was still Chuck, and when her hormones weren't running wild, she enjoyed his company immensely.

Finally, Christmas Eve arrived and Jane Ann joined Charity, her husband Ed, and their two little ones at the Henzel ranch, as she had every year since her own parents had retired to Florida. Lugging her overnight bag in from her cherry red Jeep, she called her greetings and raced up the stairs to the bedroom she used every year. Throwing open the door, she found Chuck standing in the middle of the room wearing nothing but a towel.

She gasped and stared open-mouthed at the stunningly sculpted muscles on display for her avid ogling. Everything about the man was perfect, from his ridged six-pack to his well-defined pectorals. Even his calves were beautifully sculpted. He looked like he'd been chiseled out of marble. Warm, inviting marble.

She managed to yank her gaze from his gorgeous body to his face and close her mouth before she drooled on the carpet.

His gaze locked on hers and his eyes darkened with a predatory gleam. She didn't know whether to run from him or throw herself into his arms. He took a step toward her, then stopped, closed his eyes, and inhaled deeply. When he opened them again, the dangerous gleam was gone.

"Hey, Janey," he said. "Guess Mom didn't tell you she'd rearranged the sleeping quarters?"

Jane Ann felt a deep need to tell him she was more than willing to share the queen-size log frame bed with him, but managed to stifle the urge. Good thing too, since Charity came running down the hall and stopped behind her at that very moment.

Charity took in Chuck's state of undress, reached past Jane Ann and pulled the door closed, then grabbed her friend's arm and hurried her down the hall. "You're bunking in the kids' room this year," she said, her voice high-pitched and a little strangled. "We've got cots set up for them in our room."

Jane Ann swallowed, saliva seemed to have pooled in her mouth, and agreed. "Sure. No problem. You sure you and Ed don't mind? I could share with Jilly and Jerry." Twins, especially the boy-girl variety, seemed to run in Charity's family.

Charity laughed. "No way would I put you through that. They'll be up at the crack of dawn and bouncing off the roof beams. Santa's coming, you know!"

Jane Ann laughed with her friend and the tension of her encounter with Chuck seeped away. But the memory remained. She figured the image of his near-naked body would be scalded into her memory for the rest of her days… and especially her nights.

That evening after dinner, each family member—and Jane Ann was considered family—was allowed to open one gift. The four-year-old twins, Jerry and Jilly, each chose a present from Uncle Chuck. Jilly received a necklace and bracelet set made of sea shells, and Jerry got a set of wind-up trucks. While the kids played with their new toys and the adults watched indulgently, Chuck pulled Jane Ann from her chair by the fireplace.

"Come with me," he said quietly.

Jane Ann nodded and followed him from the great room with its beautifully decorated Christmas tree into the hallway. As they neared the front of the house, he paused in the arched entry to the formal living room, and taking her by the shoulders, positioned her under the center of the arch. Glancing up, she saw a sprig of mistletoe above her head. Returning her gaze to Chuck, she raised a quizzical eyebrow.

"I need to check something out," he said quietly, his voice deep and rumbling. Slowly, his eyes never leaving her face, he lowered his mouth to hers.

Jane Ann's heart pounded furiously. He was going to kiss her. Chuck, her almost brother, was going to kiss her. Her mind raced. Should she pull away? Turn her back on him? Put her hand on his chest and give him a push? But she knew that if she touched that marvelously chiseled chest, the last thing she'd do was push him away.

Before her frazzled thoughts could settle on a course of action, his lips were on hers, and her arms were around his neck. She'd never know how they got there, she certainly hadn't intended to kiss him back. But kiss him she did. With pleasure. And thoroughly.

What started as a gentle touch of his lips to hers soon deepened. His lips were so inviting, so much softer than she would've guessed, not like kissing sculpted marble at all. She not only accepted his kiss, but leaned into it, pressing her lips to his, her mouth opening on a soft sigh of pleasure.

Evidently he took that sigh, her open mouth, as an invitation. His tongue immediately invaded. She tasted him. Coffee and chocolate cake and a simmering spice that was uniquely his own. Not to be outdone, her own tongue pushed past his, tasting him more deeply. As their tongues danced, his arms pulled her so close to that marvelously sculpted chest that she could feel the pounding of his heart. Her arms twined around his neck, her hands massaging his head beneath that close shorn hair.

Her heart raced; her body thrummed with desire; her hormones squealed in delight. This. This was where she belonged. This was exactly what she'd always dreamed of finding. Her perfect man.

Chuck.

Her eyes flew open and she wrenched herself from his embrace, panting with the exertion of leaving that hot and heady space. What was she doing? Kissing Chuck? She couldn't kiss Chuck! What would Charity think?

Chuck blinked, and then licked his lips with a sexy twitch of that oh so talented tongue. "I knew it," he growled and took a step to close the distance between them. "I knew you were the one for me."

She shook her head. "We can't," she said, her voice so breathy even she could barely hear the words.

He herded her into the living room and backed her against the wall. Hemming her in with a hand on each side of her head, he asked, "Why can't we?"

She closed her eyes to block out the intensity of his gaze and took a deep breath. "You're practically my brother."

"I'm no such thing," he growled. "You're Charity's best friend, but you're most definitely not my sister." He leaned in and nipped her lower lip with his teeth. Playfully. Oh so gently. "I've never even considered doing that to Char, but I've been dreaming of doing it to you for years."

Her eyes popped open and she stared at him open mouthed. "For years?" she asked, closing her mouth quickly lest he take advantage and kiss her again. She wasn't sure she could hold out against a second soul-shattering kiss!

"For years," he repeated, his eyes still dark and predatory. "I've dreamed of getting you alone, but every time I came home, you were off with some other guy." He closed his eyes and swallowed, "And then Charity wrote that you married the Yellowstone guy. I thought I'd lost you forever, and I'd never even had the chance to tell you."

She stared up at him. Recognized the pain he'd experienced, and saw him, truly saw him for perhaps the first time.

Chuck.

Charity's brother, but not hers. Never her brother. No kin to Jane Ann Kremetz. Just the love she'd been waiting for all her life.

"Tell me what?" she asked, placing her arms around his waist and pulling him closer.

"That I love you," he said, and pushing her against the wall, he kissed her thoroughly.

CHAPTER FIVE

*W*hen they returned to the great room a few minutes—
or maybe it was a few eons—later they found that Ed
had taken the younger twins up to bed. Charity looked at them with
wide eyes, then squealed and rushed to Jane Ann's side. She didn't
need their words, she read the truth in their faces and their entwined
arms.

Hugging Jane Ann fiercely, she said, "Finally! He's been pining for you
since high school."

Jane Ann broke the hug and held Charity at arm's length, noting the
tears sparkling on her best friend's cheeks. "Truly? Why didn't you say
something? You could've warned me!"

Charity laughed and swatted Jane Ann's arm. "Seriously? Since when
do I do his work for him? If he wanted you, he had to figure out a way
to win you."

Jane Ann shook her head and laughed. "I'll never understand siblings."

"Sure you will," Chuck said, hugging both of them at the same time.
"You've got a sister now."

"Hey, now," David Henzel called from across the room. "What's going on? You planning to let your mother and me in on the secret?"

Ellen Henzel tsked. "Honestly, Dave! Anyone with eyes can see that Chuck has finally made a move on Janey." She stood and crossed the great room to stand before daughter's best friend. Taking Jane Ann's chin in her fingers, she gazed into the younger woman's eyes. "And it looks to me like Janey didn't mind a bit!" She laughed, hugged Jane Ann, and said, "Welcome to the family, sweetheart."

Then David Henzel was beside Jane Ann as well, patting her shoulder. "Best Christmas present ever!" He grinned, winked at his son, and said, "California's going to feel a lot more like home with Janey there, isn't it, son?"

Jane Ann's face paled and her eyes widened. California? Who said anything about California? Jane Ann was Montana born and bred. She couldn't move to California! Why, who would plan the Christmas Stroll every year if she wasn't in Bozeman to do it? Her breathing was suddenly fast and shallow as panic flooded her system. She was hyperventilating!

Desperately, she looked around for Chuck and locked eyes with him. He'd stepped back to give his family room to welcome her, but now he studied her, his gaze calm, but concerned. He cocked at eyebrow at her and opened his arms. Her panic eased and she stepped past his parents and into his embrace.

Montana wasn't her home. California wouldn't be either, nor would anyplace else his military career took them. This was where she belonged, safe in Chuck's strong arms. She could face anything— even California— as long as they were together.

Jane Ann leaned into Chuck's embrace and smiled, remembering how he'd almost knocked her down at the Christmas Stroll. Raising her face to his, she kissed his cheek and then rested her head against his chest. He'd definitely knocked her off her feet this evening... and she

ABOUT DEBBIE MUMFORD

Debbie Mumford specializes in speculative fiction (fantasy, para-normal romance, and science fiction) as well as mystery and historical fiction. Author of the popular *Sorcha's Children* series, Debbie loves the unknown, whether it's the lure of space or earthbound mythology. Her work has been published in multiple volumes of *Fiction River*, as well as in *Heart's Kiss Magazine, Amazing Monster Tales*, and many other popular anthologies. She writes about dragon-shifters, time-traveling lovers, and detectives—whether amateur or professional—for adults as Debbie Mumford, and science fiction and fantasy for tweens and young adults as Deb Logan.

Join Debbie's special announcement newsletter list and receive a FREE story!

To learn more, visit Debbie at:
debbiemumford.com/
Or send her an email at:
deborah.mumford@gmail.com

facebook.com/DebbieMumfordWrites
amazon.com/author/debbiemumford
bookbub.com/authors/debbie-mumford
twitter.com/deborah_mumford

ALSO BY DEBBIE MUMFORD

Kristi Lundrigan Mysteries:

- DELECTABLE MOUNTAIN QUILTING (NOVEL)
- IN A PICKLE (NOVEL)
- FOOL'S PUZZLE (SHORT STORY)
- WILDFIRE! (SHORT STORY)

Gus and Ghost Short Story Series:

- SEVENTH
- SEVENTH: FIRST FRUITS
- DEATH OF AN ALCHEMIST (UNCOLLECTED ANTHOLOGY)
- SEVENTH: THE SAMHAIN DILEMMA
- DARK OF THE MOON (UNCOLLECTED ANTHOLOGY)

Logans of Lastalrig Series:

- HER HIGHLAND LAIRD (NOVELLA)
- HER HIGHLAND YULE (SHORT STORY)

Red's Series:

- RED'S MAGICK (SHORT STORY COLLECTION)
- SEEING RED (SHORT STORY)

Signs of the Prophecy Novels:

- YOUNGEST
- SEEKER
- CHOSEN (COMING SOON!)

Sorcha's Children Series:

- Sorcha's Children (Omnibus Edition)
- Sorcha's Heart (Novella)
- Dragons' Choice (Novel)
- Dragons' Flight (Novel)
- Dragons' Desire (Novel)
- Dragons' Destiny (Novel)

Supernatural Yellowstone Short Story Series:

- Reality Bites
- The Cat Lady of Yellowstone

Uncollected Anthology Short Stories:

- Death of an Alchemist (UA Alchemy)
- The Wedding Cake (UA Magical Arts)
- Dark of the Moon (UA Paranormal Pirates)
- In the Banyan Copse (UA Unexpected Histories)
- Old One (UA Magical Quests)
- Have Hoard, Will Seek (UA A Diversity of Dragons)

Universal Star League Short Story Series:

- Voyages Into The Black (Collection)
- The Warbirds of Absaroka
- Awakening the Warrior
- Incident on the Odyssey
- The Queen's Captive
- The Lost Colony
- Freighter Families in Space

Witchling Short Story Series:

- Witchling
- The Solitary Sorceress
- To Protect a Princess

Stand Alone Novels:

- Second Sight

Historical Fiction:

- Her Highland Laird (Novella)
- Her Highland Yule
- Incident on the High Line
- Miss Bainbridge's Summer Adventure
- Miss Bainbridge's Christmas Party
- Sisters in Suffrage
- The Trail Where We Cried
- The White Dragon and the Red

Short Story Collections:

- Love in a Flash
- Tales of Bygone Days
- Tales of Love & Magick
- Tales of the Unexpected
- Tales of Tomorrow
- Tales of Disastrous Deeds

Short Fiction:

- A Grove of Mountain Ash
- A Walk with Georgia
- An Alien Adventure
- Astromancer
- Because of the Christmas Stroll

"WDM Presents" Anthologies:

www.ingramcontent.com/pod-product-compliance
Lightning Source LLC
Chambersburg PA
CBHW030845030726
47495CB00005B/1386